Karel Tjerssen of Spiderglass was looking for something very special: a weapon. A two-edged weapon. He had been looking for it without even realizing for a very long time. Now all the ideas had gelled. It was time to go to Witwaterstrand to see if the seeds he'd planted had grown the way he wanted. Trouble was, there was all that lightless black vacuum to cross to get to it. Karel was twenty-three, broad-shouldered and lithe; blond, with eyes clear as zircons; and by his own efforts he had graduated top of his class. With his immense fortune, he was everything any man would want to be – but he was scared stiff of flying. Let alone lifting off from the mother planet into the black void beyond.

'This is a new dimension for SF'
– *The Guardian*

'Here's one new voice in SF that's not going to go away too quickly'
– *Blast*

Also by Anne Gay in Orbit

MINDSAIL
DANCING ON THE VOLCANO

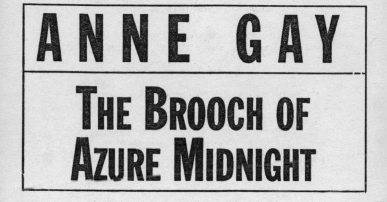

ANNE GAY

THE BROOCH OF AZURE MIDNIGHT

ORBIT

AN ORBIT BOOK

First published in Great Britain in 1991 by Orbit
This paperback edition published by Orbit in 1993

A CIP catalogue record for this book
is available from the British Library.

ISBN 1 85723 037 X

Printed in England by Clays Ltd, St Ives plc

Orbit
A Division of
Little, Brown and Company (UK) Limited
165 Great Dover Street
London SE1 4YA

To my daughter Marianne
who taught me to walk in the clouds

and

To my sister Janet Calderwood
who showed me the pictures in my head

With love

CONTENTS

INNER RING

1

Cold as starlight, the naked cliffs enfolded her. There was hardly any atmosphere on this asteroid so far from the sun, but she felt the schist grating underfoot and the sound of it came up through her bones. High on the slopes the schist winked silver in distant sunlight, each stone limned with dark shadow, a pattern like mackerel scales.

Jezrael inserted herself cautiously into indigo canyons, avoiding dead ends. Her height made her feel huge now, conspicuous. At the corners of her perception were the dancing fronds of the blue tower in her skull, but it kept her on the map, the slight artificial gravity letting her leap over craters that were marked in the memories replaying in her mind. Someone else's memories.

Afraid, lonely, she tracked her way towards the Gate. Somewhere up ahead the red cross-hairs in her head-map would centre over reality and she would be there.

And *there* was where a man and a woman had, separately, died.

A dead-eye swivelled, no higher than her knee, its thick flat fans of leaves spreading out to catch what little light there was. The matte foliage was the same shape, the same colour as the stones.

Jezrael was rattled by it. She hadn't seen the dead-eye although she'd been watching for them, knowing they'd be camouflaged in the unplanned design of light and darkness, but when her shadow fell on it, its frozen stalk uncurled to reach for the sun. Only then did she spot it.

And she was frightened by her own inefficiency. *So the targets are watching me. How many dead-eyes have I already passed? How many times have the targets seen me*

3

through them, used them to plot my position?

But before Magrit and Nils had died they had taped their memories to their ships, even as Jezrael was doing now. The Company Research and Development team had analysed the memories and said, 'Take the dead-eyes' water away and they won't work.'

Jezrael dropped her shadow full on the plant's eye, and wondered if her targets were watching and laughing at her even now, seeing her face curving down over their biological spy, sneering at her features appearing oblate and distorted through its eye.

The thing uncoiled farther, straining up to catch the light. Where its bony stalk thinned under the eye-bulb she drove in a spike. Then she glued a squeeze-tube as long as her arm to the end of the hollow spike, pumping a paste of anhydrous chemicals into the stalk to suck moisture from the plant.

The dark and glassy eye opaqued slowly and death spread along its fibre-optic roots. Somewhere at the end of maybe kilometres of root-net, someone was watching the dead-eyes wither and blink out all along the system.

Jezrael moved back, accidentally touching a leaf; it puffed into powder around her boot. Jezrael didn't allow herself to think of Magrit on a level the machine-chip in her head could read – she didn't want the Company thinking she'd gone soft – but on a plane below consciousness Jezrael was grateful to Magrit for more than this information. She wondered if Magrit had thought her machine-memories were worth dying for: the ability to kill a plant seemed like such a stupid reason to die.

I really miss Magrit. Not like Nils. . . . For Nils had been something different. Jezrael could cope, most of the time, with knowing she had sent Nils to his death. But Jezrael didn't want the Company to know how she felt. Some parts of her she wanted to keep to herself – especially from Karel.

Now all I have to do is make sure I don't get spotted by another net of dead-eyes. . . .

The map in her head unrolled further as Jezrael

4

threaded through the maze of frosted valleys, climbing to where a canyon spilt down from the lip of a crater. Three hours it took her to get there; she hadn't dared land closer to the Gate.

Three hours. That was what all this was about: speed of transport. The difference between rescue and salvation for a score of planets. When she stepped over Nils' frost-wrapped body, chill sank inside her skeleton.

Reality all but meshed over Magrit's memories: Jezrael had reached the Gate and its selfish guardians. Peering over the notch in the crater, she sprawled flat to see her enemies.

No. Not enemies. Jezrael squashed out of her mind the anger for Magrit and against the people that were betraying humankind. *Not enemies. Targets.*

There was nothing but the shades of night in the penumbra. In the dark reaching sky she saw only the crystal veil of stars and the distant yellow sun that was scarcely bigger than a star itself. It was a view that should have made her think of home, and it did. Home was a thought that hurt, a wound she suddenly wanted to heal. *If I live. If only I have time, maybe I can. . . .*

Jezrael shivered. She scanned the crater, wincing as the asteroid's tilt suddenly flooded the rocky bowl with sunlight. Concentrating on the cross-hairs that overlay her head-map, she saw a red X mark the spot. Sunlight danced orange glare into her eyes; she still couldn't see the traitors who were killing millions, spearing them with starvation, mocking them with untreatable disease.

But she knew they were there and an unscratchable itch fretted at her back. One man and woman, according to what the Spiderglass Company knew. Again she thought of Magrit, dead, and of the bones of Nils pressing out against his skin as his flesh lost moisture and shrank, mummified. And Nils was – had been – good. One of Jezrael's best executives despite his crude methods. Not as good as gentle Magrit, though, who never hurt a friend in her life.

5

The tower in Jezrael's hair started to catch messages. Jezrael began to see them as they came through the antenna, plunged down the connection from helmet to tower to the optic centres of her brain. They filtered through her synapses as though they were some addition to the visible spectrum of electro-magnetic radiation: or – she saw them interpreted as blue.

One of the targets was thinking about closing. Of the other there was as yet no sign.

The moving target felt vaguely feminine and wholly dangerous: it felt light-years older than Jezrael's biological age of twenty-five. Jezrael had to force her breathing to steady, to calm her sudden quick-stepping pulse.

She turned her head slightly to find the source of the blue light, her eyes flicking over the crevasses of shadow on the slope below. The slope itself was dazzling. She shaded her visor against the glaciers of sunlight on white rock, which showed a sparkle of rime here and there.

Fear prickled in Jezrael's armpits and adrenalin flooded her major arteries. Her skin went cold as blood was withdrawn to survival systems. The smear of fright from other wounds, other battles that were not of her choosing, spread across her interior landscape and an unedited trace of Magrit's own fear fought its way through subliminally, winding Jezrael tighter. That just screwed her determination into a fiercer knot, but nevertheless there was too much at stake for this to be merely vindictive.

Jezrael swallowed her instincts, said on all circuits to the unseen warrior: 'Let's talk.' And felt the other woman's midnight urge to violence.

'No talking, Company. Leave or die.'

'Just let me talk to him.' Jezrael worked up more spit so she could even out her voice. 'I won't hurt him. Please let me talk to him. We need the Gate. There's people out in the stars dying –'

No answer, just vicious intention crystallized like a sapphire dagger.

Uneasily, Jezrael took out her sword. As it left its scabbard the vibro-blade activated.

The other woman leaped from ambush above her, slow in the light gravity, her own sword already sweeping down for the kill.

And it wasn't a vibro-blade. It was a coherent beam, not just of light. Its heat was sheathed in steam that shone pale in the bowl of sunlight against the blackness of the sky, and each glowing droplet was there to protect a 'virus' that ate through metal or cloth or skin, poisoning as it went.

For Jezrael time seemed to warp the stars, to pin her in diamond-clear slow motion. Because the woman had the drop on her.

'My name is Ceriad,' said the warrior, still astride the ether. 'And the Gate is Dwillian. So now you, Company, can let them back on Earth know who it is who's stopping you raping the worlds.'

Jezrael watched the beam come closer and knew she was going to die. That's what came of pride – or lack of common sense. *I should have brought projectile weapons like everybody else. Only I thought if I didn't look like a walking arsenal that maybe they'd talk to me. There's been too much death....*

There could be no rescue, not even revenge. If the Company bombed the asteroid they'd lose the Gate. She wondered, and she didn't bother to shield her thoughts from the recording-machines back on the ship, she wondered if she would see Magrit or if it would just be a long black bed in which she'd sleep forever at peace. And she thought of what her parents might be doing at this moment in Witwaterstrand. Or her sister. *Chesarynth ... where are you now I need you?*

And this Ceriad rode gravity, her poisonous bow-wave rushing outwards from its skyborne centre, beginning to fall as a deadly rain towards Ayesha Jezrael Brown.

Still some core of hope deep in Jezrael's being wouldn't give up. Reflexes trained in the laser-dance (how her mother had hated laser-dance!) whipped up her sword and braced its vibro-blade to pierce Ceriad's neck, knowing she would be dead herself when the beam struck. Maybe....

I don't care now what happens to me. If only I can take her out, the millions might be fed.

The red-winking time-sensor in her head flickered its data across her vision: three-seventeen p.m.

But Ceriad's venom licked out at her, an acid tongue that glowed.

A smile burst suddenly on to Jezrael's face, surprising her; a joy so fierce it was like a flame.

Why?

And the warrior-woman's beam floated, fatal, closer....

2

On the day the Nomad War started, Chesarynth Brown wasn't thinking of death, either death that she would cause or the kind of death that would happen to her.

From beyond the horizon, carried on the long wind of dawn, the scent of China flew over the steppes. It breathed its foretaste of gold through the grille over Chesarynth's window and touched her.

She sighed, not knowing why her concentration was broken, and jacked out of her terminal. Surely the Company could forgive her living – briefly – in real time? *Anyway,* she reassured herself, *the computer will keep the thought-chain for me.*

But she had to check that the pattern of symbols was safe in the tank, because she didn't trust herself.

Chesarynth drifted to the window. Unconsciously fiddling with the gold socket on her left forefinger, she pushed back her brown wavy hair, but it was short enough to swing forward as she leant out over the sill. Working her muscles to ease the ache in her back, she inhaled the East. Down in the courtyard, a nightingale sang in the pomegranate tree. Not a single light showed in the second-hand palace but, beyond the roofs of the other wing, spotlights glared on the sheds where work never stopped – it was Chesarynth's job to see that it didn't. Come Ramadan, come Christmas, come Yom Kippur, Chesarynth let the spiderglass pour from the plant. Hard as steel, ductile as silk, proof against corrosion or the endless cold of space, spiderglass fibres even carried optical images. When she'd first arrived, she went two or three times to see the spiders she loved, but they were

9

man-sized with bloated tarantula-haired bodies skittering about on multi-jointed legs. Chesarynth couldn't take that: the difference from their gentle, pollen-yellow minds which she saw when she interfaced with them. External and internal reality.

The lights assaulted her eyes and Chesarynth looked away. Blinking to clear the after-image, she looked Eastwards to the perimeter. The wall was black against the faintest paling of the sky, as if it would fight back the heat of the coming day, but there was a prick of a red gleam by the gate to Tashkent.

Chesarynth laughed silently. A minute later she was creeping down the path, her sneakers making no sound on the tiles between the passion-fruit hedges. In eight minutes she could walk to the perimeter wall. She did. She saw the guard's cheroot glow red and his face gleamed for a moment in the still, dark air, but then he saw her and the ruby light disappeared behind his cupped hand. They both knew he was not supposed to smoke on duty.

Chesarynth smiled; she also knew she couldn't stop him unless she watched him every minute of every shift. More: she gave him another cheroot and said in his own language, 'If it is the will of Allah that cheroots exist, is it not also the will of Allah that they burn?'

The difference between them was, when she said it, it was a joke. Nazrullah believed it. Their boss, who called himself Sikander Bahadur, would have had them both re-oriented, but Sikander was asleep with one of his wives. Chesarynth was free – for a while.

Nazrullah, the guard, said, 'Moheb is patrolling the oasis area. I saw his gun-barrel in the moonlight. There's no sign of the nomads yet, but be careful. Maybe today, maybe next week, but they'll come, and some of us will die.'

Chesarynth nodded but it was an old threat, worn with constant telling and stretched thin by years of emptiness. Neither of them really believed it. It was a some-day thing, a sort of perfunctory fire-drill.

The guard swung the gate open for her while she

checked the infra-red monitors, but even from the height to which the wall rose she couldn't see any nomadic warriors. And more to the point, the top brass never used the surface road.

For the moment it was safe.

Slipping down to the dry river bed through the pre-dawn gloom, Chesarynth opened herself to the night. She hid behind a thorn-bush to watch two gazelle drink from a rain-water pool. There was scarcely enough for the doe and her faun where once whole herds had drunk. Chesarynth wondered what had happened to the stag. When the faun shied at his dark reflection, Chesarynth smiled, letting peace wash through her in the ancient heart of Asia.

Too soon the stony soil began to reflect the light that grew. Still Chesarynth lingered, loth to go back to the problems that waited for her, the problems of personnel, politics, matériel, that somehow never seemed quite real. They were just toys, shiny beads in a game of intellectual chess she played with the computer, pretty necklaces of symbols in the tank. She held herself immobile, listening to the sounds of the dawn, letting herself just be.

Until the gazelle clashed their hooves in panicked flight. Danger!

The nomads had come.

Chesarynth ran at a half-crouch, taking advantage of every dip and gully that she knew, heading for the Tash-kent gate. The contorted terrain kept her from sight, just as it hid the nomads. It had to be the nomads – Chesarynth was sure they had come for their stolen water, convinced she could smell their rank, mangy camels over the scent of dust and shrubs. On the lightening air she heard the creak of harness and the scuff of the camels' pads.

Unless it was just the dawn wind rubbing leaves on twigs and stirring the sand between the rocks? *Stop panicking*! she told herself. *Why should it be the nomads*? Besides, she realized, she couldn't hear the alarm. Surely, if it was the tribesmen attacking after so long, Nazrullah would have sounded a warning?

She rose cautiously out of a deep fissure not a hundred yards from the wall. Along the crested horizon the sun was bowling yellow light to flatten the scrubland. The brittle sticks that had been spring flowers cast long, broken shadows but she could see no other movement, not so much as a lizard.

Then Nazrullah showed in the gateway, beckoning with his whole arm, a wild, frantic gesture. Even now she could see nothing dangerous but there was Nazrullah, his shirt flapping like semaphore. Chesarynth trotted towards him, still not really believing all this, and something buzzed past her to spang on the stones. Bullets!

It really was the nomads.

In terror Chesarynth fled. Nothing like this had ever happened to her before, not in her childhood in Witwaterstrand, nor on Mars, nor her time here on Earth. She pumped her legs so fast she overran herself and tumbled forwards, scrambling to her feet, so close to the safety of the gate that she could see the smoke streaming from Nazrullah's dropped cheroot.

And in that second when she was clawing to stand, to run, a heat-seeker whistled over her body to slam into Nazrullah's. He sat suddenly, folded like a pocket-knife, and Chesarynth dragged him inside. When she clashed the gate shut it smeared his blood on the tiles.

Chesarynth slapped the alarm and all along the wall the high-voltage wires began to sing their counterpoint. But in guilt she knelt beside the guard, seeing the red soak through Nazrullah's bright, torn shirt and weigh down the hem of his waistcoat. The wound was in the groin and life welled out of the artery with each pulse of his blood; she couldn't stanch it though she tried. His face was pale with shock, its cheerful roundness not yet lined with pain. Chesarynth knelt, stroking his shoulders as he looked in surprise at his fingers splashed with crimson. Her lips twitched; no words would come but surely she ought to say something above the clamour of the alarm?

'Hashish,' he mouthed.

Chesarynth felt a dreadful sense of failure when she couldn't understand what he meant.

He tried again, a little louder, adding, 'Under shirt.'

Against a rising background of screams and explosions she finally worked out what he wanted. For the first time in the three years they'd known each other she slipped her hand inside his clothes, and embarrassment filled her at this act of intimacy with a man she had killed. She felt around, amazed at how smooth his chest was, how soft the folds of his stomach. In an incongruous plastic bag above his waistband she found a cube of something. Before she could ask he nodded, urgency growing in him as the pain began to bite. It was too small a piece to break so she bit a corner off, spitting out the bitter taste, and pushed it into a broken cheroot.

She lit it for him and watched his brown eyes darken while he sucked in the smoke with a greed she found hideous because she had caused this pain he wanted to leave. Some of the tension went out of him and he began to shudder. The attack seemed very distant despite the mortar-shells whistling overhead.

'Sorry. I'm sorry, Nazrullah. I –'

'Not your fault. Insha'Allah. Like the cheroot.'

She closed her eyes at his joke. Nazrullah took another great, ragged breath, his lips a dreadful grey. The cheroot fell from his fingers and she snatched it from his shirt before it could burn him.

Under them the ground heaved and twisted. A rumble below the threshold of hearing shook them. The wire on the wall stopped its hum but now the mortar-fire punctuated a new sound: a fierce, high-pitched screaming that Chesarynth had no words to describe.

Nazrullah said, 'Paradise. Jihad.'

Chesarynth felt a new guilt: that she had taken her attention from him. It seemed as though if she stopped thinking about Nazrullah he would die.

At least this time when she replayed his words inside her head they made sense. She shifted him sideways,

13

supporting his back against her chest, and found his rifle. Slipping aside a wooden peg in the gate, she uncovered a loop-hole and jammed the gun-barrel through it. Then she held his hand to the stock and pressed his finger on the trigger.

Chesarynth moved to look at his face and his lips essayed a smile of gratitude.

'Thank you,' he said, and she held him like a lover. Then he added, 'Allah u akhbar.' God is great. And she knew he believed he was bound for Paradise because he had died in a holy war. A pity he was on the wrong side.

Nazrullah had left pain behind and Chesarynth abandoned him, not accepting that any of this was happening, but sprinting for the armoury because Sikander Bahadur must not have anything to blame her for. Not when Nazrullah had died to cover up for her.

Not five minutes had passed since the attack started; only the ground-staff had arrived at the concrete bunker where the guns were stored, though inside the sleeping-wing of the palace Chesarynth could hear the office-workers shriek conflicting orders at each other. Hadn't she said time and again that they should practise what to do when the attack came? But the Company liked to pretend the nomads would never rise against them (half the Board paid them Danegeld) and Sikander just wanted a quiet life.... Anyway, none of them really thought a bunch of Iron-age wild men would ever dare –

Chesarynth skidded round a corner to the armoury. The gardeners were milling around the door, since none of them had the key. Chesarynth jacked into the socket by the lock but the usual surge of expansion didn't reach out to her through the wires in her finger. The door wouldn't open.

Of course not! she told herself savagely. *That's why the h.v. wire's not on – there's no power. We can't even call for help*! (She wouldn't even think about the colourful strands of logic she'd left half-woven in the computer-tank, not stored so it looked like she'd only gone to the toilet and not deserted her post. All of it lost now the power had gone down.)

There was no sign of Sikander and she ordered a handful of the men to swing a wooden bench into the door. It split and she kicked a broken panel aside, but a two-foot splinter ripped her calf. The men pushed past her, crowding to get at the guns. They didn't help her; they didn't listen. Fighting (she knew they thought) was men's work. They were all jabbering at the top of their voices.

Slapping a field-dressing on her leg, she snatched up a heat-seeker gun because she knew she couldn't aim. In fact, she wasn't even sure she could point the thing at another human being, especially not now she'd seen what one had done to Nazrullah. Revenge was one thing. Do-it-yourself revenge was another. . . .

Chesarynth made for the tunnel, because that led to the only way help could get to them; the underground mag-lev which came up under the palace. Crouching, zig-zagging along the paths through the pretty gardens, she had to hurdle bloody corpses and the bodies of the dying. All around she heard the sounds of battle; at any moment she might run into combat. A bullet spanged against the palace wall only a handspan from her face. Stone fragments peppered her face.

Ducking into the admin-wing, she left the bloodshed and the sun. As she ran down the deserted corridors, windows imploded under the gunfire but rattan blinds caught the glass and dropped it in a spray of sounds. At every corner she dropped to the floor to peek around the angle, cautiously because of the glass but still acquiring bloody shards in her flesh, knowing the tribesmen must be down here somewhere to have set off the earth-shaker she had heard. But how had they got in?

Deeper, where even the emergency lighting had failed, the air began to thicken with dust. Air-shafts dropped a faint radiance here and there, but mostly Chesarynth had to probe her way through a heavy gloom. It was strange not to be able just to jack into a socket and have the environmental controls surge into bright obedience.

Odd noises came from far ahead. *Maybe help's already*

come? Maybe someone's trapped in the mag-lev? But Chesarynth knew she was just hoping. There was no way anyone could have sent for help. *I could have done it if I'd stayed at my console. I'd have been there when the alarm sounded. Nazrullah wouldn't be dead. . . .*

Blundering along in the blackness, the racket ahead seeming now closer, not fading into insignificance, she wondered if she was only trying to find a way to keep out of the slaughter in the sun-washed garden. . . .

Blocks of stone littered the platform. Foot by foot she groped forward, finding by touch among the rubble the place where the platform gave way to a service-path running beside the rail. She was frightened of falling on to the single rail, unsure exactly how the monorail propelled the train. She told herself she was being stupid: the power was cut, wasn't it? But supposing some bright spark switched it on again?

As she crept along the service-path in almost total darkness, hugging the wall, she heard the screech of metal on metal cutting through the confused sounds of fighting, and over it all, one single man roaring.

Chesarynth clambered up a mass of fallen debris. Glowing columns of dust rode a shaft of light down to the blockage, and she realized the nomads had caved in the ceiling.

Fierce sunshine flooded her vision as she peered over the wall of fallen stone. A ragged hole in the roof dangled a fringe of tribesmen on ropes, sliding down to attack the train that shouldn't even have been there. And in the mêlée was Karel, the youngest director on the Board.

Of course, he wasn't really involved in the fighting. He was scrambling up to safety atop the train. She watched him, a man almost two metres tall, kick a puny nomad who tried to cling to his leg. The nomad fell sprawling, skull crushed between the carriage and the platform. The impact made her wince.

Hesitantly, she aimed at a warrior sliding down a rope. The laser-sight showed her her target, a bud of light on the man's chest. Eyes closed, she pulled the trigger. When she

16

opened them again, the man had gone. She hoped he wasn't dead. But another man swung over the edge to take his place and she found out how hard it was to hit a living pendulum.

Improbably, Karel spotted her above the mass of fighting, his eyes drawn by the flash from her rifle-muzzle, but he snatched away his glance in time to see a scimitar chop up towards his ankle. He threw himself backwards, legs waving energetically, and rolled to a half-crouch. His assailant clawed his way on to the carriage roof and all Karel could do was retreat.

It was strange to see such a powerful man so helpless, but to the tribesman it was merely justice. How the tribesman knew that this was his people's cruellest enemy Chesarynth couldn't guess, but she knew Karel had blocked just about every suggestion she'd given Sikander to pass on to the Board. Karel wouldn't offer the slightest reparation to the tribes whose water Spiderglass stole. But the Spiderglass men were losing and her own life was on the line. Chesarynth pointed the heat-seeker at Karel's assailant and shot him.

'Get to the generator!' yelled Karel. 'Power on!' Then he was falling under a wave of nomads, kicking, lashing out, a scimitar in his hand now. 'Do it!' he ordered, and then ignored her.

But the generator was surrounded by nomads armed with beam-guns, knives, old rifles. She could see it all from the windows of the office-wing as she raced outside.

Chesarynth wheeled and dashed up the stairs, hearing Sikander Shah bellowing, stranded in the lift. And on the half-landing she knocked out the fancy grille and leaped to the roof of the generator-shed. She ran from shadow into light that stabbed at her eyes, and headed for the trapdoor in the flat roof.

The trapdoor flung open from below. Chesarynth fell back, her head ringing on the stone. Concussed, she couldn't think straight. For the fraction of a second she was back in the past, far out in orbit in Witwaterstrand and it was the only other time she'd almost been killed.

17

And Jezrael her sister had saved her.

But when she opened her eyes a nomad was plunging his knife towards her ribs. His old-fashioned watch hypnotized her gaze: three-seventeen p.m.

This time she didn't even know where Jezrael was....

OUTER RING
Where did it all start?

1

Jezrael heard Eiker say, 'We don't want you.'

Cheap flickering lights split ozone from the atmosphere and drenched her left shoulder in harsh brightness, but she leaned her head against the angle of the alley so bars of shadow slashed her face. She was fighting hard to keep her expression unreadable.

Jezrael was just nineteen; she knew she shouldn't have been inside the junk-heap asteroid that was Bidonville. She wished she'd stayed home, at the edge of Witwaterstrand. From there Bidonville looked like any other place in town, a crusted bead of platinum on black. *But no*, she thought, *not me. I had to sneak upstrand to see Eiker's troupe laser-dance, maybe join in one last time. Maybe get hired. My only chance to get away from this dump and I screwed it up.*

Eiker said, 'You hear me?'

Jezrael made herself look up at him and it was he who couldn't meet her gaze. He fiddled with the remote control embedded in one wrist, his thumb clicking the buttons on and off, on and off. Away from his laser-suit the buttons set in his flesh did nothing but make him look inhuman. The hair on his forehead did its own little jig in the wind from the dance-bar's air-vent, but Jezrael watched the tiny movements of his eyes as he tried not to see her. *He wasn't like this when I got up on stage at the end of his set. . . .*

'You hear me, kid? We don't want you.'

'Why not?' she asked, without meaning to.

Eiker moved restlessly, his whole body shifting in the weak gravity-spill from the bar, but Jezrael put her hand on his arm below the rolled-back cuff, pegging him

21

between the walls of coral. His muscles were warm and wiry under her palm, his skin damp with sweat. 'Eiker, why not?'

'Because you're not good enough, Jez, that's why not. You hear me? You can't cut it.' Eiker unclamped her grip with his free hand, fierce because he didn't want to face what the laser-dance had done to him, and she was making him see. She found it in the hard planes of his face, attack as the best defence. He ground his finger-ends into her wrist but she welcomed the pain as a distraction. She felt too young to handle all this, out of her depth.

She watched his lips say, 'You've got the seeds, but you won't change. I offer you enhancers, inbuilt remotes even, but no, not you! You want it all!'

Jezrael felt his anger, felt his other hand seize her shoulder and the remote set into his flesh dug against her collar-bone.

'You'll never be good enough, kid. You want to go swanning across the solar system reaping applause and then come back home to mom, only this time she'll be proud of you. That's what you want, but it doesn't work out that way. You want to go laser, you have to go all the way. You got to sell yourself, burn yourself out 'til there's nothing left but the core-fire. You can't come back.' And it was his anger at being cut off from his own past that he poured like lava over Jezrael.

Eiker pushed her away, a man of whipcord and gristle. Onstage he had looked handsome but close up she could see the harsh lines around his eyes, disdainful eyes dark with anger. Jezrael was slammed against the wall, hating the tears that began to leak down her face. Loose trash floated upwards where her feet scrabbled for purchase.

He spread his hand wide, catching her throat on the tough web between fingers and thumb. The coral of the wall grated her scalp.

'You'll never be that good, kid. You'll never get out of Witwaterstrand. And even if you do, you'll crawl back home up to your neck in babies and puke, because you'll never change. Now get the hell out of here.'

22

Eiker jammed her head up, back against the wall; then let her go. He turned away, upwards, as if she were a toy he'd forgotten to play with. Above the pumping of the air-vent Jezrael couldn't even hear the kick against its hood which sent him shooting up towards the far rim of Bidon-ville. That side was a wasp's nest of salvaged hulks cemented by coral; half of them were trade-bars where Jezrael would never dare follow. Eiker embraced his *now* with desperate ferocity; he didn't look back.

But Jezrael didn't go home.

Nineteen and no good. I'll never be that good.

Jezrael moved dejectedly away from the dance-bar, stepping through the gravity-leaks and the reek of beer and drugs without registering them. Overhead, in the arcing upper hemisphere of Bidonville, brash, blaring signs spilt downwards from the Wasp's Nest where Eiker might be drinking and laughing and never thinking about her. And in the hollow centre of the man-made asteroid, caught in the no-man's land between warring gravities, trash eddied in the air like wounded birds.

Jezrael slipped through the air-skin, out of the mess of scrap metal that was the lowest slum of the whole asteroid township. From outside it didn't look so bad: the proud beaks of salvaged ships stood out jauntily from the shadow-stippled coral in a random but not unattractive design. Their viewports winked with the coloured lights of homes: clear red, soft amber, warm neon. But Jezrael was on the outside looking in.

Driven by ingrained habit, she slotted the round end of her belt-line into a long hard cable of spiderglass. One of the strands that gave this asteroid cluster its name, it curved silver into the distance. Stabbing in the co-ordinates of the school-asteroid, she felt the belt engage in the magnetic track. It led her too slowly for her anger and she pulled herself hand over hand along the limb-thick glassy cable, feeling the knob of her belt rattling at the junctions where side-strands clustered and flared off to the other spheres and barrels and star-shapes that were downtown Witwaterstrand. Now and then she passed other people

23

slotted into other grooves in the cable, some above her and some beside or below. The difference was they all seemed to be in laughing groups; fragments of their happy chatter sparked bright in her suit's audio-circuits. It forced a bitter taste of loneliness into her darkness.

A couple of times, blind to her over-familiar surroundings, she let the knob of her belt-cable crash carelessly into somebody else's. A man swore at her but it was obvious that she wasn't going to do anything about it so he pulled himself down to slot his belt-line into another groove.

Using hands and feet to propel her, Jezrael poled up to the school – this late, it was practically deserted – and slipped into the stock-room behind the gym. Beams and bars and torn matting floated behind jury-rigged clamps. That was where she'd learned.

Breaking into the locker that held the laser-dance controls took her too long. She was too angry to concentrate. At every false combination she hit the cabinet in frustration. A sharp edge of extruded plastic cut the side of her hand and that was right, too.

I'm not good enough. I deserve to be punished.

But Jezrael broke the combination – five Chinese tonemes – and slid the control-drawer open from behind the wad of dirty washing. The gym guy was so predictable! She practically snatched the laser-dance body-remotes out of the drawer then slammed her angry hands hard on the main controls.

Programming for basic rage, she flipped out the main lights that came on when anyone came in. Only the feeble safety-lights remained.

So what if I don't take enhancers? Drugs are stupid. And who needs built-in remotes anyway? What do they save – a micro-second? I don't want to be more of a freak than I am already.

She slid the remote-bands on to her wrists and ankles in the dark, by touch. Running to the centre of the room, she all but zeroed gravity as the first subsonics shook her bones. She rose in a kick that would have killed Eiker if it had connected, but he wasn't there. It didn't connect.

24

Nothing she did connected.

Half-way between a dance and a fight, Jezrael reacted to the dark rhythms, cannoning off the walls, the floor, the ceiling. When she triggered the remotes, her actions primed the beat.

Slowly she got it together, moving through three dimensions, then she brought in the bass-notes one by one, sound and harmonics, fighting fiery above the killing beat. Her body became a sonic weapon: one thrust of her arm and a soaring note rose like a spear. A double kick was the shock of an earthquake. She swam fiercely through three dimensions, and when the notes came in a river of burning sound Jezrael brought in the lights.

First they were shapeless, lances of pain in bleeding reds, the orange of volcanoes. Then the controls on Jezrael's limbs warped the lances into a pattern that was fury incarnate. Bright as magnesium, ugly as the emotions that wrought it, her rage seared the darkness but there was no catharsis for Jezrael this time. Given form and sound and movement, her (self)hatred etched more agonizingly into her mind.

The acid light twisted into the shape of Eiker's soul: hot pride and spiky anger, a face that was almost like Eiker's with his thousand-year-old eyes.

Almost like, but not quite.

I'm not good enough!

Jezrael forged a lightning-bolt of sharp and primal blue to slam it into the image. Overload: it exploded and the music screamed its agony, but the light died, the sound plummeted, shrank, and the embers of it all wrapped Jezrael where she knelt in despair, rocking herself, alone, and the music cried in the pulse of the dying light around her.

Footsteps: the light crept up the spectrum, the footfalls pulsing ochre. Jezrael looked up and a yellow flare lit the room for a second, then sank as she stilled.

He sat cross-legged, facing her. The gym-guy. Dael. 'Feel better now?' he asked softly.

Ribbons of light flamed through the room, bouncing the

walls closer as she reacted to his words. Dael snaked out a hand to adjust the prime-control on her left wrist, on the artery from her heart; her pain was hurting him. The room darkened, the walls seemed to recede until there was a dull glow in the centre of it all, like a sleepy camp-fire in a cave. 'Got it out of your system, Jez?'

'Yes,' she said, but amber roared through the dimness when she wiped her eyes on the back of her hand.

'No,' he said. 'Think I'm blind?' More softly he added, 'That was some show.'

She shook her head. 'No, it wasn't! I'm not good enough!'

'Want to tell me about it?'

Jezrael slid the remote-bands off her ankles and wrists. She didn't want to advertise her emotions. Now there was nothing but the faint luminescence of the safety-lights and she didn't have to see Dael's face looking at hers.

Silence trapped her; it stretched full of words she couldn't say because they would unleash too many memories with barbs.

Dael said gently, 'I saw you down to Bidonville yesterday, and again today.' His voice held the pattern of his Chinese home, soft vowels half-voiced between the consonants in otherwise idiomatic English. And if she had looked, she knew she would have seen his eyes like drops of melted tar under the blond fringe of his hair. Even on Earth he didn't fit in; much less in the asteroids, but it wasn't his nationality, it was his uncertainty. Jezrael thought that was why he tried so hard. He said, 'You were laughing then, but not now. Is it because Eiker has gone?'

'No. It's because I haven't.'

'Were you in love with him?'

She smiled, very bitter, very cynical, starting to feel the romance of her suffering as one does at nineteen.

'No, Dael. With his dancing, yes. Complete understanding, down below where words start. He'd move, I'd move, he'd move again and it was like painting a picture or making up a song and every note and light and movement fitted –

26

'I thought I fitted. I thought I finally belonged.'

'You do, Jez. You belong here.' (She heard his own edge of bitterness sharpening his words.) 'What more can you want? You've got your family, a job –'

She thought of Eiker: *You want it all*, and she did. Or at least as much as other people had. Words exploded from her: 'My parents want me to be somebody else, my sister's perfect, and if you think I always wanted to work on a prop-line you're crazy!'

'I thought you'd like working with plants.'

'Well, I would if they'd let me do the thing properly, but no! They can make more loot out of callus-prop than meristems –' She stopped; Dael looked blank. 'But you wouldn't understand, would you? You're from Earth.'

He glanced down, hurt, and she was sorry, but there was so much she was sorry about that it didn't seem worth finding all the words to tell him. It was all too much effort. Just being alive took every erg of energy she had left; there was none left over to spare on other people. She was amazed Dael bothered to waste time on her.

Dael said, 'You've got friends.'

'Friends! What do you know, Dael? They let you hang around with them so's they can use these lasers; they just keep me around like some cheap tart. When they're stoned I make them sound-pictures to get them higher, and they pay me with a little conversation when they feel like tossing it my way. I'm a prostitute, something they can use when they're in the mood. That's all.'

Dael tried to protest but she drowned him in words; she shouted her anger so fiercely that the remote, drifting abandoned, still picked up the vibration. Sudden topaze flared fitfully; each flicker etched into Dael.

Jezrael could feel his pain: some people stay naïve all their lives. He'd come here straight from some college on Earth one hundred and twenty degrees of arc ago, four months the way he'd measure it, and you'd think it was yesterday. He still thought day and night were time and not geography. She could feel she'd grated a nerve in him but he wanted to deny it:

'It's not true, Jez. They're not like that – well, not all of them, anyway.'

'Listen, Dael. You want to know what your friends are like? When we were kids at socialization school, they thought we were really funny, Chesarynth and me. We didn't speak the same as them, we were here before the factory came. They didn't know mass from mister when Nutristem shipped their folks up. Hell, our dad grew half of the homes they live in. Cheap rush jobs like Nutristem ordered, and then they'd screw up the feeding and the walls'd grow out of control, or the lights'd die, and they'd say it was our fault.

'And they were so scared! All the time, about everything. D'you know what scared people do? They hit out at you. Just because you're different and you're there. You know what they did to Ches – my sister?'

Dael shook his head; in the light gravity his hair spun slowly outwards, not quite settling. One of Jezrael's tears took eons to fall, a slow bright microcosm of grief.

The pain of that memory went too deep for words; Jezrael shied away from its sharpness. She trapped the words behind her lips, and Dael felt shut out, rejected.

Another silence grew, ponderous, vegetal. Both of them had run out of things to say. One day, Jezrael would apologize, but it would be too late then. The damage was already done, sinking into Dael's mind like lye. Things he knew but dared not think about, or ask.

The mellow chime of the quarter-bell cut the silence. Jezrael leaped up. 'Is that the time? Oh, hell! The groans'll kill me!'

Her leap took her half-way to the door; she punted off from the gym-bars but caught herself in the doorway long enough to say, 'Sorry I broke into your locker, Dael. And thanks for listening.'

Suit discipline. She almost didn't bother with it, but that would have been stupid. *I may be crazy*, she thought, *but I don't want them thinking I'm stupid.*

Boosting her launch with a muscle-wrenching kick

against the rough coral of the school-asteroid, Jezrael recklessly clipped her belt-line into Main Strand as she skimmed above it, hardly caring that if she had muffed it she would have gone spinning off, endlessly tumbling between the man-made planetoids around her or falling into a long dive towards death in the sun. Crescents of light crowned some of the larger asteroids on her left, or built them a plinth of fire; their bulging centres were black with the shadows of the asteroids on her right and astar with the luring lights of commerce. Almost everywhere she might have looked, above or below, radian strands angled out to inhabited coralline beads. Main Strand itself plunged from darkness to a sun-polished thread where sunlight burst between the shops and blocks of coral. The blue-green crescent of Earth played hide and seek with her behind the man-made spheres; Andronicus, the other asteroid cluster in the complementary Trojan orbit to Earth, was only a faint twinkling among the galaxy of stars.

None of it impinged on her.

As she hurtled carelessly along, she coded for her home-strand. Impulses localized in the groove she had entered pulled her along, stopping only when they encountered cross-directives from other travellers' belts.

It was late, though, late enough for the workers from the Spiderglass plant to be flooding out to their homes. Wide though the Main Strand was here, near the centre of Witwaterstrand, and many the possibilities in zero-gee of ducking higher or lower than the factory-hands, she still had to unclip and reclip a dozen times. Lines would tangle as people turned to talk to their friends; besides, the new consignment of worlders hadn't yet got used to the traffic up here. Normally traffic didn't bother Jezrael; now she was in a hurry it did.

At the end of Main Strand she took a fork, her visor darkening automatically as the full blaze of the sun broke upon her round the corner of the last huge block. The workers were branching off above, below, to either side, like pollen blown from a flower. Clumps of people formed buds that burst apart in good-byes, their suits a shine of colour against night and day.

Jezrael wouldn't take the time to wait. She unclipped, dived upwards to a radian, shooting past people's heads. The manoeuvre was safe enough with so many homes and stores around, but the worlders ducked and knotted their lines in panic. A score of voices roared into her suit-radio:

'Did you see that?'

'Are you all right?'

'Jeez!'

'She must be out of control.'

'Here, catch my line!'

But she was swimming through their net of lines, past them, away.

Downstrand, as far downstrand as you could get, Jezrael poled up to her parents' place. She scarcely even noticed the sign that said – in hologram, in radio – *Homes Grown*.

The Browns' place was an oblate spheroid, trailing a constellation of beaded wires. She and Chesarynth used to call it the lion's mane, from a picture in their copy of *The Big Book of the Earth*. Every time one of the 'beads' grew big enough to be hollowed out and lived in, Jezrael's father would sell it and her mother would set up the biomod to suit the customer.

Take anaerobic bacteria and coral polyps. Make them symbiotic and alter them genetically for the growth-rate you want; a little re-arrangement here in the DNA for extra strength in the shell to withstand vacuum and a range of temperatures down to absolute zero; devise a feeding mixture and add a wire around which the polyps can accrete, like growing crystals on a piece of string. Bathe it in pure sunlight, and you've got the basis for an asteroid you can live in. It's already in your chosen orbit and if you let it, it'll grow as your family does. Or your business. And at a fraction of the price you'd have to pay for hauling a shell of metal to just where you wanted it.

The advert was dense, old-fashioned, the colours fusing a little with age. Jezrael had always wanted her father to

30

change it for something with a little more zest, but Owen Brown had never wanted it to be as gaudy as it was when he first bought it and the music sang through you whenever you went by. He preferred its softened version, the voice slowed down to a friendly drawl. It sounded less like an insurance salesman, he said. Jezrael and Chesarynth thought it was just plain dowdy. When they'd brought boyfriends home for the first time, it had been an embarrassment.

Unclipped, taking a chance that her mother wasn't monitoring outside for her arrival, Jezrael took off. Weaving between the nodes that would one day be homes, she cut corners and jumped straight towards the front door.

She slipped through the air-skin and unsuited. No-one called out to her; no-one asked, 'Have you had a nice day?' Jezrael was glad her parents weren't around to nag, but all the same she wished someone was there in the background, for company.

Nineteen and no good. I'll never be that good.

'What time is it?' she asked, and the bio-crystal computer answered in its avuncular voice, 'Twenty eighty-five.'

The gravity had been left at Earth-normal, her mother's preference. Jezrael's legs ached from the strain of her laser-dance; her mind was weary from emotional exhaustion. And she still had to feed the walls.

She got the sprays from their place in the kitchen. Walking listlessly from room to room, feeding the growths that made the light, Jezrael asked, 'Any messages?'

'Some business ones. A new family wants a five-room home over on Diamond Strand and the Poitevins are still complaining that their kitchen walls won't stop growing. Khota Lal wants a porch put –'

'I meant,' Jezrael said, 'any for me?' Her voice quavered a little. She hadn't realized until now that she was hoping Eiker would suddenly call and say, 'Come back, we need you.'

The computer said, 'No, Jezrael.' (Her arm, with the

31

feeding can, stopped describing its regular arcs; one swirling pattern on the wall glowed a warmer rose.) 'None for you today. Sorry.'

After that, Jezrael didn't even notice what she was doing. It was a miracle that the designs on the walls stayed anything like the same.

Belatedly she said, 'Are the dust-bugs out?' and when the computer answered 'yes' she had him pitch the whistle that called them irresistibly so the tiny mechanoids wouldn't be underfoot. She got dinner out of the freezer, something that would flash-cook when her parents came in, stuffed her sprawl of holo-cubes into a suck-sack in her room.

And then she ran out of things to do.

It was late when her folks got back. Jezrael's mother finally found her resting her head on the calf's flank in Eden. It was their one luxury: a farm-asteroid with dual gravity. A centripetal gravity allowed them to use the whole interior skin as a garden, and another, adjustable, gravity-source held a private sun in the exact centre of the asteroid. Jezrael's father had grown it big enough for a cow and a calf, and some birds grown from expensive ova-banks. There were vegetables and nut-bushes, orange and lilac trees, and overhead, in the glowing ball of water that diffused its own version of sunlight, neon fish swam with rainbow trout.

'Didn't you hear me, Jezrael?' (The shadow of a cloud passed over Jezrael's closed eyelids; that was her mother.) 'I've been calling and calling you. Dinner melted all over the counter. Where have you been?'

'Hi, Mom. I was here. Sorry about dinner. What time is it?'

'Twenty-three seventeen. It should have been night in here long before this. It's not fair on the animals. You know I don't like you messing about with the systems in here.'

Jezrael stood, taller than her mother but the same general shape, somewhere between slender and plump.

She blinked, yawning and stretching, trying to emigrate from her interior world and make contact with her mother's reality. 'They'll be all right, Mom. They've just had summer, that's all.'

'Don't be flip with me. You know I don't like it. Now switch it over to twilight so the poor things can get some sleep, and get in and sort out the mess you've made in the kitchen.'

'Yes, Mom.'

Her mother gave a fine theatrical performance of someone looking around her. 'Where's your suit, Jezrael? Don't tell me. You poled across without it. You'd better come back in the spare. How many times do I have to tell you not to forget suit-discipline? You're old enough to know better. And make sure you bring the spare back over here before you go to bed. I don't want anyone getting caught in Eden without it. Clear?'

'Clear. Sorry.'

Her mother walked out, her suit's heavy shoes bruising the grass-stems. However long she lived here, Eiral Brown would never really get used to it. To her, Earth with its hills and its gravity and its mobile air would always be home. Witwaterstrand was just the place where she lived.

Jezrael mooched over to the control-panel in its niche by the door. Gently twisting the rheostat, she made the golden sun fade. It softened to ruby, then to rose, and she held it there a while. The hens clucked over the chickens, white wings outspread to gather them into shelter. An echo answered the rooster's tentative call, and in the sweet-scented evening blackbirds sang good-night from the lilacs.

With the warmth still lingering in the air, Jezrael jigged the gravities. It was gravity that held the water-ball in the centre; she lessened its force the merest fraction. There was a stopper on the centre's control-disc but she didn't turn it quite that far; she didn't want to drown the farm.

A fine rain began to fall. The soil still remembered the heat of the day; where the rain kissed it, a light mist steamed upwards, back towards the gentle sun. Jezrael had made clouds. She switched the centre-grav back on full and the rain stopped.

Now she flicked the light brighter, just for a second, and the clouds stood edged with banners of gold. Jezrael inhaled that perfect moment; peace was moist earth and lilac, and she tried to hold it in her lungs, but she had to breathe out and night had to fall. Moonlight was not something the farm did very well.

Sighing, Jezrael pulled on the cumbersome spare suit, though for the few seconds it would take her to pole back home she didn't think she needed it. Neither vacuum nor the absence of pressure would kill her in such a short time in space; some of the gang she hung around with in Bidonville gambled with the void, daring each other to see who chickened out first and ducked back inside. *Not me, though. Too sensible? Or just too scared?*

Into her fragile serenity poured thoughts of the outside world, a jagged scar on her mind. *Too straight for Eiker, not straight enough for Mom. I'm not good enough at being what they want me to be.*

It was nearly tomorrow. All she had to do was survive the hidden depths of the night and she could face up to who she was going to live as.

Jezrael looked back once at the calf nestled up to its mother, her glance a caress. Then she draped the helmet cosmetically across her shoulders (unfastened), and slipped out through the air-skin.

2

Karel Tjerssen of Spiderglass was looking for something very special: a weapon. A two-edged weapon. He had been looking for it without even realizing for a very long time. Now all the ideas had gelled. It was time to go to Witwaterstrand to see if the seeds he'd planted had grown the way he wanted. Trouble was, there was all that lightless black vacuum to cross to get to it. Karel was twenty-three, broad-shouldered and lithe; blond, with eyes clear as zircons; and by his own efforts he had graduated top of his class. With his immense fortune, he was everything any man would want to be – but he was scared stiff of flying. Let alone lifting off from the mother planet into the black void beyond.

The recliner pushed up hard at him as the hired non-Company yacht reached escape velocity. He felt his face seem to melt, his cheeks flow down, his mouth split in a rictus of gee-force. His heart thudded in the cage of his chest and the eyeballs sank back in his head, sending odd-coloured lightning spearing through his brain. However often he told himself that space-flight was perfectly normal, each take-off felt like it was the one in which he'd crash. This time the helpless bag of soft tissues that was his body would be hurled back to earth to be smashed to shapeless bloody pulp. And enough people wanted him dead that the slight risk of accident in take-off could be magnified by several orders of magnitude. They'd got his father, hadn't they? And probably his grandmother.

Not only that. Wasn't there some thing or other that just – disappeared ships? What was it the workers called it? Some superstitious name they gave it? The Gate, that was it. The Gate to Heaven. *How stupid can you get? Might as well believe in little green men from Venus.* Still, ships had been disappearing here and there, just winking off the monitors, not even wreckage left behind. Nameless fear pushed his anxiety-level up another notch. *I'm getting as bad as a worker,* he told himself bitterly, but Karel wouldn't take tranquillizers in case they'd been doctored, or in case he really did crash and needed to stay sharp to survive.

Besides, he thought in self-disgust, *I'm supposed to be in line for chief of security and I won't get it if my dearly beloved relatives on the Board find out I'm such a coward.*

So Karel, many-times-great grandson of the Spiderglass Founder, tried to hide his fear even from himself by turning his attention outwards. As the pressure eased slightly and he began to be able to see through the blur of acceleration, he stared out of the viewport at Crystal City. No longer obscured by Earth's atmosphere, it gleamed like a bauble on a child's Christmas tree. With the planet receding, with the height he might fall growing greater by the second, he remembered the first time he had seen the city circling inside the orbit of the Moon close up. Must be about eleven years ago now ....

'Look out the window, Grandmama. It's like a star made of glass!' the twelve-year-old Karel had exclaimed. His excited shout filled the yacht's stateroom, quiet but for the musical hiss of the samovar.

Ignoring the indulgent smiles of her ladies-in-waiting, the grins of the bodyguards, Alissja Tjerssen reproved the boy. 'It's vulgar to stare like that, Karel. That is what workers might do.'

Karel swung away from the sheet of spiderglass that made up the viewport. Against the vastness of star-hung space he was a short, defiant figure, a pale exclamation mark in the cheerful room. Round-faced, he still managed to glare almost as haughtily as the Lady Alissja but he sounded sulky even to himself. 'Why, Grandmama? I thought you wanted me to be happy. I thought you brought me here for my birthday treat.'

Alissja, a beautiful woman who seemed no older than thirty, held out her hand for the tea. Her taster stirred the sweet lemon paste into the drink with her analyser, then sipped and waited; neither the analyser nor the dull-brained human found anything wrong with the drink. The Lady Alissja smiled and thanked the woman graciously.

'Why, Grandmama?' the boy persisted, scowling when the taster would have interrupted by handing him his cup.

Alissja dismissed her attendants; the three guards stayed, but nobody ever paid them any attention. Since they were under hypnotic compulsion they were incapable of repeating anything they heard. Alissja sighed, carefully, not stretching the new skin of her face. 'Because, you tiresome boy, workers do not care what emotions they display. They don't see how we can control them through their wants and expectations.

'You are different. You are an heir of Spiderglass, the largest empire of Earth. Reacting visibly like that could be dangerous, inside and outside the Company. Isn't that what your deportment tutors teach you – the purpose behind decorum?'

Karel shrugged. 'If workers are allowed to be happy, why aren't I?'

'Of course you're allowed to be happy. It's just that when you grow to be a man, your pleasure will be someone else's reward, your displeasure their punishment. You must learn to keep it all inside, tidily, ready for when you want it. There are many things you'll want to keep hidden so you must practise. Now drink your tea.'

'I don't want to!'

'That'll teach me a lesson, won't it?' she said calmly.

Karel stalked disdainfully back to the viewpoint, watched by the three guards, protected by all that scanners and shields could do, safe from the vacuum in the warm bright world of the Tjerssen yacht.

In the airless dark beyond, Crystal City slowly blossomed against the bulk of Earth, firing continuous bursts of solar energy down through the smog of atmosphere to the power stations below. The satellite city was enough to capture anyone's attention: a diamond of sparkling petals, a circling castle belonging entirely to Spiderglass. It wasn't as big or as old as Steel City that lay over the horizon behind them, but its icy perfection was entrancing. In it were labs, theatres, grand hotels and recycling plants. Home to tens of thousands, the office to not a few. But most of all, it was a spun-sugar wonder that shone with the fires of nascent day.

'Do you like it, Karel?'

'It's beautiful, Grandmama.'

'And it's yours.'

The blond boy spun so fast his hair flared out around him, a crown for a king. 'Really? Do you mean it? You're not teasing, are you?'

Lady Alissja smiled, the dimple she'd had put in one cheek working according to specifications. So it should, the amount she'd paid the plastic surgeons who had re-modelled her. 'No, Karel, I'm not teasing. Your father's branch of the Company built it.'

Now Karel came to kneel at the Lady Alissja's feet, his face transfigured. He gazed at her with rapt, loving eyes. 'Oh, thank you, thank you, Grandmama,' he whispered, his voice sliding an octave in the middle of the phrase. A blush he felt rising made him awkward.

'But, Karel, you may not have it until you are adult in behaviour. There are plenty in Spiderglass who covet it themselves. Sit and have your tea. We'll be landing soon.'

Karel drank, obedient now that he had his present, smelling the soft perfume of authentic musk and rose and citron that was his grandmother, heiress to half the wealth of Spiderglass. There was the slightest sharp tang of fixative about her piles of silver-gilt curls, the merest hint of the nutrient creams that fed the perfect, grafted skin of her face and neck. Neither Karel nor Alissja thought of the worker whose skin that had once been. The sweet, cloudy tea steamed fragrantly. Everything was normal, familiar, pressing down his shameful fear of space-travel.

And Karel, receptive, never even noticed as his Grandmama cued his subconscious learning-centres with his personal code.

'Karel, learn this now. You must learn this now.' Lady Alissja's voice chanted soothingly, cadenced to lull the boy still further. 'You have secrets. I have secrets. Everybody does. We all have things that we want to hide from one another, or even from ourselves. We all like to pretend that we are universally loved, that we are good and kind and noble. We think to ourselves that if only we had the chance, we'd show heroism such as hasn't been seen since the days of old. And we think that people admire us.

'But often we delude ourselves. We blame others for our failures when really it was our fault. We fail of resolution, of carry-through, if you like. We let the moments whirl away our good intentions. Or we allow ourselves to be lazy, or to become careless. We believe we are perceptive but we don't see the pain we inflict on others. And how can we, if we can't even acknowledge our own secret face? We think we are satin when really we are harsh as gravel.

'And you must learn, my Karel,' she said, stroking the soft cheek of the boy at her side as she no longer could now when he was awake. 'You must learn to be gracious, to be kind, to be polite even to workers, even when you don't want to be. For the day may come when they are all that stand between you and certain death and if they don't like you, they won't lift a finger to save you.

'And you must learn too that you can be hurt through your desires. If your enemies know what you want, they can take it from you. And half the time you won't even know who is your enemy and who your friend. So no, Karel, don't make your feelings into a vulgar display. Keep your thoughts and desires to yourself or you offer your enemies a loaded weapon pointing straight at your heart. And when you are old enough, you will remember about your secret face, the stranger that you keep inside you, and the stranger that watches you out of the eyes of even your closest kin. Now wake up and finish your tea like a good boy.'

But it wasn't the stranger inside that Karel remembered best about that day, nor his first sight of the Crystal City that would belong to him one day if he survived.

No, what stayed with him was shame.

Still vivid in his mind was the explosion that ruptured the viewport as his grandmother's yacht tacked in to dock. The spiderglass shattered into dust, flying across the room, knife-edged sand that killed his grandmother and slashed Karel's skin to ribbons in the microsecond before it was sucked out again in a pearly cloud as the atmosphere fled roaring into vacuum, and the two guards who were dragged out with it, their bodies hanging dark against the shimmering cloud before they too exploded, staining the opal red.

Karel felt himself tumble, flying head over heels across the stateroom, dragged helpless in the howling gale towards the window on death. He saw the other guard cartwheel past him and Karel cringed, scrabbling for a handhold to save himself. Who cared about the guard? He was mean anyway. Twelve-year-old Karel grovelled frenzied hands into the depths of the sofa that wedged itself slantwise across the viewport and the guard spun outwards with a shriek of despair.

But the shame wasn't that he hadn't tried to save the guard's life – though that's what Karel would have liked to think. What could he, just a boy, have done against the raging vacuum?

No, what had sickened Karel was that for the fleeting seconds it took the glass shards to flay the Lady Alissja, her clothes had been ripped from her plasti-sculptured body and he hadn't been able to look away from the perfectly shaped, bleeding breasts of his own grandmother.

Nothing was ever proved one way or the other – an enemy of Spiderglass or some rival within the Company itself. For years Karel had thought about it but the only answers came to him in nightmares, peeling back the skin of their faces as Grandmama's face and body had been peeled by the blast, and underneath the bloody flesh of uncles or cousins were the secret faces of strangers.

'Eh? Oh, fine, thanks. I was just dozing,' twenty-three-year-old Karel said, groping back through the impressions of the last few moments since the crew-man had obviously asked several times how he was. 'Get me a coñac, will you?'

The crew-man turned to obey. Karel added casually, 'Oh, and a coffee with fresh cream.' It would never do for the worker to think that he needed a stiff drink just because of a take-off. Still, it wouldn't matter; Karel was planning to fix the crew anyway.

Later, with the coñac a hot fire unkinking his guts, Karel thought about the two-edged weapon he was on his way to make. A weapon that nobody else knew about. A weapon so secret that it didn't even know it was going to be a weapon.

Karel waited until he was alone. Breathing deeply, he forced himself to relax, centring on the rhythms of heart and lungs, intent on the chug of them as though he were a baby listening to the music of the womb. Back then there was no limit to the paths he might choose. Using the openness that came to him he brought himself forward through time as his tutors had shown him, concentrating on his body-image, perfecting it. Behind his closed eyelids he could see the tanned, muscular triangle of his torso, the unlined forehead above the brown-blond eyebrows. The tiny muscles around his eyes relaxed; he fed oxygen to them, imagining it strengthening him, making his face younger, more innocent than it would ever be again. And his eyes were a bright, clear blue, pale as glaciers in the sun.

Calm now, receptive now, one well-shaped hand moved sleepily to take a pin out of the flowing white shirt he wore. To an observer it must have seemed as though he were playing with the jewelled pin, admiring it, scratching an itch or two on the inside of his wrist.

What he was actually doing was acupressuring memory access codes so that a conscious pathway formed to areas of the brain most people could never use. The connections were manufactured from non-soluble fibre that wouldn't show up on X-rays. Mental enhancement was the primary discipline Karel had studied at the Spiderglass laboratories that were supposed to have been dismantled on the Moon when Ole took over the Company.

Seemingly asleep, Karel concentrated on reviewing his plans. All the obvious steps had been taken over the last three years under the noses of Berndt and Theresien and the rest of the usurpers on the Board, with their full approval.

The other steps they knew nothing about at all.

Now, with perfect recall, Karel viewed the sisters he had chosen precisely because nobody knew he knew about them. What connection could there possibly be between him and some obscure family in Witwaterstrand, where he had never been? The taller girl, strong, brittle, blond hair, hysterical, intelligent but under-achieving because of her rebelliousness.

A word here, a word there, always under cover, and he thwarted the two possible avenues of achievement that were open to her. He'd had someone book a laser-dance trio for a jet-set party in Madrid, providing there was no change to the line up. Then Karel had had the go-between's memory altered a little to include waking up in the wrong bed; Karel had done it himself and it had been artistic. So the guy was never going to talk about why he'd booked Eiker when it was Eiker he'd been in bed with....

And it hadn't been hard to have the culture-shippers put Nutristem under pressure to provide more and quicker because the Spiderglass colonies set up by Karel's father were alleged to be starving. Rumours were child's play. The Junoesque blond girl wasn't going to be entangled in anything worthwhile for the foreseeable future....

And Mars! Mars had been a piece of cake. The government of Mars had practically wet itself when they heard Spiderglass wanted to invest. What easier than to suggest a few practical aids in self-sufficiency in return for a little help? It hardly changed the system anyway. Made it a little more efficient, maybe. Made recruitment easier for the

Company. Karel hid a frown. And for their enemies, Madreidetic. But you couldn't make an omelette. . . .

Sure, some of the students at the university might be a little hard-up but they'd still get an education, wouldn't they? And none of them need actually starve. The quota system based on loans set up five years ago was perfectly fair. And it would stop them helling around in the puritan cities. The ecofreaks on Mars were real pleased about that.

Karel laid it out neatly for them, this bait. Of course they could jig the results if a certain girl from – where was it? Witwaterstrand? – would end up at Mars-U. The short, slim, darker girl was a workaholic anyway. She'd only need a nudge or two when the time was ripe.

Karel changed the rhythm of his breathing, brought his heart-rate up a notch or two to break out of the light memory-trance. *The best of it is,* he thought sleepily, *nobody even knows the plans are in my head, and they sure aren't anywhere else. My dearly beloved uncle and aunt, who probably killed my grandmother and almost certainly did my father in, don't even know there's a two-edged weapon pointed at their hearts.*

And its twin name is Brown.

3

At 07.99 next shift, Jezrael went to work. Or rather, the artificial construct, the personality that other people had built out of her body and her abilities, went through the routine that her parents and her teachers and her employers had decided was best for her: that was what went to her job. Her body carried a headache with some numb being inside it.

She drifted towards level forty-nine of the vast, tubular factory. Above and below her, other workers in their rainbow airsuits were arriving almost like bees at the entrance to a hive: each group of drones had their own flight-paths, their own entrance.

Not exactly flight-paths, though. It was too dangerous just to drift around in space. Every worker was on one of the hundreds of monocellular semi-rigid cords that gave Witwaterstrand its name. In the centre of the asteroid colony, the strands had romantic names of heroes or nebulae or the home-places on Earth, but around the Nutristem labs the threads were just numbers, and each worker just hooked on to thread twenty or whatever. The greater the number, the lower your status. And Jezrael hooked her suit on to thread number forty-nine.

Jezrael used hands and feet to slow her impetus or she wouldn't have been able to pass the air-skin that was formed by a combination of bacteria and physics. The air in the lock had a surface tension great enough to stop any mere molecule of gas escaping and elastic enough to allow large bodies through – providing they were moving sufficiently slowly. It felt like walking through a balloon and the very idea tended to upset earthers when they came up to Witwaterstrand, but it was what Jezrael had grown up with. It never made her nervous to look out through a transparent hole and see the stars.

Once inside the transparent air-skin, aseptic light seemed to grind on her eyeballs that were dry with lack of sleep. Jezrael wished she had something else to do but work here, only she hadn't. She took off her suit and muttered a few greetings, and mooched disconsolate to her work-station.

Light, warmth, moisture: the propagation lab was as safe – and as boring – as a womb. Thought was hardly required, just a mindless sort of concentration so that her hands did only what they were supposed to with the fiddly bits of plants. Abstract logic was impossible in that sterile atmosphere. So Jezrael didn't think. Only last night she believed she'd found an escape, her way out of Witwater-strand. Only last night she'd thought she was worth something in her own right. Then Eiker –

Thinking hurt. Lulled by the wallpaper music, she suspended it.

There came a break in the soft, monotonous music. Jezrael lifted her head, freed from the half-hypnotic state the prop-lab engendered in its drones. With such repetitive tasks, Nutritstem Inc knew two hours was the maximized concentration-span, even using wallpaper music. For seven minutes Jezrael and the others were free in the emptiness left by silenced subliminals. And in Jezrael the nothing flared into grief.

Jezrael walked amid the others, surrounded by their chatter as they headed for the suitroom. It had struck her, at first, how strange it was that the short breaks were taken in the suitroom, next to the toilets and the sterilizators, where the day-glo suits ballooned from their pegs in front of the star-view through the air-skin.

'It's weird,' she had said to Ild, the fat, jolly woman they had told to take care of the newcomer on her first shift an orbit and a half ago. That was eighteen months in Earth terms or for Chesarynth, getting on for two Martian years. But Jezrael didn't want to think about her sister's success either when all she was herself was a mere factory hand. She had asked, 'And why seven minutes?'

Ild sat on the shoe-locker and a tab fell out of her hands. She had to open her legs wide to make space for her belly between them when she bent to pick the pink tablet up. Jezrael tried to get it first, for politeness' sake. The two of them clashed heads and Big Ild laughed at the girl's apology. Though Ild was a section supervisor there'd been no hint of it in her manner. There still wasn't.

'Not strange at all, Jez. It takes a minute to walk here, a minute back, and five minutes for a breath. You couldn't get up to the cafeteria in that time. Want one?'

But Jezrael was too straight to take a breath.

It was the same now, eighteen months later, and no-one had come running to give her a job dancing laser, or any other job at all.

The men congregated at the far end, nearest the toilets, whispering risqué stories and betting with each other or some of the older women, ostentatiously facing the air-skin as if to prove some childish boast: *I'm not afraid the air-skin'll rupture and we'll all be sucked out into space.* It had taken a while for Jezrael to see how all those Earth-borns really were scared about that.

Jezrael still sat in Big Ild's protection, hiding her in-securities under the tide of Ild's gossip, and Ild snapped a tab for a quick hit that seemed only to make her laugh more than ever. Now, though, Jezrael knew why Ild laughed all the time, why she didn't care what she looked like, why she even borrowed the psychotropic story-cubes Jezrael's friends from the dance-bar sometimes lent her.

Watching hilarity grow as the pink tab spread its breath through Ild, Jezrael knew a sudden envy. The way she felt today, she'd have liked to try that compressed euphoria, only there wasn't enough of her left to interrupt Big Ild's story.

'Well, I could have died,' Ild was saying jocularly. Two or three others were listening too. 'There was E.D., my awful wedded husband, weaving 'is way out of one of them bars in the Wasp's Nest in Bidonville, and there was me, scraping to make ends meet, pawning me engagement ring to get a new suit for me baby. 'Course, I was new up here then, still petrified of the vacuum. I felt so guilty when I saw him. I didn't know where to put meself.'

Jezrael had heard this one before, knew its every cadence and dropped aitch. The other listeners were equally familiar with it, but Ild told it so well, with innate timing and practised vocabulary, part of Ild's life that hurt the big woman so much she couldn't help talking about it. Yet the memory was so painful that Ild had to dress it up as a story, pretend it didn't cut her, pretend she didn't care. Jezrael asked herself if one day she'd do that too. The story of Eiker....

'Go on then, Ild, what did you do?' someone asked, stepping into the trap of the dramatic pause Big Ild had left.

'Well, I felt terrible. I felt bad enough just going into Bidonville in the first place, let alone into the Wasp's Nest to pawn the ring me beloved' – the word dripped irony – 'had sacrificed so much to get. I knew he had, because he'd told me all about it on the trip up from Earth, how much it had cost. I felt like a traitor.

'But kids don't stop growing just because you've only got one lot of money coming in, and I didn't dare ask E.D. for any more. Didn't seem right, like, with him out working all the hours under the sun, so tired after a shift that he was staggering when he came in through the door. We wasn't more than twenty, the pair of us.

'So one shift when he said he wouldn't be back 'til twenty-three, there was this rush job on at work, he said, and we could do with the money 'cause he'd had to borrow the rent – well, I slipped into Bidonville, that awful place, hating myself, going red as fire every time some drunk started tapping me up. And then I saw E.D. coming out of a bar by the pawn-shop, arms round these two blokes who was helping him handle the gravity-shifts 'cause he's not that good at it even when he's sober. And the stink of liquor coming off them! You'd think they was a distillery! He'd always told me it was the smell of one of them chemicals they use on you at Spiderglass. And I used to believe him.

'Well, I tried to hide but there wasn't nowhere I could go. Even drunk as he was, I knew he'd seen me.'

It was Jezrael's turn, helping Ild to perform for the others, the magician's apprentice. 'So what did he say, Ild?'

Ild laughed, and when she laughed all her fat laughed with her, wheezing up and down like a concertina flexilock. 'Say? He didn't say nothing! Just sort of looked the other way as if he was dead interested in the adverts coming off the wall.'

Ild had her audience hooked now. The six-minute warning-muzak broke out, a prod in the background that no-one actually acknowledged in words. They just drifted to their feet and began pushing back towards their workbenches. Someone asked, 'So what did you say?' and Ild laughed again.

'I never said nothing neither, just sort of walked past him as if I wasn't there. But I went back next shift when I knew he'd be at Spiderglass, and I sold the pawn-shop woman my ring. Got me baby's suit and a new data-cube player and E.D.'s never asked where the money come from. He wouldn't dare!'

And Jezrael, looking back from the crowded doorway, wondered if everyone was like that: say one thing and do another, the way Eiker had said she would be a big star if she came with him, but when it came time to leave he said, 'You're not good enough.' Did you have to keep selling yourself, making out you were what they wanted, one long compromise with no chance of winning?

The subliminal music started again, soft but compelling her to her work-bench among the crowds of others. One last glance back through the hanging suits showed the cosmos, black and crystal shimmering through the transparent air-skin, and the only big star was the sun.

Along about twelve seventy-five, when her stomach was beginning to think about eating, something touched

Jezrael's shoulder. She jumped and dropped the plant she'd just propagated, but the jar only fell a few milli-metres and the tiny cutting stayed secure in its rooting medium. Seeing then that it was one of the management, Jezrael felt foolish, but the woman apologized for startling her. It was not what Jezrael expected from the hierarchy; it made her nervous.

'Can I just check your prop?' the woman said, moving to do it anyway so that Jezrael almost overbalanced in shifting aside.

The woman wasn't anyone Jezrael knew, just someone in the wasteful flowing clothing of the managerial staff. She wasn't wearing a cap; she didn't even spray her hands. Whoever she was, she simply unsealed the plantlet in its jar, and prodded the little bit of green with her finger-nail. The cutting skidded across the nutrient jelly, leaving its growth hormones in a faint verdant trail behind it where they wouldn't do any good.

Jezrael's lips tightened so that she wouldn't accidentally express her anger. Surely the woman must know she'd wrecked the sterility of the prop-jar? That the poor little cutting was damaged now beyond hope?

But the woman merely screwed the lid back on the jar and shelved it with the rest. She even had the cheek to press Jezrael's quality-control seal back in place.

'Supervisor Ild informs me,' the woman began, measuring Jezrael with her eyes, 'that you have some ideas about improving quality. Come and see me in your lunch-break. Seventeenth level, night-side.'

And the woman walked away, just like that, not even giving her name, as if she were so important she didn't need to say who she was. But Jezrael couldn't puzzle it out just now; the metal arm that curled out from the back of her work-station had lassoed a dozen culture-pots from the conveyor belt and they were piling up dangerously. If she didn't do something soon, they'd be smashing on to the floor.

At thirteen the wallpaper music stopped. The conveyor belts stopped. For a moment, before the workers could react, the only noise was the cellular strain of plants growing, and though Jezrael had considered it time and again, she could never hear it. She just knew at some level that it must exist.

Then the reaction-time was over and the workers began talking of lunch, and dates, and arguments they'd had the free-shift before. It filled the down-time of factory life. The sound crashed over Jezrael, swept her along in an ocean of babel and shuffling footsteps.

From the next aisle, a few metres nearer the tube, Ild called through the open parts of the work-station, 'You going out today then, Jez?'

Jezrael ducked to yell back, 'No, not this shift.' No more sneaking out at lunchtime to meet Eiker, maybe dance a little laser with him or just blow the froth off a couple in some nearby bar. Not this shift, nor the next, not ever.

'I'll save you a place then, will I, love?'

'You can buy me a soup-bulb, if you like. I've got to go and see some baggy up on seventeen.'

Ild and Jezrael were past the end of the benches now, where they met like radii with the tube as the focus. All around were workers from their lab, queueing for a turn on the grav-lift where little pink strands of motile light separated the tube into sections so no-one travelling up or down accidentally trod on the ear of the person below. Sheet metal made vertical barriers between the fast and the slow lifts. No-one else was waiting for a fast ride up.

From her place in the line of hungry workers, Ild called, 'Why, what you been doing then?'

'You got me,' Jezrael answered, shrugging.

A man behind Ild said, 'Have I got you too?'

Jezrael never quite knew how to take Lew, whether he was really as crude as he made out, or if he was just trying to flirt on the principle that all women want fat old men to flirt with them. This time she was safe because he wasn't within touching distance, but she still couldn't think of anything to say to him or his insinuations.

She stepped into the fast shaft, alone, feeling that once again she'd wimped out by not saying anything to Lew. *I bet he's laughing.* But more important worries assailed her. What did the baggy want her to say? The truth? Some new revolutionary system that would improve quality without losing output? What had Ild got her into?

Promotion. If I can convince her, maybe we can stop sending out mutations. (The plain, shiny walls distracted Jezrael. On this fast lift no-one had the time for the long streaks of graffiti that the cleaning machines had to burn off the slow shaft.) *Then I'll get promotion and I won't have to listen to that cotton-wool music any more. (Or don't they have anything to complain about in exec-land?)*

A deep red sign warned her that floor 17 was coming up; the shaft was pulling her so fast she only just made it off in time. Jezrael stepped through the cold draught where the air-streams collided and found herself in a padded corridor that swelled to accommodate a human secretary at a desk.

She pressed the button to attract his attention but his awareness was locked inside the machine. It gave Jezrael the creeps. She pressed the stud again. When nothing happened she waited, and waited, wondering about pressing it a third time, but before she had made up her mind he jacked out of his terminal and said, 'Jezrael Brown? I'll inform Ms Chowdhury that you're here. Please take a seat.'

He waved her to a bench that was moulded out of the wall-padding. Jezrael got to know it very well in the fifty metric minutes she had to wait. She was amazed to notice that the lights were electric, not bioluminescent. Her mother made much prettier lighting systems. *When they accept me on the staff, I'll tell them. Maybe Mom'd like a big commission like this....*

There was also some self-congratulatory advertising 'literature'. Fortunately it wasn't very loud, though the words kept flashing out at her long after she had put the brochure back on the padded table. Jezrael spent the time instead trying not to feel hungry, and marshalling her arguments in her head.

Finally the clerk sent a glow-track that directed her

down long, uninhabited corridors. It wasn't like a true Witwaterstrand place. There were no plants and only trite Nutristem pictures of orchards or waving corn to break up the spaces between the doors.

The glow-track flowered against a door. When Jezrael knocked and walked in, she saw that Ms Chowdhury didn't rate a real window, just a warped old holo of Witwaterstrand. She hadn't even got an office all to herself, just one desk in a circle of others. Standing opposite her, waiting to be noticed, Jezrael felt she was the focus of all eyes. It didn't help one bit.

'Oh, there you are, Serael,' Ms Chowdhury said at last. 'Sit down. Now, what's this theory of quality control your supervisor claims you have?'

Ms Chowdhury's cool incivility showed Jezrael – in retrospect – that this baggy didn't want competition from mere lab-workers. At the time Jezrael thought it was only that the woman was working too hard to waste a single moment on courtesy.

'Serael! I haven't got all shift.'

She hasn't even got my name right!

Jezrael sat quickly on the low chair across the desk whose polished acres held only a small recessed keyboard. The holo was so off-centre that Ms Chowdhury seemed to be sitting among the coral knobs of Witwaterstrand, her loose hair a chiaroscuro corona of the sun. Jezrael felt reduced to insignificance; her regiments of logic dissolved and blew away. It made her babble.

'I work with the new Mars-plants every shift and I can see that when we work on callus material – you know, when you deliberately damage a plant so it sends growth hormones to the wound, you know, so it repairs itself, well I can see that it gives you faster propagations and more of them than if you work from the growing tip, but because the callus is designed as a sort of, well, scar, there's a lot of ones that don't grow right. They might look all right but they don't give you any fruit at the end of it and there's people out there going hungry –'

Ms Chowdhury didn't focus on Jezrael, but at a

point just behind her, not so much intent as disinterested. Jezrael found the way Ms Chowdhury's opulent figure sat as still as a vase unnerving, too. Only a slight artificial breeze stirred the flower-patterned robe; the quality-control woman totally failed to react to what Jezrael was trying to say.

Jezrael swallowed. Her argument limped along lamely. None of the other five people in the room said a word, and not one of them seemed to be doing anything but listening to her.

'I mean,' Jezrael said desperately, her thoughts unravelling. 'I mean we should go back to axilliary meristems. I know you don't get quite so many cuttings but more of them are viable in the long run.'

Still no response. Anger flared in Jezrael. 'Look,' she shouted, leaning forward as if she could get closer to Ms Chowdhury that way at least, but Ms Chowdhury was sitting serene in the black and silver holo, far away, unreachable, her eyes in the stars.

'Look! It's not just some fancy company name that's at stake here. It's people on Mars finding that suddenly the food-plants they've bought won't feed them! You could be killing thousands! People could be starving to death because of you, can't you see that? Or suffocating because your mutations don't give off oxygen like they should do. Don't you care about any of that?'

Ms Chowdhury uncrossed her legs; the obsolete skirt she wore floated, resettled. She put one elegant hand on the polished wood of her desk – it wore Saturn's rings like a jewel – tapped her ugly long nails arhythmically. 'You're being a trifle over-dramatic ... ah ... Serael. Better to meet our quotas on time with a reasonable degree of success than slow deliveries down to meet your perfectionism, wouldn't you say? Better to let people have some food than none until your perfect clones come through?

'On your way out, think of the costings. How under the sun do you think fledgeling colonies could afford stock with a hundred percent guarantee? Unless, of course, you've got some sort of a faster-than-light transport system in your pocket, like this mythical Gate you people out here in the boon-docks seem to believe in?

'No? Well there's no other method of cutting costs. We don't want to price ourselves out of the market, do we? Without us, how could half the population of this orbiting rabbit-warren afford to eat? The stores would close, and the clothiers, and who'd pay for the school or the medical centre? Witwaterstrand would be a ghost town, now wouldn't it? You really should think things through.'

'But you didn't give me a chance!'

Ms Chowdhury's face arranged itself in a beautiful, mocking smile. 'I listened to every word you said. Without interruption. Your argument just didn't stand up – you should have brought a stake up with you.'

Faint laughter came from the other baggies. Jezrael flushed in embarrassment. She stood, sure she would fall over her feet on her way out because they seemed the size of those polished wooden desks. As she closed the door behind her, she heard the woman say, 'Really! These people must be lobotomized to get a job here. What do they think quality control's for?'

Choosing the slow lift down so she could compose herself, Jezrael wished she had a print-spray. There were plenty of things she could think of now to say to Ms Chowdhury. *Lobotomized! What about their flaming subliminals?* The whole dinner-hour had gone, wasted.

She was late back on station. Jezrael didn't even check to see whether her pay had been docked; about that, at least, Nutristem was efficient.

She had to fight the subliminals so she could drink her soup at her work-station. It didn't even taste good.

4

There was a five-minute inter-active letter from Chesarynth when Jezrael got home. Her father must have seen it
flashing on the old-fashioned flat screen; it was timed at
fifteen forty-seven and was only valid for three hours, but
he hadn't bothered to start it.

Jezrael made a moue of disgust. *You'd think he'd care
enough about Ches not to waste an inter-active. Does he
think she's made of money?*

The unusualness of it struck her with a pang of worry.
*Wonder why she lashed out on anything this expensive.
Hell, I hope she's all right.* But Jezrael didn't dare start it
without her parents' permission. They'd go crazy if she
did.

Presumably the computer had told him the inter-active
was logged on, but there was no sign of him. He was
outside somewhere, probably tinkering with the irrigation
system.

Jezrael flopped on the moss-couch, feeling ungainly but
defiant, especially since her mother wasn't there to nag at
her. She wanted to be anaesthetized so that she could
forget the injustices of the past three shifts but her mind
was on a treadmill, recycling the arguments with no practical solution in view. Her rage was savage and she knew
the only person it was damaging was herself but she was
still bound to the treadmill.

There weren't any messages for her either, at least not
interesting ones.

The letter from Chesarynth sat there, flashing. (Her
father must have turned the sound down again. He didn't
like the computer interrupting him.) Jezrael tried to ignore

55

it but in the end she couldn't. It had to be big news or Ches would simply have had a one-way message compressed and squirted across space, the way she always did. Yet it didn't seem fair for Jezrael to have the whole letter to herself when it was addressed to all of them.

An itch of jealousy bit Jezrael. *Maybe she's won another big academic prize.* Jezrael tried to ignore it.

Finally, she swung her feet to the floor and said, 'All right. I give in.'

Suiting up, she slipped through the air-skin, automatically going slowly as the skin wouldn't let fast-moving bodies through. There had to be some protection against meteorites – and the kind of 'friend' who threw biolight diseases in to make the walls stink or go neon purple.

Jezrael didn't hook her belt-line on to anything. She found a savage pleasure in weaving between the shining pipes and the rough grey polyp-clusters that would one day grow big enough to be homes. For a fee, Owen Brown would even arrange to have the homes towed to anchorage anywhere on the growing sprawl of Witwaterstrand.

She found her father where he usually was, cursing to himself in the balance-pod where the irrigation pumps were. It was the hub of the whole home-growing farm system, a hedgehog of bristling feeder-tubes and the mechanisms inside the cramped pod were supposed to balance out the nutrients so the seedling polyps could grow into proper asteroids, and it was a sore point between him and his family. From there all the homes he grew sprouted out along dekametres of spikes. Jezrael crawled inside the hollow sphere.

'Hi, Dad.' She pulled herself over, weightless, to squat beside him. 'How you doing?'

Owen Brown screwed another segment on the scraping-tube. He had to concentrate; it was awkward in the confined space. It was a while before he registered his daughter's presence through his irritation.

'Hi. Probably some sort of polyp degeneration in the pipe-corals, wouldn't you say? There's a house-bead halfway down number seventeen that looks like it's not getting the right balance of nutrients.'

He raked the scraper as far as he could up the inside of a spike. The noise was amplified along the hollow tubing; it sounded so threatening that Jezrael was sure the pipe would rupture and globules of nutrient would explode out into space with their air. She was glad for once that she'd put her suit on before poling over.

Owen jiggled the scraper one last, vicious time then began to pull it out and unscrew it joint by joint. Given the freedom of zero-gee, the tube-segments clashed like cymbals when he dropped them all around the inside of the sphere. Jezrael rescued them one by one. The impetus her father's temper gave them could wreck the whole pump system. As it was, chips of coral were already ricocheting off the walls.

'Why don't you get Mom to fix it? She could build a virus –'

'I can do it!' he snapped. 'It'd just take a minute, if you'd let me get on with it. I don't want her interfering.'

'What about Ches' letter? It's an inter-active one,' she said again, 'and it's going to run out in about twenty minutes.'

'Your mother can answer it. I'm busy.'

Jezrael snagged another pipe-segment that was floating towards her head. 'She's not in.'

'Well, you answer it then! Oh, hell and damnation!' He jerked the scraper-tube up and down but it was firmly wedged inside the pipe-coral. Then the handle came away, leaving the umbrella-end jammed up in the spike. Her father's forehead crimped and he ran his fingers through his short greying hair. 'Oh, shit.'

Jezrael left him cursing in the stale air and went to write to her sister.

At this time of year Mars was less than three minutes away. Since Chesarynth was only a student, she couldn't afford a proper holo-gramme, or even a phone-call. The most she could run to was a squirt-letter maybe once in thirty degrees. To have an inter-active letter – well, it must really be something important to pay that much.

Jezrael primed the computer and turned it up. 'Hi, Ches,' she said, and the computer turned her message into sound and print, compressed it, and squirted it across three light-minutes of inner space like an orange-pip.

'It's Jezrael. Hope you hadn't given up on us. Mom's at work and Dad's swearing at his pipe-corals. Work's still boring as hell and some stupid baggy will insist on callus-prop in the Mars-room so if you ...'

What can I say? So if you can't breathe, or you're starving, maybe it's my fault? I don't want you to panic, Ches....

'Oh, damn it, who cares about work? How're you doing? Answer.'

Three minutes there; three minutes back. Jezrael fetched herself a cup of apple-juice and sat looking at her sister's picture.

Chesarynth was a couple of years older than Jezrael, and much, much prettier. She had a sweet, heart-shaped face and a little pointy chin that she hated. Jezrael would gladly have swapped it for her own rounded features. When they used to go out, it was always Chesarynth who got the good-looking guy. Worse than that, Ches was far too nice-natured to go off and leave her. She'd always say something totally embarrassing like, 'Sorry, I'd like to go, but I can't leave my sister.' *As if I needed it advertised that I couldn't get a decent boyfriend!* The trouble was, Chesar ynth meant it well, so how could anyone get cross with that? And anyway, most of the time Ches was the one person who understood how she felt.

Jezrael smiled at her sister's picture. The little sliver of holo on the sofa-table showed a girl with shiny, sculpted waves of rich, deep brown hair.

Chesarynth's voice interrupted her. At the same time the computer printed out a hard copy.

'Hi yourself! You sound really fed up, Jez. I wish I was there with you.' Chesarynth sounded strange; Jezrael put it down to distortion. 'I miss you. I miss Mom and Dad too, but I miss you especially. They keep piling the work on. There's this bonus-scheme now we're in the second year: come up with an eco-conversion idea that works and they'll stake you to a bigger bit of land and some more seed. The idea is you'll be able to grow enough not just to feed yourself the basic grant-ration they allow you but even have some left over to pay for tuition and clothes and stuff. Some of the third years are actually paying their own food to anyone who'll do their crops for them. They're just wasting away trying to fill their crop-quota and keep up with their work. Is Mom there? Answer.'

'No, Mom's out – she'll be a couple of eons yet. She's installing some new lighting-virus she's come up with. It's another mood thing, makes the lights shift colour and gives off odours to relax you or turn you on or whatever. I called it a sex-ray but she didn't think it was funny. Anything wrong? Answer.'

From the static holo on the table, Ches smiled back at her. They'd gone together on Ches's last day in school. Some enterprising holographer had set up a portable booth in the gym and they'd each paid him to take the other's likeness. Jezrael knew that while Ches was waiting, she was looking at a picture of her.

School. Not only pretty and kind, Ches was smart academically. Jezrael remembered one teacher, the dotty Cosmology woman, who always called her Jezrael whenever she did a kind of average piece of work and Chesarynth if it was good.

Over the light-minutes Chesarynth pleaded, 'Promise you'll lose the letter before the groans get in? There's roaring inflation here – some sort of problem with the plants not being fertile – and my grant just can't keep up. Most of this term I've been doing someone else's crop-quota as well as my own because I needed the food but I can't take it any more. I'm desperate. It's horrible, Jez. I'm too tired even to sleep. I even borrowed someone's psycho-vid – you know, watch this and the sublims'll put you out like a light – but I kept thinking what Mom always said about sublims being dangerous 'cause you never know what they're telling you to do. I was so screwed up that it didn't work anyway. So I've contracted. Answer.'

Jezrael's stomach froze, leaving a hollow ball of anxiety. 'Who to?'

Six minutes. Six metric light-minutes while the question lagged in the ether, and the answer dragged its way back. A dull knot of tension pulled pain into the base of Jezrael's head, stiffened her neck. *Don't let it be –*

Subjective time elasticated, telescoped. Jezrael found her fingers were dragging at her cheeks, and forced her hands into her lap, but they wouldn't rest quietly there. She clasped them tightly together and the skin whitened where her nails pressed into her flesh.

'Jez? Promise you won't let the groans see this letter? It's Spiderglass.'

'Spiderglass? Oh, Ches! How could – no, scrub that. You must have been desperate. Why didn't you ask me for money? I'd have sent you some. My poor honey! When is it' – the computer pinged for end of transmission time; the inter-active letter had run out – 'going to be?'

5

More than three orbits before, while her younger sister was still at school, Chesarynth had left Witwaterstrand carrying her mother's hopes and dreams, her father's expectations....

Chesarynth Brown didn't count the Adaptation Hospital. For the first time since she had come down the tube from the ship, she set foot on the surface of Mars with nothing between it and her but the soles of her boots.

No walls, no view-screens, no more trendy men on holos giving orientation class to all the would-be students. And no clothes or artificial air either – or at least, not much. She didn't know how the others felt about showing acres of skin, but Chesarynth felt embarrassed all over, as though what she was displaying weren't so much her body as her inadequacies.

Big and red and purple and green, the vast outdoors confronted her face to face, and she wished it wouldn't. There was too much of it altogether.

Standing shivering in a crowd that huddled nervously together by the mound of baggage, she chatted idly with two boys and a girl who'd shared her side-ward. Across the cold, lumpen landscape, people kept coming up to the batch of student adaptees. One by one they matched images on their portable memo-screens with the adaptees and took them away. *It's always somebody else*, thought Chesarynth, trying not to let her apprehension get the better of her as the crowd thinned.

In quick succession the girl left, and then one of the boys, led off by supercilious second years who'd be their room-mates. There was only Chesarynth and one of the boys now, anxiously watching, not wanting to be last.

The tiny sun shone distantly, sliding lower through the cold haze of atmosphere that was still strange to her. Chesarynth and the boy had run out of things to say now; there was no humour left in the jokes about being late for your own funeral. Together, unspoken rivalry keeping them from standing quite side by side, they willed someone to come and get them.

Chesarynth held her breath that came so hard in the thin air: from between the ordered banks of vegetation came a girl, running. Chesarynth smiled inwardly, hiding her relief and pride.

But the picture on the girl's memo-screen matched the boy instead of her.

'So long,' he said. 'Don't worry. They're bound to come and get you soon,' but his partner was dragging him off. He picked up his bags and there was only Chersarynth's left. Over his shoulder he made keep-in-touch noises but the girl kept saying, 'Come on,' and 'Hurry up, won't you? Some of us have got quotas to meet.' Then they were gone between the pyramids of plants that made air for Mars, and Chesarynth was left behind, alone.

Even the sun was leaving the sky and still no-one came. She loitered, really cold now, unhappily wondering if she ought to go in and tell someone, but it seemed like an admission of failure, somehow. Besides, she didn't want to be a nuisance.

Indecisive, she hung around on the steps, wondering what to do. *I bet this wouldn't have happened if I'd been able to get into Earth-U,* she thought. *I wish I hadn't failed the scholarship. . . .*

Then the shadows grew to embrace her in their chill. All in a rush she grabbed up her other bag from its lonely pile of one and peered at the buildings on the sun-fired horizon.

Mars didn't go in for glow-tracks. (The handsome holo had said such extravagances were unecological and anti-survival; in the historic romances she was ashamed of enjoying, the heroes of revolutionary Russia would have sneered 'bourgeois' in just the same way.)

Chesarynth looked around: there was no-one else in sight. Fumbling to check the air-gems were still set across her chest, she stepped apprehensively away from the shelter of the hospital porch, sure she would get lost. Briefly she wondered why that student had sold her them the other day. If the looping strands of diamond in her flesh were that good at making breathing easy, why hadn't he kept them? But her unacknowledged terror tore her mind away from her coruscating skin.

The huge open spaces that she had to cross made her feel like a bacterium on a wall; she had forgotten how slow walking was if you really wanted to get anywhere. At home, up in Witwaterstrand, you could just kick off from any surface or let one good pull on a rope propel you dozens of metres. On Mars, with the blocks of the University backing against the distant hills, and her two packs dragging behind her, each step seemed very small.

And as if that wasn't bad enough when you'd got all that weight to schlepp, you couldn't even turn the gravity down.

Then the ground danced under her feet. Chesarynth screamed; obediently it stilled, and then she knew it couldn't be the ground. Mars was a planet, wasn't it? And planets stay still, at least their surfaces do. *So it was me. I'm going mad.*

She pretended there was an end to the sphere of sky above her, something to hold the air in, but there wasn't. They were working on an air-skin – they'd said – but it wasn't finished yet. And clumps of white vapour shifting across the aching deep blue made her dizzy. She felt she might fly off the world at any moment; there wasn't so much as a belt-line she could hook on to keep her safe.

Looking downwards and repeating chunks of the orientation to stop her mind from flying off, Chesarynth trod carefully along the paths between tall pyramids of plants. When she had gone two hundred paces, she had to stop. Inside her head, her panting echoed off the walls of her skull. It had been nice of that student to sell her air-gems but they didn't seem to be doing much good. Still, hadn't he said they'd need time to grow into her blood-vessels? Maybe the pain of them was a good sign.

I just need a breather, she told herself, *it's just that I'm not used to air as thin as this.* But even when she took a long drag of expensive bottled oxygen the pounding of blood in her ears was still as loud.

Because however much she tried to hide it, she was afraid of the outdoors. It felt *wrong* to be outside without a suit. The way the air kept lurching past her was frightening, however often she told herself it wasn't a meteor-strike or a leak. If she'd had clothes on, even, it might have been better, but you had to let the oxyvirus have as much skin-surface as possible to work on; for the sake of hygiene she wore small briefs; for the sake of mystery, a halter-top on her labouring chest. And, with her ankle-boots, that was all.

So, funnelled in invisible rivers by the ziggurats of plants, the cold air jerked past just about every fraction of skin. Chesarynth could feel the tiny hairs on her arms standing up, bowing left and right like crazy dancers. Tiny prickles of fear answered the wind's caress on her stomach and back and breasts; and in her ears her blood stomped like a cossack. There were pins and needles inside her head and neck and she had the horrible feeling she was about to die between the vegetal pyramids with no-one even knowing she was dead. Ready-made, the picture sprang into focus in her inner vision: her corpse staring wide-eyed into the dark untidy sky, lying there for days.

Chesarynth sat, elbows on knees – lying down would be too much like being dead. She felt alone, and afraid, and very small; she hated the way her body looked now. It was fat, and red with the oxyvirus, and didn't seem to be hers at all. Even her eyes felt dry and stiff behind their plastic coating.

I'll be all right in a minute, she told herself, but herself wasn't convinced. She wished Jezrael was there; she'd have known what to do. Jezrael wasn't afraid of anything. But

Jezrael was forty million miles away, and Chesarynth was alone.

'Oh! – are you – You'll be all right in a minute.'

Chesarynth jumped, actually rising a little in the half-grav that Mars always used. Above the roaring in her head and the bright balletic air, she'd neither seen nor heard the person come round the angle of the path behind her.

'Don't worry – and don't breathe any more of that tinned air now, either. You're hyperventilating, at least I think you are. Fizzing in the head?' Short fingers pressed her wrist. 'Pulse gone crazy?'

Chesarynth nodded.

'Thought so. I take it you're a new bug? A-huh. You're overdosing on oxygen – awful, isn't it? I remember I did. Cup your hands and use your top to breathe in and out through. Breathe slowly. That better?'

It was. The person touched her and Chesarynth was startled, but the gentle rubbing up and down her back acquired a sense of comfort with frightening rapidity. Frightening, because whoever it was might stop at any moment and Chesarynth would be alone again.

'All right now?'

Chesarynth looked outside her internal world and saw a girl the same age as her, maybe nineteen, little, with bright blue eyes and an explosion of black curly hair.

Chesarynth swallowed, tried a smile. 'Well, if you're using "all right" in some sense of the word that I haven't come across before, I suppose so.'

The dark-haired girl giggled in a friendly way. 'What's your name?'

Chesarynth told her, and her sleeping-hall and room-number when she asked.

'Oh. Well, I guess the state you're in is my fault. I'm your room-mate, Loretta Sibo, and I was supposed to come and get you, only I didn't key my last assignment in on time and the tutor was giving me an ear-bashing so I was late, and I've forgotten my memo-pad. You're supposed to come and get the new bugs after last lecture, and I didn't. I'm sorry, only it's the first time I've had to get anybody. I've only been here a year – a Martian year, that is. I haven't had to do this before. Will you forgive me?'

Chesarynth nodded, a visual back-up to her own froth of nervous talk: 'Yeah, it's OK, I think I am anyway. Don't worry about it.'

'Don't you worry about it either, you'll soon get used to it. Look, I'm really sorry, OK? I guess it's my fault you bought the air-gems too' – Loretta nodded her dark head at the quartz dying in Chesarynth's skin.

'Your fault? What d'you mean? Shouldn't I have got them?'

'They're just a waste of time, that's all. They don't help you breathe. It isn't air they live on, it's blood.'

Chesarynth began to panic but Loretta patted her arm maternally. 'It's all right, it's all right, never mind. They'll fall out in a day or two and you'll be fine, don't worry. I'm still breathing, aren't I?' She smiled brightly, repacking the precarious heap of Chesarynth's things on the hand-cart she'd brought. 'Anyway, look on the bright side. You can always sell them later so long as nobody catches you at it. D'you think you can walk if I pull the cart?'

And, between the piles of plants that were every shade from green to purple, they crossed the grid-walk of paths to Orion Hall.

At sight of it, Chesarynth stopped. Ten stories of glitter faced her, a vast reflection of sunset sky with already a spatter of stars among the mirrored clouds. Here and there blocks of white light shone out where windows were lit from inside. And the tessellated plant-life stopped like a carpet that had been cut off.

It was like walking towards a hologram of a jewel.

Loretta flung open a door on level seven and said, 'East, West, home's best.' She didn't even seem out of breath from walking up fourteen flights of stairs.

Chesarynth stepped inside, dropping one of her packs where she stood. The walls of their room were an ugly sandstone pink, totally bare in between a couple of small holos. All the furniture was the same colour, as if it was meant to be camouflaged, and everything was square, or oblong, or some shape with rectangles. After the living corals of Witwaterstrand with swirls of coloured light softening their organic curves, the artificiality of the room was oppressive. There wasn't a green thing to be seen.

'So what do you think?' asked Loretta.

'It's a bit hard to take. You see the outside ...'

Loretta kicked the door shut. 'I know what you mean. Sort of bleak. From the outside the solar panels shine and this place looks kind of weightless, you know, ethereal, like moonbeams, and inside it's solid. Back home in Bolton we haven't got anything like it.'

'Amalchem Bolton?'

'Yeah, Amalchem Bolton, glittering capital of Northern Europe.'

'Where all the medicines come from?'

'Yeah, that Europe.' Loretta sounded ironic.

Chesarynth tried not to look shocked. *Why under the sun would anyone from Earth come to Mars to study? There has to be something going on here....*

But of course she couldn't ask about something as mysterious as that. Maybe there was some humiliating secret in Loretta's past, or more likely her family's. Chesarynth hunted round for a change of subject, not hard on her first day at Mars-U in a room that seemed naked in its barrenness. There wasn't a plant in sight. 'It's awfully spartan.'

'Don't sound so sad – Chesarynth, isn't it? I wish I could find that memo!' Loretta was rooting about in a heap of clothing dropped under the desk. 'You've got to laugh at it. They've almost all got this paranoia about diseases and things. My uncle's just like that, can you imagine it? He sits there in front of his computer-terminal at home and pontificates about how if we let bio-light and stuff on Earth all the bacteria would suddenly mutate and take the planet over, you know, take me to your genes sort of thing.'

'But ...'

'I know. I went to Andronicus last year and they had biolight and everything too, but the powers that be reckon it's all right if you're on an asteroid, that's a closed system so you could isolate mutating bacteria. They just don't want alien growths' – Loretta dropped her voice to a parody of the mysterious – 'on the loose all over their nice tidy planet. And as for all the eco-freaks who've got their hands on Mars....'

Chesarynth smiled, trying to look cool and cosmopolitan while feeling quite the opposite. Andronicus was the other asteroid group built in the complementary Trojan orbit sixty degrees the other side of Earth from Witwaterstrand and somehow it was a much richer place than her own home. Andronicus was the pinnacle of the arts, the centre where cubes were made for all the asteroid colonies clear out to Jupiter. For all she knew they even exported to the new star-colonies. And not just the hypno and psychotropic ones that Jezrael had sometimes sneaked home. They did light-poems and soap-operas, and Loretta, an Earther, had actually been there. All Witwaterstrand had was Spiderglass and Nutristem. Chesarynth couldn't imagine anyone from Earth passing up Andronicus for a backwater like Mars, but she was too self-conscious to admit it. So she just said, 'How come you haven't got any ordinary plants or anything?'

'Wait 'til you've done your quota for the garden-master. I'm sick of the sight of greenery and you will be too. Look, I'm hungry, how about you?'

'I don't know. Where do we eat?'

'We're lucky – it's not far from here, only a couple of blocks. And you won't have to report to the garden-master until tomorrow.'

Chesarynth barely had time to wonder 'Who?' when the brunette was sweeping her out of the door on a tide of verbiage.

'Got your grant-card? Good. Let's just hope it's up-to-date. What with jet-propelled inflation, mine's just about up to a sandwich.'

Between forksful of rather stringy beans, Chesarynth

gulped for air and tried to tune into the animated conversations Loretta began with other students. She was not sure enough of herself yet to risk asking, but most of them seemed to be moans about the quota, or the gardenmaster. All in all she was beginning to feel more than a little apprehensive. Whoever he was, it was apparent he more or less held the balance of life or death over the students. Chesarynth, always afraid of authority figures, felt fear creeping its cold fingers over her bloated skin, the dying stones in her breast. *What will he do about these? Oh, no! I'm in trouble before I start!*

Panting in the thin air, Chesarnyth ran her fingers over the gems. They were asleep in frond-like curves, a living grey scar in the red welts of her breast. And like Loretta had said, they didn't seem to be helping her one bit. All that pain for nothing. *Come on,* she thought, *you can do it. I feel like I'm drowning in this sea of carbon dioxide.* But they did nothing but hurt.

All through the meal the talk wandered to other areas of the mysteries that were Mars. Like rivulets each tiny trickle of talk joined forces with the others so that as they walked back to their hall under the sky that was a haze of purple-red-black, Chesarynth seemed caught up in a cataract of frightening strangeness.

Loretta was happy enough, though, to do the talking, to show off her knowledge and her caring with nothing more than the odd breathless agreement from her new roommate. You couldn't help liking her. Chesarynth plodded along, glad for the arm that was linked through hers, to the dazzling oblong of light that spilled out of the black mirror hall, resting often on the long flights of stairs up to the sanctuary of their beds, her throat dry, her eyes burning under their unaccustomed plastic lenses which seemed to draw moisture from her corneas rather than keeping it in.

She flopped, yawning, on to her bed that seemed made of bones to stick into her red, swollen flesh. The unrelenting gravity pressed her leaden limbs into the soft plastic. Each breath was an effort.

Only then, isolated in her personal darkness, did she remember the garden-master and the fear he already inspired in her.

But whoever he was, the garden-master could wait until tomorrow.

6

Karel smoothed a hand over the cabin wall, turning it into a mirror. For more than a minute he looked at his reflection. Tall, muscular, Nordic pale hair brushing his shoulders, Nordic pale eyes squinting a little against the brightness of the lights. Then he snapped his fingers at his personal bodyguard, a gentle girl called Magrit who had long been in love with him. It suited Karel that way. He liked to keep her on edge by drawing closer to her then rebuffing her. It kept her alert to his slightest whim.

Impatiently he snapped his fingers again but she was already moving forward, sweeping up the robes he had laid out on the bed of his stateroom. He saw the way her eyes gleamed as he shucked out of his casual outfit and stood naked waiting for her to hand him his disguise. His gaze met hers in the mirror; Magrit blushed but Karel merely smiled sardonically. He liked the way it added to her discomfiture.

This robe was opulent but discreet. Iridescent cream over a marginally darker shade, the inner sleeves tight with a point over the back of each hand and the outer sleeves hanging stiff and wide, it whispered discreetly of money. Lots of it.

But the crowning glory was his mask. He had been assured that on Mars a breathing mask with contact-lenses could pass every security scanner that technophobic place possessed. Undoubtedly the face part moulded Tjerssen's features. It even seemed transparent but it bleached the colour of his skin, darkened his eyes. In fact it also imprinted a false retina-pattern over his own so that to the uninitiated he could be Berndt Tjerssen – if Uncle Berndt

71

had been young and slim and two metres tall with an interface socket on his forefinger.

But Karel was quite up to this challenge. How else could he have got so close in so few years to the place on the Board that he coveted? Not only that: he had even helped refine the technology of it himself in his base on the Moon. The base that Chairman Ole thought was no longer there.

So Karel triggered the hologramatic device in the helmet.

Suddenly he was short and fat and the grey strands of his hair were combed over his bald spot. Even his hands were mottled and wrinkled; nobody could see the gold interface ring that Karel had bullied the lab doctors to insert before he'd attained his majority. 'You'll regret it,' they said. And, 'It makes you look like you're some sort of worker.' But Karel had never regretted it and now he was grateful because it had been in the interface that he had solved the problems of building the disguise. So long as nobody actually touched him they'd never know the difference. Karel smiled and the mask smiled with him.

He looked to Magrit for approval but she gave him none. She was watching the disc of Mars become a globe.

He felt a childish urge to switch the disguise off and shout 'Look!' before he triggered it again but he remembered his grandmother and shut the thought away behind his outer face. Instead he chose a subtler way of punishing Magrit who could gaze in wonder through the viewport without vertigo wrenching her guts when she should have been admiring him.

'Come here,' he said. A laryngial vibrator modulated his manly voice to Berndt's choirboy whisper.

Magrit turned, blenched. Long ago Karel had supervised the planting of the spiderglass tower in her skull. And he had taken the opportunity to implant his own view of Berndt in her: a monster, a lecher who took pleasure in strangling young girls even as he brought them to orgasm.

And now Berndt, it seemed, was smiling like a cherub at her even as he pulled open the seal of his robes.

Gentle Magrit, who had taught Karel a hundred ways to kill, dropped into a fighting stance. She looked sick.

Karel laughed – Berndt laughed – and even as she threw herself at him in a drop-kick he swayed aside. As she twisted mid-air he caught the glassy tower in her skull a glancing blow. Only a light one, but it was enough. Magrit screamed in agony, fell helpless.

Karel flicked the disguise-switch and bent over her, artificial concern pasted on his own face. Fires of pain writhing through her head, Magrit clung to her saviour.

'I thought you knew,' he said. 'I thought you'd realize it couldn't possibly be Berndt, even if you didn't see me change. Apart from anything else, can you smell Berndt here?'

Magrit couldn't. 'I – I'm sorry, Karel. I should have noticed – Berndt always reeks of those incense-pastilles he burns. I could have killed you and it's all my fault. Please don't send me away. I'll do better next time.'

And inside Karel was a secret satisfaction.

There had been long negotiations with Mars. Karel had had the best artists in Andronicus labouring for months to search their files – and his own – for recordings of Berndt. Of course, they didn't know who Berndt was. Or they said they didn't, for the twenty thousand credits. And from all the fragments they had reconstructed a series of wonderful cube-recordings. Also of course, Karel was the one who chose the words they put in the puppet's mouth.

Needless to say the artists were then 'recruited' as Spiderglass drones. Karel had supervised the operations himself, cutting through their brain-tissue to plant synaptic stimulators. One artist was a refuse recycler now, happy with his work out in the asteroids. Karel couldn't remember what he'd done with the other one.

So now came the first face-to-face meeting between the Minister for Internal Affairs, the Chancellor of Mars-U – and Berndt Tjerssen. Who naturally was not Berndt Tjerssen at all despite the heavy incense that wafted from his creamy robe.

In a discreet inner room in County Hall, Ecoville, the courtesies were just finishing.

'And now to business,' said Madame Chancellor. 'Under normal circumstances the loan-quota system is ideal for all concerned. The student is self-sufficient, the active farming work keeps him or her fit, we don't need to pollute our environment with filthy machines, and he or she reaps the benefit of the best education system outside Earth.' Her voice trailed off, depressed.

'And of course the off-world currency they bring in helps to maintain a positive balance of trade. But these days –' the Minister shrugged.

'But these, of course, are not normal circumstances,' Karel-Berndt said helpfully. 'I believe you said on your cube that you have something of a problem with inflation?' Karel was polite, businesslike. He was well aware of the economic problems Mars was facing. They were to some extent inevitable in such a set-up. And the real Berndt had long ago made it Spiderglass policy to tip the scales the wrong way for Mars. That way, the local government depended more and more on the students' contribution to money supply. It made it all the easier to buy into the action, control local legislation. Berndt was not totally dumb.

A pity he hadn't foreseen Karel floating vast sums of worthless currency into Mars through various interested and the interest was fifteen per cent – parties. All in the name, the secret name, of Berndt. There was practically nothing to link all this with the Company and nothing at all that pointed to Karel himself. It was just one fraction of his long-term plan for Berndt's ruin.

But getting rid of Berndt the murderer – however satisfying that might be – wasn't enough. Karel had to make sure that when he went, Berndt took Theresien and Oskar down with him. Ole was one man he could deal with on his own.

The Chancellor and the Minister said more than they probably intended because Berndt seemed so sympathetic. When he had let them run on long enough he broke the flow with a positive plan of action and they practically fell on his neck.

'With garden-masters that you can control, you also control the student. They each, each of the students that is, have to send you a psych-profile with their applications, yes?' He smiled, began a nod to encourage their swift agreement.

Madame Chancellor followed his lead, nodding and smiling at what she thought was a sweet old man.

'Then, dear lady, let me show you an ingenious little idea the Company has come up with. Yet another practical application of spiderglass. It has to do with motivation. If you know how to get the best out of your students you can increase their quotas, help them work more efficiently. It will cut down the time that they spend with undesirable elements in the shanty-town round the spaceport, cutting off one source of revenue to those same undesirables.' Karel-Berndt cut to the minister. 'Thus also benefiting internal affairs, do you see?'

The minister saw. Already he was figuring percentages.

Karel-Berndt waved one pudgy manicured hand. A strong scent of rose and patchouli drifted through the air. 'And by making sure of your garden-masters you can eliminate agitators. I – ah – I gather that a certain garden-master has been preaching technological revolution? With the system I'm offering you, all that can be a thing of the past. He could, rather than being neutralized, actually be made totally loyal to your ideals.'

Karel's outer face smiled blandly,. 'Perhaps, then, you would think it poetic justice if we were to demonstrate the system on him?'

'Not so fast,' said the minister, his austere features arranged in disapproval. 'I want to know what you will get out of this.'

Karel held his hands up in a display of innocent rejection. 'Me? Nothing, sir. But if there should happen to be some failures amongst your hard-working students, some who don't want to work for the good of Mars, perhaps we might be allowed to recruit from among them?

It would help us and it would get them out of your hair. And naturally, though I know it must pain you to think it is still so, there are certain goods which even your worthy compatriots are unable to supply. I think, in exchange for permission to recruit, we would be able to offer you sufficient recompense for the food these lazy fellows won't be growing. How does that sound?'

7

The garden-master.

Nothing Chesarynth had ever seen had prepared her for anything like the garden-master.

Next morning, her first proper morning on Mars, Chesarynth woke heavy-eyed and nauseous from a troubled doze. She hadn't been able to sleep for the eternal light in her bedroom, nor had she dared switch it off because the oxyvirus needed light to work. Fed up with listening to her restlessness, Loretta had flung an old mask at her in the middle of the night, but the eyemask pressing on her face was a constant reminder that others could see her and she couldn't see them. Fear and insecurity made poor bed-fellows through her first lonely night but she was too shy to disturb Loretta who exhaled in dainty snores.

Gradually the light from the window came to rival the electric glare inside. Relieved to be able to move around at last, Chesarynth stumbled out of bed, reeling from the shock of gravity.

Fragments of nightmare surfaced to scratch at her confidence: the old fear of moving air that meant *Danger! Atmosphere escaping*! and the fast beating of her heart as it tried to make her lungs draw in oxygen that wasn't there. She hadn't yet given the virus time to accommodate her system to dealing with the excess of other gases; her head ached dully with surplus carbon dioxide. Besides, the air-gems had lost all their rainbow sparkle; they just sat in her skin, hurting now the analgesic had worn off, not helping her to breathe at all. A vague, pervasive feeling of anxiety lurked just below the surface of her mind; a physical anxiety at cellular level to add to the normal

77

nervousness of strange surroundings and her need to prove herself at Mars-U.

Changing, bone-tired, she knocked into an angle of the desk, something she hadn't done since she was a toddler; clumsiness in space was anti-survival. Loretta stretched herself awake.

'Sorry, I didn't mean to disturb you,' scarcely impinged on Loretta's yawns. Nor did 'Good morning,' or 'Did you sleep well?'

Loretta the Earther bumbled around the tiny room, cannoning into everything in sight. Chesarynth with her precise movements, could scarcely believe it.

Pale sunshine speared into the room and across the static-bound dust on the computer-screen. She noticed a message appear.

It was the time for her appointment with the garden-master. Loretta mumbled something about not falling for the con, but Chesarynth was in no mood for paranoia, especially from someone who didn't even like plants enough to let their beauty brighten such a bleak room. Besides, she hadn't entirely forgiven Loretta for how bad she'd felt yesterday on the long drag over from the hospital. But the vibrant colours washing across the sky outside filled Chesarynth with excitement; they lured her into her bright future on Mars. If she made them her excuse to get away from Loretta for a bit, it still didn't dim their rose and gold beauty.

Transferring the garden-master's map to her portable memo-screen, Chesarynth cheerfully set off early for her appointment. Her first tutorial was at ten; she had three-quarters of an hour to make it. Plenty of time to see the garden-master if she didn't get lost.

But it was easy to find the garden-master's office-block. It lay at the focus of a dozen paths, a long, low red building, the pyramid gardens narrowing as she approached it like giant arrows. And with the map he'd sent her on the memo, she had no difficulty finding the precise door she wanted either. She hadn't so much as seen him and she was grateful to him.

Before she'd even started to look for the bell, he called 'Come in,' his voice welcoming.

She walked hesitantly through the outer door of the low, red-walled building and into a welter of green growth. Inside did not seem like inside; it was a jungle. Creepers screened tree-trunks with viridian lace. The mass of branches was a soaring upreach of leaf-jewelled arms captured in a baroque act of prayer, the floor a textured mat of plants which lovingly embraced her feet.

Chesarynth took no more than three steps before the garden-master's forest ensorcelled her. Its living presence halted her. She half turned but already there was no sign of the walls, no prosaic door. Such banalities had vanished behind the deep pillars of the trees with their silken or crinkly skins of bark.

This unexpected world, dense with life, was vast, its odours rich and overpowering. Chesarynth felt herself dwindle into insignificance, the same way she felt in her father's lofty presence. Caught inside the garden-master's domain she could not go on; it was too great an intrusion.

Again that voice, vibrant as an oboe, resonating strangely through her, calling her on: 'Come in, Chesarynth. You'll always be welcome here.'

And she would have followed it to its source, gladly, but she couldn't see how. On every side were the splayed emerald hands of fig-trees, the needle-fingers of palms. The violent colours of blooms exploded on her vision but that voice called again and a kind of path through the vegetation led her into a clearing by a window. Outside was dust-blown Mars, but here, in this secret seclusion, a young man turned to face her.

His smile was a thing of beauty. He looked into her eyes and it was as if some switch was tripped inside her mind. Weird sensations trickled through the channels of her brain, making her dizzy. *He likes me! He thinks I'm wonderful – me!* And still that odd feeling surged through the cells of her being as though electrical impulses were twiddling the dials of her mind, tuning her in to the peculiar knowledge that after years of being a disappointment to her family, this stunning man actually thought she was great. Tears sprang to her eyes.

Chesarynth stopped. She felt tongue-tied and clumsy. The Martian tan looked attractive on him while it made her feel like a root vegetable with an IQ to match.

'Do sit down,' he said. 'Make yourself comfortable.' He waved to a place just in front of her that certainly wasn't what she would have called a chair, not even a moss-sofa like her mother had grown.

Instead Chesarynth sat on what appeared to be a fallen tree-branch. Its smooth trunk lay by a pool in whose depths swam fish that gleamed with their own rainbow light. The man sat opposite her, trailing one hand into the water, and the fish flocked to him, an opalescent aura of adoration. The huge, creamy-white trumpets of lilies haloed his head, sending highlights over his golden hair.

At second glance, he wasn't young. Perhaps he was in his mid-thirties, perhaps older; there were laughter-lines around his eyes and mouth and not a hint of a wrinkle anywhere else, but he wore wisdom and humour with a kind of acquired grace that could only have come with maturity. He was strong without being over-muscular, and his skin seemed to have been polished smooth by life. His shorts were the same colour as his skin, and Chesarynth was embarrassed all over again at her lack of clothes.

For, more than anything else, the garden-master was beautiful. And the odd knowledge was imprinted on the circuits of her mind: *He likes me!*

'You understand, Chesarynth,' he began, 'that every inhabitant of Mars over the age of reason is expected to make a viable contribution to our economy?'

She nodded, listening most to the warm melifluous tones that wrapped his sentence. Its content was secondary. Besides, she thought she knew what he meant.

'This means the students as well. We on Mars believe that every human body needs a variety of activity to keep it functioning properly. So we tailor everyone's workload to make time for them to be creative in more than one field – ah, that was a bit feeble, wasn't it, that pun?'

Again that rising tone of his elicited a nod and a smile from Chesarynth that mirrored his own somewhat rueful one.

'This way we not only look after our people's health, we can also ensure that we don't have to depend on irregular and expensive supplies of foodstuffs from Earth or the asteroids. And, may I say, improve on quality and freshness. None of us here like the idea of irradiated foods that have been treated who knows how many times.'

As he talked, he smiled at her, his wonderful blue eyes looking into hers. His body-language was open, inviting her to share his vision, his care. And it showed off his musculature. Even Dael, the gym-master back in Witwaterstrand, didn't have a body to match this one. Chesarynth's embarrassed gaze wandered back to it however often she tried not to stare.

'I hope you don't mind, Chesarynth, but I've been looking through the holo you sent here, you remember, the one instead of a formal interview?'

She nodded a third time, but it didn't matter, this being struck dumb, because he made her feel wanted. For a while she could actually forget about being red, and bloated, and tired down to the bone from the gravity that nailed her endlessly to the planet's outer skin.

The garden-master went on, 'I was fascinated to see that your parents kept a farm-asteroid of their own. Did you really help out in it?'

'Yes,' she started, then had to clear her throat. 'We enjoyed helping out, my sister and I.' She would have said anything just then to earn his approval. All her life Chesarynth had ground away at her studies, trying to earn approval. Somehow she had never really noticed a man before, except as a status symbol: look, I must be OK, I've got a boyfriend. She said huskily, 'It was like – like being part of the circle of living things.'

'That's great!' The garden-master's enthusiasm was her reward. 'I hope you'll get just as much pleasure working in your own field here. Would you like that, a field of your very own where you can grow what you want? Within limits of course!' He laughed, inviting her to share the joke, because of course she wouldn't want to grow anything anti-social like narcotics. 'And I'm sure you'll appreciate the help that'll be to your grant. You do understand that part of your grant-loan is in the form of food and drink? And that you have to repay part of it by growing a quota of foodstuffs to help our fledgeling colony?'

'Mmm. I think it's a wonderful idea, being able to help feed a new society. And I'd like to grow mainly salad-stuffs and fruit, if that's all right with you.'

'Of course it is! It's terrific to find someone who cares enough to have ideas of their own. Salad-stuffs, eh?' He wandered across to a map made of micro-organisms, which grew beside the vine-framed window. Chesarynth watched his shoulder-muscles shining ever so slightly as he lifted a hand to trace across the map. The sunlight flooded across him, and a leaf-shadow danced over his hip.

She drifted over to join him, embarrassingly aware of how close his naked skin was to hers, but he smiled down at her – he was only a little taller than she was – and he asked, 'How would you like to have this bit here?'

He pointed to a patch of dull red near the wrinkled dun-colour that represented the hills. Only some of the squares around it seemed to be green, and she knew an urge to make her land as verdant as they were, anything to please him. She felt the tiny brown hairs along her arm rise to his magnetic field.

'Think it over, Chesarynth. It's near the hills, so there's some run-off water, and they'll protect your garden in the winter. We have some pretty fierce winds then. And you're close to a sun trap too – it should be ideal for soft fruit. Do you think it would suit you?'

She was sure of it.

'Any help you want, you know, just come and ask. And once I have a bit more time to spare, I'll come across and see how you're making out, if you like. I want you to be happy here.'

Of course she liked.

'By the way, how are you making out with your acclimatization?'

She didn't want to seem a wimp. Besides, his sympathy was so genuine – she thought – that she'd have broken down in tears if she'd even started to describe how terrible she felt: a permanent ache in the chest, the oxyvirus that seemed to have solidified like blubber just under the angry red skin. So Chesarynth smiled bravely. 'Oh – er, all right now, thanks.'

'That's great! So many people don't really give it a chance; they just chicken out. But once you're used to the oxyvirus and it's used to you, you'll never want to be without it. The trick is, not to worry about it.' He carefully avoided looking at the opaque air-gems.

He sighed a little, and all at once she was feeling sorry for him. Bowed down by the weight of his responsibilities, he said, 'I'm sorry, Chesarynth, I'd really like to have more time for us to get to know each other, but' – he shrugged and grinned – 'Mars wasn't built in a day. Look, I'll put your seed-stocks and quotas and stuff on the memo-screen in your room, all right? Get your room-mate to show you where your field is. But anything you need, just ask. I'll make time to get it sorted out somehow.'

And she shared a smile of complicity with him.

Outside, the chill sunshine sparkled on the frost over the hills but Chesarynth was happy in a way she had never known was possible. Now she had two friends here and her apprehension was gone. She knew she'd make out all right at Mars-U. She'd make her own little Eden, and the garden-master would be the Adam with whom she could share it.

Time now to get across to her introductory tutorial. Inspired, joyful, she imagined herself at the end of her course graduating with honours, and her mom and dad finally holding her, smiling through their tears, proud of her at last.

'What a con!' Loretta looked at the field in disbelief.

She and Chesarynth stood in the shade of a vast tower

that held a mirror-dish. To either side were tents of plastic that rattled in the wind; under them the soil was parched and bare. The university was a good quarter of an hour away, backed against the red-brown hills. A raw wind dried up any dew that might have fallen.

Even farther, so shrunken with distance that it was only a pricking of lights in the fading afternoon, was the nearest town of Ecoville. A cheerful ribbon of yellow glows across the equatorial plain was the long road to town. Sometime Chesarynth would like to go and explore but Loretta had told her they would have to walk and in the thin cold air the idea began to lose its attraction. *Maybe sometime when I've got used to gravity you can't switch off.*

Loretta stamped around, kicking at the cracked ground, making wordless noises of disgust.

Chesarynth was still too out of breath to answer. It was the end of her first day at the university and she was exhausted. She would never even have found the place if her room-mate hadn't taken her. In fact she would never even have gone to look for her field if Loretta hadn't insisted she get started right away, while there was still some daylight creeping soft and red over the icy horizon.

Loretta went on indignantly, 'How could you be so dense as to let her fob you off with this?'

On the cracked ruddy land before the hills, Chesarynth stared at her room-mate. 'Her who? And what's wrong with it anyway?' She waved chilly fingers vaguely at the oblong of dead land, the promised land the garden-master had gifted to her for her own. 'It just needs some plants to give it life –'

But Loretta was tugging at her black curls in wild exasperation. 'Her the garden-master, who do you think? It's miles from –'

'The garden-master's a man.'

'Yours might be, you sap, but mine's not. It's all part of the con. You know that routine about the holo-interview and how informal it all is? You don't want to believe that. They analyse it to death, take you to pieces to see what makes you work. In my case, it's this woman who's supposed to be like my mother, and I'm scared stiff of her. You, it seems, would work harder for some guy you fancy.' She watched Chesarynth try to hide a blush, but with the oxyvirus emphasizing it, it wasn't so much of a blush as a scarlet acclamation.

Loretta clicked her tongue in impatience. 'I warned you, but you didn't take a blind bit of notice. Didn't you feel something weird happening inside your head the minute you clapped eyes on him? Like somebody had shot about four million volts through you? It's conditioning, you sap!'

But Chesarynth kept stubbornly silent. How could she explain to Loretta that the way she felt wasn't some cold machine programming? It couldn't be. The garden-master was too nice to let something like that happen.

Retta sighed her exasperation. 'OK, OK, it's true love and the moon's made of green cheese. Don't stand there all moony-eyed. The point is, you've been taken for a ride whatever you feel about it. You want to find some guy to do you a swap for a patch somebody else has pioneered. Look at the state of this land – it's never been touched! There's not a scrap of humus –'

Chesarynth said, 'That's why he wants me to have it, so I can make it green!'

But Loretta the wordly-wise carried on, '– so it'll take you all your time to grow weeds, let alone a respectable quota. And it's miles from hall, miles from the sludge, and you're between two complete no-hopers. I mean, look at this crap!'

Loretta pointed to the two pathetic fields either side. Under the transparent plastic awnings the beds were raised to catch as much sun-warmth as possible, just like the memo-screen recommended, but the few plants were feeble, spindly things that straggled along the soil, pale and moribund.

Trying not to catch the other's pessimism, Chesarynth said, 'So mine'll look even better when they're grown.'

'So yours'll be robbed blind, you mean! How else are these bugs going to stay ahead? Have you found out who they are yet?' Loretta moved to read the nearest sign. 'Rastac something – never heard of her. Who's this other one?'

She stamped over to the other down-at-heel greenhouse, dropping to her knees in the cold breeze of dusk to rescue the name-board that had fallen from the sagging frame. 'Look at this, Ches! This one can't even be bothered to fix her sign on right. What's it say? Leika something, it looks like. A complete waste of space, if you ask me. All her stuff's dead.

'And you're just about straight under a sunflower' – Loretta gestured extravagantly at the tower with its reflector that arced across a third of the dark Martian sky – 'so it'll give you more shade than light, if it doesn't come down in the next tremor. Show me your memo?'

The portable computer-screen showed a quota of two hundred kilos.

'See what I mean?' said Loretta. 'You're a new bug; you don't know hardly a soul. You'll never make it.'

Chesarynth's pride was stung. 'The garden-master obviously thought I could!'

'Oh, sure. And if he told you you were a spaceship you'd jump straight off into space! Can't you see what they're trying to do to you? Your best bet's to wave your cute little ass at the first corporate student you see, because sure as hell you won't make a two-hundred-kilo quota on your own.'

'Is that what you do?' Chesarynth asked coldly.

'Yeah, of course it is! What do you think I am, stupid? Callum gave me fifty K last harvest or I wouldn't be here. I mean, think about it, Ches. If you do raise a crop, and if it doesn't grow wings and fly away in the night, it'll be because you spend every spare minute of your life out here in the shadows. How're you going to keep up with your work?'

'Easy! Stop trying to scare me.' And Chesarynth thought, *If the garden-master believes in me, who cares what this wimp thinks? She doesn't even like plants. I'll show her. This place'll be beautiful, like our Eden at home....*

And up through the ground under her feet she felt – she heard in her bones – the dull graunching rumble that was her second Martian earthquake.

Weary weeks later, in the dawn, before even the sunflowers had begun to lift their heads to greet the reflected dawn that a string of satellites bent down from beyond the horizon, Chesarynth forced herself to get up from her bed. The translucent blanket was at least a psychological protection against the outside world; she was loth to leave its shelter.

Shivering, she dragged her growing hair back from her face. Protective colouring: like a chameleon, she was changing her appearance to look like she belonged. But on Witwaterstrand, ordinary people didn't have long hair. It always escaped and its tickling always annoyed her. A hasty wash in the blessing of hot water while she and Loretta got in each other's way – Loretta was too used to the freedom of Earth spaces to be very aware of anyone else's spatial co-ordinates – and the two of them shambled out to the fields.

Loretta had called hers the Unlucky Strike.

Chesarynth left her there and made her way, yawning through the cold air, to her Last Stand. Rastac was just leaving the next plot; Chesarynth stepped aside for the girl whose beautiful Maya features always seemed so strained, but Rastac stopped a moment to admire Chesarynth's ice-moolah.

'Four leaves, huh? Be ready for transplanting soon. I can just imagine biting into that crisp white root when it's ready, can't you?'

Vaguely alarmed, Chesarynth said defensively, 'Yeah – if it ever gets that far.' The thought that was always lurking in her mind decided to spring out through her mouth. 'Seen anything of Leika lately?'

'Nope. You?'

'No. I don't think I've ever seen her. Oh well, better be getting back to breakfast.' But Chesarynth found ways to loiter until Rastac was too far away to steal from her.

87

Because sure as Mars was cold, someone was robbing her blind. And how come the invisible Leika's veg grew in such neat, profuse blocks if she never did any work on them?

Shivering, Chesarynth shrugged. *Not my problem. I haven't got the strength to worry about that. God, I'm tired!*

This morning it was so cold that you could trace the underground thermal grid, dark with moisture against the white plaid of frost that glowed unnaturally under the sombre red of the sky. Even though she wore nose-plugs, the icy air burnt Chesarynth's nostrils and her eyes stung under the contact-lenses that covered the whole front of their curve.

Inside the tent of plastic, she smiled with satisfaction at the little oxyboxes where her seedlings were fighting for life. There was perceptibly more growth today; better than that, today was the day the garden-master would expect her report. She would see him again. A pity he'd never had time to come out here and visit her, but he was so busy, poor man, it was hardly surprising.

Just the thought of him stopped her for a moment. She crouched, hands forgotten in the cold damp soil, astonishment sweeping over her again at the memory of his perfection. Chesarynth didn't understand why he had this effect on her; it was more than some childish crush. And it had been so sudden. *(Recollection was almost tangible: she relived that amazing moment when she had seen him for the first time, the solid, sun-kissed warmth of him in his cocoon of emerald leaves, the way she had felt him inside her mind the instant she had looked into his ice-blue eyes. Nobody had ever done that to her before. It was weird. Abnormal. But after a lifetime's pointless striving to win her parents' approval, he had just looked at her and his presence inside her mind had told her that he really, totally liked her. Besides, whatever Loretta might say, how could she dream of giving up feeling this good? Because of the garden-master, she mattered. She was worth knowing. And whatever regulations made him impose on her, Chesarynth couldn't help but adore him.)*

88

Struggling to compose herself enough to get some weeding done, Chesarynth absently watched her chilly hands at work, but her mind was far away. She'd tried everything to find out more about him but she hadn't managed to dig up a single fact other than that he was wonderful. For all her efforts she didn't even know his name.

Day burst over the plain; a great glowing incandescence leaped across her from the next sunflower, its rays slanted so low that it passed under the tower overhead and caressed Chesarynth's skin. Joy fizzed up inside her, a secret joy that she could not have shared with anyone.

Around her white coils of mist danced up from the soil, from the plastic, and the dazzling jewelled frost sang a symphony of colour. The sky paled to amethyst. Life was an ecstasy, her life, the life she had nurtured from the tiny seedlings in their Nutristem packaging. Maybe it was even stuff that Jezrael had cultured, loving it for her sister. How could Loretta be so cynical?

Easy. Loretta's garden-master was a mother, strict, sparing of praise. But Chesarynth would see her own garden-master today, luxuriate in the warmth of his smile, carve its shape and resonances into her mind so that she could call up its luminance any time she liked. And she would have to hide the echoes of pleasure that sang through her body every time she saw him.

What did it matter that the air-gems had dried up in her flesh, leaving a looping scar as one by one they withered and fell off? That even after four weeks her skin was still puffy and red with the Martian tan that could only have been named by an ad-man? Or that her course-work in biophysics was harder than she could have imagined?

She hardly even noticed the rumbling ripple of an after-shock that sped over the land from another Marsquake.

In just a few hours she would see the garden-master.

8

The evening was gold and rose; for the first time since she'd been here Chesarynth felt warm as she walked back from the refectory with a bunch of friends from her biophysics seminar. She smiled in sheer pleasure as the sunset painted copper strands in her brown hair. Everyone was enjoying the spring; you could hear it in the laughter floating on the flower-perfumed breeze.

Loretta was walking up ahead with her boyfriend, the corporate student, though she didn't seem too happy about holding his hand. Suddenly she turned to face Ches's gang. Skipping backwards to keep up with him, she said, 'Hey, Ches, Callum says why don't we all go to Hell?'

'What, now?'

'Oh, come on, Ches. Don't be so boring. I bet you've got all your work done down to the last jot and tittle, let alone combing the fronds on your carrots.'

Everyone laughed, even Chesarynth. It was true. For the time being she'd actually got caught up and it felt great, even if it couldn't last. Somehow, though, she could have sworn there'd been more carrots and a lot more leeks only the day before....

With an effort she forgot her worries; it was time she had some fun. Still, she wasn't sure about going to Hell. It sounded rather like the Wasp's Nest back in Witwaterstrand and her mother would die if she knew Chesarynth had ever been there. Not, of course, that she ever had – well, maybe once, with Dael, to see Jezrael laser-dance. But her mother didn't know about that.

While Chesarynth was hesitating, Alexei said slyly, 'I went by her Last Stand this morning. You are right: all the carrots have partings on the left-hand side.'

More laughter. Loretta said, 'Oh, go on, Ches. We won't tell, will we, Callum?'

Callum, sleek and self-satisfied, was too bored with the subject to deign to reply, but Alexei said, 'I will take good care of you, *da*?' And in stereo he and Retta whispered that Callum was happy to pay.

'Oh, I couldn't!'

'Don't spoil it for me, Ches,' hissed Loretta. 'You don't have to drink anything if you don't want to.' She dropped her voice still further to plead, 'And he'll be much nicer if you come too.'

And despite herself, Chesarynth let them persuade her, even when Rosalita and Sanjay said they'd rather stay in hall.

'All right, OK, I know when I'm beaten,' she said. 'If you're sure it's all right, that is. Besides, Rosie, I'm not going to play gooseberry with you and Sanjay. See you around.'

Chesarynth and Alexei, Loretta and Callum weren't the only ones on the road to Hell that night. As the sky darkened, there were sudden knots of voices coming from up and down the road. It was companionable, walking arm in arm four abreast. Overhead swung the bright globes of lights, so that the way was a shining ribbon. All around were the darkling fields and the scent of moist earth, with here and there some weary soul dragging themselves back from their labours, but the road was alive with gaiety and Chesarynth was suddenly very glad that she'd come. For the first time the nagging ache of homesickness vanished.

She turned her head a moment and was struck by the ugliness of the university buildings behind them. 'Look, Retta. Doesn't the university seem drab from here?'

'It always did, you idiot. Don't you know that yet?' But affection took the sting out of Loretta's words.

And Chesarynth was glad to turn away from the collection of squat, graceless blocks that bulked angular against

91

the naked hills, because ahead the lights of the town were beckoning. Already Ecoville had stopped being the tiny cardboard cut-out it had always seemed when she rested on her hoe for a minute at the Last Stand. Now, its buildings had grown to become three-dimensional.

'Feel that?' asked Loretta as a warm breeze stretched out to them from the streets ahead.

Chesarynth nodded rapturously. It smelt of housedust and flowers, dinners cooking and machine-oil. It smelt like Witwaterstrand – almost. But before nostalgia had more than brushed her mind, she was caught up in wonder at the first real street she had ever trodden. For a while the endless drag of gravity seemed worthwhile.

'Looks puritanical, doesn't it?' commented Loretta.

Alexei nodded, his sparse, ragged hair tickling Chesarynth. 'The main town is.'

'Well, you've got lots of other outdoor cities to compare it with,' said Chesarynth, reasonably. 'I wouldn't know, but the way Mars is run, I wouldn't be surprised. In fact I'm amazed that they let Hell exist at all.'

'One day it won't, but they haven't figured out a way of stopping it yet,' Loretta answered. 'They can hardly ban all machines on a world that's dependent on space-ships, can they?'

'No politics, please,' said Alexei. 'It would spoil my appetite.'

And everyone laughed but Callum.

They walked closer, stepping into the streets that sprang so suddenly from the red-brown plain. Chesarynth went on, 'What gets me is that all the buildings are cubes. The places my father grows are sort of beautiful, flowing – I don't know. Even Nutristem has curves, but this ...'

'Don't stand there gawping,' muttered Callum. 'You look like a tourist. I want some action.'

All the same, Chesarynth couldn't help noticing that the buildings were isolated, each in its own separate block: the town hall, the library, the conservation centre, with none of the looping strands that were the highways of commerce and friendship back in Witwaterstrand. Even the self-righteous ergonomic houses were primly angular. And the goods in the store-displays were worthy basics, not a luxury among them. Small wonder the citizens were all at home.

'Oh, isn't the heat great?' said Loretta, sighing with pleasure. 'You'd think they'd put this many thermal grids under the fields, wouldn't you, if they cared as much about the environment as they say they do?'

Then, past the dark reflections in the shop-windows, Callum led them out of the orderly, empty rectangles of Ecoville. He glanced around, as if spying out proctors, a familiar movement that made Chesarynth nervous.

She hung back. 'Are you sure it's –'

'*Da*, is OK.' Alexei squeezed her arm; on the other side Loretta was smiling encouragingly.

'Oh, come on!' Callum sneered his contempt. 'Of course it's all right, you're with me, aren't you?' He strode impatiently ahead and it was left to Loretta and Alexei to reassure her.

'I come here all the time,' Alex said. 'It's not actually against regulations. So long as you behave yourself – you're not planning a riot, are you?'

The girls smiled at Alexei's feeble humour. Loretta added, 'Don't worry, Ches. Even if a proctor comes, they're not going to touch a corporate, are they? Besides, they hardly ever come to Hell. They daren't.'

She speeded up, dragging Chesarynth after Callum's retreating back. Unconvinced but unable to justify her reluctance, Chesarynth could only follow.

Without waiting for them, Callum turned a corner and they half ran to catch up as he plunged down a side-street.

It seemed a parallel universe reached out to enfold them. This wasn't the impersonal indifference of the main town. Ship-salvage metal walls bulged out at them so that the sky above Chesarynth was a smoky canyon. Stars were obliterated, but they weren't missed. Neon signs of red and purple and electric blue punctured the shadows, and each had a smell: pheromones and blossom radiated brashly from brothels, drug-smoke wove with wine and stale beer from the dim amber of bars. Jangling songs clashed from a dozen broken-down cubers and over the muted roar of drunken conversations a sad violin wept Mozart's liquid tears.

The lurid ambience punched a hole in Chesarynth's mind. Excitement fountained up, drowning out her preconceptions; she exchanged smiles with Loretta. Alexei looked in his element, his glass eye reflecting the polychrome glow.

Then they rounded a shadowy corner and burst into daylight, though it was night.

'Oh!' said Chesarynth's mouth of its own volition. Skies of pale summer arched blue in sunshine, and there was a lulling sound rising from the ripples of a lake. She gazed at the colourful gondolas bobbing on the waters; in each were laughing groups beneath striped awnings of red and white or yellow, a bright contrast to the living green of hills. Small life-forms sang across the cloudless bay, their wings flashing silver in the sun. And sweet old-fashioned music trembled with the threads of conversation.

'Oh, isn't it beautiful?' Chesarynth said again. 'I've never seen open water before.'

Callum grimaced in disgust. 'You're not now, either. What are you, some kind of nut? It's just a holo. This way.'

He led them across the marble quayside, and pigeons danced aside into the peonies.

'Even if they are holos,' she whispered to Loretta, 'they're beautiful! Look at the iridescence on that bird's neck.'

'Have you seen their feet? They're coral-coloured. Fancy real birds having plumage like that.'

'Are they ...'

'No, they're holos too. But they're supposed to be exact copies.'

They stepped down three white stone stairs on to a gondola that waltzed beneath their weight and drifted gently out towards the distant grassy hills that slept in the sunlight. Callum and Alex keyed drinks from a console in the bulwark – neither of them would accept Chesarynth's offer to pay – and they sat back in flowery swinging chairs that echoed in movement the lapping of the waves. Chesarynth wondered how Alex could afford anything like this, but the thought was soon chased away.

'Seen what you're wearing?' asked Loretta.

Gone were her plain shorts and halter of plastic. A silk gown of gentle mauve caressed Chesarynth's skin. Pearl-stitched flowers hemmed her wrists and low neckline. And Loretta was a graceful flame of rose with flowers nodding in her black, glossy hair. Even the boys were in piratical velvet and lace.

'You look lovely, Retta!' Chesarynth sipped her drink whose flavours were elusive. 'I could stay here for ever, couldn't you? Listen to those bells across the water.'

'It's supposed to be the angelus ringing out across an Italian lake. It really gets you, doesn't it?'

Callum claimed Loretta's attention then, flirting rather crassly, and Alex was lost in his own private world, but it didn't matter. Even when she had finished her drink, Chesarynth was quite happy to watch the limpid reflections of the flowers on the quayside and to trail her fingers through the satiny waters. She pictured the garden-master sitting opposite, smiling at her, sun-dapples striking up from the waves. . . .

All too soon their gondola glided back to the quay. Callum led them away between crowds in the bright clothing of a dozen eras and out into the shadows.

Chill and black, reality struck them hard. Without the illusory sunshine, the grit swirled by vicious winds around their ankles stung angrily. Chesarynth and Loretta were subdued but Callum and Alex were seized by a brittle gaiety, singing an ironic fighting-song. And since they were the ones who were paying most, the girls couldn't gainsay them.

Not only that. Behind their sharp laughter came frightening echoes as shadowy figures took it up. Chesarynth and Loretta would not have admitted it, but they were too scared to go back on their own.

They began to pass people wrapped in old scraps of

plastic, huddled under any shelter they could find. Some were whimpering in their sleep but those who were awake stared suspiciously as though someone might snatch the only thing they had left. Alex, already rather drunk, drifted along inconsequentially. The girls kept closer to Callum, though it wasn't the stares that unnerved Chesarynth most, it was the faces.

For they were not the flat harsh red of the Martian tan, like everybody at the university. Instead they were lacquered masks that glinted in the neon lights, masks white as geishas or black as Congolese. One boy, no older than ten, wore a big red nose with a carnival smile painted crudely on a face cut from an oil-can. Above the holes of his eyes, above the orange frizz on his forehead, there was a scant fluff of diseased hair on his own head. One foot had only four toes.

But those who had not yet taken to masks wore their own faces all awry. Men with no ears, women with noses of tin, smears of ruby like a second mouth in the middle of a forehead, grating back the laughter that rose maniacally from Alex and Callum.

A sari'd Hindu with a caste-mark in her forehead and a topaz in her nostril walked past, cradling her son. She smiled, normal, welcoming, at the girls but pulling her cloth of modesty over her face when Callum looked her way.

A bar, a drink. Another place, and Callum scowling when Chesarynth wouldn't drink again. Loretta had given up all resistance; she swallowed smoke she didn't want then coughed it all out again in a scarf of motes that gleamed where a beam of light fell athwart it.

Laser-music caught Chesarynth, its resonances stirring her body. She watched the figures jerk symbols under the strobes of the null-gee dance-floor and thought *I wish I was Jezrael! I wish I could fly like Jezrael then I could be a part of this*. For it was the alienation that unnerved her most. Strange to think that a corporate student, the purest of the pure, paid a good wage by the company who was funding him, should feel so at ease in a place far removed

96

from his tidy, well-planned life. From the corner of her eye she glimpsed Leika, slim and vibrant, long black hair shining, the centre of a rowdy group, then the shifting dancers hid her from view. Not knowing where Leika was any more made Chesarynth feel even more nervous.

A man jerked her to her feet. He was so big, radiating so much suppressed violence, that she couldn't deny him one dance. Out of the whole set she made one or two body-riffs (copied from memories of Jez) that she felt at home with. For the rest of the song, a long and awkward inhibition held Chesarynth stiffly.

As soon as the music faded she propelled herself out of the null-gee. The big man followed her, still looking as though he were on the verge of breaking into a fight.

She said, 'Excuse me. I have to go to the facilities,' and hung around in there 'til she was sure he must have gone.

But when she came out she couldn't see Loretta, or Alexei, or Callum. Alone, she felt the atmosphere more hostile than ever.

Desperate to find them, she was pushing past a crowded table in the frightening smoke-filled dungeon where the air was solid with sound. Some African woman grabbed her.

Chesarynth tried to pull away. The woman yanked at her hand so that Chesarynth fell on one knee (without the money to pay, she'd always have the scar of the broken glass she stumbled on). Ready to cry, Chesarynth hit out instead.

But the African caught Chesarynth's skinny hand in her powerful one and pulled her closer. The oxy-crimson face was lacquered in black stripes, a ruby tiger with strong white teeth, and the yellow whites of the woman's eyes stared into Chesarynth's from a hand-span away. And some oddball dissonance of speech jarred on Chesarynth's hearing.

'I'm not gonna hurt you, girl.'

'You already have!' Chesarynth's blood shone scarlet as it slid down her knee.

'I meant real hurt, like the kind these gentlemen would

like to give you. Look at them!' The woman's speech was slurred, each consonant like a ski-slope for the contralto voice to swoop down. Though she didn't shout, her words carried against the racing pulse of the music and the cymbals were her exclamation marks.

'Look at you! Look at your hands.' (A man at the next table toppled slowly to the floor and lay there among the broken glasses, smiling in his sleep. His thigh settled across Chesarynth's foot, but the African held her still in a grip as fierce as an electro-stick's.) She forced Chesarynth's hands up to eye level as if they were some alien specimen for them both to dissect.

Frightened, Chesarynth looked, and saw her hands suddenly as the African woman must have seen them: wrinkled and reddened, half of Last Stand ground into their calluses. Where were the beautiful nails that she'd been so proud of at home? In their place were ugly, lined stumps with a forever rim of Mars.

'Now look at me. Look at all of us. Skins all ashine, girl, plump and rounded with health. You see anybody here with her nose stuck in some memo all day? You see anybody here that look like you? Do you?' she insisted.

Knuckles cracking under the pressure of that grip, Chesarynth said, 'N-no.'

'That's 'cause there ain't any.' And suddenly it occurred to Chesarynth what the thing was that didn't match up: the dull speech-patterns of Hell smeared across the woman's syllables that were as perfectly cultured as pearls. 'I'm telling you, girl, you get out of that university. It's not doing you a bit of good. The guys that run this planet, they got you all sewn up tight in a little sack, and you reckon that if you're good, they're gonna let the seams out once in a while so's you can breathe.

'But they can't, you hear me? There's twenty-five hundred of us in Hell here or some other equatorial city, maybe more if you count the crazies up in the ice-deserts. And there's not more than five hundred of them proctors on the whole planet. Can you see that? So they force failure into your brains and then they got you. You think anybody gonna make your stupid quota?'

Chesarynth found her head shaking 'No' at this woman's whim, and hated her for the dirty ideas she was pouring into her head. She didn't want to hear all this. She wanted to find Loretta and go home.

But with the strength of the drunk the woman pressed Chesarynth's hands until she agreed, and Chesarynth thought what a failure she was.

The African smiled fiercely. 'So you get into debt then you gonna give your head to the cleaners.' One tiger-eye winked. 'You gonna hide your failure from your momma and contract to some interplanetary monopoly so they can put a tower in your head and plug you into some machine, then farewell and amen to all the life you could have known.'

Chesarynth tried to protest but the tiger-head snarled and she recoiled. The African woman laughed in her face. 'You sort your head right, girl. I mean, look at this Mars! You got inflation, you got food that ain't fit to feed hogs, you got water that eats out the pipes and the cisterns, and you got farmers starving to death planting out clone-stuff that's been zapped by so much radiation it don't know which way is up. Why do they buy it? Some fat cat somewhere has him a mighty smart contract and a bank balance that could buy him the Earth! Then you got some damn puritanical Luddite government out here that says using a tractor or an agri-bot is a sin against the whole human race.

'And what do you bugs do? You whisper yes and amen – ain't you doing that with me?'

Chesarynth nodded again, the woman's rag doll.

'And you run yourselves ragged poking away with your dibbles and pruning-forks when you're supposed to be studying. How you gonna do two jobs? What are you, some kind of schizophrenic? Or some spying proctor-spawn?'

The knotted fear in Chesarynth's throat gave her no chance to reply before the woman continued.

'And you come here shouting your mouth off about

some bug that's shrunk?' (Chesarynth wondered how she'd got into this conversation which made no sense.) 'You ain't gonna get no answer from Hell 'less you stop letting the government squash you!'

The red-black woman flung her away and Chesarynth fell sprawling atop the drunk, his body a jellified mattress. His arms rose to feel her, his fingers crawling over her bare flesh like the tentacles of an anemone. Above her the smoke hung in shining strata, and the tsunami of sound surged into her. Repelled, she struggled to her feet but that rhythm faster than heart-beat slipped up into her bones and slid an earthquake through her body. She couldn't think straight; even her mind had been invaded by the alien ideas of sedition.

The drunk crooned and clung to her leg; Chesarynth couldn't shake him off. A splash of blood from her knee coalesced on to his face and he slowly licked it from his lips, his tongue ponderous and vegetal. Inside her abdomen, her secret organs writhed.

The African woman said, 'Yes, I seen her, maybe.' (Again that top-drawer accent sliding above the basement words. Chesarynth still didn't understand what was going on.) 'She blazed like Halley's then three towers dragged her out.'

Chesarynth felt the drunk begin crawling up her leg, his breath hot on her thigh. She couldn't push him off, but the African said, 'Joe, I told you before. You leave folks be or I'll tell your head of faculty where-at you are. And you, girl. Run along now and play at being perfect, and don't you descend on Hell again until you know which side you're on.'

And it was better to chance the cripples in the dark than to stay where twisted logic skewed your view of the once-neat world.

9

Magrit heard it all.

It was an extension that she had allowed Karel to add to her bluetower, an amplifier so subtle it could detect vibrations through the floor. All you had to do was get close under where the speakers positioned their chairs, and with her security status that was eminently possible. More, such a simple means was beyond the imagination of the old guard on the Board: Chairman Ole, the Lady Theresien, Oskar or Berndt. They checked the conference room for electronic bugs, had it soundproofed and screened for spy-beams, the lot.

Then, to prove how keen and worthy he was of promotion within Security, Karel had one of his personnel check that nothing had been inserted between the floor of the boardroom and the ceiling of the office below. Nothing had been – as he could demonstrate to one of Oskar Tjerssen's minions who stayed to keep a hostile and suspicious eye on Magrit.

So, though Karel wasn't senior enough to be on the Board himself, a recording chip in the back of Magrit's skull picked up every word that was said through the tiny oscillations of the steel joists and the consequent microscopic motions of the air in the room below, where Oskar's man watched Magrit for trickery.

All the man saw was the relayed sunlight dancing rainbows through the swaying fronds of her tower. He thought it was beautiful. But such a shame for a pretty girl like that to be dehumanized that way. She looked like she had some futuristic sculpture welded to the top of her head. It was a thought that helped him stave off the boredom of guard duty.

And that was how Karel heard Lady Theresien say, 'Are you sure about that, Ole?' Her accented voice rang out through Karel's living-room, striking faint echoes from the range of spiderglass towers he had hung along the wall opposite the sea view. Unasked, Magrit turned the volume down on the playback machine. Quieter now the patrician voice went on, 'I wouldn't have thought it was safe to promote a mere child like Karel to the Board. After all, it's known he thinks one or more of us had a hand in the demise of his father. For all I know he blames us for the death of his grandmother in that dreadful space-accident too.'

'Guilty conscience, Theresien?' Ole said in tones spiked with malice.

She arched her pretty brows at him. 'Not at all, Ole. But just look at things from his point of view. Through his grandmother, the boy's father should have been next in succession. And now you are Chairman instead. I'm sure that if he does blame anyone it is you.'

'Touché.'

Oskar, his stocky body tilted back lazily in his chair, drawled, 'And I believe it was you, wasn't it, Ole, who had his little lab on the Moon closed down? "Uneconomical" is a pretty thin excuse if you ask me. I bet our boy wonder resents rather thoroughly you throwing away his toy.'

'That,' said Ole with a touch of hauteur, 'was the best means at our disposal to clip his wings. Who knows what he might have done with all this psychological engineering? As it is, he's harmless.'

'Personally I can't stand all these subhuman towers walking around. What's to stop them running amok? They give me the shivers.'

In the aqueous light of the marine hideaway Karel lifted one blond brow at Magrit. She looked down in confusion.

'That, Oskar, is entirely beside the point.' Lady Theresien sneered at her illegitimate half-brother.

'Well, what is the point then?' Oskar said.

'The point is that having rendered him harmless we now offer him a junior position on the Board. The most junior position that we can give to family.' Berndt, who had been waiting to get a word in edgeways, looked pleased at making this contribution.

Theresien said sharply, 'We don't want him on the Board at all.'

'Oh, but we do,' Ole answered. 'We want him where we can keep an eye on him. And we want him not to be able to swing a block of votes, which he could with almost any other position. And there's an end to it.'

Not without a protest, Theresien subsided. The non-family members of the Board were called in and interminable discussions went their usual way.

Karel listened to the rest of the recording, Magrit on duty at the triple-thick spiderglass door of his undersea home. He paced past the angular green couch, the solid turquoise cube of the glass table. Not until he had endured a lot of unprofitable routine discussion did he find something else interesting on her data-chip.

Karel and Magrit heard the shuffle of people leaving the boardroom in Ole's wake. Then, his eyes moodily surveying the gaudy fish of the reef, Karel suddenly sat up.

Because, her voice echoing in the empty boardroom, Theresien said to the chief of her personal security team, 'There's something about that boy that unnerves me. I want him watched. I want his computer files checked, his movements, everything. And that bodyguard of his, Margarita or whatever her name is. Because that boy is going to be more important than any of them realize. We wouldn't want anything unplanned happening to our golden boy now, would we? And if he were to have a little accident, I think one of our people ought to be there, don't you? Just to lend a hand, as it were.'

Magrit stood, her back to the window, her eyes wide. She gazed at Karel with apprehension. In that moment, backlit by the sun shining down through the tropical blue lagoon, he thought she looked beautiful.

'She wouldn't –' began Magrit and Karel changed his mind.

'Shut your mouth. Of course she would. Don't you know anything?' He had stopped pacing. Now, responding to the death-threat, Karel the golden seemed like a lion at bay. 'She can do what she likes so long as Ole doesn't find out. Bring me the computer trolley. I need to think.'

So Karel jacked in to his private off-line computer, checking first for foreign bugs in the matrix, but he couldn't see any. Nor feel nor smell nor hear them. But still he knew that somewhere Theresien's team was stalking him through the symbolic forests of data.

And Magrit was left feeling shut out.

Moodily she checked and rechecked the approach scanners, using other systems that Karel had welded into her mind: radio, infra-red, radar, sonar. Even plain old-fashioned sight and hearing.

But there was nothing, only the plain refractive walls of Karel's hideaway that flashed through subtle shifts of colour every time a cloud crossed the sun so far above, or a wave tangoed with the light. Beyond, in the clear waters of the lagoon, corals of red or mauve winked in and out of view behind shoals of angel-fish. The only thing that disturbed them were small sharks.

What worried Magrit was the knowledge that somewhere, someone was homing in on Karel, coming to help him have his fatal little accident. Theresien's net was large: favours owed, debts called in. Or Berndt with all the senators of other industries at his beck and call. In all probability Magrit would never recognize the assassin who might be making his stealthy approach even now. The same someone who was planning to walk through her to kill her love before ever she had a chance to break through and *mean* something in his life.

And there was nothing she could do about it.

10

Another dawn.

Retta mumbled, 'Leave me alone! It's the middle of the night.'

Chesarynth grinned, stepping out of reach of the flailing arm. She threw a cold wet flannel on to Loretta's pillow. It dripped through the black curls into Loretta's tight-shut eyes.

Wordless, she threw it inaccurately back.

'Well, you asked me to wake you up, Retta. You might show me a little gratitude when you've got all that weeding to do. Besides, don't you want to come and see if I've got any sugar-greens left?'

Ricocheting off the main memo-screen, the soggy sloth dropped to the floor. When Chesarynth, laughing, bent to retrieve it she noticed that there was a light flashing on the screen.

'You, Chesarynth Brown, are a low-life reptile.' Loretta struggled upright, disentangling herself from the transparent blanket. 'In fact, you haven't even attained reptile-hood. You are a blob of invertebrate protoplasm, probably a fore-runner of amoebic dysentery –'

'Shut up a minute, Retta.' Chesarynth was pressing keys on the memo. 'I've got a message coming in.'

'Probably just another love-letter from that disease of a garden-master you're in lust with.'

'Oh, go fry a snowball. It's from Jez.'

'Can I see?'

'Seeing as you can't even spell "privacy" much less understand it, who am I to stop you?'

But Chesarynth didn't mind at all, really. After all,

Loretta shared the messages from her brother with Chesarynth. Any contact at all from the outside world was better than none. Together they watched the message – a flat audio-visual prerecording, cheaper than a letter because you couldn't answer it directly so there was no transmission-time to pay, and much cheaper than a real videophone conversation – and saw Jezrael smile at them from a different world.

'Hi, kid,' she said, her hair a rumpled riot of colour in the lights of a laser-dance bar. 'Sorry I can't afford a real letter but the groans'll be sending you one soon and I'll chip in with that. I suppose you're all settled in now – your room-mate sounds like a laugh. I'd love to meet her. Your garden-master sounds too good to be true. Bit of a cop-out, though, isn't it, chasing after the staff? Isn't there any talent your own age?'

(The screen blanked out momentarily; Jezrael had edited some hesitation or other. Then the picture crackled into life again, dimmer this time.)

'Hey, Jud,' Jezrael yelled. 'Don't put the lights out yet, I haven't finished in here.' (No change in the dimness; Jezrael's skin shone with sweat in one slanting yellow gleam as she turned towards the unseen bar-owner.) 'Yeah, Jud, thanks a bunch. Same to you.' She faced the recorder again, her hand relaxing from a rude gesture into the dark dance-hall.

'Things are still pretty much the same around here. There's no pleasing the groans, but you could've guessed that. Dael's still pining for you but he's got his eye on the new environmentalist just in case he gets over it. I'm still plugging away at Nutristem but they're really weird there. They want quantity even if it's crap and I don't know how long the quality-bods will let me do my stuff properly. Maybe I'll have a chance to get out of here sometime but 'til then.... Dad and Mom are still arguing about the irrigation system, but what's new?

'I'll tell you what's new. They've got this great laser-dance troupe in and I'm trying to get an audition. The lead dancer is really something else. He's got to have studs

106

in, but even so, he's amazing. And he looks like I'd ordered him, only he's a bit kind of lived-in. He let me jam with him this evening so I'm high as a satellite.' She grinned again, her whole face lit up from within.'You know? I even got a round of applause! I couldn't believe it!

'Mom and Dad still don't like me doing this – big surprise – but you should hear them bragging you up every chance they get: "my daughter, the star of Mars-U". And their latest plan is to get me into some finance office because I'd meet a better class of geek in there. They reckon that's the only way I'll get ahead, meet some well-heeled creep who's dead from the neck down. Nice to be appreciated on my own merits, hey?'

'I miss you, you know. Bet you've got all your assignments keyed in from now 'til solstice. The groans are making me do an extra course in my free time but I don't understand the questions let alone the answers. So just every now and then I kind of tiptoe away. Mom was livid when she found out but Dad just kind of went glacial, you know how he does. It's no fun having to take all the flak on my own.'

The screen went black; from nowhere Jezrael shouted, 'Jud, you son of a space-cat, put the damn lights on! Oh well, guess I can take a hint. Take care of yourself, Ches my love, hope you've got someone to stop you working too hard. And that you've caught the bastard who's been nicking your crops. For my money it's that inscrutable Leika, but what do I know about the price of fish?'

Loretta pressed the stop-key. 'You mean you've told her about me? And mentioned Leika in the same breath? Yeuch!'

Chesarynth grinned up at her, her face lit by the still picture of her sister on the screen. 'Sure did. Told her you were twins.'

Loretta responded by snatching up her pillow and batting her over the head with it. Both of them knew it was impossible; Ches had only seen Leika a couple of times, just kind of hanging round the fields, or skulking

107

round the coffee-shop, but in place of Loretta's freckled prettiness, Leika had some hideous disease that pocked her skin with weeping sores and where they went beyond her hair-line, the lush dark waves became bleached and stubby.

Fending off Loretta, Ches said sarcastically, 'If you've quite finished, I want to catch up with my correspondence.'

'Of course, your worship. Allow me to key you back in to your letter.'

Jezrael's round-chinned face blurred into movement. Her voice slurred back up to its normal cheerful pitch. 'Why don't you fly me a line some time? I've sent you a little something if you check your account. It's not much, I know, but –

'All *right*, Jud, don't get your wires crossed. See you, honey – if the lights ever come back on.'

Loretta smiled and pressed the SAVE key. 'She sounds great, your sister.'

'She is. She's got everything I haven't. She doesn't let anything scare her, she's really good at making friends and having a good time. All I ever did was work and she still got nearly the same grades, but Mom and Dad never saw it that way because she's always getting into trouble. That's why they said it was no use her staying on for Higher Studies, and she said she would only on condition they let her laser-dance. Stalemate. Looks like she'll have to drop out after this semester. So now she's pinning all her hopes on being a professional dancer. Hope she does better with this audition than she did with her last one.'

'C'mon, Ches, wake up. You've got friends. What about me and Alexei?'

Chesarynth picked up her portable memo. 'You and Alexei? I didn't know you fancied him.' And she skipped out of the door before the outraged Loretta could wreak her revenge.

Happy, she walked through the dawn freshness, sharing her pleasure with her friend until Loretta turned off to the

Unlucky Strike, then enjoying her happiness on her own. Even when Leika brushed past her without a word it didn't spoil Chesarynth's mood.

Things weren't so good at the Last Stand, though. In fact she'd renamed it Last Ditch because that's all it was. A hole in the ground with a tent of patched plastic around it.

Staring at her ripped-up patch, Chesarynth threw her spade down hard in disgust. 'You bastards! You absolute sods!' she yelled. Once again some busy soul had dug up a whole batch of her seedlings; there was nothing left of the sugar-greens she'd unboxed only the day before. 'That was the only thing that was doing OK. Loretta was right. This place is too far away from anything!'

Still cursing, Ches trudged wearily to the sludge. At least she didn't have to hoe now so she could cart some more of the sanitized liquid compost over from the nearest pipe a twenty minute walk away. 'If they bother to turn our section on, that is. I bet there's a queue too.'

Of course, there was. Standing in line with her barrow, at least she could talk out her frustration to the people she usually met. Some of them had had sporadic thefts as well, but not on the scale Ches was experiencing. There was some half-hearted sympathy but nobody took much notice until she announced to the world at large. 'How come there's never a proctor around when you need one?'

All around her the slumped red bodies stiffened. Rastac, three places ahead, said in alarm, 'Don't you go getting mixed up with proctors, Ches. I mean it.'

And others nodded wide-eyed agreement.

But when she had schlepped the barrow back Chesarynth's anger returned full-force. Her soil was so devoid of humus that the liquid leached away almost immediately even though she dug little walls to keep it in. 'It's a complete waste of time!' she railed, watching it run away between the sickly, straggling ice-moolah that was about all they had left her. 'Another kilo on my rotten quota – and for what? I might as well give up now. Just look at this rubbish! Whatever am I going to tell the garden-master?'

Furious, she glanced round but the few who were

already at work under the plastic sheets looked perfectly innocent. Somebody wasn't but there was nothing to tell who. The two greenhouses beside her were untenanted but there were signs of digging around Leika's blocks of sugar-greens. They hadn't been there yesterday morning but who knew what Leika was doing when?

Maybe, thought Chesarynth, unwilling to face the truth, *maybe she's just done some hoeing for once.* Whatever, there wasn't enough evidence to hang a cat.

She ran over to Loretta's patch with the sun casting stretched shadows before her. Overhead the sunflowers were turning their plastic reflectors to catch the rising daylight; as she dodged between the crackling walls other shadows ghosted beside the first one.

She didn't need to say anything when she got there. Loretta took in her angry, dishevelled appearance and said, 'Again?'

'Yes. My new sugar-greens. There aren't even any footprints that I can track. It's been raked off again.'

'Did you check Rastac's place? And Leika's? I thought I saw her sneaking back as we came out, though what she can do in the dark beats me. Here – I'll come with you in case anybody asks what you're doing there.'

'They wouldn't,' Chesarynth said bitterly, 'Nobody ever notices a damn thing.'

None of Rastac's anaemic, ill-tended crops was sugar-greens. And later, all the garden-master said in his warm, caressing voice was, 'Poor you! And yes, Leika has also booked out some sugar-green seedlings.'

Again Chesarynth felt the familiar melting inside her head as she looked at him. Whatever Loretta might say, the garden-master couldn't be conning her – or how could she feel like this every time she saw him? His hand just happened to stroke her arm as he turned to the wall-map, a sympathetic gesture that lingered more than mere accident would allow but not so long that it was indiscreet. Chesarynth cursed the accident that had placed him in charge of her. She was sure that if they'd met any other way –

110

The garden-master shared a rueful smile with her. 'Maybe if you spent more time on your field, Chesarynth, nobody would be able to steal your crops.' But he grinned – it pierced her heart – to take the sting out of his reproof. 'Never mind, Ches, things aren't so bad. Your ice-moolah should pay off what it'll cost you to replace them, because I'm sorry, but I can't let even you have more cuttings for free.'

Stuck.

Chesarynth stared at her assignment on the memo-screen a moment longer then gave up in disgust. She sat on Loretta's bed because Alexei Min was lying on hers, the soft plastic of her blanket draped over him, its folds a rainbow tent peaking where his feet rested half-way up the wall. Outside the window, sun sparkled on unseasonal carbon dioxide snow against the blue of the sky, and the snow-crystals vanished, turned to gas, the second they touched the warmth of the earth. In the summer air there wasn't even steam to mark its going.

Chesarynth stared out through the triple glazing.

The long bright road that beckoned her on to know-ledge when she first came to Mars-U had dropped black barriers on her, one by one. She was stuck on Mars, glued down by the clinging quagmire quota.

'I am sorry, Ches.' Alexei spoke slowly, carefully, each word perfect. That's how she knew he was drunk. 'I can't explain it any better than that. Why don't you take a personal tutorial or two? It's only fifteen kilos. If your ice-moolah lives up to expectations, you can afford it. Just put it on your quota. It is no problem. I do.'

Chesarynth watched the snow fall in the sunlight and die like meteors. Personal tutorials, one to one with a real live human professor, who'd let light in on the dense maze of biophysics lectures –

'Anyway,' Alexei said, nodding and nodding like a toy, 'it is fun. It is jokes. Lectures only show you how it looks and feels and *smells* to do the experiments. They never really explain anything.'

And, paralleling Alexei, Chesarynth kept looking out of the window as she said, 'But Alexei, fifteen kilos!' All the same he knew she was getting desperate. 'I can't make the Last Ditch grow anything right. I mean, look at this weather! I've patched my oxyboxes so often they look like a broken mirror and they're still leaking.'

Alexei's red fingers reached across to brush hers. His real eye, the blue one with brown flecks in it, swivelled round to look at her. Its prosthetic companion didn't quite make it that far. Chesarynth, used to organic replacements, had to concentrate on not looking away. She wondered why he'd never had it fixed but she didn't have the courage to ask.

'You'll do fine,' he said, sounding as if he wanted to mean it.'I'll help you as much as I can.'

'Thanks, Alexei,' Chesarynth said wearily. 'I appreciate it. If I could only concentrate – but I'm just so tired. I can't get used to weighing so much all the time.'

Loretta exploded into the room, preternaturally cheery. 'What, you two still loafing about? Come on, come on! I've found a buyer for those do-do air-gems! You have still got them, haven't you?'

'But I can't' Chesarynth shouted. 'I've told you, I'm not going to sucker anybody else. Air-gems don't work and I'm not going to rob some poor innocent bug, OK? It wouldn't be fair. Besides, I thought it was illegal.'

'So don't. Anyway, it's only illegal if they catch you.' Loretta was already rootling through Chesarynth's orderly drawers, searching for the withered air-gems that blood would make plump and sparkling again. 'Well, I'm going to, Saint Ches. I could do with a decent meal even if you couldn't.'

Chesarynth stared out at the diamond snow again, bored with yet another replay of this argument. The light painted a dead blue glaze on her eyes. 'You won't find them, Loretta.'

From under the organophoam mattress came a muffled 'You wanna bet?'

But Loretta didn't find them this time either. She

slammed out again, then put her head round the clashing strips of plastic that did duty for the door. 'Are you two coming to eat, or what?'

The only trouble was, Alexei couldn't help her. Half the time he missed lectures completely because the machines made his hangovers worse; the other half, even he couldn't make head or tail of what his body should have learnt. In Witwaterstrand Chesarynth wouldn't even have talked to him. Here he was at least someone who cared – even if he wasn't the garden-master.

And the blurred cubes in the library weren't much help, either.

Then she had a brilliant idea.

She'd tape the lectures on a portable cube-machine. It would be hard, she knew. She'd only get the verbal and visual lines on a micro-miniaturised cuber – there was a second-year mech-eng girl down the hall who could knock one up for a few kilos – but at least she'd be able to play the lecture over and over 'til she got it straight in her head.

Then she'd have to fight the synergetic conductors that relayed to her synapses exactly what it was like to operate the subatomic waldoes, or at least block them long enough to switch the cuber on, but after that she could concentrate. Maybe that way, tired as she always seemed to be in the CO_2-heavy air, Chesarynth could work out what the hell was going on.

Another biophysics lecture – slime-mould reactions it was, according to the day's memo-screen. Alexei came along to watch, though Chesarynth was as nervous about him giving the game away as she was about the whole operation. Still, he meant well.

In single file they shimmied through the crowd to two adjoining glassy bubbles. Alexei's fake eye winked grotesquely as Chesarynth parted two plastic petals to climb into a contour-seat.

Over the chattering in the segmented lecture-theatre, the lights dimmed a little in the visible spectrum. Amidst the last fading whispers Chesarynth heard the usual flurry of clicks as people clipped the synergizers into place on heads and wrists, and the cold fingers of the medullar connection sliding through her hair tensed the muscles at her nape.

It was twilight on the banks of contour-seats, but up beyond ultra-violet some particles were left to pipe the tune for the oxyvirus' dance. Chesarynth's seat began a preparatory tingle as the synergizers tuned in to her body-frequencies. Down at the focus of the amphitheatre she saw the fat, bored technician scratch his thigh and turn the lecturer on.

Chesarynth fought the alien subconscious control long enough to press the On button of her illicit cuber. Nobody had ever said, but just having it here made her feel guilty. She glanced furtively through the transparent walls of her seat. Everybody else seemed paralysed, or dead. Their eyes reflected the swirling colours in the air above the boxy lecturer. She'd never noticed that before, that deadness. She'd always been part of it.

Her guilt-sweaty palm activated her cuber.

But as soon as she'd switched it on, hidden as she was in the shadows between the bubbles of other red-skinned students, a fierce buzz sounded.

In confusion Chesarynth bent to fiddle with the thing, sure it was only some stupid feedback looping through the cuber. Pain stabbed through her head as the synergizer, adjusting and readjusting to her every movement, fuzzed her responses.

Still the buzz whined in the air above her as if she were some bug to be shot dead by irradiation. Everyone turned to stare at her and she tried to pretend it was nothing to do with her, but some cold robotic arm angled down from the ceiling. At the end of its black head a flat eye recorded her embarrassment and its fat unmoving mouth said, 'You are student WF1397/41 Brown Chesarynth.'

Down at the front, the fat technician keying the lecturer stopped it. It died in a series of whirlpool colours and electronic sound; the synergetic motion faded from her body, from everyone's body, leaving nausea in its wake; the subtle array of scents that were supposed to cue memories splurged into olfactory diarrhoea. Up and down the rows of benches, students gagged and retched.

A proctor oozed his way between canopies like the cells of an orange, heading towards her, not even apologizing for the giddiness his sudden motion caused. Like all the proctors he had long hair dressed in a jewelled spike so that the hair sprayed up from his crown like a fountain, and in the middle of that black cascade a small, glassy aerial tried to hide.

Only nobody but proctors wore their hair like that.

A shiver swept Chesarynth, planting a seed of icy paralysis in her stomach.

Tall, chunky, inviolate, the proctor reached over to peel apart the canopy's rim and hold a stick over Chesarynth's head. It came so close she ducked her chin. He brought the stick lower still, forcing her to maintain her uncomfortable crouch. At that angle she could hardly look up but she could feel the tip of the thing as a psychological soreness where her skull-bones had fused after birth – and his stick wasn't even touching her.

The robot's spider-arm sucked the cuber out of her hand so fast its speed burnt her skin. And, in a voice no deader than the robot, the proctor said, 'WF1397/41 Brown Chesarynth, the garden-master will see you – tomorrow.'

The garden-master was beautiful still in his sorrow. And he was so, so sorry as he fined her ten kilos. His gentle fingers wiped away her tears of contrition. Then, with the late Spring sunlight haloing the jungle mist around his head, he added, 'Don't worry, Chesarynth my – friend. I'll help you. Why don't you try these ground-cherries?' (An image hovered momentarily in the air beside them so that as they turned to see it, his shoulder brushed hers ever so lightly. The fruits were tempting as pomegranates, luscious red and plump on the vines. Their scent had escaped from the sherbet of Paradise.) 'They're a new hybrid from

Nutristem; I've just been waiting for a chance to give them a trial. They're good heavy croppers, they say, and they don't take up much room. With a bit of luck they'll more than clear your debt.'

Chesarynth reached out words to snare the life-line· 'Oh, thank you! Only –'

Her garden-master smiled. 'I know – how can you pay for seedlings that have been transported forty million miles?' He lowered his voice, put his lips so close to her ear that the hair on her temple felt his speech as a caress. 'I tell you what. Why don't you pay me back when you make your first harvest?'

The fine was ten kilos; the cost of the ground-cherries, another eight, and the Last Ditch wasn't prospering. Then she'd had to pay the mech-eng girl ten kilos for the cuber.

And worst of all, Chesarynth knew it was she who had put that look of pain into the garden-master's eyes. The memory of it sandblasted her self-worth like the dust-storms of the equinox; *how could I have done that to the only real man I care about? Who ever cared about me?* She felt she was hardly fit to live.

It wasn't worth it. From now on, she'd go straight.

The one-to-one tutorials for the rest of that term came to another forty five kilos.

After all that, Chesarynth was so depressed that she blew seven kilos on a micro-letter foil to Jezrael care of Dael via the very next ship, since a solar storm was blocking all other forms of communication. Then, of course, Chesarynth was terrified that her parents might snoop around and find her desperation in print.

At least Jezrael still loved her.

And the garden-master was so nice, even after all she'd done. She would never, ever let him down like that again.

Darkness. The darkness of a midsummer's night.

Chesarynth peeped from the doorway of her hall and saw no-one about in the starlight. Leaving Loretta innocently asleep, she slipped out into the cold winds of night.

116

One hundred and fifty days into failure. Half a year in Witwaterstrand, but on this quicksand prison of Mars it was a scant quarter of a year. The remaining year and fifteen months stretched out before her like a prison sentence in a shrinking tunnel. Despair gnawed at Chesarynth – she wished now she'd paid more attention in Mental Hygiene classes in school but it hadn't seemed important then, just a pleasant, chatty loafing time that you didn't do assessments for. She couldn't remember what she was supposed to do about despair.

Gliding down the stairs, trying to be invisible, she felt fatigue as a physical weight on her aching shoulders. She braced herself for the black cold of outdoors, the frozen cube of darkness that lay beyond the glowing crystal of her hall. And the hollow of night in Mars-U wrapped her in its icy caress.

No-one there.

She ducked between the pyramids of alien plants. Adrenalin was a nova in the absolute zero of fatigue. There seemed to be vast spaces in her head, isolating one idea from another, with shooting stars as messengers from each lonely ball of thought.

She didn't think she'd make it. The constant weight of Mars sucked at her legs, dragging her down, slowing time so that it seemed she would never be free of her endless plodding through a morass of duties, from the lectures and seminars that she had to prepare for – or have her quota upped another ten K – to the routine schlepp out to her field. And each time she had to spend longer to nursemaid her crops or guard them, she had to pay the penalty for skimping her studies: an increase in her quota. She was up to two hundred and seventy kilos even after the seventeen sacks of Mars-beans she had already turned in to the garden master's smiling approval.

Scurrying furtively into the night, Chesarynth felt as if her guilt were a flowing target for unfriendly eyes. Its flush under her skin was a foil against the black air that was not so far off freezing.

She glanced round apprehensively as she pulled the

barrow from its hiding-place in a plant-pyramid. Bit by bit she'd filled it with scraps and human waste, anything to put humus and nitrogen in her soil. Now it was time to take it out to the Last Ditch.

The secret load in the wheelbarrow dragged her shoulders down. Chesarynth stumbled as she tried to pick out the star that was Witwaterstrand in the blue-black sky of Mars. One hundred and fifty days she'd been here, one hundred and fifty days of growing wretchedness, and home was retreating every second. She couldn't even send a holo-gramme; the asteroid-cluster was in the incandescent shadow of the sun.

Rounding the corner of someone else's greenhouse, the plastic gleaming dully in the darting moonlight, Chesarynth stole a moment to stop and wipe her forehead. Her hands didn't feel as if they belonged to her; they'd grown horn layers over the scars of her blisters. Loretta had been right about the ground, anyway. Surely she couldn't have been right about the garden-master, though. *She's never even seen my garden-master.* But the thought was freighted with shadows of worry.

Sighing with an exhaustion that dimmed her anxiety, Chesarynth picked up the handles of her barrow and staggered off again, peeking like a thief around the night-dark fields.

She wished she could afford another letter back home. It would have been great to speak to Jez, tell her that now she understood why Jez had always thumbed her nose at the authorities, but what if Mom or Dad saw it? *They worked so hard to send me here. Maybe it's just as well I can't find the money. They'd see the state I'm in....*

The barrow stopped suddenly and she walked into it. The balloon wheel at the front was caught on something she couldn't see in the dark and it worried her. The wheel was designed to go over just about anything, and if there were something obstructing it, it meant she was off course. She was so tired she could have wept.

Under the blazing crystal stars everything looked the same. It even sounded the same, the plastic green-house roofs crackling and billowing in the breeze that never seemed to stop. Squares of plastic just above head-height that dust weighed down until they sagged in exhaustion. Their undersides – if you were lucky – dripped condensation back on you, and there was the constant stench of raw manure that you weren't supposed to use because it could start off all sorts of epidemics, but what else could you do? You'd got to fill your quota somehow and where else could you get humus and fertilizer in one for free? And in between, rearing above the well-trodden paths, the sunflowers, their silvered polythene nodding sleepily to the thunder of another 'quake.

Chesarynth back-tracked, shivering with cold and fatigue. Stood on the balloon-wheel to get a better sighting. Yes, there was her sunflower, the end one before the notch in the hills. She was so tired she hadn't even noticed that she'd walked past the end of the path that led to her field. And someone else was moving stealthily this way. Moonlight – she thought it was moonlight – gleamed pale on their hair.

What can I do? Shall I go to my field and dump the stuff there? What if they catch me with it? Would it be safer if I just chucked it all on somebody else's patch?

The answer was obvious. Whoever it was, a spy or some other poor slob behind on their quota, they were three squares back and one over. If she ran, if she didn't get lost again, Chesarynth could get her load safely buried on her field and be far away before they caught up with her. And why should anybody else get what she'd so painfully brought all this way?

Chesarynth broke into a stumbling run, glad she was too far away for them to make out who she was. The hoarded scraps of food slopped about dangerously close to the rim of the barrow but she kept them aboard, feeling cunning. The liquid human waste splashed up at her, stinking, but she didn't lose much. All you had to do was dismantle the toilet in your room a bit, put a sheet of semi-permeable plastic across – there was quite a run on the black market to get it – and complain to your room-mate how nothing ever worked properly any more. You didn't want them cashing in on it – or splitting to the garden-master. Chesarynth hated even the idea that she was letting him down by doing this forbidden thing, but if she didn't make her quota she'd be letting him down again that way too. She remembered the way he'd looked at her last time, such disappointment in his gentle eyes....

She rounded a corner, breathing hard. Above the wisps of cloud, Phobos stood still, just barely distinguishable from the other stars because of its crescent-phase. She looked all round, her heart pounding so hard it seemed to shake her ribs, but there was nobody behind her. The person with the pale splashes in their hair was out of sight but still her pulse roared and there were tingles under her skull. *Don't let it be another panic attack don't let it....* But she hadn't got time to concentrate on having a panic-attack.

Furtively she scrabbled away the topsoil from her latest raised bed, the one nearest to the hills at the end of her patch. She shovelled the wizened dead radishes away with the rest, part of her quota that had never really got above ground. *I was so sure they'd take. I'd have been able to cart them back for the garden-master. He'd have been so pleased with me.*

She threw the soil on to a sheet of plastic. Condensation rained on her, but at least it wasn't the icy rain that stung her skin when she wasn't under cover. Another crafty glance round. No-one.

That would have to do. She upended the barrowload of raw sewage and rotting vegetables into the hollow she'd made, then quickly emptied the plastic sheet so that the dry soil fell over her raised bed. At least it partly deadened the foul smell. Tomorrow she'd be able to seed the ground. She'd got to do something to keep her quota up. And maybe this time the garden-master would take notice of her, instead of looking through her like he had last time, when she'd taken him the few miserable bunches of radishes that had survived.

Because whatever she was doing, the garden-master

was in her thoughts. His image holo'd itself into her mind when she was in lectures, his voice replayed in her head across the scrolling words on her screen as she studied or wrote assignments. Sure, the boys on her course were OK. But they were just boys. And the garden-master actually seemed to like her.

Still nobody in sight. She scuttled across to her quarter of the toolshed she shared and quickly shoved in the barrow. Then she played hide-and-seek back to her block.

Had she locked the shed?

Of course I have, she thought, as she had thought a hundred times before. *I shoved the barrow under the plastic, stuck my head out of the door to make sure it was all clear, then I locked the shed like I always do.... Didn't I?*

So how come I can't remember if I locked it or not?

Because I always lock it every day. Wait a minute, what did I do with the key?

Chesarynth was too tired to decide. But surely she would have locked the shed? Her grant wouldn't hold out forever if she kept losing tools.... Once she'd left a trowel out on what was supposed to be her strawberry bed. She'd been too busy to go back that morning, but she knew just where it was. Who would even see it stuck upright in the hollows between the rows? And after lectures when she went back, it had gone. The garden-master had been so sympathetic when he'd seen her that she'd told him all about it. He'd been so sorry he had to make her give part of her grant to buy another one....

Now, with her guilt emblazoning the darkness, Chesarynth didn't dare go back. It would only draw attention to herself.

On her way in from the fields, she glimpsed other figures lurking about, their skins red-black in the night so that they looked like demons from some ancient ballet by Prokofiev. Working by the light of the sunflowers, that was all right, everyone did that, but not night-flying. Chesarynth had never thought she would come down to this.

Past the beginning of the fields, past the last of the

pyramid-beds with their pale moon-flowers giving off a haunting, bitter smell. At least it was better than the revolting fecal odour that seemed ingrained in her hands. Chesarynth tried to saunter down the frosty paths as if she had every right to be there so late into the night.

Relief: she was back on the campus, where the geothermal lattice underground spread its dark geometry through the whiteness of the hoar. Reaching the lines of halls, she saw there were still some late-birds, boys kissing girls against the stored warmth of the solar panels. The music of a party somewhere. She could have been coming back from some date, or the concert. That was it! The concert!

Only what if somebody asks me what they played? Gate-crashed the party, then. Don't know whose it was. But nobody's going to ask me, are they? And Loretta wouldn't split on me even if she knew I was gone.

Above the buildings of Mars-U rose a reddish halo of lights. She assumed a nonchalant walk, thinking of the times Jez had swept back into the library at the end of a study-period, pretending she'd just gone back to fetch a pen she'd left in her locker, look, here's the pen, that proves it. And nobody knew she'd stolen a few moments to laser-dance, well nobody but Dael and her sister, *and we'd never tell.*

The stairs were almost too much for Chesarynth, but she made it by determination. Loretta was in bed, snoring faintly in innocence, one hand over her eye-mask as if to shield it from the light.

Chesarynth scrubbed herself, wincing at each splash, cringing when the water hammered in the tap, but Loretta slept on. Clean at last, Ches flopped on to the bed, throwing her damp boots under the desk then turning to face the wall. Usually she found it all but psychologically impossible to get to sleep in the stored solar glare, but now she could hardly keep her eyes open anyway. She forced herself to slow her breathing, match it to Loretta's in the hope of masking the snores.

And the door slammed open.

Both girls sat bolt upright, the sound piercing them. They unmasked. It was the hall proctor, and the proctor was armed with a stick. An electro-stick whose pain was stored in Chesarynth's fontanelles, and it cued remembered nausea from the remembered stink in the lecture.

'Recording,' said the proctor aloud, presumably so the tower in her hair could pick up and send the recording to some –

'WF1397/41 Brown Chesarynth, you are accused of engendering disease by using untreated waste on your garden. Do not attempt to deny it as we have an eye-witness though she prefers her identity not to be revealed at this time.'

It didn't matter. For there behind the proctor, half hiding in a doorway, stood a girl with moon-spewed patches pale in her hair.

Leika.

The proctor's tone was inhumanly calm as she went on, 'WD0798 Sibo Loretta, you are accused of complicity. Accompany me please.'

And as the girls stumbled into the corridor, Leika smiled behind their backs.

11

Another raise in her quota (the garden-master smiled his sorrow, of course, from under his halo of lilies); more resentment from Loretta, more useless sympathy from Alexei. He kept coming up with schemes for wreaking vengeance on Leika but she was lying low.

'Does not matter,' slurred Alexei a couple of days later. 'I have seen her in corpo's block. Why don't we sabotage her memo? Or better still, steal it and sell? We make profit, she's in trouble –'

'No!' yelled Chesarynth in alarm. 'We'll only get in deeper. Anyway, she's got what she wanted, hasn't she? And they've moved her field. Don't know where she works now.'

All the same Alexei invented more and more bizarre plans for revenge which became so outrageous they kept the girls in half-horrified stitches.

Until one day he and his oddball eye disappeared.

At first Ches and Retta just thought he'd gone on a massive drinking spree. Then time passed, and more time, and their anxiety grew because they couldn't find him anywhere, even in Hell. One night all his personal belongings simply vanished, and his bed was reassigned.

But they were too exhausted to worry for long. Assessments and quotas, quotas and assessments, and still things vanished from their plots as they vanished from everyone's, sooner or later. Only somehow it always seemed sooner from Chesarynth's Last Ditch, and she was too tired – and too cold – to stand guard all night for month after month. Her quota grew, sharp and heavy, like one of her father's coral houses, and there was no time for anything but digging and study and snatches of sleep.

Goodbye, Alexei.

But the real rock-bottom – Chesarynth thought – was eleven months later, when the gravity of the solar slings dragged Mars to aphelion and winter.

Same scenario on a frost-jewelled night when sleep cradled Chesarynth in the bright floating crystal of the hall. Three proctors, this time, slamming aside the stiffened plastic sheets of the door, pouring out a cruel dazzle that burned away the cobwebbed dreams when Chesarynth, bewildered, yanked aside her eyemask. Fierce as molten iron the glare burned from the proctors' electrosticks, the wild radiance spraying up and down her body and Loretta's through the transparent covers until each private cranny of their flesh was lit up like a tourist map.

Chesarynth yelled curses at this visual rape.

But Loretta didn't even ask 'Why?'

In the garden-master's jungle a different path was open. Chesarynth and Loretta, still shivering with the sub-zero chill of night, felt a wave of moist, odorous warmth sweep out to engulf them. It coalesced on their skin, moist, tiny beads indistinguishable from nervous sweat, oppressive.

So was the silence. It squeezed Chesarynth until her ears rang with it, but Loretta wouldn't say a word. For days her emotions had soared in arpeggios from the base-notes of gloom to fragile, tinkling laughter, but she'd never answered straight at any of the times Chesarynth had asked her what was wrong. And Chesarynth had stopped asking, but now she wished she hadn't.

Still the silence, so complete that she jumped when a dried-up leaf fell skithering through the branches. The proctors had disappeared, taking their cattle-prods with them, but they hadn't gone away. The uncanny not-quite-humans were still somewhere about, still able to see her in some way that wasn't mere physical sight. Chesarynth could feel those strange eyes piercing her with impersonal contempt from some secret place.

The thought rushed into her mind, milling among her other crowded worries: *How can anybody let that happen to them? Let someone put that alien tower through their skull and have its wires weaving through the soft grey flesh of their brains?* Turn them into something that could torture nonchalantly –

Chesarynth stopped thinking about it. It was too scary, came too close to home. . . .

In a gloomy clearing where creepers and dark Spanish moss sagged from the shadows of trees, the girls waited, not quite alone.

And waited.

'Do you think –' began Chesarynth, the words pressed out of her by the dreadful weight of no noise.

'Ssh!' Loretta stood, back to Chesarynth, not even touching her, a cold and hostile stranger.

This time there was no cosy fallen log to sit on. Instead, half-seen through the murky gloom of a starless chamber, there was just a close wall of trees thin enough to be the bars of some cage. Underfoot the damp struck chill through Chesarynth's shoes. The boggy smell gathered thick in her nose until she thought she would vomit. She felt terribly alone, cast out into utter night of guilt through complicity in some unknown crime, but every time she tried to speak Loretta hushed her fiercely.

At last two voices spoke, their cadencing identical, the same timbre, only one higher and one lower. And one voice plugged directly into Chesarynth's mind so that she couldn't quite hear the words of the other, only echoes of her mother's anger like a carpet grimy from years of down-treading, that spread its hateful dullness upwards through the ambiance of her thoughts.

The garden-master spoke to her, spoke inside her, from a patch that showed paler against the slimy black boles. One minute he wasn't there, the next, he was. Chesarynth wondered who else might be watching hidden in the black forest. And she resented Loretta's being there to spy on her when she was with her beloved garden-master, felt her own behaviour change, felt the distance that sprang up between herself and him where there had never been distance before.

It was all Loretta's fault.

He said from very far away, 'Oh, Chesarynth, I'm so disappointed.' (And underneath, the archetypal mother said the same thing to someone else, and Chesarynth knew she had earned the same reproach. She hated herself.) 'I thought,' he said, in tones like drying honey, 'I thought that you of all people ...'

His voice trailed away, impossibly soft but clear and crystalline, like the jewelled trail of a distant rocket, fading his once-bright hopes of her.

Chesarynth remembered his smiles, the way his eyes seemed to look right inside her, freighted with the love she had never quite managed to win from her parents. Her body pulsed memories of the sensation his nearness bred in her, but she had gone too far this time – whatever her crime might be – guilt withered all her hopes of him.

Not quite all. His voice, sliding on a sunbeam of promise in the darkness: 'But I know you won't ever do anything like this to me again, Chesarynth.' (Underneath, subterranean, the same words as maternal threat going echoing back down the tunnel of the years to childhood.) 'I don't believe what they say. You do care, don't you?'

She wanted to shout, 'Yes! Yes!' but the dark feminine undercurrent of disapproval was sucking at her ankles.

'Conspiracy to deal disease, Chesarynth. What if it had been you that caught the disease? I couldn't have borne it, seeing you wasting away, your skin dingy, your eyes dull, and what could we have done about it? We don't even know what it is yet.'

Chesarynth managed to say, 'Neither do I!' but it was as if he didn't hear.

He went on, 'Cholera-based, we understand. The viruses are analysing it for us now, but they're still at the digestion phase. How could you even think of a disease as protection for your crops? What if some rogue rat had gone foraging round your plot and caught it? What if you two had started an epidemic? Everyone in your hall –

127

everyone on your course – what if that's happened to your friend Alexei Min? How do you know he didn't catch it and now he's off dying somewhere, alone, helpless, out under the cold sky? How could anyone as gentle as you –' (underneath she heard that dark vindication of female disappointment: "How could anyone be as stupid as you?") – live with themselves after that?'

'But I don't understand!' The words shouted themselves into the stilly gloom from Chesarynth's mouth, and she was shocked at the sudden force of them.

So cold, so sad, her beloved garden-master sighed, 'And now you lie to me. Oh, Chesarynth, you don't need me to say anything else about it. You know what you've done, and worse, what you might have done.'

'I don't! Oh, I don't! I couldn't lie to you.' (She was five, crying at her mother's knee.) Chesarynth could have thrown herself at his feet to beg forgiveness – but she couldn't even see him. She wanted to hear his little jokes again, the cheerful good humour they shared to make the best of it when she made her pitiful reports every ten days. She wanted him to stand so close beside her that she could feel the warmth of his body ruffle the electrosphere of hers.

But he was just a cold, distant voice now, isolated and full of pain, cut off beyond the universe of her loneliness. She had put herself beyond the pale.

As if he hadn't heard, he said from the far rim of the dark ocean of morass, 'They want me to punish you, and I just couldn't.' (Her mother's unhappiness was bitter in her mouth.) 'But ...'

A thunderous luminescence ripped through her skull-bones, vibrated each of the liquids in her body – blood and brain and guts and eyeballs – at its own conflicting frequency. Catherine wheels of fire roared around the edges of her vision, and the swamp-oaks were a hell-black net of shapes wrought by insanity at the bottom of a pit.

Her bones were rivers of coruscating pain. Mouth and nose, ureter and womb, burnt blinding, deafening, a jangle of bright acid. Breath was beyond her, snatched by the glittering maelstrom of vertigo that whirled around and inside her.

And her skin was the surface of the sun, each pore turned inside out, ten thousand incandescent flares leaping from the burning well of gravity to escape then fall from space, plunging back into the thermonuclear furnace of her pain.

She could not move. There was no direction that was not pain.

She could not speak.

She could not think.

She knew she was dying and the thought died in the shining darkness.

A long, long time later, she was infinite, and the universe was endless pain. Then the world of agony receded until she had limits, and the slow, arrhythmic earthquake was her heartbeat which shook only her.

Then she was Chesarynth.

A sound: '... stop now.' Was it ... it must be ... a voice that was the path back to life, and it was the garden-master, her beloved garden-master, who had freed her from the dark jewelled chaos where she had been.

And she knew the only reason she was not dead was that the proctor had obeyed (or had she only remembered what she wanted to have heard?) and taken the electro-stick away.

Beneath the wreathing bog-oaks his face ballooned: the garden-master. His hand swam into view like a playful whale, touching her forehead to check her temperature, the tips of his fingers smoothing down her cheeks with a tenderness that made tears slide weakly into her hair.

He still cared.

Blessed be the garden-master's name.

When she dragged herself back to hall, she was alone in her room. There wasn't even a sign of Loretta, but right at that moment Chesarynth couldn't have cared less if she never saw her room-mate again. All that pain, all that torture, and Loretta had never once said that Chesarynth had nothing to do with the diseases she had cooked up.

Flinging herself on the bed, too exhausted even to pull the blanket over her, Chesarynth willed herself to sleep.

It was late the next afternoon when she awoke. Loretta was sitting on her own bed, looking at her, dark circles ringing her eyes. She said, 'Let me get you a cup of coffee, Ches.'

'To hell with the coffee. Just tell me why.'

'Why what? Why anything?'

Chesarynth lunged off the bed and grabbed Loretta's hand hard. There was no resistance, even though she knew she must have been hurting her. 'Why you didn't tell them I had nothing to do with it.'

'I did, Ches.'

'You can't have done or my garden-master would never have let them do that to me.'

'I did but they didn't want to believe me. I told them I was sick of my stuff going missing every time it got nearly ready to harvest and I told them it was only a sign anyway, just a sign to scare people off. Just a little bit of bacteria in a neat little box pegged on the sign of my plot. OK, so I wrote that I'd seeded my crops with it, but I didn't! I hadn't, honest.' Tears were leaking tiredly down Loretta's face, snail-tracks in the worry-lines that drew her cheeks downwards. 'And I had put a container-virus there too so even the bit of stuff in the box wouldn't get out of control. I wouldn't really start an epidemic – what do you think I am, crazy? But I've been running illegal compost for humus, the same as every other mother's son around here, and apparently there were some bugs in that, so they didn't believe me. They had all the evidence they wanted. Do you really think I'd sell you out like Leika to get them off my back?'

Since that was exactly what Chesarynth had been thinking, she had no answer. Wasn't that the sort of behaviour you'd expect from somebody who'd abandoned her in Hell? Loretta might have said time and again that they hadn't been able to find her that night, and that they thought she'd gone off with the big guy, but she should have waited to make sure. Chesarynth had had all night for her fantasies about not being able to make real friends to surface again. She still wasn't sure about Loretta, anyway.

There was one other question, though, that had been spinning through her dreams all night. 'So how come all of a sudden your corporate student isn't going to bail you out? With all the stuff you said you took from him, what d'you need to go back to muck-slinging for?'

Loretta smiled lop-sidedly, but the smile slipped from her face leaving a wounded expression. 'I thought you'd noticed Callum doesn't come around any more. His hall proctor told him to stop hanging around with a dead-beat like me who took him to nasty places like Hell. Told him he could be dropped from sponsorship for mixing with undesirables. So he kissed me off and took back his stuff and I'm back in the clarts like everyone else.

'But don't worry your pretty little head about me, Ches. I've got a plan that'll see us both through. . . .'

The solstice passed and the weight of the cold gathered momentum and steamrollered on. Way beyond the hills the sun-satellites still gleamed out against the dusk but even their radiance was smeared by the atmosphere. *Nothing's bright and clean any more*, thought Chesarynth, *not like it was back home. Nothing's right any more. And I can't do anything right.*

She shifted from foot to foot, shivering outside the refectory. Clad head to toe in second-hand insulators with a layer of thin air trapped next to her skin, she was still chilled to the bone. She couldn't even see Witwaterstrand in the bleary blue-brown sky, but in her transparent clothes everyone could see her. At least her bag was opaque, an out-of-place cheery yellow that suddenly seemed too brash. All the same it hid her frightening secret, the reason that Loretta was meeting her here in the first place. If she ever came.

Another group of students pushed chattering into the

doorway, jostling for their turn to get in out of the cold. They eyed Chesarynth askance and she went up on tip-toe, trying to look as if she hadn't been stood up; surely that was her friend, just beyond them, she could see her over their heads. The only trouble was, Chesarynth was sure she hadn't fooled them. Who'd want to come and see a worn-out red-skin like her? Even Loretta hadn't showed up.

Five more minutes, that's all I'll wait.

The students went in together and she leant back, lonely, against the solar panel, caught out in her feeble deception. Acutely aware of her red, puffy flesh that was only smooth where her bones pulled it tight in poverty, Chesarynth cursed Loretta. And in the bag clutched tight under her arm were the grey, withered raisins of her guilt.

Five minutes passed, then ten, but still Chesarynth didn't have the moral courage to go. She despised herself – but she hadn't got any more friends. Too scared of losing even Loretta's erratic companionship, Chesarynth stood miserably in the ice-cut dusk.

Another fleet of freight-liners shrieked overhead, blasting her ears with sound.

Why did Loretta pick just here to meet me? Why couldn't she have picked somewhere warm? But the background to the thought was *Why do I have to stand here – with this – where everybody can see me?*

So to shield herself she wove fantasies of the garden-master from the strands of her memory. *At least he cares*, she thought, and imagined what it was going to be like when one day he really did hold her and she felt the smooth muscles of his chest against her body. He'd long forgiven her for the sin she hadn't committed; he was again grateful for her hard work, sharing her pleasure – deepening it – in her vegetable successes. He wasn't at all the way Loretta said he was. It was only a matter of time, really, until she was no longer his responsibility. Then he would be free to act in life what she read in his eyes, in the way he constantly brushed against her, in his caressing, velvety voice....

She shifted in the gathering darkness, squatted to hug her body-heat to her. People were coming out now, and a hot breath exhaled around them from the canteen, laden with a cargo of spicy food-smells. Starving, she sniffed the air jealously. The landscape was sad for her, a mournful grey with mist racing in streamers over the frozen ground. She could have cried. But Loretta had told her to wait outside in the winter cold, and Chesarynth was too unsure of her friendship not to.

She didn't even see Retta when she came.

From out of the windswept twilight, Loretta threw a handful of moondust at her. Startled, Chesarynth ducked automatically; Loretta laughed as the soft shining fabric billowed over her friend.

Chesarynth laughed too, a laugh that changed to the sound of delight when she stroked the shimmering plastic and felt the warmth of it kiss her fingers. Flowing seams curved in random rainbows that were almost pictures.

'Where'd you get it from?' asked Chesarynth, slipping the transparent heater-cloak over her and sealing its heat voluptuously around her.

'Never you mind about that. Now come on. We mustn't keep the customers waiting.'

Walking naughtily along the warm covered ways that were really only for tutors, Loretta pulled another heater-cloak from the file she carried under her arm. Folded, the cloak was an ethereal opal no more than the size of a portable memo-screen, but it was so sheer that it opened out to a voluminous bell-shape. Chesarynth wondered where Loretta had got the money to buy them, but already she was too attached to being warm. She didn't ask.

And every time they saw a proctor Chesarynth's body would shrink in remembered pain. How could they not know what she was about to do?

'Gyorg said he'd seen Alexei the other day, with two good eyes and a tower in his hair.' Loretta had to pitch her voice loud as yet another ship screamed overhead to the landing-field not six miles away.

'You what?' yelled Chesarynth.

'Gyorg – said he'd seen Alexei. He reckons Alexei contracted so's he could buy himself another eye. I don't think he would, though.'

Chesarynth half ran to keep up as Loretta ducked into a service-tunnel at the back of the Media Arts complex. 'You know Alexei – he'd do anything when he's had a skinful. D'you think they have an escape-clause for people who contract without really meaning to?'

They were in a subterranean corridor now, smooth foamy walls blushed with the native rock. In here the wind couldn't reach. The stone absorbed sound so that they seemed to be walking without so much as a footfall; their voices were swallowed into the uniform pink light. It was like moving down a giant throat. Chesarynth wished she'd never come.

'Nah.' Loretta's scorn came out as a whisper; Chesarynth was glad she wasn't the only one feeling insecure. Loretta tried again, louder, as if to prove her identity. 'Nah. I reckon once you've shrunk, you've shrunk. That's it. No way out. I mean, there can't be that many people desperate enough to go for it in the first place. They wouldn't let you go once they'd got you. I still don't think Alexei would do anything that drastic, though. He's probably down in Hell somewhere, totally plastered.'

Loretta was hanging back too, now. They walked very close together for mutual but unacknowledged comfort. Left, right, down spiralling ramps; Chesarynth was totally lost. At first there had been signs saying things like 'Level Four', but since Level Seven the ramps hadn't been marked. They were so deep beneath the surface that even the roar of the ships' jets didn't penetrate to them. Chesarynth felt the weight of the building pressing down on her; the air was blood-heat, dead, still. At least she'd stopped shivering.

Surely I can't be doing this? Only her guilt seemed substantial, and she hadn't even done it yet, suckered some poor new bug with the promise of an easier life the way she'd been suckered back when breathing meant the chemical terror of hyperventilation under her loathsome red skin – though what she carried in her yellow bag was proof that she was going to. *But I'm desperate*, she thought, and then she thought of Alexei who one day had dropped out of her life.

How desperate was he? Could I ever get that bad? Bad enough to contract? No, of course I couldn't. Only she was frightened to discover that she didn't feel too sure, and each step down into the roseate intestines of the building took her farther away from her past life.

'Here,' said Loretta, and stopped suddenly. 'Wonder if anyone's here yet?'

Chesarynth looked outwards from her fear. They were in a huge room, so huge it ought to have been a cavern, and there was a vast, blocky thing suspended over them from stone and metal columns. The columns ended in scratched metal runners that stretched into the flesh-tinted distance. She could smell oil and electricity.

Loretta led her boldly under it and Chesarynth could imagine it falling, pinning them, pulping them. Its megalithic mechanical mystery was threat embodied.

She swallowed. 'What is it?'

'Marsquake cradle. What do you think stops all the buildings falling down every time they shove in another load of scrap to beef up the planet's core? It's the price we pay for breathing.'

Chesarynth whispered back, 'I don't get you.'

'Oh, come on, dumbo. Thirty years ago this planet had ten per cent less gravity than it has now, so it couldn't hold even this pathetic atmosphere. All the oxygen just kept flying off into space. So they pour in heavy metals down this great tube sort of a thing into the core to add to the planet's mass. Now we got marsquakes but we got air, OK?'

Chesarynth didn't like to admit she'd never thought of that. She had assumed the constant tremors were part of being on a planet, except that it was a part nobody liked talking about because they were ashamed of it. Witwaterstrand never did things like that and she wished with intensity that she were back there. She wondered where

Jezrael was. Dancing, she hoped, with another laser-troupe, one that would take her with them to stardom on Earth. It had taken Jezrael a long time to get over her disappointment from the last lot.

Suddenly, among the labyrinth of ruby shadows beneath the spring-legs, some hideous blood-stained being moved. She screamed; Loretta elbowed her and she felt foolish. It was only a man.

At least, after her first fright, Chesarynth assumed it was a man. Against the light his torso was a massive, warped cone narrowing to short, dumpy legs. Out of his grotesquely broad shoulders grew two ordinary arms that seemed out of proportion by contrast; on his head Chesarynth thought he must be wearing some sort of helmet made of mesh.

But it wasn't just the ruddy darkness that shaded him with red. As he stepped forward into the light she saw that he was the colour of blood. Clotted whorls of crimson knotted beneath his skin; streaks of pus-yellow flared along his veins. And the tight-packed flesh of his face was the same septic salad of pigments. It didn't need the wash of musk-and-acetone odours from his body to make Chesarynth feel sick.

He came embarrassingly close, smiled, and said, 'Your manners are showing.'

Chesarynth made herself look away in shame.

Still in that conversational tone, he asked Loretta, 'Has she got the stuff?'

Loretta nodded, her dark, glistening curls brushing the net of wires on his skull.

'Will she do it?'

Again Loretta nodded. 'We've got a memo-screen down here too.'

He laughed, and the girls both winced at the force of it in the silence. 'What Spider says he'll do, he'll do. You don't need to check it, but I guess you're going to anyway. Lay it on the line for her.'

He couldn't cross his arms over the bulk of that gory chest so he laid his hands over each other. The finger-tips

136

just reached his dimpled wrists. And all the time that Loretta spoke, Chesarynth tried not to look at him, or to seem as though she weren't looking at him.

'You still want to sell those air-gems, don't you, Ches?' Loretta said huskily. 'Well, Spider's got this amazing deal for you.'

Now the moment had come, her body's memory of fear made her tremble. Fear and guilt – and greed. She tried to convince herself she wasn't guilty: 'I'm not doing anything that'll hurt some poor other bug.'

'Don't sound so defensive! You won't have to; it's simple. All you have to do is give Spider the air-gems and help him activate them, and he'll fill almost all your quota for you.'

'With stolen stuff from other people's plots? Leave somebody else with a tonne of quota round their necks like Leika's done to me? And what about the proctors?'

'Slow down, Ches! Stop jumping to conclusions.' Loretta's voice was a fierce hiss but you couldn't have heard it ten feet away. 'You don't have to do anything like that. Spider's got other plans for the air-gems, haven't you, Spider?'

He nodded, the wires gleaming on his skull. Their multi-coloured insulation looked like a crazy bird's nest, the soldered joins like spashes of guano. Iridescent ampoules shone, sickly cats'-eyes showing the way to –?

Chesarynth said, 'So how is he going to pay me? Put a guard on my plot? Dig for victory?'

'No, you idiot. And before you ask he's not going to dump five hundred kilos of carrots in our hall-room either. Shut up and listen, all right?'

Chesarynth nodded.

'Right then, it's simple. Spider's a major chip in Hell because he can interface with just about any computer on the planet.'

About to ask the obvious question, Chesarynth was hushed again. Loretta went on, 'In specific, he knows his way around the government computers, and the central one for Mars-U. So you give him the air-gems and he wipes most of your quota off every board it's on: your tutors', the grant office, the proctors', even your beloved garden-master's –'

'But he'll notice! Then I'll –'

Spider interrupted. 'He won't notice. Believe me, whatever you think your relationship with your garden-master is, he can't notice, it's impossible. If I had the time I'd prove it to you.'

'Why?' Hostility loaded Chesarynth's whisper.

Spider put his loathsome head close to hers, and the girders were his web around him. 'Why won't it notice? Or why'm I doing this? What do you care? Just say yes or no. I haven't got all shift.'

Chesarynth bent her head, scrubbed her rough hands over her harassed face. Defeated, she lifted her gaze to Spider. 'OK, if you're sure. Here they are.'

Far off there came a sound from the outside world, the rumble of jets at the spacefield. It was such a familiar noise that Chesarynth scarely even noticed it though all other external sounds were cut off by the maze of tunnels. She unsealed her bag and poured the cascade of grey, withered stones into Spider's hands.

Loretta handed her a knife. 'Now cut your hand. Go on, don't just stand there! You have to bleed on them to get them glowing again. Oh, give us it here! I'll do it.'

And pain sliced cold through Chesarynth's palm while her blood – bright crimson with the oxyvirus – dropped shining on to the mass in Spider's hands.

The deep-throated rumble sounded louder.

And the air-gems swelled, sucking in her blood, her life-fluid plumping up the wrinkles, polishing the dead grey rhino-skin until the air-gems were gems again, sleek, metallic grapes glowing with health, polished with red reflections of the marsquake cradle's web of steel.

The cavern shook with sound, a tremor that was so normal nobody noticed it. It passed on, growing fainter.

Spider's smile was wicked. He tossed the air-gems, cupping them in one palm. Then, with a finger-nail, he slit his thigh. The purulent yellow flesh parted; down below the creamy-white fat was a pocket swimming dry amongst the shoals of veins.

Like a lipless mouth it opened to swallow the shining beads; Chesarynth gagged at the thought of part of herself encased in Spider's flab. A squeeze and it was as if the thigh-mouth had never been.

He sneered a wider grin. 'Come down to Hell, ladies. Learn what squeamish is really about.

'But in the meantime, set your memo to the grant office. What you're gonna see now is a Corot among computer artists. Only don't talk, OK? I don't want to get my circuits in a twist.'

Taking not the slightest notice of the girls, Spider hunkered down, back to one of the pillars, wriggling his backside into a comfortable position on the steel runner that crossed the floor. His head was in the crimson shadows; ghosts of sparks chased each other around the tiny crystal ampoules in his wire crown.

For a long time, it seemed, nothing happened. Chesarynth got tired of her fear. She wanted only to get away from this repulsive law-breaker, back to her own life above ground. She didn't want to be around if any suspicious proctor came poking about. Besides, there wasn't the slightest flicker from the memo on the figures of her debt.

She dragged Loretta over to a corner and whispered, 'What the hell does he think he's doing?'

'You know the proctors talk back and forth by radio telepathy? Well, the guys who adapted Spider when he ducked out of law-school –'

'He's a student?'

'Ssh, Ches! Yes, he was a student. But he got hammered by the quota too, then he tried politicking to change the system so they jammed up his oxyvirus somehow. Haven't you heard of him round campus?

'Someone in Hell sort of fixed him – that's why he's got those enormous lungs, sort of an experiment, I think it was, only they rewired other bits of him at the same time. They tried to make him a sort of tower – like a proctor. Well, someone who could screw up their communication system on the same mental frequency, but they hadn't got the same gear so that's how come the crow's nest on his head.'

Chesarynth grabbed Loretta's arm in a painful hold. 'You mean he's in touch with the proctors? What have you got me into?'

'Get off! You're hurting me! Of course he's not talking to them! If he was, he wouldn't be down here peddling stuff, would he?'

'Well, what did they want with their own personal tower?'

'Don't you ever watch the news? Half the guys in Hell want nothing better than to gum up the government. Inflation five hundred per cent, all this slave labour in the fields, strikes illegal, rigged elections, folks just disappearing even if they don't just starve to death, and the towers going round like some kind of thought police – wouldn't you blow them all back to vacuum if you had the chance?'

Chesarynth glanced nervously across to Spider, still sitting, still with a corona of lights sparking round his polished skull. In the black depths of the memo-screen in her hand, nothing moved. She looked back along the corridor they'd followed but she saw no proctors there – yet.

Close to Loretta's ear she whispered, 'So if he's not talking to the towers, what is he doing?'

'He's jacking in to the government computer system.'

Chesarynth, rapt in a kind of horrified fascination at a human interface who didn't even need a finger-socket, said, 'What do the people who adapted him think of how he turned out?'

'Nothing.' Loretta made sure Spider was still too busy to be listening. 'When he woke up and found out what they'd done to him, he killed them. Tuned in to their domestic environment network and froze them. When they did the autopsy, the two adaptors still had salad in their mouths, fresh as the day it was picked. He iced them that fast.'

'Hey, Retta, look at the memo-screen!' Chesarynth

waved it maniacally in front of her friend's eyes. On the black background, the scrolling columns of Chesarynth's quota were going wild. The orange numbers were on a loop, flickering through the sequence of nought to nine over and over again.

They had scarcely noticed the slow rumble of the foreshock minutes before. Now, in the dead silence of the tunnels, the world grumbled again. The girls looked at each other, wondering. Surely that couldn't be jet-backlash, not this far down? They looked uneasily at Spider but he was frowning intently, concerned only about what was happening between his head and the government nets.

Then he howled out a grating laugh. He said avidly, 'Now watch this. This is the part I like best; where those bastards get –'

Then the major shock struck.

12

The distant rumble swelled, turned the air to an ocean of dust. The floor rose, subsided, tossed them up again. Even the walls undulated. Fragments of ceiling fell. Darkness shattered around them, hatching fear from black night.

And the noise was a solid Stygian wave that battered Chesarynth until she fell upwards against the wall. In all that maelstrom not even gravity could be trusted. There was nothing to hang on to that stayed still; the planet's skin was in revolt.

Eternally beaten by sound that left her bleeding, Chesarynth could not even scream. Dust like gravel cascaded down her throat, clogging her airways with a spume compounded of blood. She could not breathe in or out and the scream built up inside the blackness of her head.

Jezrael! echoed through her mind, and the terror in that cry was distilled to volcanic heat in the cauldron of her silence.

Chesarynth knew now – and the knowledge was ground into each cell of her being – that she was nothing. In the roaring, shuddering darkness she could do nothing. She couldn't save herself, or find Loretta. Nothing she did could put the world back as it was. She could die and nothing would be altered. The insanity of Mars was omnipotent, untouchable.

And still the grinding of tectonic plates juddered through her long after her hearing had been murdered by the deafening crescendo. She didn't even hear the ice-sharp screech of stone on metal that was the seismic cradle being hammered slantways on its track. Things fell on her unseen, unknown, pains. And still she was stifling.

Chesarynth slammed her back against the wall and breath exploded from her, a river of sparks behind her eyelids. She coughed her lungs clear. Even when the dazzle of asphyxia had left her vision, there was no other light to see.

Then the unknown night stopped pattering over her with its mad, sharp fingers. The roar passed through the walls, a poltergeist of monstrous dimensions, taking the tremor with it.

The rock around her rested, untrustworthy.

And, eons later, a faint rosy glow burst out, crystalline dust-motes dancing gilded by the light.

It was enough just to be.

Eventually she moved. As the air cleared she saw Loretta staggering over rubble, clawing blindly at the haze of dust. They found each other and clung tight as sisters making up after a fight. The warmth of a living body was relief like a tsunami pouring in through their hug.

Chesarynth thought Loretta couldn't speak. Then, through the haloed brightness she saw Loretta's lips move to form her name. She saw the straining tendons of Loretta's neck, and knew Loretta was shouting. And it was Chesarynth herself who could not hear.

The question was unthinkable: *Will I ever hear again?* All the same it would not stay quietly in her subconscious. It yelled itself over and over, dancing images of fear and endless loneliness in front of her thoughts so that she could not forget it however hard she tried.

Together, Chesarynth and Loretta stumbled through the dust-clouds towards the steel-sprung pillar, feeling the kinship of humanity with anybody who had lived through the 'quake, even Spider.

His body was there. Only most of his skull had exploded when the ground-wave had thrown him on to the shining rails at the same time that it had forced the cradle off its track. His neck ended suddenly under the pillar. Blood had fountained around him; so had his noxious lymph, in feculent yellow gouts. Drops of his body-fluids fell from the spring web on to Chesarynth's hand.

143

She screamed – and felt only a tearing in her throat. But Loretta, appalled, clamped a hand to Chesarynth's mouth, then stooped to unseal Spider's thigh-pouch, reaching inside his dead flesh to rescue the air-gems.

Chesarynth turned away, sickened, and her boot crunched on one of the glassy ampoules that had been the diadems in his hideous crown.

She lurched away and Loretta caught up with her. Together, speechless – what was there to say? – they threaded through the net of tunnels. In some, electricity crackled in darkness from broken circuits. Others still cast a calm pink glow that seemed horribly out of place.

And on to the still, dead air crept a dread reek of smoke.

Now a high-pitched sound began to ring in Chesarynth's head, like someone drilling fast through her bones. She glanced sideways at Loretta, who didn't seem to notice it.

Maybe my hearing's come back, thought Chesarynth, but she had been so long in silence that it didn't seem right to speak. She didn't like to admit to herself that she was too frightened of not hearing the answer. Besides, it took all her attention to clamber endlessly through the smoke-wreathed piles of detritus.

The temperature rose; the labyrinth of fractured walls stretched on, a harlequin of light and darkness laced by acrid smoke, and through it all whined that whirling spear of sound that drove her mad.

Surely we should've got out by now? thought Chesarynth. *What if the fire catches up with us?*

But what they caught up with was worse than any fire because it destroyed the only thing that could have made her whole again – her hope.

Still lost. It must have been midnight on the outside – Chesarynth suddenly thought of checking the time on her memo-screen, then she remembered that her memo-screen was back there, an identity-tag near Spider's corpse. There was no way of going back for it now. But

144

hours must have passed and no-one was coming to help. No-one knew where they were. Tension was a being knotted into Chesarynth's guts. It fought to get out; she fought to keep it from swallowing her.

Loretta slumped against a corner in the light, resting, and Chesarynth knelt beside her, wishing she could talk out her feelings, put them in words that would float them away like bubbles on the air. Yet she dared not tell Loretta how small and frightened she felt, because she had no way of knowing what Loretta's answer would be. *What if it's only me that feels this way? Retta would think I was pathetic. I can just hear her laughing at me, telling all our friends what a wimp I am....*

It was Chesarynth who felt impelled to move again before Loretta was ready.

Back on their feet, they slogged their way through the maze, jumping wires that crackled and danced with live current, just waiting to catch them. Dimly now, Chesarynth could hear her internal world: the laboured pump of blood in her eardrums, riven through by the sharp screech of tinnitus. But she still couldn't hear Loretta.

Another tunnel, black as despair. They followed the wall with their fingertips, Chesarynth in front, Loretta, admitting defeat, holding tight to her shoulder. There were recesses in the bulging rock that must have been doors, but none opened out to offer them escape. They couldn't even see a catch, or feel a handle.

Sound splintered; between its shards Chesarynth heard, as if far off, a smash of plastic: someone was breaking through a door.

And flamelight dazzled her as the plastic beneath her fingers shuddered. An axe pierced it, half-seen, missing her by a hair's-breadth. A great jagged tear blossomed with flame that seared her face.

Then the cruel sharp light was blocked by a man with his hair on fire. He lifted empty hands and brought them down in a chopping motion, and a foot beyond his reach the axe-blade bit through again in someone else's grasp.

Uncomprehending, Chesarynth jumped back. Loretta

screamed as the door slewed on one hinge and caught her forehead. She went down and the door half tumbled on top of her, swinging at a drunken angle. A man, naked but for flesh-coloured shorts, burst screaming through the doorway, dropping the axe. At the same time the man with the empty hands made that same dropping action, leaving nothing to fall to the floor as he, too, plunged screaming at the gap.

Then, backlit by the flickering hellfire, the two men jammed each other in the doorway. It would have been funny if it hadn't been tragic, but their shoulders stuck for a moment, and their wide, staring eyes printed themselves in horror on Chesarynth's mind, with their black mouths twin circles pumping forth animal cries of fear. And all the time the man with his hair aflame made no movement to put out the fire that was blackening his scalp.

Inside the room other men and women were jostling, screaming the same wordless cry. Black figures trapped behind waist-high consoles, they were old and young, strong and fatherly, flirtatious girls, sweet-faced mothers. Their terror blocked the flaming air.

Chesarynth pulled herself together after that first split-second of shock. Yelling, 'Stop shoving!' she yanked at the burning man, pulled him free and smothered the flames on his head. She threw him aside to slither over the dangling door –

And saw in terror that as he staggered sideways, so did every one of the people inside the writhing flames.

'Climb over the desks! Climb over the desks!' she shouted, and when her words penetrated through the roaring, crackling fire, the people did.

Even the ones who weren't behind the desks made climbing motions, and the same scream came from all their throats, deep or high. The two she had freed tried to shin up the far wall of the pyre-lit corridor.

All the same, Chesarynth and Loretta forced their way over the shattered plastic into the room. Bodily hauling the living dolls over obstacles, they pushed them out into the black hallway, deafened by the sliding octaves of screams. Red, orange, golden, woven with inky smoke the room was a chaos out of nightmare. Acrid stenches roiled from smouldering plastics on chairs and desks. Console-screens exploded glass that ripped into the marionettes, sending higher screams wailing through the infcrno. And each shriek was perfectly cadenced to the terrified chorus, pitched over clashing arpeggios that swooped and tumbled identically until Chesarynth, unable to bear it, slapped the nearest doll's face.

The whole awful concerto stopped instantly, uncannily, mid-breath. Only the crash of burnt furniture broke the background rush of flames.

Chesarynth and Loretta looked at each other; the leaping firelight showed the same blank incomprehension to both of them.

Shrugging, Chesarynth said, 'Which way is out?' but it wasn't Loretta who answered.

A dozen arms lifted to point back along the way the girls had come. In as many different keys the dolls' voices chorused, 'That way.'

And when the girls headed along the black passage, they went alone, while the same wordless whimper of abandonment sobbed in each doll's throat.

Chesarynth swallowed, glancing back in disbelief. Tentatively she said, 'Follow me.'

It worked. The fire-scarred marionettes shuffled along behind them, moving their feet left-right-left like a platoon marching. In the chequerboard half-light Chesarynth couldn't tell one from another. Only, if one stumbled, they all did, whether there were an obstacle there or not. And the fire spread in their wake, an implacable pursuer.

The girls halted in the gloom at the first intersection but their weird escort didn't. Assuming that the dolls knew what they were doing, Chesarynth and Loretta trailed after them – until they all piled up, marking time, against a wall.

After that, either Chesarynth or Loretta would ask every few yards, 'Which way now?' and hope that the next

147

turning, the next chamber, would not reach out to hug them in its burning fingers.

So, question by question, their silent inhuman guides led them room by room to the exit.

Dawn light pounded their eyes when they staggered into the quad. Chesarynth helped Loretta crawl from the blind black tunnels into the fierce brightness of the day. People were rushing about being busy in the aftermath of disaster, taking not a blind bit of notice of them. Others were slumped bundles of limbs, disaster-shock pegging them motionless.

In the blue icy air, with the frost forming on their rags of clothing, the girls looked at each other as if to check that they really had survived. Chesarynth saw that Loretta's heater-cloak had grown new blooms, the dull red of dried blood, like her mother's chrysanthemums back home in Witwaterstrand.

Blinking in the dazzle, her nose beginning to run as the sudden cold stung her eyes, she gazed at her own cloak. Its opalescent beauty was marred with filth, too, and she felt like weeping for its loss, because she hadn't even had it long enough to tell which were the cloak's flowers and which the patterns of her blood.

Seconds had passed; it felt like far longer. There was a slithering rockfall from the rubble at the corridor's mouth behind them, and somebody bumped into them.

Chesarynth and Loretta steadied each other and turned to stare curiously at the marionettes crawling out where the light didn't dance with fire.

Loretta shook her head in astonishment, a grin of self-mockery building up to bitter laughter.

And tears slid down Chesarynth's crumpled face. Because underneath that smear of soot, one of the dolls was – *it can't be!* – her garden-master.

13

Back in their room, Chesarynth slicked out of the blood-stained heater-cloak. For once she couldn't care less about efficient use of space; she left the thing on the floor, stepped over it, crawled into bed.

She pulled the covers up over her head, wishing they weren't transparent. It seemed to her that her innards had been drawn out of her body, not just her emotions, and she lay quivering, feeling that she had been flayed alive. Rage and shame corroded her. *How could anyone do this to me? How could I have let them? After all Loretta's warnings, I . . .*

Etched on the inside of her eyelids was the blank, doll-face of her garden-master, empty as a gourd when no-one was pulling his strings.

She flickered her eyes open again so that the sight of her room could whitewash *that* scene. (Loretta said softly, 'Ches? Are you OK? Ches?' But Chesarynth was too raw inside to answer.)

Besides, her garden-master was still there. Each curve and muscle of his face, the blue of his eyes pushing out the sweep of his eyelashes – even smeared with ash she had known him, once he clambered out into the harsh sunlight. Only he hadn't known her. The one who made him the person she loved was not inside him. He was somewhere else (she was sure it was a man). Could another woman have ever done that to her? But what about Retta's garden-master? And surely only a woman could know just what to do to make her feel that she would die if he didn't – oh, God! She had fallen in love with a *woman*! And, somewhere, the doll-master was laughing at her stupidity. Chesarynth probably saw her a dozen times a day, and each time the woman would know just what was going on inside her.

Chesarynth moaned, so vitriolic was her shame. And Loretta had warned her – she had known all the time, only Chesarynth wouldn't listen to her.

Long after Loretta's soft breathing showed she was asleep, Chesarynth held herself still, all but the shivering. Then Chesarynth lay trying to remember how to breathe. Push out your ribs, let the air in, don't forget to let it go. But her diaphragm seemed paralysed and each breath was an effort. Too much of her mind was occupied in resenting the fact that she couldn't talk to Retta about it, because Loretta had known and Chesarynth hadn't believed her. Anger was a magma glowering red and deep inside her, unreachable salvation, but shame was stronger now, lurid yellow like the flames. *How could I be so stupid? I deserve this. I must do.* But she couldn't talk to anyone about it.

And somewhere, in many electronic memories, her quota hadn't changed at all despite her blood on the air-gems, and Spider's pointless, headless death.

Apprehension followed her for the next week, built its home in the emptiness inside her where once her dreams of the garden-master had lived. But in the crazy days of reconstruction that followed, everyone was too busy stemming the floods from the blown-out thermal grids to care about Chesarynth. Besides, there were people with real injuries – she had to help carry bodies from the wreckage to the hospital. Loretta would look at her oddly from the far end of the stretcher and Chesarynth knew what she was thinking. Compared with those mangled women, Chesarynth had no right to feel traumatized just because the man she loved wasn't a man at all.

What was her fear beside their torture?

Irrationally, she would shout, 'Stop staring, Retta! Leave me alone, can't you?'

Then Loretta would shrug and wait for her mood to change, or go off with Giovanni or Sanjay – Rastac was long gone – leaving Chesarynth more miserable than ever.

Anyway, no-one found out that Spider had tried to rejig her quota – or at least, she felt, no-one had found out yet. And it seemed that nobody had identified as hers the portable memo-screen buried in the seismic cradle by Spider's headless torso.

The closest anyone came to it was the garden-master at his most winsome in his leaf-jewelled glade. He said it was a shame the marsquake had wrecked her memo-screen, here's another one, that's ten kilos please.

Chesarynth trembled with revulsion as he smiled deep into her eyes. He was connected up again to the person or thought-amplifier or whatever it was that acted like a tower hidden inside his skull. She was uncomfortably aware now of the unknown manipulator who knew all about how she felt and why she did the things she did, who knew the weakness inside her, and she was ashamed of her soul's nakedness.

But the garden-master was saying, 'Don't be upset, Chesarynth. There's still plenty of time – you'll make your quota yet. I'm told you're picking up your studies well too.'

She couldn't respond. Now she knew it was there, she saw the deliberateness of his ploys. Inside she was sick of watching someone else press her buttons and provoke any reaction they wanted. With the garden-master's smiling warmth a pressure on her skin, she wanted to forget all that had happened and take the pleasure he offered as though all this weight of bitterness didn't lie behind it.

'Don't be upset,' he murmured. 'Won't you let me help you?' And as if there were nothing wrong, he was still plunging his plastic blue regard into hers, taking her hand in his – at a cold command – leaning forward this time to kiss her as she had dreamed of for so long.

Their mouths seemed to pass a magnetic spark between them. His tongue touched her lips and its delicate tickling melted her, but at the same time she tried to pull away because she felt she was going to be sick at the thought of a woman's tongue in her mouth.

Something wrenched inside her head and the conflict was gone. Disappeared as if it had never been – and yet Chesarynth felt some pang of loss, though she couldn't have said what for. Forgetfulness spread through her and there was only the kiss, the touch – but somehow it wasn't what she had thought it would be. The magic was gone.

She left his verdant office with almost all her usual reluctance. Her body revelled in the memory of the garden-master's embrace – briefly. But when she was outside again, with the clean sharp smell of plants growing in their orderly pyramids, the habit of loving the garden-master had lost its support.

Chesarynth was aghast at her momentary disloyalty. But there was something inhuman about the garden-master – wasn't there? Yet how could she love any other man? The boys on her course were childish, callow, and she felt cut off from them. And what about Loretta – she was different too now, wasn't she? Or was that more of Chesarynth's own paranoia?

No, the fight had gone underground. It was hiding in her subconscious, rocking the foundations of her sanity. Still, she had to try and carry on a normal life – if life for a student at Mars-U could be normal. She wasn't going to let this place beat her.

Summer of the second long Martian year.

'Don't let the bastards grind you down, kid,' said the message from Jezrael. A hard copy of it was folded into the case of Chesarynth's portable memo. She rubbed her fingers along it for luck.

Loretta stood beside her in the sunshine, a thin Loretta in old, patched boots that made her legs seem stick-like, knobbly. Chesarynth knew they all looked the same, all except the corporate students, but they didn't have to take this exam today. Even so, the image of those boots and the spindly legs rising from them struck Chesarynth as pitiable today.

'Stick it to 'em, Ches.' Loretta gave her arm a friendly squeeze. 'They've whittled us down but you'll show 'em.'

And one by one the meagre group of students moved in for their exam. Chesarynth left Loretta standing forlornly, her turn not for another month. Chesarynth wished, not for the first time, that her surname didn't come at the beginning of the alphabet.

In a dim, blood-heat cubicle contacts were fastened over her head, her chest, her hands. The technician didn't answer when she tried to make nervous small-talk. He left and the smell of his sweat was combed from the air by filters. Light fled; in the weak gravity of this strange womb she couldn't even feel the electrodes, so soft were they, so well padded the contour couch.

Peace was pushed into her then, an artificial peace that came at the bidding of some chemical compound; her anxious heartbeat slowed to rest. Then a light-pattern sprang wheeling into the darkness over her couch, its smell keying a Pavlovian response. She was sure her fingers had moved in the manner that would correct the genetic defect presented by the light-shapes if she were linked to the sub-atomic waldoes. She smiled.

A different sub-atomic pattern, a different odour – her fingers danced their ballet and the DNA spiralled as it should have in a healthy organism. Chesarynth couldn't believe her luck.

But soon the questioning light-symbols whirled faster; more complex mechanisms replaced the beginner's work. Now formulae hung in the air, incomplete, shifting so rapidly she hardly had time to twitch the answers. She began to feel her inadequacies, the gaps in her understanding. Theory was one thing but the applications were becoming incredibly convoluted, far beyond anything she'd studied. She wrestled with logic and syllogisms, fighting to keep up with the twisting light.

And won. Time had been suspended, somehow. It didn't seem long until the walls and ceiling paled but she had done well, of that she was sure. She laughed aloud in sheer pleasure, stretched luxuriously. Was that it? Could that really be all?

Outside, blinking in the cold sunlight, Chesarynth

looked around. One or two other examinees were being led away by chattering friends – all the few surviving students at Mars-U were friends – but there was no Loretta to meet her. She waited, stepping restlessly from foot to foot on the raked gravel. Late afternoon sunlight carved shadows for each tiny pebble; the pyramids of oxygenators waved luxuriant fronds against the horizon.

Then Loretta came running, late as usual, and swept her up into a bear-hug. 'Hi, honey! How was it? You still alive? Sorry I'm late but ...'

'... but you're Loretta – yeah, I know. It was OK. I've done it! I've survived! I've beaten Mars-U at its own game.'

'You look like the cat that got the cream.'

'I can't believe it. I've actually finished my course.' Chesarynth tried to look decently worried, but didn't succeed. 'Now I've got the rest of the month to pay off my quota.'

'Who cares? Even if you don't, you can pay it off when you get a job.'

That night there was another suicide along their corridor. Sonobe died as she had lived, tidily, repressed, one of her long hair-pins skewered into her brain through her ear, and she never made a sound.

Chesarynth sat staring at the screen in her room and Loretta was beside her. She didn't know where she'd be without Loretta. All their old friends seemed to have disappeared, gone home, contracted, but at least Loretta was still there, a little crazy now, given to fragile laughter in the empty hall that had once rung to lots of voices.

'Do – do you think they've made a mistake?' whispered Chesarynth.

'Maybe, maybe.'

Loretta leaned closer, one skinny hand on her friend's shoulder. 'One point nine doesn't sound much like you.' Two was the lowest mark possible. A pass was 1.5. 'I thought you said the exam was OK?'

'I did. It was. I'm sure it was. But it can't have been, can it?'

They contemplated the horror before them. Chesarynth leant her head on her hands. 'I can't go home, you know. The groans can't afford to pay back the tuition fees, let alone the quota. I'll have to re-take.'

The wide vista of the future narrowed down to an endless tunnel of assignments and a quota like a ball and chain. Chesarynth tried not to look as though she were crying.

She was thin, her buttocks hollow as an athlete's from all the walking to her field, the bending, the lifting and carrying. It couldn't be from all the unhappiness that ghosted along beside her, the feeling that she was going crazy and she didn't know why.

She dreaded waking up.

Every morning now it was the same. She dreamed she was up and dressed, that she was late and running to her field, and that when she got there, her precious spindly vegetables were gone: the pale green shoots of onions, the persistent vines of courgettes that never lived long enough to be marrows, the strange, leathery tops of carrots that were forever dark and weird – all gone. Nothing left but holes in the cracked earth (there was a water-shortage this summer; the tremor had ripped up the reservoirs).

Holes all empty as the eye-sockets of a skull. Holes ripped in the earth of Last Ditch, staring at her malevolently, waiting to bury her underground. Holes the scavengers had left her despite the traps she set, the rogue rats she had found by the spaceport and chained under her greenhouse. But in her dream there was nothing left under the crackling ripped plastic but the awful staring holes. The only deterrent she never, ever tried was the cholera-mutation Loretta had perpetrated last year before the electro-stick turned her through three and a half dimensions.

And then Chesarynth would wake, late. She really had overslept because she was so exhausted. She really did have to go through it all again, the getting up, the dragging on her clothes, the running hungry, always hungry, to her field so far away under its crackling ripped plastic in the constant shade of the sun-flower. And her thoughts would unravel, frayed by anxiety that never left her even when she slept.

Then, when she got there, something else would have gone for real. Now she didn't even have her suspicions of Leika to cling to; Leika had just disappeared in the middle of one day, while everyone was either in their fields or in lectures. Sure, the thefts had slowed down. But they hadn't altogether stopped. Mind whirling in an eddy of uncertainty, Chesarynth didn't know what would go next.

And one day it was Loretta.

Usually one or the other would straighten her back at the end of the evening's labours, lock up her tools and anything that was even nearly big enough to be eaten, uncage and tether the rats, then drift over to her friend's patch.

'Chilly, isn't it?' one of them would say, and the other one would top it with the worn-out punch-line: 'Shut up and close the door. It's cold outside the fridge!'

Tonight, her seven hundred and tenth day at Mars-U, Chesarynth worked after the sun had gone down until she was practically gardening in braille. She looked around but there was no sign of Loretta; if she'd been coming she would have been here at Chesarynth's patch by now.

Chesarynth packed up, leant one shoulder on a stake that was meant to be supporting a clump of shooting-beans from Nutristem, only they hadn't grown. Now the pole had only a skull-and-crossbones painted sign: 'Ches's Last Ditch', and she didn't care if the proctors told about it.

Fed up, Chesarynth squinted around her, willing either Loretta to appear, or the energy to crawl over to Retta's 'Unlucky Strike'.

Even with the delaying action of the giant mirrors, the penumbra was thickening over the plains, and where it thickened, it was cold despite the sub-soil geothermals.

Spidery turrets held the silky silver diffusers that caught the sunlight; far above, the satellites that beamed it down were strung around the equator like diamonds. So there was still a milky river of daylight though the sun had set over the hills a metric hour ago. Now some of the diffusers were out of direct line-of-sight altogether and hung their heads like flowers in shame. As the atmosphere responded to the change in temperature, evening breezes sprang up and rippled shades of argent across the diffuser-bells; the sun-flowers were dying in the moonlight.

Loretta wasn't at her patch, either, when Chesarynth finally made it that far. Nor was she in their room, but there was a message scrawled on the dust that static electricity always stuck to the memo-screen.

'I've shrunk, kid. Give 'em Hell. I'm there' – the last word was squashed diagonally across a corner – 'already.'

Shrunk. Contracted. Sold out.

Loretta had given her head to the cleaners. They said – but what did they know? Maybe they'd all got it wrong – they said that when you contracted, they paid off your debts with enough left over to go and blaze a trail in Hell, your last night of being you. After that you were an un-human, a thing walking around using your two legs, but you weren't there inside it. Your mind got washed out and where the liquid flowed through your cortex, there grew the wire roots of a tower.

Chesarynth's first thought was guilt: her own. Loretta hadn't made it past first harvest this year. Even with the scraps of food her friends saved for her, the shoot-to-burn spy-eyes Conchi had cobbled out of stolen parts from the physics labs, Loretta couldn't make her quota. She was so far behind with her crop-payments that she couldn't even afford to eat.

I could've done more to help, Chesarynth thought. *I could've* – but the thought was truncated. There was nothing more that Chesarynth could have done. Her own quota now included borrowings against next year's grant – inflation was four hundred per cent and rising – and she'd spent half this week keying in a project for Loretta while

Loretta sat up in her field, watching her Mars-mallows with a sharpened hoe in her hand. Chesarynth had said, 'I'll watch your crop,' but Loretta was past trusting anybody that much. Slit-eyed with sleepless suspicion, she had taken a nightwarmer out to her 'Unlucky Strike' and sheltered from the wind against her shed. And the battery hadn't lasted and the cold had numbed her to sleep. Now some other sleazy bug had cashed in Loretta's crop and even the rats were gone. Loretta had shrunk.

Maybe it wasn't too late? Maybe she was still doing the comet-act down in Hell?

At the thought of her friend in danger, Chesarynth slammed out of their room and ran down the stairs. The thermometer in the hallway said 'Fifteen degrees' when she asked it, but outside the wind-chill factor had reduced it to maybe five. A faint mist lay silver in the starlight where the warm breath of the soil met the air.

Cutting through between the deserted teaching-blocks, she dodged out of sight every time she heard voices; flattened into corners when there were footsteps, and the footsteps were worst. Tutors talked in words; the proctors with the towers in their heads didn't need to. And they said, all the students said, that the proctors even knew what you were going to do before you did it, because they could read your thoughts before you'd finished thinking them.

Paralleling the hills, Chesarynth kept to the roadway where the stored sunlight burned in dazzling haloed globes. If she hadn't been doing much, she'd have chanced the textured shadows of the fields where there was less fear of detection. But she was walking so fast the night-winds cooled her sweat. At this level of activity, it was better to be where the oxyvirus had light to work with.

It was maybe a kilometre and her feet seemed on fire at the end of it, but the pain up the back of her legs was worse. Even that was nothing to the fear that she might never find Loretta, or that if she did, Loretta wouldn't be human any more. And the worst thing was that the unhuman seemed quite content to be that way. The danger was so close to Chesarynth that she could feel a ghost-tower stabbing her brain.

In the town it was warmer. A denser geothermal grid underlay the centre streets and there were plants that seemed like a picture-cube of Earth, not like the scarred imitations out on the campus fields. There were people laughing, each brightly lit window a frame out of someone else's life. Homes. A pang of homesickness trembled through Chesarynth; she could have wept just to see Jezrael pole round a corner, the one person she knew would always be on her side no matter what. And tears did escape down her sunken cheeks at the memory of all the times she'd lost her temper with her little sister over nothing at all. Even if they didn't find Loretta, it would still have felt better, just knowing that Jezrael was there to help her try.

But Jezrael had left school and Mom and Dad had chained her to a job in Witwatersrand that suited their image of her and Jezrael was shrivelling inside sixty million miles away.

And now Loretta had left her too.

Chesarynth couldn't find her, though she searched all night through the black streets of Hell where even the proctors went in threes. She went from bar to bar, trying to escape the drunken maulings in the dives where everybody wore the masks of rebellion; a naked-faced prey for any refugee to mock or grope. At each one she showed a tiny holo: Loretta with her brother back in Andronicus, Loretta laughing, smooth-faced with cheeky freckles under beautiful black luxuriant curls.

Of course, no-one in Hell had seen her. If Chesarynth had asked them what planet they were on, they wouldn't have said 'Mars'. Hell was no place for truth or honesty; such things belonged back in the bright cheerful homes that looked like an advert for Mars, the world for wholesome families. And even if they had seen her, Loretta would have been masked, or at least painted. If you wanted to celebrate or burn your sorrows in the comet's tail, there was no point in cutting yourself off bare-faced.

People with nothing to hide wouldn't be in Hell in the first place.

Before dawn, when Chesarynth was in despair, pushing past a crowded table in a frightening smoke-filled dungeon where the air was solid with sound, some African woman grabbed her.

And locked in a wheel of *déjà vu*, Chesarynth knew the only way out was the way Loretta had taken.

14

The wind was whistling round her ankles, the first wind of autumn that was a ghost of the winter-winds, laden with the sharp taste of their frosts, and where it swept over the ground it left behind brush-strokes of ice. Three months since Loretta had contracted and over the defeat of the second harvest's failures, the rumour leaped like a forest fire: there was a recruiter.

There was a nest of recruiters.

Spiderglass's chief was here.

Salvation was at hand.

The trouble was, nobody knew where to find it.

Chesarynth groped for consciousness after another bout with the proctors' electro-sticks. She couldn't even think what this one had been for; of late all the kids in her year who weren't corporates but had still managed to survive this far had succumbed to visitation after visitation. It had long since stopped making sense. All that kept them going was dogged determination: they had made it this far; they weren't going to give up now no matter what Mars-U threw at them.

Right now, Chesarynth couldn't think of that. It was all she could do to remember who she was and what the single idea that stiffened her was: she had to beat the system. Not to let her parents down. Not to be shamed in front of Jez, or her class.

Gathering the scattered shreds of her identity, Chesarynth made herself anew around a core of unfocused rage. In time it came to her that she had arms and legs, heart and labouring lungs; that her eyes worked (and oh! the

161

blessed feel of being able to see again, though to wake lonely in her barren room without Loretta was no fun); that the amnesia caused by lightning flaring through her nervous system was temporary.

Groping past *Who am I? Where am I?* she stumbled mentally against a thick black opacity that she could not peel aside. There was something she had to remember, she knew that, but she didn't know what the elusive something was. It had something to do with the garden-master – fire washed down her synapses again, just thinking of him, a fire whose heart was pain. The trouble was, she had thought of him so much that he was mixed up in everything.

She tried to sit up. At first her muscles only twitched but she rested, imprisoned by Mars-U in her body, longing for a drink, and fear was in her. She tried not to need it, frightened at how far she had slipped, knowing only too well what her mother would say, but the taste of akvit was in her dry mouth, its bite fierce in her throat. It would meld her back into herself.

At last, with the first ugly light of dawn smearing the sky, she fought off her paralysis. As soon as mobility came back, she downed a shot from the can Loretta had hidden before she – shrank. *Just one,* Ches thought, *just for the shock.*

Then she took another swallow of the spirit.

With its heat in the hollowness inside her, Chesarynth set off down the road to Hell, its golden globes paling before the onslaught of the day with its long burden of labour. They led her on down the road she had almost chosen. Ignoring the cold, repressive tidiness of Ecoville that once she had thought so fine, she pursued her desperation into the more human slovenliness of Hell. She needed escape and there was only one place she could go.

She was well aware that what she was trying to escape was herself but the hologram bar embraced her in its impersonal welcome anyway. This time it wasn't a lake but a cavern: warm, gems glinting from its stony walls, rivers of golden fire dancing through the dark, and the music was a cushion that wrapped her in peace.

Heat. Heat to still her shivering. She drifted over to the lake, but it wasn't a peaceful pastoral scene any more. Instead the lake was the dull crimson of lava and sparks speared molten upwards. No scent of sulphur, though; it was as if apple-logs and pine were burning cosy in a homely grate.

Stepping between the stalagmites on to a platform that was hard and shiny as an obsidian coin, she was wafted upwards to a safe eyrie where a heated pool reached out to her in silent welcome; it shone with a warm light hidden in its depths. Chesarynth slid into its gilded steam, letting another drink soften the contours of reality. She could feel the water laving her parched skin; when she reached up an arm, scented droplets ran like beads of amber from her fingers. It didn't matter that she was only adding to the overwhelming weight of her quota; she had almost made up her mind anyway.

What would it be like, not to have to spend shivering nights and days at the Last Ditch, breaking my back to feed that robbing son-of-a-bitch? (Almost but not quite the unknown had the face of the garden-master and she shuddered.) *To sleep all night in a bed that didn't give me nightmares? No more midnight wakenings with a cattle-prod (her thoughts slalomed from words into pictures, feelings: the shock of the door slamming her awake with the hard-faced proctors impaling her nerves on needles of fire). What would it be like to contract? Would I meet up with Loretta? Would we even recognize each other? They say that if you're a proctor, you can talk to all the other proctors even if they're somewhere else. I'd never be lonely again ...*

The thought cut off, unwilling to contemplate the horror of being so inhuman that she would have nothing to say – nothing that didn't involve mechanical obedience to some vast machine plan, whatever painful injustice it dealt to somebody else.

They always look so bland, so dead-pan; I've never so much as heard a friendly word from any of them. Imagine a

163

*whole life with no more conversation, no more friendship
to stop you going down beneath the weight of life alone.*

But would I even have a life of my own?

The memory of the electro-sticks came back to her, the
disassociation of mind from body, the disintegration of her
personality beneath that nova of blinding, coruscating
pain.

Chesarynth leant sideways a little, trying to distance
herself from the frightening ideas in her head; relishing the
kindness of the bubbling gilded waters, looking out from
her remote ledge down to the other glowing pools, each
with their knot of friendly people, or their uninhibited
couplings, the murmur of their conversations as soft as the
sound of bees in the lavender of Eden – still the thought
wouldn't leave her in peace.

*Could I turn one of them inside out with an electro-
stick? Could I sink low enough to do that? What if they
asked me to prod someone I know? Would I still recognize
anybody so that it would matter?*

What would that tower feel like? She ran a hand through
the damp mass of her dull brown hair, trying to imagine
meeting that cold, glassy ugliness with her fingertips. *Does
it hurt when they put it in? When they peel back your scalp
and drill through the bones of your skull?* Invisible needles
bored into her brain, cold, dead worms of metal rupturing
her personality. Her essence would drain away down the
wires; there would be nothing left of Chesarynth –

*Nothing left of the pain. Nothing left of the failure. What
am I worth anyway? I've let mom and dad down; Jez would
hate me if she saw me now. If I go back home before I
qualify, they'll have to pay the grant back – and* (the
thought was like the rock of Sisyphus, a boulder rolling
endlessly over her) *my quota. They couldn't pay the debt
off; it wouldn't be fair. I'm useless. Worthless. I couldn't
even stop my best friend shrinking. . . .*

With an effort she wrenched her mind from its self-pity
to the womb-like restfulness of her holo-bar pool. Its
warm, golden glow shone all around her, giving her an
illusion of well-being, of firm, undamaged skin, of peace.

164

Beyond the lip of the midnight ledge she could see other glowing pools, turquoise, ruby, emerald, and the scent of rose and citron was in the air. Reckless for once, she dialled another drink.

This one didn't slide obediently into the slot. Just as she was getting impatient, thinking she'd have to re-dial and wondering whether it was some sort of omen telling her she'd had enough to drink, a man stepped up from the abyss. He came and squatted on his heels beside her pool, skin shining warm in the glow from the water. Silently he held out a crystal goblet and, surprised, she took it.

'Thanks,' she said, but he didn't go away.

'Do you mind if I join you?'

She took refuge in flippancy. 'I didn't know I was coming apart.' Internal resonances shook her as the remark shook the surface of her calm. All her fears swamped upwards, a tidal wave of anxieties let loose by the electro-stick earlier in the night: failure, debt, terror in the face of the unknown, and grief for Loretta, for Alexei, for Sonobe, horror lest Loretta end up something like the Spider in his clotted envelope of flesh – or she did. And, too, there was that phantom memory – something horrible about the garden-master and her own disloyalty that made her think she was on the edge of insanity.

'Hey, don't take it so hard, I didn't mean anything by it,' said the unknown softly, but it was just his lips. Somewhere inside him she could feel the fierce vibrations of satisfaction. Chesarynth didn't know where it came from, but she was as sure as she could be that he had picked his moment, picked his words with care to sting. *So he has to know who I am? Has he been watching me, waiting for me to crumble?*

No, that was ridiculous. All the same, she didn't trust him – but then, how could she trust herself either?

He said with pre-packed sincerity, 'I just wondered if you'd like some company, no strings attached. I'm on my own, you're on your own, so I thought I'd ask.'

He certainly knows which words to pick: on my own. I'll always be on my own now, won't I? And the echoing loneliness reached out; the strings funnelling her into a dark future.

She nodded, reinforced it with a muttered 'Mmmm', not wanting to admit that suddenly she was afraid to be alone with her subconscious.

'That's great.' He stepped out of well-made shoes – Chesarynth wondered if they were his own or some concoction of the holo, and then whether he was really there or just some window-dressing the holo-bar had sent up – then he eased into the golden waters and she thought, *What the hell?* There was a strange metallic ring, winking gold at the end of his finger.

In his scanty Martian clothing, he wriggled down, sending gleaming ripples towards her. 'Aah, that's good, isn't it? Unknots the kinks.'

'For a while,' she said.

'That's all you can ask, isn't it? Pleasure in the moment, because all life is trivia.' He'd put his drink down to get into the glowing pool; now he snaked a hand behind him to get it, not even looking. 'Slainte.'

'Salud. That's a strange philosophy, isn't it? Is pleasure really all there is?'

'No, of course it's not. There's also the great mystery of the universe, the whyness of which, helping as many people as you can, earning your daily crust and a bit of jam if you can. But in the meantime if you can have a bit of fun now and then, why not?' (She wondered if she were to be his bit of fun, or whether his purpose was what she wanted and dreaded: recruitment.) Unconcerned, he swallowed, and his Adam's apple bobbed gleaming in the light. Above it was a beard streaked brown and blond.

Student, thought Chesarynth in an abrupt volte-face, then instantly revised her opinion. *No. He doesn't have that hang-dog look about him, and he's too old to be a new bug. Unless he's corporate ... but how can I tell in here? The holos could paint him anything. How can I fix my future if I can't trust myself?* And there was that self-doubt again, the poison of Mars-U in her system.

'My name's Karel. How about you?'

166

She told him.

'Student?'

'Yes ... no. Not any more. I' – it was hard to say it but she'd better get used to it – 'I flunked, and ...'

'And your quota's got out of hand.' He carried on speaking and she knew he was giving her time to get over her admission of failure, but she didn't think she ever would. 'It happens all the time. It's the system. I'd change it if I could. It breaks more people than it helps. The ecofreaks don't seem to realize that they'd actually have a better university, get even more trade on-planet, if they'd let you work a sensible way with machines and joint effort so one student didn't end up robbing another one blind just to get enough food to stay alive. But the government here wants it that way. It's dead but it won't lie down.'

Chesarynth nodded, betrayed by his apparent sympathy. 'That's what this tiger-woman told me in a laser-bar the only other time I came to Hell. Said there were hundreds –'

She broke off, casting covert glances at his bushy hair, aware she'd been indiscreet.

Obligingly he turned his head: no tower. 'Believe me, you're safe with me.' There was some look in his eyes that she couldn't fathom; looking at the crinkles of laughter around them she got distracted. The two messages he sent out conflicted – kindness and some secret satisfaction. It put her off-balance, and she knew that was what he wanted. What she didn't know was why.

'So what do you do?'

Karel smiled, lit up by some secret amusement. 'I recruit, amongst other things. Students. You, if you like.'

That was it. Naked, out in the open. And she knew she was about to contract. For good or evil, for ever and ever, she'd sell her future to this man she couldn't fathom. There was nothing else left.

Chesarynth pulled back until her spine was pressing into the soft padding of the pool-rim. She asked suspiciously, 'What for?'

'For Spiderglass.'

15

Karel said, 'No, Magrit. This is one trip you can't make with me.'

'But –'

'No, I said! I don't want you. You've got to stay here and make like I'm still in Andronicus. You can stall them for a couple of weeks, can't you? Got all the recordings and so on?'

She nodded dumbly, still reeling from the shock of hearing him say that he didn't want her. The pale rippling walls of the lagoon-house seemed to swallow up his words into a cavernous maw but still his intention spun through, echoing across the distance to her.

Not that Karel noticed. 'Well then. You could be really useful to me. Nip out to Andronicus in a couple of weeks rigged up as me, lay a good trail for them to follow, but keep them guessing for a while. I've got to put off accepting my seat on the Board 'til I've got a better power-base. I never thought Theresien would move so quickly.'

He turned his back to her so that she could fasten the day-suit's seal running along his spine. It was a double blind, that: a tight dove-grey suit such as any worker might wear, but with its closure at the back to show that he was rich enough to afford servants. It was the sort of thing that any of the disaffected younger sons of industry might wear to show their rebellion. 'What I really need,' he muttered, 'is something that'll let me know what people are going to do before they do it.'

Magrit let her hands linger a few seconds more than necessary over the delicious hollow where his spine went down into the small of his back. Absently she said, 'I'm sure you can make some adaptation to the tower for that as well.' A sudden mental picture assailed her: Karel, body torn apart by someone neither of them suspected. Concentrating now she added, 'I'd be happy to have it fitted so I can keep you safer.'

Karel walked away impatiently. 'Yes, yes. I've already sent specifications out to my lab. They're working on it.' He stooped to pick up an authentic animal-skin carry-cube but Magrit had anticipated him. They bumped heads.

Karel glared at her, too angry for words, bent again to pick up the cube as Magrit backed off and stood fretting. He clicked his tongue in impatience.

'In the meantime I've got to go and catch that shuttle. It's stupid having to be just a plain joe that they won't keep ships for, but I need to make my connection so just get the hell out of my way, will you?'

In three minutes he was gone. When he came back he would be somebody else - but not by his design.

He jumped shuttle at Steel City, leaving a patsy who was only too glad to imitate a son of industry for a while. Food, well-aged wines and tasty women were enough of a reward for a drunk who just happened to look a bit like Karel. Especially seeing as Karel gave him a psych-implant that would last long enough for a two-month spree.

'You mean,' said the thirsty drunk, 'I'll have the gab? I'll be a real class act?'

'Oh, yes,' Karel said, offering a second small drink with Andronican enhancers. 'You'll be just like me.'

And the drunk stayed on the shuttle from Steel City to Andronicus revelling in Karel's cabin with its luxuries. Right up to docking time the drunk failed to realize he wouldn't have any memories of this. In fact he wouldn't have any memories of his own at all. He would be cast-iron certain that he was Karel of the House of Tjerssen.

The shuttle pulled in to the airless docks of Steel City,

one very happy drunk amongst its passengers. Only moments after the shuttle docked a cargo vessel took off for the asteroid belt. And, since freight-time was money, the haulier made the journey almost as fast as any passenger ship would have done. Though it was the first time Karel had travelled in anything but a private yacht or a liner, he found the week didn't hang too slowly on his hands. There was the relief of not having animators try and make him jolly. It just didn't have much in the way of deck-games, that was all.

Eight days later the haulier closed in on the only hotel in that section of the asteroid belt. Karel joined the captain to watch the landing. Though there was nothing he could do in an emergency, it would have been even worse in his cabin. Not for worlds would he have admitted that the silent rumbling shadows of jagged asteroids nearby terrified him worse than the very fact of being adrift in a sardine-can in the void. So he feigned interest with his surface mind while inside some primitive part of him cowered and chanted the prayers of desperation by a caveman's ritual fire.

There were other bulk-freighters around under the transparent glistening that meant a force-shield was holding off the rattling hail of ice-pebbles but the place spun quiet in the endless night. A few young bloods, dicing death between the sharp debris of the Fifth Planet, saw the haulier and buzzed it but the captain had played chicken with them before. She ignored them totally and held to her course. Most of the bloods scrambled out of the way at the very last moment but one butterfly-winged delta left it too late.

Karel's mind fell apart under the missile-attack of his terror. *I'm going to die!* The words screamed inside his head, dissolved his organs into liquid breakers that threatened to spew all over the command-deck. It was with relief he saw that the delta was going to hit the force-shield instead of the haulier.

Shrieking 'Bastards!' over the com-link, its pilot smeared his expensive toy all over the force-shield. There was a moment of incandescence that flared over half an arc of the force-shield as the haulier occupied the only landing-window. Then the rest of the jewel-coloured deltas flocked through in the haulier's wake, their pilots yelling their chorus of mockery above the loser's anger.

'I'll get you for this, you son-of-a-bitch!' the crashed pilot said bitterly.

The haulier captain flicked the com-link to transmit and answered calmly, 'Daughter-of-a-bitch, actually. I'll buy you a drink when we dock. Now get off the frigging air, will you?'

Karel tried to cover his shock. 'I thought he was dead.'

'Not him. They like to think they're real fly-boys but the only thing they fly is remotes. What else did you expect from poncy industry bloods? Sure, they've got emoters in their deltas so it makes them feel like they're really aboard but they wouldn't actually risk their precious skins.' The captain had a habit of saying 'actually'. It was driving Karel crazy. 'They're all safely stashed in the bar. Now shut up and let me think, will you?'

The echo of himself and Magrit dissipated Karel's relief of actually landing. *Christ*, he thought, *she's got me doing it now.* As soon as he'd had a drink or two to calm his shattered nerves he left the rich teenagers to their cocktail-swilling competition and went to his room for a long, hot bath.

Except that here the water had to be hauled so there was no bath. A particle-vibration shower wasn't half as relaxing. Besides, never having had to use such a basic facility, Karel got one of the particles in his eye. It did nothing to improve his temper.

And so he spent the best part of three weeks jacked in to his computer, enjoying the beauty of ideas distilled down to their essence. Stringing beads of symbols, shifting thoughts through three apparent dimensions, he finally came up with a solution to all his problems.

Still in the computer matrix, Karel relaxed and looked at his answer from every conceivable angle. That pattern

171

in the south-west quadrant would fix Berndt – always gratifyingly open to blackmail where bribery wouldn't work – and there were the permutations if Theresien lined up her tame senators, Oskar his connections with Antarctic Waters Incorporated or a dozen other industries. All Karel had to do was sharpen his double-edged weapon and the whole thing would be under control.

Karel set his computer to time-delay his instructions via the hotel network and the several Earth- or Mars-bound ships that were currently in dock. He checked on the progress his Moon-lab was making with the imminence-awareness modifications, ordered that Spiderglass in Southern Mars would try it out on a captive or two.

He even went so far as to arrange a message-drop for Magrit on Andronicus. *That should keep her happy*, he thought, and enjoyed his own graciousness for a while.

Then he jacked out of the interface, allowing himself the luxury of smugness. His hotel room might be a bit basic but tonight he would open some of the special treats he'd brought to keep him company in his exile. *After all, I've not just saved my own life. I've also got the company ready to topple my way. It'll take time but revenge is a dish best served cold. Now all I have to do is turn up at the right time for the big showdown with the Board – while they last.*

A pity, really, that Karel had arranged his future and the Company's so neatly. It might have worked.

Except that the lift he hitched on a vital supplies vessel took him in exactly the wrong direction.

Five and three-quarter days it took him to get back to Phobos. Or Deimos. Karel couldn't be bothered with little details like which of Mars' moons was the relay station for Earth. The ship would hardly take him to the other one, would it?

Then nine hours of irritation in the waiting room. There'd been a delay on a charter flight and a crying baby that kept sicking up everywhere. Voices grew shrill in the weightless crowds because there was so much noise nobody could hear the calming mantras the relay station scattered across the air, or see them since so many bodies were aloft.

All in all Karel was glad to reach the relative sanity of an inward flight. At least from a speck of a place like Deimos (or was it Phobos?) there wasn't the gee-stress of acceleration. True, it wasn't actually a passenger run but he'd slid his chic plastic across some useful palms and got the first ship inwards. Bribery was definitely one of the more useful skills he'd learned from his tutors. Besides, after being cooped up in the asteroid hotel with a lot of chinless wonders he was good and ready for the peace of a vital supplies vessel.

Poling hand over hand through the airless cargo-decks in a borrowed suit Karel checked out what the competition were freighting. Maybe he'd get a line on some profitable angle he could exploit. Dim lights flicked on at his approach, faded behind him.

Most of it was exotic foodstuffs, cash crops from the astcroid cities when they'd have been better off growing basics for themselves. *Some people never learn*, he thought with mild disdain.

These little crates held medicines cultured in Nutristem. (He wondered idly how the locals there liked the name of an industry taking over the old place-name, Witwaterstrand. Wasn't that supposed to be some sort of joke? A rip-off from the place where the diamonds came from in Africa-Rand? But progress was progress. Long live industries!)

And crawling between stacks of pegged-down boxes Karel came across illicit plastiflesh from Mars. By the way the hologramatic logo blurred he could tell it wasn't the real stuff, just some cheap and probably mutant imitation for folks who wouldn't shell out for decent paint-jobs. Doubtless it would wreck their polluted skins even further, give them some horrible disease (he'd seen pictures of its effect on the news).

Karel shook his head at the stupidity of workers. *Why don't they just save up for quality stuff?* he was thinking when the thing happened.

173

It was as if his brain shifted through a fourth dimension. His stomach jogged like in an elevator, and for a brief moment it was as if he'd left part of himself behind.

It's nothing, he told himself, though the sweat prickled out all over his body. *I bet it's perfectly normal. I'm just being paranoid because I hate this goddamn flitting about off-world.*

But at the same time he was aware that something was wrong. Around him the crates seemed to stretch, leaving ghosts of themselves or becoming ghosts. The chains clanked taut. And all the lights blazed on at full power as though the cargo were being offloaded. Even sound seemed elastic; the slow hum of the ship's engines just aft of the cargo-decks – *Christ! It's going to blow! Why didn't I stay in the crew-room?* – dopplered.

Dizzy, he grasped one of the stays and clung to it like a monkey and stayed there for what must have been several metric hours.

Only it wasn't. Though his limbs were wracked with cramp as though he'd been hanging on all night, the sirens blazed out to snatch at his adrenal-glands.

And the pre-recorded whoops and klaxons paled before the captain's voice: 'We have hit a space-time anomaly. Emergency stations. This is not a drill.'

When the crates solidified once more to stay relatively still, Karel unpeeled his fingers from the stay. Eventually, poling along by the usual zero-gee kicks and shoves, he made it as far as the cargo-access.

But of course it was sealed. It had to be, to keep the precious air from spilling out of the inhabited parts of the ship.

The trouble was, Karel was on the wrong side. And since he'd borrowed the air-suit without asking, nobody knew he was in the vacuum of the cargo-hold. The unheated cargo-hold. The shielded cargo-hold where sound would not penetrate.

Nobody answered his frantic calls over the suit's radio.

Don't panic, he told himself mentally. They'll notice I'm

not there. Someone will come and get me soon enough.

But the air in the suit grew stale and hot. Even though he'd had the scent-glands of his armpits and feet doctored they couldn't keep up with his nervous sweat. It was the second time Karel Tjerssen had come up against the tyranny of vacuum and he was afraid.

Pounding the door with a wrenched-off bale hook, screaming until he could taste the blood in his throat, Karel slumped alone, unnoticed. Unmissed.

Weightless he drifted between the ranks of cargo. Black suns flared across his vision. There was a roaring in his ears so loud he thought the engines were really blowing this time. Like a lizard pants for water he panted for air

But there wasn't any. There was nothing but blackness and an endless falling to death.

16

For ninety degrees of arc, almost three months, Jezrael stayed worrying in Witwaterstrand about the inter-active letter that Chesarynth had told her to destroy 'accidentally'.

'What is it?' her mother kept asking her, growing more and more irritated. 'Surely you're not jealous because Chesarynth's got such a good job? If you'd ever settled down and got on with your own studies, you could have done nearly as well for yourself. Pull yourself together.'

But what Chesarynth's ordinary letter had said when it arrived after its trip on a freighter was only that Chesarynth was working for Spiderglass.

Not that she had contracted. Given her head to the cleaners. Become an un-person. Shrunk – even if her parents had been in touch enough to know what that meant.

On the ninety-first degree of arc Jezrael quit her job. She sneaked back home when her parents were out, left a message on-screen for them and told the computer goodbye. Then she closed her Nutristem cash-account and left Witwaterstrand to moulder in its sun-drowsed frozen corals, heading out for the colder orbit of Mars....

'It's here, Vrouw Koch, under your sled-chair.'

'Then pick it up, Jezrael,' the old woman said sharply. 'And don't sigh like that! You're not a martyr. You chose to do this job. So if you're going to be a nurse, even for a few days, be a nurse and don't complain.'

'Yes, Vrouw Koch, sorry, Vrouw Koch,' and if Jezrael's new employer detected the sarcastic flavour of this unwonted humility she was wise enough not to say so.

Jezrael handed the old baggy the tube of plastic face that she had petulantly insisted was in her squeeze-bag. Ten minutes of searching punctuated by impatient reprimands had not improved Jezrael's temper, but around her was the reassuring thrum of the ship's engines, and she would only have to put up with the old hag for another few hours. Already the faint but acute squeal of braking thrusters proved that their destination was getting close. For the thousandth time Jezrael wondered where on Mars her sister was. And what her parents must have said when they found the message she'd left on the computer. A tsunami of guilt swelled, receded. Underneath was a mountain of joy: *I've done it! Even if I'm not gonna be a laser-dance star, I've managed to break free at last!*

The real nurse – a mechanized package built into the sled-chair – uncoiled one of its arms, shoving Jezrael aside. 'Time for a nice sponge-bath,' it said through the same metal larynx Vrouw Koch used. It wasn't concerned with Jezrael but with the rich old lady into whose autonomous functions it was plugged.

While it swabbed and dried and dusted with anti-friction powder, Jezrael moved politely away. She was glad of the respite; while the machine had control of their communal larynx, old Koch couldn't bully the help.

The viewscreen in the tiny stateroom absorbed Jezrael. The planet ballooned, sunlight glancing from the one visible ice-cap. Barren tundra lay like dead, wrinkled skin across the planet's cranium. Only around the equator did blotches of colour vary the landscape: ochre gave way to maroon, to penicillin green. Jezrael could almost taste the dryness of Mars.

A necklace of glittering sun-catchers hung, crystals of fiery beauty around the old planet. Where they crossed the neat stencilled line of nightfall, the black crescent dented beneath the weight of their river of light. There the greens were brighter, starred by the shine of greenhouses.

Jezrael felt a frisson: Mars was closer than she had thought. Almost, now, her first landing ever. The thrill of

177

her first-ever space flight had long ago given way to boredom.

The engines changed their note, sliding on a scale of powered anxiety: now Jezrael knew that the safety-net of space had broken and she was falling through its tattered mesh into the gravity well of Mars. If that whine meant the engines were failing, Mars would reach out invisible arms to crush her to its rocky bosom. The risk only gave piquancy to her sense of daring.

Stronger than that, though, and brighter, was an overlay of excitement: *This is real! It's not just some cosmography simulation with the rest of the kids chewing gum in the back row. This is it! I've actually made it out of Witwaterstrand, whatever Mom said, however dumb she thinks I am. That swollen orange monster is a real live planet.* And, in a kind of mystic wonder: *There's people down there who don't know me from a hole in the ground. Nobody to tell tales to Mom and Dad. I can be whoever I want to be. I'm free at last.*

'Jezrael,' said Vrouw Koch peremptorily, seizing control of the voice-box. 'I didn't pay your passage just so you could stand there like a tourist. The nurse is going to disconnect my spinal socket for a moment. Do you think you could help me into my new robe without tearing it to shreds this time? I want to look my best when I see my son.'

No Martian tan for La Koch. When Jezrael handed the old baggy over to her son *(you're welcome to her)*, she was breathing expensive oxygen through a discreet tube. The actual cylinder was built into the sled-chair, hidden under the voluminous folds of the woman's robe. It was the first practical use Jezrael had ever come across for rich people's un-ergonomic clothing.

Jezrael herself bought a mask from a slot-machine in the spaceport. Trying it on in the facilities, she felt bold and exotic. She'd chosen plain black – not that there was much of a choice within her price-range. Extensors on the back fitted transparent eye-protectors from which she

178

recoiled, blinking, but the extensors kept on patiently until the contact-lenses covered her entire eye-ball. They felt gummy and rough and the whole idea of them gave her the creeps, but it was better than having the moisture boil off your eyes in the low air-pressure.

Used as she was to the constant shifts of gravity in laser-dancing, Jezrael found no real problem with her weight. It just seemed silly not being able to turn it off when you got tired but if that was how they wanted to run their planet it was their look-out. Besides, it made her feel very cosmopolitan.

Looking around at the locals with their lurid skin-tones, she also felt radically overdressed, but she wasn't willing yet to abandon her sensible Witwaterstrand blue-suit that fitted her so snugly. Somehow it didn't seem right that they were all running around in their birthday suits. Still, with luck, she wouldn't be here long enough for that to cause a problem.

The trouble was, Mars was big. Nor did they seem to have computer-directories around here. And breathing the air that her mask filtered was hard work. *Never mind,* Jezrael thought, *I'll get used to it. But first, I'd better find somewhere cheaper to stay than the spaceport hotel.*

Ecoville made the same prissy, angular impression on Jezrael as it had on her sister, but Hell felt more like home. More precisely, the chaos of neon and bulging walls reached out to hug her with its memory of the place where she felt her skin fitted: the Wasp's Nest.

Down a dark, light-fractured alley that made her feel no more lost than anywhere else – a wonderful feeling, this first exploration – a sign beckoned her. It must have been as old as the one her father had bought so long ago: Homes Grown. The grainy old holo shone, pushing out a warm ruddy gleam of soft lighting in private alcoves; voice-music with the heart-beat of a laser-dance sang of love grown comfortable as favourite shoes. And the scent-sphere, even bounced around by the stale mugginess of the alley, lured her with the smell of salad and coffee with liqueurs. It didn't matter that she had to step over the legs of sleeping beggars. Maggie's Bar was home.

Strange to be in a bar alone, not even friends coming to meet her to work out the latest routine together. No laser-dance yet; in the absence of pre-packed emotions Jezrael was glad of the company of her own. A breathless excitement lifted her up, a feeling of daring, of triumph that she had escaped a lifetime's surveillance by her parents. Even the ache of missing Chesarynth was a round, shiny part of this tapestry of joy: *I'll find her*, she thought exultantly, *then maybe the groans will be proud of me for once.*

Unconsciously swaggering a bit, she threaded through the empty tables that were waiting for the evening rush. She bellied up to the bar and found they also rented beds; Jezrael was amazed at how easy it was to check in, an anonymous, accepted part of this scenario.

Her coffin was in the third row up, hard to climb into in gravity. Jezrael chinned herself up, scraping her knee as she rolled over the threshold. She cursed, wishing she were in the null-gee of the dance-arena downstairs, but at least there was enough room to sit upright, and the air contained less carbon dioxide. Once her carrycubes had been stored behind the panelling, Jezrael was oppressed both by the name of the coffin and by a shadow of claustrophobia, but one of her credit cards fitted a slot and the concave walls became a tawdry landscape. A pity she appeared to be on a cliff in some earth-bird's nest; vertigo was something Witwaterstrand hadn't prepared her for.

That, and a wash, about exhausted the coffin's possibilities until it was time to sleep. But Jezrael was too pepped up by excitement to waste time sleeping now. Dropping through the open doorway, she sealed the porthole and set off to the university.

On the long, bright worm of the road with cold darkness hiding the landscape, happiness still floated her spirits above the ties of gravity and breathlessness. What did that matter if you could be out under the stars with nothing between them and you? It was a fantasy fulfilled, and if all

180

the scenery were hidden by nightfall, imagination made shining wonders of the dim shapes around her. When she saw lights beckoning to her across the darkling plain, she slowed, wanting to leap forward in excitement, wanting to freeze the moment to savour its rarity. Jezrael was glad she hadn't had to have the oxyvirus that Chesarynth had written of; she remembered how Ches had described its effects.

The glassy block she came to stunned her: it looked like a prism festooned with constellations, pierced with lights of life. Drifts of vapour gleamed pale in its dark mirror; they would be clouds, she decided.

But the inside was as dull as Nutristem. And Jezrael could hardly stop staring at the skinny red people. Wounded souls stared out of their haggard faces. She knelt to fiddle with the slide-fastener on her thermo-boots until she had recovered her composure. Only then could she ask questions of these people, barely a year her senior, who seemed so old.

There was no computer-directory here either. The offices were closed. That year's students had all left, except for the corpos, and Jezrael knew enough to know that her sister hadn't been one of them. And it sounded like bad news asking a proctor; her informers quailed at the very thought. At least someone told her where Orion Hall was.

She found Chesarynth's room, third from the end, seventh floor. Nobody was in.

Tapping at other doors, hating the plastic panels that rattled noisily at her knock, Jezrael found no-one, or people who cursed her for waking them, though by Jez's book it was early yet. Nor was it merely jet-lag; an old-fashioned wall chrono told her it was barely nine-fifty. And none of the people she disturbed had even heard of Chesarynth Brown.

Some-one knew though: a youth with knobbly joints in his pipe-cleaner limbs. He was Eurafrican, his hair a ginger nest, and his eyes were a beautiful rich brown. In some other place and time she would have found him

181

attractive; just now he was a specimen to be dissected.

He knuckled crusty sleep from his eyes and said, 'Ches? Yeah, she was here – that room on the left.'

'Oh, damn it. I thought it was the one opposite.'

'Wouldn't make any difference,' he said. 'They've vapourised too. Didn't even make it past late harvest.'

'Do you know who took Ches?'

'Nope. When people contract, they generally don't want anybody to know, maybe 'case they come back as a tower. All I know is, there was some rumour that she'd shrunk. Didn't seem likely – she was too bright, worked too hard. But the quota – well, who can tell anything about someone else? I'll just barely make mine if I'm lucky.' He yawned prodigiously and in the time it took him to stretch, caution stepped belatedly into his mind. 'What's it got to do with you, anyway?'

'I'm her sister.'

Scratching his hunger-swollen belly, he digested that one in silence for a while. Jezrael gave him time to get used to the idea, hands in her pockets, standing loose, relaxed, open to possibilities. Finally he said, 'You're not going to go away, are you?'

'Nope.'

'Well, I guess you'd better take me for a coffee. You pay,' he went on, as if to make it doubly clear. When she accepted without hestitation, he added, 'and something to eat.'

'Sure. Assuming you've got something to add. I'm not leaving Mars without her' (the enormity of her task suddenly broke over her, heavy as a mercury cascade) 'or at least a good idea of where she's gone.'

'Be right with you.'

Since all he had to put on was boots and an old heater-cloak whose novae were dim with mud, he was right. He said nothing as they walked two or three blocks and she gave him time in the shivery night to come to, assemble his memories. Jezrael had never been so cold; Witwaterstrand was never like this. Up to now she hadn't really believed Ches's stories of people wandering round half-naked.

The night-shift was on in the café; half-light in shades of purple and amber rubbed over the scratched tables, and worn plastic chairs. Here and there in the echoing room were a few people, almost all of them on their own; one or two were asleep but the others looked desolate, abandoned. They roused her to obscure pity.

Some poor slob of a half-asleep student served them, her mind on the calculus glowing green on her pocket-memo. The skinny boy ordered what seemed to Jezrael huge quantities of food. It came luke-warm but tasty, and the mahogany scents of spice rose rich on the thick steamy air. The prices looked steep to Jezrael, but what did she know of life on a colony? She had nothing with which to compare them. It made her wonder what prices must be like out in the new star-colonies.

He ate with concentration for what seemed a long time, and she watched him after she had finished. 'D'you mind?' he asked, reaching for the scraps she had left, and he cleared her plate too. Jezrael wasn't given time to object.

'Be my guest,' she said satirically, but he seemed impervious to irony and she leant back in the chair, feeling it creak into comfort as torpor eased through her. It had been a long day.

A monumental patience kept Jezrael still, elbow aslant on the table, her eyes veiled. Watching the wrinkles come and go around his mouth as he chewed, she had a sudden image of Vrouw Koch building herself a new face from the tube of plastic make-up, polishing the creases from her old arms. What right did that flabby old woman have to smooth skin? All she'd ever done was be born into the hegemony that ruled Charismachem A.G. Jezrael wanted to putty over the crevasses in this young boy's face, smooth out his worries, but she couldn't. She could only wait until he was at his ease, smothering a belch behind his hand. He met her gaze.

'Thanks,' he said, then didn't know what to tack on to his beginning.

'You're welcome. Do you actually know where Chesarynth went? Or even who she went with?'

183

He shook his head. 'Hard to keep track, so many come and go. Maybe if you ask her garden-master. Do you know which one it was?'

'I know it was a man, looked about thirty, thirty-five I think, blondish, good-looking. He was really sympathetic, she said.'

'Oh, one of them. Narrows it down a bit. Which office was he in, do you know?'

Jezrael's turn to shake her head.

The old-looking boy shrugged. 'Probably wouldn't make any difference anyhow. I shouldn't think he'd help you even if he knew.'

They sat looking at each other, wondering which path to lead their conversation down.

Jezrael backtracked. 'What do you mean, so many come and go? Surely it's fairly rare for a student to drop out when she's expecting to do re-takes?'

'Nope. There's maybe a dozen, a half-dozen at least, deaf it out any week you care to mention once the first flush of novelty's worn off. It's the quotas. Rotten system. But unless you can afford to go to one of the earth universities you're stuck with Mars. Well, there's always Andronicus but it's not a real university, just media stuff.' His voice was scornful. 'Anyway, they sell degrees there. Not worth the plastic they're printed on.'

More silence, and Jezrael could see she was losing him to a rising tide of somnolence. She tried another tack. 'So did you know her room-mate, Loretta? Loretta Sibo, I think it was.'

'Yeah. Little freckly brunette, always thought she was up to anything only she wasn't. She let them beat her. She was one of the suicides, wasn't she?'

One of the suicides? Jezrael said the first thing that came into her mind: '*One* of them? How many are there then?'

He waved a hand in a sweeping gesture. 'You take any hall, seven floors, maybe twelve rooms each side of the stairs, twelve on both sides of the corridor, that is. How many's that make? I'm too beat to work it out. Seven hundred or so – double rooms, see,' he added as Jezrael's eyebrows rose. 'Then there's halls right through up to sigma from alpha, plus a few named after companies.' He saw her surprise. 'You thought Orion was a constellation? It isn't. It's a toothpaste manufacturer; you haven't sensed the adverts? Big sweep of night sky with Orion striding around, the constellation that is, a great feeling of openness and a cool fresh breeze, and I mean fresh, all kind of woodsy, and there's this guy walking along in the dark with his dog, real hero of the wilderness stuff, then you smell real woodsmoke and hear some real folksy music and there's this house with a rose-garden and honeysuckle and all, and the door opens and light sweeps out to welcome him with some cute kid in her mother's arms. Boy, you want to see that mother! Young, a real beauty queen, and the dog rushes up to play with the kid and the woman gives the man a real welcome and he smiles at her with a piano-ful of gleaming white teeth and you can smell the pheromones a block away. Then it says "Orion" in this deep sexy guy's voice and there's a smell of freshness and mint in a wet garden so strong your mouth'd feel clean after a garlic sandwich, and that's Orion for you.'

Jezrael could perceive the picture even though she'd never had a multi-sense set. The groans didn't believe in them. She said, 'But the suicides?'

'Oh, yeah. Well, in each hall you can count on maybe ten or twenty suicides a year. Then there's the ones who just vapourize, fade away, vanish, kaputt. One day they're moaning about the quota like any other bug, the next they're just an empty space. You never see them again. Vapourize, see? My room-mate went a month ago.' Real emotion wakened the boy's features briefly, a sharp unhappiness, but it faded again beneath his repletion.

'Mmm. My sister said that Loretta contracted, though.'

'Well, she'd have known better than I would. But I don't know who was recruiting that week. See, we have recruiters in and out like other people have biolight – get it? Like crawling over the walls. Only because of what they do, they don't generally advertise. Not much to be proud of, if you ask me, shrinking people. My room-mate called them soul-suckers.'

Jezrael searched through her memories of Ches's letters, the rare hologrammes. 'What about some Russian guy, came from Petrotextiles way? He did biophysics, same as my sister, I think.'

The boy yawned again, crooked teeth flashing in the coloured light. It suddenly occurred to Jezrael that she hadn't even asked him his name, much less where he was from. When he could finally bring his jaws together he said, 'Doesn't switch any pixils for me. D'you know anything else about him?'

'He drank too much. Oh, and there was something wrong with one of his eyes that he'd never had fixed.'

The boy nodded, his hair so compact it moved as solidly as the flesh on his forehead. 'Alex, that'd be. Bugged out around the same time as Loretta – or was it before then? Yeah, I guess it was before. Always seemed to have money to go to Hell whenever he wanted. Strange – he was way under quota but it never seemed to worry him. He just kept on shelling out for a shot. Don't think I saw him sober except maybe once or twice, but it was hard to tell.'

Jezrael thought that going to Hell meant getting drunk. There were no signs on the higgledy-piggledy streets where she'd found her hotel. She homed in on the rest of what he'd said, somewhat incredulous. 'What do you mean, it was hard to tell? You can tell whether someone's drunk or not, surely?'

'Not the amount he drank. See, you drink enough and it scrambles your wires permanently. Even when you haven't had a shot for days, you still act a little bit crazy. Folks like that, they don't all fall around, see.'

Jezrael thought a while, and the boy wandered across to get another coffee. He seemed to blend into the darkness, reappear in the oases of light: now you see him, now you don't. She thought of her sister and the dull ache of worry shifted up a gear. Jezrael could hardly sit still.

'So,' she began as he slipped his knees under the table,

186

'd'you know what happened to this Alex? Or to anybody my sister knew?'

'Nope. He just vapourized. Blazed a comet's trail across Hell and that was the last anyone saw of him.'

'Don't you care about all this?' she yelled at the boy, then immediately apologized. 'I'm just so worried about Ches. She's ...' and Jezrael couldn't think of a way to say how she felt about her sister that didn't sound maudlin or embarrassing.

The boy shrugged. 'Wouldn't do me any good if I did; people still just come and go around here. All I care about is making it through to finals. You want to get anywhere, you got to have a degree. It doesn't matter for people from Earth. They all got connections, every second uncle is some corpo big-shot, runs Automex or something single-handed. So no, I don't care. Anybody can't handle it, that's their problem.'

Jezrael slumped, straightened up her spine again immediately. 'I don't suppose you've got a picture of any of them, the disappeared?'

He shook his head again, slumber padding up inside his eyes until his neck could hardly support the weight of his skull.

'Would the university?'

'Maybe. Pictures, retina-scans, genetic blueprint. Dozens of copies in the quota office, faculty desk' – he yawned again and his jawbones cracked with the effort – 'garden-masters, any of them.'

'So where –'

'Don't ask.'

'Why not?' said Jezrael belligerently.

'Was it me, I wouldn't ask. It just feels wrong, that's all. Dangerous. Maybe dangerous for your sister, too. If they have shrunk her, they're not going to let anybody know. Maybe they'd erase her completely. One thing's for sure, they're never going to let you find her. If you go to the proctors they're just going to turn you inside out with their electro-sticks 'til you don't even know where *you* are, let alone her.'

'Can't you –' began Jezrael desperately, and stopped. What could he do anyway? What could she possibly ask him to do?

'Whatever it is, I can't.' His voice was flat, uncompromising. 'Do you think I'm going to stick my neck out for you? You don't care about me – you didn't even bother to find out who I am.'

He stood abruptly, sliding sideways out of his seat. He looked wild, desperate enough himself. Some anxiety had chased the sleep from his body. 'Look,' he said, leaning forward across the table so that she shrank back a little from his red-brown face. She could smell tired sweat on his skin, coffee on his breath, and his throaty voice soared in anger. 'Look. Don't you think the authorities know what's going on around here? Did you think they wouldn't notice that many people disappear? Have you thought about this at all?'

The girl behind the counter stared at them, her chin underlit by the green numbers on her memo. Uncomfortably, the boy dropped his tone to a whisper. 'Sure they know it. But they're not doing anything about it because it's big business. They let enough through that they can publish pass-lists right across the solar system and next year my name is going to be on it. Apart from that, the recruiters can have a field day, pick the students right off the vines. You think they'd be able to get normal people to die inside so some business can have a tower or an interface? They keep us desperate because they need us desperate. They must get a huge rake-off. And wherever your sister is, she isn't your sister any more, just some tower with a code-name.

'Thanks for the dinner, kid. But as for this sister-hunt, deaf it. Because if you stir things up you'll get both of you killed complete.'

188

17

Beneath the near-constant screaming of ships overhead, Jezrael walked free along the midnight road. It took a long, confused time to find her way back to Maggie's bar: another new experience, this not knowing where places were. In Witwaterstrand's three dimensions you could see every asteroid from every other asteroid. She'd be more careful to track her route next time, but when she made it back to the scratchy, crackling sound-and-picture sign of Maggie's place, it was a triumph that blanked out her failure to find Chesarynth.

What did I expect, anyway? I found her hall, someone who knew her, I even got to look round her room for hidden clues – except there weren't any. Still, if it was that easy, someone would already have done it.

What Jezrael did not acknowledge, because she didn't really accept it, was the strange boy's assessment of the situation. Mars-U couldn't really be that dangerous, could it?

Around her in the streets this late at night pressed the density of darkness. An atmosphere of tension shoved in at her that wasn't all a hangover of paranoia from the boy's conversation. Men (women?) hid behind masks that were grotesque, the heads of apes or reptiles or twisted gargoyles. They stood alone or in clumps, lurking half-seen in the shadows or waiting *(to rob me?)* under the lurid cones of light. Now Jezrael was glad of her own mask. It hid her vulnerability.

Ducking gladly out of the smell of refuse and humanity, she walked into Maggie's place.

Maggie himself was behind the bar: Magyar, a man with

high cheekbones and a geometrical face of flat planes. They didn't seem to be quite his own in their Slavic perfection. Jezrael squinted against the thick air that stung her eyes even through her mask and realized that his face was a paint-job. Glancing around, she also realized that practically none of the other customers thronging the place was masked, though quite a few of them were enamelled. She pulled her mask off, smothering a curse at the dry ache when the protective plastic corneas came out of her eyes.

Serving her with hot chocolate and brandy, Maggie introduced himself above the din of the crowded tables, the light-and-music chaos of the seething dance arena. Conscious of his scrutiny, Jezrael watched the dancers paint clumsy blocks of colour on the air. Maggie disconcerted her; there was a cold curiosity under his air of geniality. When he spoke it was loudly to combat the barrage of clashing harmonics coming from the ill-matched dancers. 'So you're the new tenant, huh?'

'Yeah, does it show?' Unsure of herself, she gave a half-grin that meant *I can take it but don't push your luck, bud.*

A smile ghosted across his features, curving his lips before he started to speak again. 'Sure. You're a stranger.'

'So are you – to me.'

'Touché, kid. What name are you using?'

'Jezrael Brown. I always do.'

He measured her with a passionless glance. 'So why did you pick my place out of all the bars in Hell?'

Hell. So that's what the boy meant. Quicksilver flowed the thought: *I must find out about comets and blazing trails.* Jezrael filed it for some other time. 'I saw the laser-dance on your ad.'

'Ahuh. I thought so. You have that look about you. You any good?'

No answer: what could she say? *I thought I was. Dael and the guys used me enough that I know they did too – but Eiker left me behind....* What she chose out of the maze of possibilities was, 'Give me a space when this lot have gone and you can make your own mind up.'

'Fine. That's usually not for four or five hours or so.'

Jezrael was surprised; she hadn't thought his question was anything but empty curiosity. She sipped her drink through a straw, feeling the warmth sink through her chest to expand its glow in her stomach. She said decisively, 'OK. You're on.'

He didn't seem to believe her. There was a faint quizzical – no, mocking, she decided – lift to one dark slender painted eyebrow and she added, 'Count on it.'

'I will.'

Maggie, a slim tanned figure, yet not attractive, turned to serve someone else, and Jezrael was conscious of a sense of loss. Isolation gripped her, cold talons of inadequacy and loneliness puncturing her mind. Maggie meant nothing to her but at least he had spoken to her, showed a little interest, even if it had been more of a challenge than a shared love of the art.

(A memory: her mother dabbing some new compound on the biolights in the living-room when Jezrael had come rushing back bursting with the thrill of her first laser-dance. Almost sixteen, she'd been then. She dropped her carrycube in the hall and ran in to tell her about how good it felt when she tried out the new gym-guy's equipment. Still full of the wild juices the laser-dance had given her she began to babble it all out to her mom. Mom stood, head cocked to one side, the sponge dripping in her hand, contemplating her handiwork. 'Mmm. That's nice, dear. Gym, you say?' And Jezrael had felt the energy draining out of her. Mom wasn't interested. She wasn't even listening. Jezrael said quietly, 'Then I stripped off and murdered him.' And Mom took a while to answer, 'Did you, dear? Well done. Could you just put the enzymes on the meat? I want to finish this.' The disapproval hadn't come 'til later, when Ms Brown understood the sort of people who danced laser.)

Jezrael stayed perched on the bar-stool but Maggie was too busy with his other customers to chat and she became self-conscious. Swivelling to lean back against the bar, she feigned interest in the gawky writhings of the dancers.

They were amateur, the lot of them, not watching each other so they could weave patterns together, just hanging their own private feelings on the same air like a bunch of gaudy clothes flapping on a line. Not one of them was wearing amplifier-bands; if they had been, the racket they made would have been intolerable instead of merely uncomfortable.

It made Jezrael want to weep to see one man paint his isolation bitter green though he wanted to seem cool. Over and over again desperation seeped through his bravado for anyone to read.

Tiredness began to catch up with her and she wished she could just crawl into her coffin upstairs, but she wasn't going to wimp out. She filled in the time with planning her campaign. *Maybe that student guy was right. Maybe I shouldn't ask the Uni unless I can't get any sense outside.*

In time alcohol began to raise the din, inflate the confidence if not the abilities of those who stayed it out. Maybe one of them knew where Chesarynth was, or what had happened to a man named Alex. Fear of what might happen if she asked the wrong person held her back.

Three red-skins stalked in, hair fountaining on the crown of their heads but unable to disguise the shining glass in their skulls. Jezrael recognized them at once from her sister's description: towers. Their cattle-prods were looped to their wrists. She swivelled uneasily to face the bar, trying not to catch their eye in the polished chrome that backed the bottles.

A frayed-looking woman came to talk to her, smelling of camphor, her face painted like the web of a spider and a black widow hung in its centre, black with burning red eyes painted on the woman's lip. They jigged, incandescent, every time she slurred out a word: the spider-woman asked a few questions, spurious interest, then tried to entice Jezrael outside to buy 'the find of the decade'.

'No dice.'

'Come on, kid, I'm trying to make you a fortune.'

'Philanthropy doesn't pay. At least, it hasn't for you, has it?' Jezrael played a mocking glance down at the woman's tattered, tawdry splendour and the black widow's faceted eyes lashed up and down in a mazurka of hate as the woman let rip with a harangue.

'Look, save it,' Jezrael answered. 'I know the score. You take me outside and roll me.'

Even then the woman wouldn't give in. She seized Jezrael's arm in one wasted claw; her dingy shot-silk sleeve fluttered over the girl's skin, tickling like the tiny feet of arachnids. Though the woman's flesh was soft as wet clay, Jezrael couldn't escape that desperate grip. She looked uneasily at the ruby and amber reflections behind the bar; the towers were coming closer. Drink was the last thing on their minds.

'Give up, Widow-woman. You're losing.' That was Maggie. He leaned over the bar, cool, confidential. 'Take a drink with me and quit panhandling in my bar. You're bad for business.'

Jezrael turned to him indignantly. Before she could say anything Maggie added, 'You too, kid, have a drink. And don't mind her. She's harmless. Aren't you, Widow? Harmless,' he shouted, for the woman's eyes were rolling in the spider's web that twisted into disconnecting lines. 'And don't cry. The kid's not going to fall for that. Can't you tell?'

Widow-woman slitted her eyes into a poisonous glare, the tears she had squeezed out shining, orange and wine-yellow flies trapped in the web by the bar-lights. She snatched the drink that had appeared on the counter and drained it, slamming the empty glass down; it broke and she slashed a gleaming shard across her wrist.

Jezrael recoiled, frightened, feeling the stirrings of the guilt that up to now she had kept nestled deep in her subconscious – but no blood flowed from the Widow's skin. There was only oil.

'Put it away,' Maggie told her wearily. 'We're all bored with that one.'

Widow turned, her wiry black hair a flared continuation of the radials in the web on her face. With a wry shrug she stumped away through the thinning crowd. Jezrael didn't breathe easily until the Widow had barged out of the doors and the towers had gone away, blank-faced.

Jezrael dashed to the door, a mixture of curiosity and apprehension. The Widow was rolling on the ground, head against the wall, a long thin wail fanning spittle from her lips. The towers were just disappearing round the corner, swinging their electro-sticks. Jez felt her stomach flip over but before she could nerve herself to act, a couple of cripples pounced upon the Widow with cries of pity and dragged her off, their clothes flapping like the untidy wings of some bat. Jezrael trailed uncertainly back to the bar.

'You got your own bands?' asked Maggie, deliberately offhand.

Jezrael refused to be disconcerted. 'No. I'll use some of yours, OK?'

'What if I haven't got any?'

'You will have, somewhere. I don't mind waiting while you root them out.'

'Oh, and you won't need that mask in the arena. There's enough oxygen over there – it doesn't pay me to have my dancers get sick. If you get to be one of my dancers, that is.'

So, with only a few scattered customers, backlit silhouettes huddling over their drinks in dim alcoves and staring at her curiously – one of the men was a shag-haired blond tower, crazy-eyed, who made her nervous – Jezrael played the panel of master switches to check them out. Some of them caused her trouble – a light/noise discord made Maggie snort derisively – but the laser-dance system was pretty much standard.

Standing lonely on the darkened floor, keeping protectively close to the console, she said 'Any requests?'

Maggie nodded. 'Only last ones.' Grinning at his own joke, he added sharply, 'Now get on with it.'

Jezrael threw the gravity control and stretched out flat on the empty air. Hovering horizontally not a foot from the plastic patchwork of boards she waited until action and reaction had cancelled each other out and she was still; the bands barely picked up her resting pulse to give the feeblest of flickering gleams. In her blue, tight-fitting suit she blended into the shadows. Maggie cleared his throat impatiently.

She responded to the challenge. Faint undulations along her length gave out a fitful flicker that hardly lit the walls, yet it was like the sky of Mars at sunset with the contours of her body the profile of its hills. Thunder rolled low overhead from the slow movement of her torso; it was vaguely oppressive. A twitch of fingers starred the darkling hills with the siren lights of a town. Then golden spheres of light dropped one by one across the floorboards of the plain: with mystic sweetness they lured the watchers along the road to the welcome of the town.

The town: Ecoville. A caricature of cold precision, lights sharp as icicles sprang into being while her arms moved robotic to pierce the night air with mathematical arpeggios which had never had a soul. Maggie saw the flat dead roofscape the way she had seen it: isolated, inhuman. (Jezrael heard him gasp and smiled inside. *Now to shock him from superiority!*) She sketched chiaroscuro shops, windows all empty as the red robot people stalked unseeing past her, proud in their naked skins. The only difference between them and the towers that marched through the chilly dusk was the glittering spikes in their skulls.

Then Jezrael swung her hips, shoulders counter-rotating, and as she broadened some movements, sharpened the gestures of her limbs, her chin, violins and cheap opera fought the throb of pop. She kept the tunes going and something grew in stroboscopic jerks: the fluid curves of Hell's streets. Spattered with sign-light (she wished she could paint the smells) staggered drunks and racing children whose faces were warped awry. (She smiled her delight as the creation grew denser, more sharp.)

Now a balletic crescendo: with the power on full through the bands on wrists and ankles she drew home for Maggie. Home as it should have been, with the warmth of firelight in the alcoves of his bar, with the swell of happy conversations, and friendly groups dancing to bright, soaring music. A place everybody would want to come to, and then she added Maggie himself (*not quite right*, she cursed, but still she thought he would be pleased with his handsome Slavic face, his lithe and clean-cut figure).

And the dancers made a song, an uplift of colour and harmony, that she meant to soften the hardest of Slavs. (Inside she thought *Oh! It limps on crippled feet when it should have made the stars feel pity.*) But it was too late for that, and the toe-tapping beat faded into the gentle after-glow of a summer's eve.

Jezrael drifted against one wall, fishtailed pink towards the controls, a grin for herself brightening her face.

Some customers applauded, but not Maggie. Exaltation fled from her. As she drifted down the fractional gravity she made a great play of stripping off her bands so that the nakedness of her mind was hidden. Jezrael knew she had daubed her insecurity on his dance-floor walls, and she wished now that she hadn't been showing off, then her desperate urge to belong might not have been blown up large across the canvas she had painted with her dance. Eiker was right: she couldn't dance.

By the time she could face him, Maggie had hidden his delight. 'Drink?' he said professionally.

'Ahuh. Passion-fruit juice.'

When it came in its silver-frosted glass, Jezrael gasped it down. A quarter of an hour she'd danced, and as the adrenalin sagged back out of her bloodstream the tired-ness flooded back in.

'You didn't come here just for dancing,' Maggie said.

Jezrael's chin went up. 'How do you know what I came for?'

'I saw you just now, remember? But if you don't want to tell me the details, that's fine by me. I take it you'd like to do a set every night?'

'It depends what you're paying.' Jezrael said it as if it were an everyday occurrence and not the once-in-a-lifetime jackpot; she would never let him know how much that cost her. She was just thankful she'd taken the bands off. 'Got any decent rooms?'

He nodded appraisingly and Jezrael knew by that that she should ask for more.

'And my meals. And,' she gazed into his eyes, trying to work out just what was going on behind his enamelled face, 'thirty credits a day.'

'Ten.'

'Twenty it is then.'

He laughed, the first genuine response she had seen in him. His face-paint was good: it didn't even crack. She wondered briefly why he was wearing it, why they all were in here where the air was so rich. Not like poling across Witwaterstrand unsuited with thrills laughing up inside her and the vacuum black and sucking at her skin. Eyes half-closed to stop the moisture boiling off. Ten seconds maximum to death, and the slow ones with thread veins snaking red across their cheeks. Right now it was all the same fierce elation and Maggie was still laughing.

Jezrael laughed too then stopped as Maggie added, 'And when you tell me what it is you're doing here, maybe I can help.'

But she remembered what the boy at the university had said, and was afraid of what might happen if this creature of Hell found out about her quest....

18

Days she asked questions of the wanderers in the streets, the barflies, even the crews out at the spaceport. Drunks and criminals, strays and those who'd found their true métier. Naked-faced or painted, they all gave the same answer to her hologram of Ches and Loretta and her questions about Alex: no idea. Yet she was careful never to ask anybody too close to her current life. She remembered all too well what the student boy had said. Jezrael didn't want to become one of the disappeared. Or to get Ches killed off. She hid her secrets inside her, locked away – she hoped – from the display of the dance.

Days she asked questions and nights she danced laser. A dazzle of impressions.

It was just as good as she had thought it would be. Some nights she felt high with her performance. It was as if she could reach out one goddess-like laser arm and pluck the diamond fruit of the stars. She could have drunk the whole universe which flowed from her dancing and it intoxicated her, empowering.

Men and women came to see her, to watch and then to ask her out if they liked the numbers she did at their request. She loved it all, loved the challenge of painting what they wanted to see, flashing out emotions that they couldn't express. (She thought of life with her parents.) It felt so good to be wanted and admired, to be the one people needed. What did it matter whether or not they had money? Jezrael knew she was flying the star-ship of her fate – and grew more and more afraid that some day she would crash. In the meantime she tried to stifle her guilt about leaving Chesarynth in harsh and alien hands,

198

and revelled in all her new celebrity brought her.

But it didn't have to be a flight to some equatorial city that they gave, or a seven-course meal on a river-boat upon the methane seas of Jupiter's moons – by hologram. Zuleika the Philosopher strolled with her up and down the streets of Hell to sail the seas of shared ideas within emerald shadows that smelt of cinnamon or diamond-dream drugs; Jezrael was flattered to be courted by someone so beautiful, so mature.

Plump corporate students bored her briefly with catalogues of rich parents and their self-important futures laid out like a tidy map. She played grafix in arcades and chess in warm cafés, though sometimes the earthquakes would shake the machines and the pawns would crumble into a thousand purple pixils, and Zuleika would shrug and say something witty.

And always Jez asked questions, but then the thought of what Mars-U had done to her older sister would jump into her mind and the might of the whole Martian system would flatten her hope beneath its juggernaut weight.

Best of all, with distance she sloughed off Witwater-strand like a skin. One night, in the cosy warmth of her vibrobed with fine music harping across the pale beauty of her room, she felt freedom flaming through her like the gift of the first sunrise. She remembered that afternoon, when Zuleika had led her down through the bowels of a recycling plant and out through a clear-walled tunnel beneath the growing reservoir, and in her bed she hugged a laugh to herself: *Now I know what a sardine must feel like when they take it out of its tin!* And she laughed again, thinking of the tiny fry wriggling out of their transport cannister and into the vast sealed lake. Sometime maybe years ahead they, and the algae with them, would colonize the banks of the plastic-roofed canals with forever to spread their inheritance and then the streams too could be free.

My future! It shone bright and pure as the ball of rainbow water with the sun at its heart back in Eden. *Nobody to tell me I'm wrong all the time, I'm useless, I'm only fit to marry an investment clerk. If the groans could see me now!*

For out of the inflexible chrysalis Witwaterstrand and family had walled around her flew a person who made friends, and her own happy dreams were of finding Ches then both of them settling down, here, amidst the constellations of coloured neon signs.

More and more people came to see her; Maggie said, 'If this keeps up I'll have to get a new sign – Jez's place.' There was a tinge of jealousy behind his humour; she didn't trust him personally though she knew she was good for trade.

Of course, outside the luminous world of Hell, she was practically unknown. The ecofreaks had no interest except in their pseudo-religion of work and the changing of Mars. But Jezrael too felt that way: beyond the enclave that seethed with vitality were only the dried-out husks who didn't laugh, or love, or nurture, and they were merely germs dropped down against the winds of cold dead Mars.

Jezrael grew so confident that she almost sent a hologramme to her parents. Late one afternoon when she had been about two weeks on Mars, she threaded her way out of the colourful riot that was Hell and asked her way to the Offworld Communications office. It was right in the heart of the dull grey grid of streets that was Ecoville proper. The clouds in the red-brown sky were flat and heavy, pushing a cold gale before them. It swept the streets clear of most people and plastered dust on the old-fashioned windows of the stores.

Ignoring the strait-laced gloom Jezrael walked briskly along Labour Parade until she found Off-Comm. Despite the romance of its name, Offworld Communications was the same boring cube as any of the other isolated buildings. Two regulation tubs of oxyplants stood either side of the door; the leaves were ugly green ovals ripped by the rising gusts.

Inside the locals gave her reproving glances for her mask and the pale hands that hung below her cheerful sky-blue suit. Still buoyed up by the glamour of her new

200

life at Maggie's, Jezrael was glad the lips of her mask hid the rude face she pulled.

But when her turn came at the space-channels, the thought of Witwaterstrand made her chicken out. Mom and Dad wouldn't want her mixing with laser-dancers and hanging around in bars. *I'm the sort of person they warned me to stay away from*, she told herself, clinging to the humour of it. *Anyway, they wouldn't believe I could do anything well. They'd just think I was lying.*

So she left the holoscreen blank. Instead she recorded a sound-only message saying merely, 'Hi. I'm fine, hope business is good for you both. Mars is great and I've got a good job but I haven't tracked Ches down yet. I'll be in touch. Don't worry about me, I'm fine, really I am, honest.'

Then she scrubbed the last pathetic words out and slunk back to the refuge of Maggie's to sink chocolate and brandy 'til it was time for the next show, hating herself for being such a coward.

Otherwise it was great fun being a success, though notoriety brought its own problems. A skinny furtive boy tricked out like an ecofreak gave her a daring halter and shorts made of cloth of gold, but she was afraid of his voyeurism and when he took to following her around, she tracked him home through the night after her show, and when he would have gone inside the darkened house, she whistled low.

He came dancing back up the sidewalk, nervous as a virgin. 'Ssh! My folks'll hear you.'

Away over towards Labour Parade the sound of breaking glass splintered the night; shouts made tiny with distance confused the darkness, vanished into it. Wreckers again – dissidents. The boy jumped nervously, and Jezrael made it worse. She jerked her chin at the unlit house where his parents were virtuously asleep. 'You follow me any more and I'll tell them.'

'You wouldn't!'

'Why not? You don't care about barging into my private life so why should I care about yours?'

'Ssh! Keep your voice down! They'll hear you.'

A thought struck her. 'About four months ago, did you ever see this girl?'

No, he didn't recognize Chesarynth. Nor the description of the invisible Alex. But he did say, 'Have you asked Maggie? He knows everybody in Hell whether they come into his place or not. Why? Who are these people?'

But Jezrael had vanished between the black solid houses, scared she'd ever asked.

The next night – who knows why? – trade was bad. Maybe it was because a couple of corpos had booked the floor for an hour with an offer that Maggie couldn't refuse, but they were bad. So bad that their clashing coloured projections flashed hard as lightning in the customers' eyes, and their stereotyped hop-heartbeat was uncomfortably loud and raucous. People took one drink and left but Maggie counted his profit philosophically.

Then the corpos didn't like the dead atmosphere they had created so Maggie closed the doors behind them. Jezrael's ears rang with the silence.

Would Maggie betray me? I'm known now. I've got friends who wouldn't let me vanish without a fuss. Like Zulei.

Would he let something slip by accident? Maybe the proctors could force it out of him. Maybe we'd both vanish and where would Ches be then?

But I've been here weeks and I haven't got anywhere. And that kid said Maggie knows everyone in Hell.

'Want a drink?' she asked, trying to be nonchalant.

He whipped up two orange coffee-liqueurs, saying, 'Yeah. Why do you think I opened a bar?'

Maggie debited her card and they drank. The silence still drilled in their ears. Jezrael tried to get up nerve for what she had to say.

'Right, Jez, that's me for temporary oblivion.' Maggie stacked his empty cup in the sink and switched off the machine, which died with a hiss of old-fashioned steam.

She surprised herself by saying with her parents' politeness, 'Can I ask you something?'

'I don't know. Can you?'

'Helpful to the last, Maggie, that's you. Look, I want to ask you something in confidence and I don't want you selling me out to – to anyone, OK?'

'Would I sell out my gold-mine? Kill the goose that lays those aurate orbs?'

'You'll have to do better than that.'

'Better than the profit-motive? Can't be done.'

Jezrael slid down from her stool; it folded back tidily into the front of the bar.

'OK, kid, you win.' Maggie shrugged, giving that quirk of one painted eyebrow that was his stock-in-trade. 'I won't tell anybody unless you say so. So give.'

Now the moment had come, Jezrael still wasn't sure. She found it hard to look at Maggie's face with the sharp little eyes peering out from his smooth lacquered skin. It was as if she might show him all her inner thoughts just by meeting his gaze, while his thoughts went to earth under those fake layers of plastic. Maggie waited, leaning on one elbow, his finger-nails tapping the counter.

'Look, I've lost my sister.'

'Careless of you,' he interrupted, then said, 'Sorry. Carry on.'

Between backtrackings and suppositions, Jezrael took quite a time. But he anticipated the climax: 'And now she's shrunk and you don't know who to.'

She said bitterly, 'Our worry's not even original, is it?'

'No. Shades of *déjà vu*. There's not many turn up asking around here but enough so I get the picture. Doesn't it occur to you, though, that if she wanted to get in touch, she could? I mean, even out on the asteroids they got colour holo. You think they couldn't manage a little message? So it follows that she doesn't want to get in touch with you.'

'Maybe she can't! Maybe she's just some ersatz machine!'

He shook his head confidently. 'Nah. She just doesn't want you to know where she is. Think she likes being a tower? So how come you're doing the opposite of what she wants? If you do find her, she's going to be really pissed with you, wouldn't you say?'

'Well, maybe.'

'Maybe nothing. Definitely. But you were right not to go charging in to the authorities. They got cattle-prods and stuff that make you forget your own name.'

'Do you think that's what's happened to her?'

'What do I know?' He scratched his chest reflectively. 'Actually, quite a lot. No, I don't think she'd contract to Mars-U if she hated them that much. Also if we can pin the date down a little' – he waited for Jezrael to clue him in – 'then we got the little devils. I'll get back to you on that one, all right?'

She watched him write the dates in grease from his fingertips on the shiny metal of the coffee-machine. 'You see?' Maggie said proudly. 'Now I won't forget. Nobody's going to think of looking at that, and they wouldn't know what it meant if they did.'

'Hadn't you better put it in a code of some sort?'

'Nah. A dead give-away, that is. Now it looks just like some ordinary unimportant thing that maybe hasn't got wiped off since then. In my place that couldn't happen, but how are they to know that? Living in Hell has its uses.'

'Can you tell me anything else about this Alex guy? Or Loretta?'

His face in its pale lacquer scarcely moved as he talked. She wondered how it felt to have muscles permanently plastered down like that. Maggie said, 'I knew an Alex once,' and the breath locked in Jezrael's throat.

19

A long way outside the city sprawled an industrial complex. But industry on Mars didn't meet Jezrael's expectations; it was small-scale compared to Nutristem, even, just a lot of little houses huddled in a strip either side of one of the thermal exhausts from the spaceport. Even so, Jezrael could tell it was an industry because there was a wall all around it, a wall that seemed like any other piece of chewed-up Martian rock, but it was topped with a shimmering view of the sky that meant some sort of force-shield. Who but an industry would want that kind of protection?

The ground-car hummed over the ridge and out of the night-side down into the valley and then she couldn't see the poky little houses, just the high wall in the orange flare of sunrise. She wondered what Maggie had in mind.

At one end of the wall, where you could see the noses of the spacecraft sticking out of the distant pits, there was a shanty-town on the outside of the industry, made of pre-fabs and adobe glued higgledy-piggledy together to cut down the number of separate walls that had to be built. The largest building was a patchwork of mud and plastic and stone pierced by square windows and topped off at different heights.

On the empty road the hired car slid to a halt past the usual ribbon of plastic greenhouses. Jezrael and Maggie got out, yawning.

With the long shadows of dawn cutting black across the coppery light, Jezrael thought the place looked eerie. Looking at the odd roofs that seemed almost crenellations, she stretched and drew a deep breath, but with the flat cold smell of Mars came a stench so thick she gagged even through her mask.

'What is that?' she said, recovering.

Maggie looked at her sardonically. 'Fester.'

Rubbing her frozen hands up and down her arms, Jezrael asked, 'Pardon?'

'Pardon? Where did you get that from – the Dark Ages?'

Jezrael jerked her chin up in pretended disdain; it kept at bay her anxiety. 'It's manners. That's why you wouldn't recognize it.'

He shared a grin with her but added, 'These people, they're just moochers or people on the dodge. Of course, the proctors know where they are, but it suits them to keep these guys all in one place where they can't get up to much. Saves trouble.'

'Pocket revolutionaries?'

'No – they couldn't be bothered. In fact, they can't be bothered to do anything much, and nobody wants 'em around because – well, you'll see. I hate to say this, Jez, but this is a bunch of examples about what can go wrong when you shrink.' Neither of them said anything about Chesarynth but she was a silent presence in their minds. Maggie said too briskly, 'This is where your Alex was the last time I heard of him.'

Which explained why he'd brought her here. Up until now it had just been another of his weird surprises. But she wasn't quite sure she wanted to meet Chesarynth's tame drunk. What if he got violent?

They began to walk towards the down-at-heel enclave, their shadows bending at strange angles as they encountered the foot of the wall. The smells grew stronger, more redolent.

Jezrael said out of the side of her mouth, 'It appears they can't be bothered to wash, either.'

Maggie smothered a grin. 'You're right. Keeping clean isn't high on their list of priorities. When you know them better, you'll understand why. Now just shut up, OK?'

Above them, through the grimy pits of windows, a few scarecrow figures were leaning out to watch them. It gave Jezrael an even more uncomfortable feeling. Someone invisible threw a scratched plastic door open; beyond the daylight that fell through the doorway was solid blackness. Jezrael swallowed.

Maggie grabbed her arm. 'You're going to see some pretty horrific sights, kid,' he whispered.

'Now he tells me!'

She felt her boss take away the comforting touch on her elbow but it was too late. Their bootheels were already crunching on the grit of the threshold. Then someone slammed the door shut behind them; in all the dark interior the only light was a few brave rays of sunshine which fought their way in through the cracks of the door. Gilded dustmotes painted thin stripes that died on the thick air. Jezrael tried not to breathe.

Maggie said, 'We've got something for Alex.'

A cracked voice cackled. 'He don't want to see anybody right now. He's in a board-meeting.'

Someone else unseen laughed at the joke.

'Tell you what, though,' the first voice said again. 'You just give me what you've brought and we'll let him have it soon's he's fixed the fate of nations.'

Again that thready maze of laughter whirling through the dark. Other people joined in, but Jezrael couldn't see anybody or anything. If Maggie hadn't been there she would have been even more frightened.

'Good line, guys,' Maggie said calmly, 'but it's passed its sell-by date. Alex will want to see us.'

More laughter. 'You're right there, barman. Alex would like to see anybody.'

Stealthy fingers rattled against Jezrael's thermal cloak. She shuddered and pulled it tighter around her. Something touched her hair but when she jerked her head up, the thing had gone. She couldn't even feel Maggie any more, but she heard him.

'Just tell him, will you? Tell him it's someone from Chesarynth Brown.' Her boss sounded just as composed as if he were serving behind his bar; Jezrael could only admire.

A deeper voice said, 'It'll cost.'

Now Jezrael could see blacker patches against the darkness, lumpen shadows like vultures with their necks bent under their wings, but not a face was turned towards her and she still couldn't tell who had spoken.

Maggie said, 'Of course. When we're with him, we'll pay.'

Now there was a general shout; Jezrael thought there must have been dozens of people in the noisome twilight. Hoarse voices shouting, 'Let's play!' 'Now we'll have a good game!'

What drove lightning through Jezrael, though, was the scratchy taunt that came from somewhere behind her: 'Draw us your sister, girlie! Use your laser-lights!'

Jezrael whirled round in the soot-black echoes of wild giggles. Someone grabbed her and she pulled away but the hand seized her more firmly this time and Maggie said, 'It's only me. Stick with it, kid.'

Fragments of her past speared at her through the funereal gloom. 'What was it like knowing the other kids wanted to kill you and your sister? Didn't it make you hate yourself knowing that's how much they despised you?'

(The suit-room at school, hot and crowded with unfocussed anger. Scared worlder-kids wanting to get out, knocking elbows and hips as they pulled their gaudy suits on. And not a one facing up to their terror of the air-skin yet – until Chesarynth, unaware, came in.

Rosemar erupted. She and Timkin raged at Ches, knotted a sleeve round her neck, doubled the gravity. Even weighted to the floor, the other worlders laughed. They could do it, the tall Congolese and the weaselly boy from Bolton, because violence was in them and Chesarynth was helpless. Hanging from a pipe by her neck, feet dangling useless too far above the deck. Her face mottled. Bruises flowered on her skin where the suit-metal bit. You couldn't hear her throat rasp as it tried to suck for air

208

because Chesarynth was drowning in their laughter. Dying. Dying of her killing weight because they could handle gravity and she couldn't.

Until Jezrael ran in, panicking, to rip the gravity to zero, to turn her terror outwards into free-fall pain. Rosemar and Timkin saw their blood splash in air.

Ches and Jez got away that time. But an undercurrent of hate never quite left them after that. Hate – and mockery.)

'Too good for an investment clerk? Not you! You're just factory fodder, aren't you. Torturing plant genes.' (A chorus hissed hate that solidified around her.)

'You'll never make it without some guy to be your crutch.'

'Yeah, the scum of Hell. You'd think she'd have more sense than to trust him.'

'Trust the Magyar? Nobody could be that stupid. Not even her.'

'Think you're smart, don't you girlie? Running away from home like some rat.'

'Can't be that smart, can you, girlie? Or you wouldn't be here. You'd have made it to college.'

'Not her. Too much of a dummy. Remember how she cried when they said she was too stupid to do anything but slice plants up? Remember what your pa said when your report came up on the computer? You were too stupid even to erase it first.'

Another voice sneered, 'Pa? No way. She called him "Daddy". Daddy!'

(Between, beneath and around the wild plaiting of the two main speakers' voices in the murk came a ragged chorus, 'Daddy's girl, Daddy's girl.' Harsh throats, old and thin, warped into those of evil children. It was strange that it pierced her nineteen years to dig at the childish psyche underlying her self. And down there was the pool of hurt and anger and frustration she had felt so long ago with the kids ringing her, taunting her. The bitterness poured out of its hiding-place in a corrosive fountain.)

'What a wimp! And look at the hash she made of things

in the factory. Thought she was going to change every-thing for – for Nutristem, hey? Thought she was going to be a big-shot, end up a baggy.'

'Yeah. Then her parents might not have thought she was such a waste of space.'

'What else could she be? You hear how they all laughed at her behind her back when Ild wasn't looking? Her and her pretensions! Her a laser-dancer! Look at her! She looks like a cart-horse. Talk about bull in a china shop! She'd fall over her own feet!'

Why doesn't Maggie say something? Anything? wondered Jezrael. *Maybe he's changed his mind. Maybe he'll find out what I'm really like and then –*

She couldn't finish the thought. Her world was crashing down around her, each block of confidence carefully erected over the abyss of self-doubt. All of it, shaken to its foundations, unstoppable destruction. Since she'd been dirtside she'd known the blind implacability of mars-quakes. Inside her there was nothing rising from the debris to cling to, nothing that wasn't disintegrating, untrustable.

Still the two wreckers bombed her from the shadows. 'How many times did her mother say she could never stick at anything? Even laser-dancing – remember how Eiker ditched her as soon as he'd had his fun? Her precious self was too important to take the drugs.'

'Didn't want her pretty skin all scarred by a few little studs. Eiker was right to leave her.'

'Taking her to Earth, for Chrissake. Fancy her falling for that! Stupid orbiter!'

'Dumb provincial, more like. Her go on a tour? Don't make me laugh.'

'Remember her pet mouse? She let it die.'

'Let it die? No way. She killed it. Went poling across from Eden with the poor little bastard stuck in her pocket. Forgot it was there. It just wasn't important to her. Remember how it exploded? Blood all over her clothes.'

'Didn't even tell her mother, did she? But she couldn't hide what she was. Remember what Mom said when she found out?'

'Murderer! Stupid, incompetent murderer.'

And just like when she was a kid, Jezrael couldn't answer. Because it was all true. It was all just like she remembered, even the agony of knowing she'd killed the pet her mother had said she'd never be able to look after properly, but she'd begged and pleaded that she'd take care of it, she really would. How could she answer? *And how could they know? Why doesn't Maggie stop them?* And her shame was blazoned in a corona of fire and humiliation across her dark Gehenna. *How could I ever have thought that Maggie liked me? I'm stupid! Stupid and ugly....*

'Remember when her mom sent her to socialization classes?'

'Lusty Lil!' answered the other voice, cruel and triumphant.

'Lusty Lil! Lusty Lil!' howled the unseen mob, and another sore burst inside her, spurting out its ancient pus. Rage and frustration boiled up inside her until her skin was like the rattling lid of a kettle and she was shaking with the rising flood of all the pain she'd buried and thought forgotten, but there it all was, a nightmare treasure of scorching jet-black shame.

Jezrael didn't need the evil choir. The habit of self-flagellation was strong enough. Her eyes burned with unshed tears and she said nothing. That was the trouble. She did what her father had told her to do and said nothing. 'They'll get tired of it,' he said. 'They'll stop if you ignore them.'

And she remembered: socialization class. The scene was like an etching, acid scars in the flesh of her mind, in which she was both viewer and participant. A double loser, because neither then nor later could she work out what she had done wrong or how to stop it.

The walls were dim. The biolights had died of neglect in the ancient rock of the asteroid that was the socialization class orbiting by the school in Witwaterstrand. It wasn't actually a class, more a sort of club where you were supposed to make friends, and, according to her mother, meet boys. Nice boys. Why don't you bring one of them

211

home for us to meet? Jezrael had winced at the idea. *Bring one of them back and expose him to my father's lofty indifference? My mother's superiority? Her probing questions to make sure he was suitable? The guy'd be a bug under a microscope, writhing in embarrassment. He'd tell everyone about it next day; they'd never stop laughing.*

So, in the pitiless electric glare, she'd been mucking in, scraping dead biolight culture from the walls, in scruffy clothing so it wouldn't get spoilt, knowing she looked horrible but what would her mother say if she came back home with her new violet suit covered in stains? Of course she was plugging away at the scraping and the smelly dead layer was dripping down her arm, tickling in her armpit, splashing her face. Of course her mother had told her to be sure and arrive early, nobody likes a shirker. And none of the other girls had turned up to help because they didn't want to get dirty.

So the boys looked at her scruffiness, her clumsy body, her fat (her mother always said impatiently that she wasn't fat but Jezrael knew she was). They saw through her. They said, 'Who're you going out with?'

No answer. How could she say 'No-one?' And she couldn't lie, because everyone knew everyone in Witwaterstrand. They'd know if she was lying.

'Secret, eh?' they'd said. 'Good in bed, is he?'

She'd thought, *Ignore it and it'll go away. That's what Dad always says.* But of course it didn't. It must have been her fault. Her father couldn't have been wrong.

'Look at her! She's blushing!'

'Must be good.'

'Might not be. Might be useless but she doesn't want to admit it.'

'What's it like?' they asked her, and she could find no answer.

'Big, is he?' they said.

'Are you big, Jez?'

No answer, but the tears had trembled in her eyes and she'd sniffed and wiped her face swiftly – but not unseen – on her sleeve.

'Must be big. The rest of her's big enough, isn't it? Stands to reason.'

'Then the poor bastard probably hasn't got it where it counts. How about me, Jez? Would I fit it?'

Goaded beyond endurance, she wanted only to hurt them back. She said the most cutting thing she could think of. She said, 'You? You wouldn't even touch the sides.'

The other boys all laughed at him, the one who'd asked the stupid question. Now he wanted revenge too.

'You're that big, are you? We'd better give you another name, big girl like you. What about Lusty Lil?'

And they'd laughed, and she'd scraped and scraped at the wall, wishing she wasn't crying, wishing the asteroid would explode and she'd die and they'd all die too, wishing it was time to go home because she couldn't leave or they'd know how hurt she was and that's what they wanted. So of course she'd been Lil to every boy in school, every boy she'd ever met until Dael, and he wasn't a boy anyway. He was the gym guy so he didn't count.

And it had all gone away, cowered in the crevices in her mind out of the light of her thoughts but spreading its unacknowledged blight over every vision of herself, until Hell had unfrozen her, given her self-respect on a short-term loan.

Until now. Until these faceless shadows had read it in her in this reeking poisonous night-filled room.

And they were laughing too, and Maggie did nothing to defend her so he must know how little she was worth.

Still she couldn't say anything to make them stop. What could she say? What would they listen to?'

'Who wants Alex?' An icy contemptuous tenor cut across the taunting laughter. They stopped suddenly, shrank back into silence, and it was as if mortal fear stalked among them.

Maggie spoke. *(Jezrael cringed; somehow she'd been entertaining the ridiculous hope that maybe Maggie wasn't there to hear all this because then it wouldn't have been so totally damning.)* Maggie said, 'I do. We've done business before.'

The cold voice spoke again from some point high in the room. 'What do you know about Chesarynth Brown?'

'See us,' said Maggie firmly, 'and you'll find out.'

A snap of his fingers and the shadow-speakers fell over themselves to open a window. Jezrael shrank back against Maggie's warmth; she needed it. In the harsh copper light the place looked like a butcher's shop but the slabs of meat were moving.

Maggie took her hand, laced his fingers through hers and she clung to it, following him up the crumbling adobe steps. Around her the shadow-voices tried to hide, hunching their shoulders, scuttling away from the light, flinging up arms swathed in bloody rags to cover their faces.

For there were no paint-jobs here, nor even masks. Cancers had eaten away jawbones, noses, leaving twin streaming pits in some faces. Radiation burns and blistered dead eyeballs twisted features into mutations. A woman with no legs dragged herself under a table.

Now Jezrael knew what the stench was. Gangrene.

Bile boiled up in her throat and she fixed her eyes on Maggie's back. Even if he knew what she was, he was still a link with something cleaner, something from outside this charnel shack.

Her feet slithered on the steps. Shaken, she tripped on a strip of plastic shoring and the shadow-voices laughed in triumph.

At the top of the steps was a square room, a hole in one wall open to the bleak dawn. The sky outside was bulging with livid clouds; the sun hung beneath them, a flattened ball of ruby fire, ruling lines that were pitiless to the sketchy furniture in Alex's place. Even the mummified food on a stack of abandoned plates cast a shadow.

Maggie led her to a bed where he sat beside her, facing the rickety table and the salvaged pilot's chair. Closing the door behind them, Alex walked, favouring one leg, to the pilot's chair on its swivel. He sat, a silhouette, turned away from them to stare out of the unglazed window, and a

214

quietness grew around them, a quietness compounded of little sounds.

Harsh sunlight pushed a wind across the desert, and it was the cold wind of dawn. Jezrael was amazed; she thought her humiliation must have lasted a lifetime but the scarlet lances of the sun flew horizontal in through the window, and blown sand whispered on the walls, gritted in the seams of the bedsheets. The dryness sucked moisture from her nostrils, leaving the smell of ancient dust.

Breathing, that was another thing she heard. Breathing that was raucous and vast, so slow it might have been the pulse of the planet. And even above the endless lament of wind across the desert and the crackle of plastic green-houses she could hear the whining voices at the foot of the stairs. Up here the rot of gangrene was fainter but there was a sweet metallic smell that might have been alcohol or drugs or the urine that steamed slightly in an old corroded can. It seemed that the spartan light itself was solid with echoing sounds.

Maggie said nothing but the expensive plastic of his clothes shushed softly in time with the pressure of his hands as they stroked hers. The constant rubbing at that one piece of skin made her sore and she wished Maggie would stop patronizing her, but she dared not say. He might take offence. Now that he knew what she was really like it was obvious he could barely tolerate her, and that only for the sake of his profits. From the abyss of self-hatred it was hard to see the room, hear its sounds, but she must concentrate on them now for all she was worth – not much – to drown the hollow agony of her soul.

To the left a tiny noise dared to click, magnified in the hard silent shadows; Jezrael knew that sound well from her room back home where she had hidden from her endless failure to meet her parents' standards. It was a cuber, time-programmed. She thought it must be to record something from the telecasts. Now that she knew what she was looking for in the red-and-black patterns of daylight, Jezrael could make out racks and racks of holo-cubes, a whole library of them: the sick psychotropics of

Madreidetic, poetry, home recordings. And as a faint tremor surged towards them, rumbled through and past the flaking building, bottles chimed against the symphony of shifting dust. She felt like she was breaking apart. She wished something would happen.

At last it did. Unseen beyond the high back of the pilot's chair, Alex said, 'So you're Jezrael. You surprise yourself, but you don't surprise me. I've thought about you a lot since Ches shrank. I thought you might come, but you are too late.'

Jezrael tried to say something but her voice was rusty. Unheeding, Alex went on, 'I remembered your picture. Not too pretty, no.' (Jezrael thought in panic, *He's going to do it too*, and tried not to hear her own sub-thought *How can I hate myself more than I already do?*)

'But brave. Only it took you too long to find your courage, Jezrael Brown. Your sister has shrunk and I am dead.'

A click; the voice switched off, the faint hum of the recording (she hadn't known 'til then that it was a recording) stopped abruptly.

Jezrael's hatred turned outwards and she leapt to her feet, yanking free of Maggie's touch. 'You can't be dead! You switched on that button. You walked. You're not dead.'

A ruin of laughter sandpapered through his throat. 'Drink with me then, Jezrael. In that bottle there, the square one.' Sardonically: 'You be mother.'

She stepped over to the table; it was corrugated plastic, the runnels blocked in with adobe, each with its tunnel of shadow. Its support was torn from the chassis of an old ground-car.

She took out the twist of rag that stoppered the bottle and a smell that was sharp and somehow sombre smoked up into her face, but she poured without flinching. Then she walked round to hand Alex his drink.

By will alone she stopped the shaking of her hand as Alex took the drink.

Parts of his face smiled. 'Well done, Brownlet. But I am

216

dead. Alex Arachne they call me. Spider Two.' He clinked his glass against hers. 'Spit in death's eye.'

'Cheers.'

He laughed, an ancient, tied-up sound. 'Look at me, Brownlet. Now you know why I'm dead. Drink to death, kid. He's looking over your shoulder.'

Sunlight streamed past her into the dead eyes of Alex. They too were dry and blistered, except for one weeping spot over his right pupil, but he tossed off his drink and held out his glass for another. The glass itself was another dusty can.

Jezrael almost drank then, needing it, but the smell stopped her. The bitter liquid sloshed in the can and something smiled in him. It wasn't pleasant to see.

'Whisky and strychnine, Brownlet. What can hurt me now?'

For nothing ever could. No company would ever have contracted Alex the alkie, but someone in Hell had. He bore a crown of wires that nested thicker than the hair left on his skull. Matter from his ulcerated eyeball had formed a pool on his lower lid; he blinked, and it fled down through the bloated folds of his face.

Full into his unblinking eyes the sun hurled its power. Barely shielded by the scant atmosphere of Mars, the distant Sol was still a killer. The low air-pressure had boiled off all the protection of his tears; he blinked, a habit that had outlived its usefulness, and the room was so quiet that she heard the slow scraping of his eyelids, saw the matter drip down from his lashes. Black skin cancers traced a strange geography over his face. And silvery ampoules glowed like pink pearls in the light that had killed him.

His lips stayed still, curving around the edge of the can. A jagged edge pried blood from the corner of his mouth but he didn't seem to notice. Jezrael watched the dark shine of the blood on his unmoving lips. The fingers of one hand rose to fumble through the wiry crown of thorns above his right ear to click another cube and his voice said, 'I want that system to die, Jezrael.' The recording was

217

thick with Russian violence, the words spitting out in an over-clear diction that Chesarynth would have recognized. 'The whole of Mars-U and those useless cringing ecofreaks that let it happen. I want them to die in pieces like I am doing. Fire like worms eating along their nerves in an endless conflagration of pain. To feel their nervous system dying. To know what fear is, and desperation. To eat failure, to sleep failure, every breath filling them with the strangling dust of failure, silting up their lungs. All the corporations and their fat corpo sons. Vampires. You know what vampires are, Jezrael who hangs up there between the stars? Come soon, Jezrael. Your sister won't tell you, but I will.'

All through the playback there had been a surf of background noise; Alex paused, Alex of the recording, and Jezrael could hear the sounds of a bar, drunks laughing at jokes that weren't funny, a music of clashing hate rooted in some long-dead tribal war.

'When I see you, Jezrael Brown,' – the real-time Alex laughed, the dark liquid splashing over his feeble moustache, drowning out the voice of the recording for a moment – 'I won't know this. I won't know that I'm blazing the comet's trail across Hell because in – in six metric hours I'm giving my soul to a vampire. She's not corporate but she's a vampire all the same. I get my debts paid off, my bastard quota that'll stop those' – something Russian, obscene – 'proctors flaying my connective tissues every time they want to feel something. I'll even get my other eye back, well a new one anyway, and I won't think about the poor bug that's selling it. At least I'll be able to see properly. I won't be able to call my brain my own – Christ, I can feel the wires inside my skull now and it hasn't even happened yet – but at least I'll be able to see.'

Jezrael watched the real-time Alex's mouth writhe in an attempt at laughter that had her and him both crying.

'She wants me to subvert the proctors. She gave me a platinum credit-cube valid for tonight, in Hell only. Food! It's wonderful, eating. I'd forgotten how good food can be. And real vodka, all the way from the banks of the

Dnieper. And you should see my clothes, Jezrael, real clothes in real colours because when I'm a spider it won't matter to me whether I wear that plastic shit like the ecofreaks or what, I'm not going to look like anybody their daughters would take home for tea. Worse than that, I won't even care.

'Christ, I'm scared! They're going to split my head like a melon.... I hope to God they don't cock it up. I won't think of that. It's only Russian roulette you get paid for.

'But I'll be jamming those bastard proctors. Give them a right royal pain in the brain, and that's got to be worth something. If I can only bring hope to somebody else it'll be worth it.'

On the recording, Alex drank. There was a damp and breathy giggle at his side and he said drunkenly, 'Ssh! In a minute. Busy now. Busy leaving footsteps between the stars. No. Can't send it. They won't let me send it. It's all been for nothing.

'No, she'll come. She's got to come. Ches says she loves her, but Ches isn't going to make it. They've got their hooks into her already, I can see the signs. Jezrael will come, won't you, Jez, and I won't know you and I won't be this person any more. I won't remember all this. I'll be something else. A spider. Get them, Jez. Get the bastards. Spit in the eye of death.'

Back in the room that was a hundred shades of red, sunrise on pink extruded rock, pastel plastic and sepia dust, Maggie looked at Jezrael; she could just about see him over the back of the pilot's chair but he was irrelevant in this. She was watching Alex, the nest of wires flattening at the back as he leant his head wearily on to the cracked old padding.

'Did you?' she asked.

'Did I get them? Did I hell! Didn't you see the ecofreaks out there, still stomping round like redskins, proud of their pathetic grubbing round in the muck? Won't use tractors, oh no! They don't mind using the students as slave-labour though, do they? And they've got those damn rockets dumping iron from the asteroids into the core, haven't they? And the way they're mucking around with the eco-sphere, they say there's some seriously weird stuff going on out in the ice-deserts.

'But what do they care? The companies keep a low profile around here because this crackpot government says so but they're laughing and the ecofreaks are making a fortune flogging off poor innocent bugs to the corporations after they've grown tonnes and tonnes of food for them, and still the poor bastards get into debt, not to mention the ones the oxyvirus doesn't take with, like Ches. Sometimes I think they fix it that way to trap the bright ones....

'Don't get me started on this, Jez.' Alex took another swig but the can was empty so he stretched over and took a pull from the square bottle.

'Well, why didn't you jam the proctors?'

The bottle clashed on Alex's teeth; he laughed and she saw that the gums had pulled back and his teeth were as long as a dog's.

'That was just her come-on, Jez. She was working for the corpos, all right, but not the officials, just nasty little crooks. Only this one can't afford the real tower-business. They get their shrinks on the cheap. And this' – he put his callused finger on the dry crust of his eyeball – 'she got this on the cheap too. Diseased. I got this virus, see, blocks off my memories one by one, like shutters going down. My whole life, all the things I was, all the things I cared about, one by one they're swallowed up by this great cloud of darkness. And you know the really stupid thing? I still drink to forget.'

Horrified, Jezrael could only listen to him. Layer by layer he was heaping up poison on the intricate paths of her own fears for Ches.

'See that?' Alex gestured widely, inaccurately, to the cube library. 'Good escapism, huh?' He laughed hideously. 'That used to be my life. I recorded them all, one by one, everything I remembered. I sent the embalmed downstairs through Hell to steal all the cubes they could because I knew everything was going. Now I watch them

220

over and over and it's not my life any more. They stole my life from me and I try to remember it but it's not my life any more. It belongs to someone who once sold an eye to buy oblivion and I watch it and wish I could go through it all again, but it's not my life and I forget it anyway five minutes later.

'You want to know something? When they said you were looking for me I played my entire life over or I wouldn't even have remembered who Ches was. I played it all again this morning, knowing you were coming and chunks of it are drowning in the shadows even now.

'Can you imagine that? Having to re-create yourself every day?' Alex sneered at himself, lips peeling back from those awful teeth. I have to leave myself a message or I wouldn't even know to do it. Look at this –'

He laid one hand on the table, palm up. The other hand scrambled around like some blind, seeking monster. Jezrael followed his movements, mystified, until she realised he was groping for the cutlery on a filthy plate. A rusty fork and a shiny knife. She shoved it nearer and he scratched at it until he had the fork in a tight, uncultured grip. Then he slammed the tines of the fork down until it jammed quivering in his thumb. Blood welled up, pooling blackly under the puncture in his nail. She had heard his bone break; she felt sick. No fake wound like the Widow-woman, no oil in a clever prosthesis. The fork stuck out sideways, trembling as he fumbled for the bottle, lifted it to his mouth.

'See?' he said, almost proudly, and there was a wolfish grin on his face which compelled her to horrified fascination. But when he would have slammed the bottle back down on the table, he missed the edge and the bottle smashed on the floor.

He turned angry. 'This corporation back here, just over the wall. Like an itch and I can't scratch it. Fannying around with their tacky little houses like any good ecofreak, but underneath they're all linked together and the whole damn plant is run by saps like me who shrank.'

Hope flamed in Jezrael's eyes; Alex heard her indrawn

221

breath and said, 'Nope. No sisters here. There were two corporations recruiting around the time Ches shrank. I tried to get to her, get her to run and hide in Hell, but I was too late. Like you, you're too late. Too late for Chesarynth and too late for me, but not too late for the rest of them. You do it, Jez. Join up with the revolutionaries, the real ones. It's what I should have done.'

'Why didn't you?'

'Because I'm dead, Jez. It didn't work right, did it? My conversion I mean. I got clouds in my head like white thunderheads blow up out of nowhere. For a while I was OK. I was a good little moron, did what I was told. When I wasn't in the net I was glad I could see. I told myself it was worth it, and the colours you see when you're in the jet, like you wouldn't believe. Like a rainbow, like singing opals. I'm so stupid that sometimes I even miss it. But I wasn't any good to them. I could see the net like a carbon lattice, diamonds of fire, but it didn't mean a damn thing. Then they did a psych profile and found out I wasn't a real tower.'

Anger surged through him. He slammed his hand on the table with a sound like a pistol shot and the fork hit once and vibrated, high C. 'How could I be? Pinch-rigged, held together with chewing gum. Half the autonomic functions, they're skew-wiff. Think I like sitting round with a catheter up my prick? But this weather if I don't my leg goes into ulcers.' He bent forward, cuddling his head in his forearms. Softly, speaking to the table, he added, 'It used to matter when I could still feel pain. I miss pain, the sharpness of it, the crystal purity of it. I dream of pain. It was the last feeling to go. Lasted long after sex went. And now I sit here, waiting for those gutless wonders downstairs to get up the nerve to put a sticker through me. God knows I try hard enough to provoke them. That's probably why they won't give me the satisfaction.

'A lovely, steel-bright knife. I wonder if I'll feel it? Then I won't have my own endless stink in my nose.'

The shadows dimmed, sharpened again as the day soaked up the clouds. Sand rattled on the back of Jezrael's cloak, trickled into her boots. Silence walked through the room and she thought of the dust silting up the shrink's lungs.

'Which companies, Alex?' she asked.

No answer. Alex was walking the lost trails inside his mind.

She laid a hand on his shoulder. 'Which companies?'

'Carpathia. No, wait a minute, it was Madreidetic. Wasn't it? And Spiderglass.'

Maggie drifted to his side, guiding Alex's hand to the bottles of vodka he had brought, but Alex sat back, his head lolling slackly against the anachronistic grandeur of his pilot's chair. Under the wisps of an old man's beard his throat was strangely defenceless.

No thank-you. Nothing.

Ill at ease with the lack of farewell, Jezrael and Maggie made indecisively for the door.

Alex screamed after them. 'You should have done it! I told you everything you wanted to know and this is how you repay me! I showed you the knife on the plate. I showed you it wouldn't hurt! Come back and kill me, you bastards!'

Maggie led Jezrael down the crumbling stairs into the well of stinking darkness. From the lighted doorway above Alex's voice pursued them. 'You cowards! You low-down yellow bastards. Come back and kill me!'

20

That night Jezrael didn't dance. Nor the next.

On the third night the Magyar watched her seeking her own oblivion under the bright coloured lights at his bar, and said, 'Hear that, Jez?'

'What?' she asked listlessly.

'That's the sound of customers staying away in droves. I pay you to dance, not get smashed. You don't even like getting drunk.'

She looked up briefly from her chocolate and brandy. 'You wouldn't like what I dance.' And the thought inside her head was, *You know me too well now for me ever to dance round you again.*

The Magyar shrugged, turned away. Over his shoulder he said, 'Try me.'

'When we're closed, I will.'

He didn't like it. For the laboured heart-beat rhythm carried in every pulse a foreknowledge that death was one second closer. It was not Jezrael but a corpse dancing, a grotesque thing whose every movement was ugly with the pain of living, and the pictures she painted bruised the air with the colours of self-loathing.

With bitter satisfaction she saw what it was doing to him, to the Magyar, to the man she should not trust. The same twisted pleasure burnt in self-immolation: she knew he'd sack her because she was no good, so that she was right not to trust him.

Before she sank to the drama of staging her own funeral the Magyar did something he never had before. He stopped merely standing there, arms folded. He levered himself from the pillar he'd been leaning on.

The Magyar put on bands of his own, the studs on his pulse synchronizing the controls to his rhythms. A more positive heart-beat lifted the sombre lights to amber that glowed with the promise of daybreak in the soul. Jezrael had an urge to clash rhythms with him but she held herself back, allowing him that one courtesy before he fired her.

Now he was Maggie again, sardonic, not trusting himself to zero-gee but to a fractional gravity that made him bounce as he deliberately upstaged her. He set a rolling beat with a simple bass-line and with effort made his body its counterpoint. She could feel the faults in his timing but it was close enough for jazz.

He wasn't a good dancer but even with his lights a fuzzy flare, he could block out simple emotions in primary colours. It was like a child's picture but you could just about tell through the blur of red and blue and yellow what he meant.

At least Jezrael could. She rejected it at first, impatient with its simplistic, expected message. The stars like fruit so luscious they were supposed to tempt you – but they were over-ripe, odd shapes. Bees, out of proportion over flowers that hurt her eyes, but still they hummed while they worked – if you could call that limping drone a humming. Smiles on a shadow's face and another shadow answered with a lop-sided grin.

Crude as his daubing was, he made her feel better despite herself.

The shadow reached out a forelimb that might have been an arm. For a time the other shadow rejected it, turning away in jerky disdain. The first shadow hung its head. Then the second shadow touched the first and the music went out of sync with overstated joy.

Slowly Jezrael stepped closer, timing her steps to his pre-programmed beat. She shored up his shadows, gave them colour and solidity, but she wouldn't fill in their faces. The hands of the picture touched, held. With subtle movements of her head she sketched in the background: Maggie's bar.

Then she stopped. She didn't know where to go from there.

Maggie walked to her, slowly, trying not to frighten her. Gently he slid his arms around her, held her to him, and the bands picked up the gesture and filled the dance-space with a friendly glow. The gesture wasn't planned for sound-effect but all the same it had a soothing harmony of its own. And gradually Jezrael unstiffened. She relaxed into his friendly embrace and the upbeat tempo took over its work of cheer.

He kissed the top of her head. She made no move to reject him so he kissed her again, still friendly, offering comfort, making no demands. Imperceptibly his hold tightened and her arms stole round him, hungry for the comfort of another human touch.

The light was dim now, a faint yet cheerful radiance. In the privacy of his own dance-floor Maggie allowed himself to step out of character and Jezrael could feel it. With the bands on, there was no way their bodies could lie. He could see her, Jezrael knew, and with wonder realized that he still went on holding her, giving her acceptance. It brought back subconscious echoes of the way her mother had held her on her knee when she was tiny, too small to want anything her mother didn't give.

'Jezrael,' he whispered, and the tone of it sent a caressing resonance through the bands to soak glowing into the air, 'you should have seen what they found in me.'

She didn't pretend to misunderstand. The scars of the shadow-voices were still black around her mind like the bars of a cage.

'That's not all you are, Jezrael. You're my friend, you have courage and humour, and you dance like an angel sings. You listen to the secret wounds of people and you give them what will heal.'

Her head came up in denial. 'But –'

'But nothing.' He stopped her lips with a kiss soft as a breeze; she could smell the sweetness of orange liqueur on his breath. 'Nobody's perfect, Jez. Not even me. You know what I do, a little wheeling, a little dealing. Even

226

though I've never said, you picked it up. You can't do all that and be stupid.'

Rigidity shot through her; she pulled away involuntarily and the movement was a dissonance of viridian light and a cymbal-clash of sound, but Maggie didn't let her go.

'You don't need permission to be what you want, Jez. You're your own person, not your parents' marionette, not the kid your school pummelled into a box that didn't fit. You want to hook up with a bank-clerk, then go ahead and do it, unless you'd rather not. But you're not stupid, whatever anybody says. I could call you an aardvark but that wouldn't make you one, would it?' He hugged her tighter. 'Would it?'

She shook her head and a glockenspiel cascaded bell-like through the air, sending little rainbows flying.

Now she became conscious of his body touching hers all along its length. Jezrael knew she could have pulled away and nothing would have been said, but she felt that she owed him something. Tiny movements in her muscles showed her stiffness and her awkwardness clanged a discord.

His hands dropped from around her shoulders. 'Not here, Jezrael. You can't lie to me here.' He added more softly, his words stroking prisms from the dimness, 'You don't have to, Jez. And you don't have to decide now.'

Once again she refused to pretend that she didn't know what he meant.

She stepped in closer, the minute motions of her muscles whispering in chiaroscuro that she wanted to be decisive.

He kissed her – a sound like a flight of hummingbirds and their colours shone around her. Then, with his master wrist-controls, he set a dance number playing, an ordinary dance that yet made the lights flash out in bright patterns, and she moulded her steps to his. This at least was something she knew how to do. The clumsiness of the past few days fell from her little by little as the music carried them along on a wave of sharing as powerful as ocean and the next time he kissed her, she responded. That too was something she could cope with – to a point.

Clear and melancholy as an oboe in the lilacs of Eden was her kiss but he brightened it to morning and life flowed fresh around them as they learnt each other's touch. It couldn't be love but their sharing was enough for now in her plangent chords.

In the morning she awoke to find him leaning over her, just looking.

'Hi,' he smiled, and his bedroom took shape around her through the fleeting mists of sleep.

Her face, unguarded in half-awareness, wandered through pleasure to uncertainty but she couldn't hide her self-doubt that early.

'You were fine,' he assured her. 'You are fine. You know no obligation.' His old jauntiness came back, looking a little unreal through the peeling layers of plastic on his face. 'You are Jezrael Brown and today is the first day of the rest of your life. So what are you going to do with it? What do you want?'

She rolled on to her back, one arm still flung child-like above her head. It seemed natural to hug the pillow, her forehead furrowed in concentration.

'Hey, it's OK, Jez. You don't have to decide your whole life right now. Just tell me what you want to drink.'

'I used to be indecisive but now I'm not so sure.' She ducked the hand that pretended to swat her and said, 'All right, I give in. Orange juice.'

'Where I come from, we grew oranges.' He disappeared into his private kitchen, the sound-system in his apartment relaying his voice. Jezrael heard the click of his ice-box opening, closing, the sound of somebody doing a kindness for her. It was a sound she hadn't heard since she left her parents in Witwaterstrand and she'd never thought to miss it. Or them. The amplifiers picked up his feet padding back across the floor. 'I used to pick them fresh off the tree for my brothers for breakfast.'

'Not your parents?'

'They were your basic revolutionaries.' He handed her a

glass – real glass, too, not plastic – and slipped into bed as she thanked him. 'They didn't like what Splijt Gmbh were doing with them, subliminals and so on soaking into their brains so that they were turning into zombies. A tone to do this, another tone to do that, they were programmed. Frightening. It was as if they didn't exist between clocking on and clocking off, they said.

'Then at night it got so they didn't even notice us. One morning they went off to the industry and never came back. We didn't know what to do. We were so scared, the three of us, and then the news came on the house computer that the police were coming to get us. It locked all the doors and windows and Andrej – that's my eldest brother, he must have been about ten then – smashed the comp. I can still remember the bang. There must have been about a billion sparks.'

Jezrael sat up, busily arranging the pillows around her, embarrassed now to be in bed with a man, though it had been OK last night when they came upstairs after – afterwards. The dark mass of her own insecurities reared jagged as a reef waiting for the chance to tear the heart out of her. At least with Maggie, whatever he might have planned in the long run, she could bury herself in his reminiscences for now. 'So where did the orange trees fit in?'

He smiled at a memory. 'They weren't real big trees, just dwarf ones in a tub in the front yard at this farm where they took us in. They weren't luddites, just poor people who couldn't afford machines that would keep working on the side of a serious hill. And they were getting on a bit so we ended up doing most of the work.'

Sideways, hiding behind her dyed blonde fringe, Jezrael watched him. His skin was mottled beneath the cracks in his paint. 'They used you, huh?'

'No.' He was smiling, shaking his head, glad to walk back through time to that past. 'No, they did all they could for us and we did what we could for them. Trouble is, unless you've got ten thousand hectares of good bottom land and the capital to buy decent machines, you're never going to do much more than scratch a living off a farm.'

'So how come you're not sitting on a hill on Earth with a goat or two? Whatever made you want to come and live on Mars?'

'Just dumb, I guess. I thought I ought to be a pocket revolutionary too, but I wasn't very good at it. Rather than hang around causing embarrassment to my brothers and dropping people from the revolution in it, I came here and did what I do best – drinking.'

Jezrael chuckled faintly, returned to the subject that was uppermost in her mind – the particular subject, that is, which was fit for public consumption. 'Does Spiderglass have a plant here?'

'Yeah. Out towards the South Pole. And before you ask, no, that's not one of the places I have contacts. Dumb I may be, but I'm not going to take on an industry. Especially Spiderglass.'

'Could you take me there?'

'Nope.'

'So how can I find out if they've got Ches there?'

He snorted ironically. 'Well, why don't you just walk on up to the front desk and ask them if your sister can come out to play?'

'Don't look at me like that! I might do that very thing.'

Maggie clicked his tongue in disgust. 'You think they're going to let you roll out of there on all four wheels? Even my goat would have had more brains. You go in there asking questions about somebody they've got stashed away so carefully she never even gets properly in touch and they'll turn your head into little bite-size brain meat-balls. They won't want all this shrink-stuff getting out.'

'So you're not coming with me?'

'Honey, if you've got any sense at all *you* won't go with you.'

'Can I use your holophone?'

'Jezrael, get real! You think they don't have enough power to trace your call before you've finished dialling? The only reason Mars has got a com-network at all is that Spiderglass sponsored it. The ecofreaks wouldn't have, would they? Who do you think got the contract for all

230

those fibre-optic cables? Who trained the operators? Come to think of it, who d'you think invented towers in the first place? I mean, spiderglass is what they're made of, isn't it?'

'I'm going to do it, you know. With or without you.'

'Make it without. What skin I have left, I need.'

Spiders, of course, couldn't be seen, not even on the streets of Hell. It was too dangerous. Now that Jezrael had seen Alex, though, and knew that someone somewhere was making the attempt to disrupt the proctors' transmissions, it was obvious that that someone, or maybe someone else, was trying to break into the computer network. What else could cause as much disruption at a single stroke? Irrigation, sewage, the thermal grids, what passed for an economy, Mars-U with its secret sales of students – the whole lot could go up if only the right person could get at the computer.

She was angry enough to do it herself.

But first she had a better use for the secret spider – to find Ches.

The more she thought of it the more obvious it became. Only first she had to catch her spider. There had to be one around somewhere but she had no idea where to start looking.

Maggie wouldn't even do that for her. He said, hamming up the over-protecting accents, 'It's for your own good. You'll thank me for this one day.'

'Yes, pop.'

This time it was Zuleika who helped – by cutting the cloth of Jezrael's life to her own twisted design. If Jezrael had known the pain it would cause she would never have had anything to do with the thirty-year-old philosopher – but she didn't know. Jezrael never knew anything about other people's plans until afterwards, and by then all she could do was try to survive the consequences.

Zuleika had been away about her own concerns for maybe a fortnight, but no-one was worried. Zuleika might be away for an hour or a month but she always came back. Under other circumstances Jezrael would have missed the older woman, but now it was a relief not to suffer her curiosity.

It was maybe five or six nights later that she came in out of the autumn frost with some friends to watch the show, and Jezrael didn't know whether or not to be pleased.

That evening the regulars watched the first number – a shallow love-story/song which Jezrael had based on a holopic serial. It was always popular but Jezrael knew she was risking the privacy of her fantasies and fears so now she never gave it all she had. Besides, once she had experienced what she shared with Maggie, she knew more of what love was about. And Maggie wasn't it, nor ever pretended to be. Just a friend.

So there was applause because the routine was slick and easily accessible. But it was only brain-candy; there was no real art or substance to it. Still, it was what most people wanted, though Zuleika sat in her corner by the dance-floor where Jezrael could see she wasn't impressed.

Then a regular said in her deep, hermaphroditic voice, 'Could you do us something new? Something we've never seen?' and there was a ripple of assent.

'Give me five, OK?' panted Jezrael, and took off her bands so that no-one could see her sit cross-legged behind the console, thinking while she sipped ersatz passion-fruit juice spiked with a soupçon of gin.

Other people were filling the place all the time: strangers hiding behind their masks; painted demons and dragons and queens. Jezrael recoiled from their voyeuristic urge to pry into her. There was a dense fug lying in strata that were coloured by the bar-lights. Every time someone came in their clothes were starred briefly with the unseasonal frost; if they walked close by her, Jezrael could feel the cold radiating from them but it was a relief in the twice-breathed air.

The noise-level rose with the impatience of her audience. She stood quickly once the idea had taken shape in her mind, slipped on the bands and suspended herself in a tight curl at the exact three-dimensional focus of the space

232

she had to work with. Then she spun a melody as cold and pure as the crystal harmony of space.

Jezrael filled the dance arena with the shining wonder of Eden. She was its golden liquid sun, the dance of lilac leaves as a blackbird soared from its nest. A cornstalk bent as a harvest-mouse climbed up to home, not knowing that around the sphere of life hung the aching void, aching to reach in and crush Eden until the aberration of life and light was expunged from its perfect desolation. The fragile strands of spiderglass looped across the pit of night to lace one platinum bead of a Witwaterstrand asteroid to another through endless midnight, and the music slowed to the halting drip of single plangent notes that faltered, died.

And silence rocked the room. Only for a moment. Then applause surfed over her but Jezrael still wasn't satisfied. The picture had been clear, the melody pure, but the emotion was a pale shadow of what she really felt, the twenty minutes of the dance a transient ghost of endless threat. Where was the barb of insecurity that ran through the cosiness? The death that stalked her from within? All the audience had taken was the nectar; she hadn't given even a taste of the backdrop of isolation.

Jezrael mooched over to the console, played a jet of air over her body to wipe away the sweat, anything so as not to have to face them. The bunches of people in the alcoves were breaking their conversations open to keep her in view, watching over their shoulders behind their paint and masks and glittering contact-lenses, waiting for another number, pre-packaged ecstasy, but she had none left to give.

Zuleika caught her eye, said, 'Bring up a chair, Jez, and have a drink. What'll it be?'

And when the seat and the wine were placed before her, Jezrael sank down in a gesture of concealment that couldn't work. A sharp-faced girl came up and asked for her thumbprint and autograph, but Jezrael answered wearily, 'Not that one. Give half my ID to you, and when I look up you take a retina-print too. No dice.'

233

So the girl sketched a rude gesture and left, leaving anger behind her.

'Never mind, Jez.' Zuleika's tone was soothing in the very familiarity of her cynicism. 'Everybody's got a right to make a living.'

'Oh sure. But I'm not it.'

Zuleika and her friends smiled. Wit sparkled through the conversation; the philosopher was no dummy and with her plastic beauty added on, she was an attractive package. She had never denied it.

The evening ebbed and the friends – one a gold tragedy mask – paid for everything and went, leaving Jezrael uncomfortably tracing patterns in the condensation around her glass.

'What is it, Jez?'

She tried to meet Zuleika's glance, saying airily, 'What's what?'

Zuleika waited, her elegant coiffure trembling high above her head every time someone left the warmth of Maggie's bar. When Jezrael said nothing, Zuleika murmured, 'Look at me, child. Do you see anything that isn't friendship in my face?'

'I'll tell you what I do see!' said Jezrael forcefully. 'I see plastic, but I don't see anything of you or your intentions. How do I know what's happening under your paint? How do you think that feels when you've seen everything that's inside me each time I dance?'

Zuleika stuffed the clutter of her possessions back inside the folds of her robe and calmly drained her drink. For an instant Jezrael felt desolate; she had cost herself the friendship of the one woman she was close to on Mars.

'Do you want to take a risk, Jezrael Brown? All you have to do is walk back to my place. Can you take that?'

Jezrael was confused. Head on one side, she said, 'Maybe.'

Zuleika stood gracefully.

'Hold on a minute. I'll just tell Maggie where I'm going.'

'You don't need veiled threats around me, Jezrael. You're far too transparent.'

Again Jezrael was unsure. Zuleika had seen through her ruse but it was also true that she needed to explain to Maggie why she wouldn't be dancing with him when the bar closed tonight.

Zuleika waved one elegant plasticized hand. 'Go on, Jezrael. Go and see him if you must. I'll wait for you outside.'

Jezrael took advantage of the fact that Maggie was busy trying to send a reluctant drunkard home. Maggie heard, nodded, but carried on persuading the bleary customer that he'd had more than enough. It was only as the freezing wind outside slashed at her that Jezrael realized she hadn't sorted out where she was to sleep that night. She didn't want to upset Maggie but she didn't want to intrude on him unwanted either.

Shelving that as a problem for later, Jezrael felt Zuleika slip an arm through hers and pilot her through the maze of lost souls that still blocked the zigzag streets of Hell despite the hour and the frost that was forming on their hair. At the limits of the wild town Zuleika turned into a dead end. Jezrael turned round to see only the pale glitter of hoar that polished the empty plain beyond the truncated street.

Zuleika came to stand beside her. 'D'you think the frame is worth the painting?' she asked, gesturing at the crumbling walls at either side.

Vertigo swept out of the steppes on the wings of the cold dead wind of Mars to shake Jezrael to the core. Somehow, within the limits of her explorations, Jezrael had never realised the immensity of the fourth planet. 'I don't know. It's just – empty.'

'It's beautiful.' Zuleika took a pace or two as if drawn into the vast emptiness. 'Look at it – look at the constellations in the chocolate sky. It's so clean. All our efforts, the university, the ecofreaks, and what have we done? We still haven't managed to mess it up with the rubbish of our untidy lives, though we're trying hard enough. You think Hell is better than that?' She jerked her chin at the stark, star-shadowed plain.

Zuleika didn't seem to want an answer but Jezrael clung to the specious security of what was around her. Hell at least was familiar. It was people. And Jezrael couldn't bear to face herself. Out there she would have to. So Jezrael said, 'This is home to maybe a thousand people. This is where they eat and dream and play. Hell is what keeps them safe.'

Zuleika smiled, moving a few more steps from the shelter of the buildings to where the moonlight silvered the frost on her indigo hair. 'You're wrong, Jez. Hell is just a graveyard where people try to hide from the fact that they're wasting themselves as busily as they can, so they don't have to look at what they've sunk to.'

Jezrael followed her a few steps out from the safety of the known. The wind seemed to tear her essence into fragments that whirled away over the shadowy pearl of the plain. From a starless shadow on the sky came a few flakes of snow, lost in the vastness of the eternal face of Mars. Jezrael shivered.

'So tell me what happened, Jez. What put the black hole of death inside you?'

'Let me see your face first.'

Zuleika shook her head and shadows – one red and one green – from distant neon lights danced around her nose, her eyes. A painful smile warped one side of her lip upwards, then she faced the sterile plain, keeping her back to Jezrael. 'You still don't trust me, do you? You don't know much about friends.'

And her nails began picking at the facade of Zuleika the Philosopher.

By the time Jezrael had recounted the Alex incident in a voice that couldn't keep from shaking, Zuleika's hands had fallen to her sides.

'Come and face me, Jez. I'm ready for your inspection.' Her irony was deep and dark.

'Don't be like that, Zulei. Don't you understand how I feel? I'm so scared for Ches – and for me. I'm scared of what's going to happen. I'm scared of what I am.' But she moved around, her back to the frozen equatorial wastes and the polychrome lights of Hell bursting from the dark bulk of Hell into her eyes. She saw only half of Zuleika's face; the other side was a silhouette against the acid glow.

Zulei was young. Younger than Jezrael, once the plastic stopped hiding the contours of her face. The backlit skin was smooth, unlined. It shone jade in the neon with odd shards of plastic casting shadows dark as the pits of Zulei's eyes.

Jezrael exclaimed, 'You're young! Younger than me, when you make yourself look so old.' She replayed her words, found them insulting. 'I didn't mean that. Forgive me.'

Zulei shrugged it off, drifting further into the silent, empty night. 'Now you've seen me, do you trust me?' she whispered.

Jezrael nodded, affirmed it with a quiet, 'Yes. I'm sorry, Zulei. I shouldn't have done that to a friend. It's just – it's just that the whole thing's getting to me. It's like there's nothing left in the solar system that I can cling to because nothing's what it seems to be. Not even Maggle. I don't know what's happened to my sister, what's happening to her now, and I'm scared for both of us.'

Zuleika dismissed her protests. 'Don't you want to ask why ...?' she said, brushing her fingers over the youthful skin of her rounded cheek.

'If you don't mind.'

'Not now I don't. You see, Jez, I've got nothing. I didn't have much when I came to Mars, only dreams. Youngest student ever to be admitted, all that sort of stuff. My family were so proud of me. Fancy our Zulei doing philosophy and semantics, they told the neighbours. Always knew she had it in her. Some company will snap her up as sure as sunrise, and she'll be able to help us out, she's a good girl, she won't let us down.

'Only I did. I knew how much they'd sacrificed to get me here. I was doing everything they'd never been able to. And I was a good girl. I thought I was it, wonderwoman.' Her eyes, hooded in shadow, flashed. 'When I was young I could do anything. I could have flown. I thought I could make my quota.

'But I couldn't. They knew I was a star, and a semantician at that. Just think – the tales I could have told if they'd let me get away from them. Mars-U would have been cooked. I'd have smashed the corporations that were bleeding my family back in the Atlas Mountains. So they gave me a patch out where the thermal grid was thin, under a sun-flower, and what the ice didn't kill, the lack of oxygen did.'

'My sister –'

Zuleika didn't pause. She wasn't listening, or only to herself. 'They gave me a pitch next to another dead star. Your sister.'

Jezrael leaped forward, snatching her friend's arm in eagerness, accidentally spinning her round so that the other side of Zuleika's face caught the emerald light. But for the moment Jezrael was too eager to notice such things. 'Chesarynth! D'you know what happened to her?'

Then she saw the other side of Zuleika's face and recoiled, actually took a step back in horror. For the Martian tan made a jigsaw puzzle of Zuleika's left cheek; between the ruddy smooth parts were frost-bitten craters where not even skin would grow. And the raw flesh unleashed a vapour of decay that climbed upon the winds of Mars and rode ragged around Jezrael.

Zuleika nodded. 'I'll tell you. I'll even take you to her, but I had to be sure of you first. But let me explain something otherwise you won't understand.'

Unconsciously Jezrael stepped sideways to hide her vision from that contaminating sight. Still, she had achieved her quest, and joy and eagerness kept her listening to the young–old girl. 'Anything.'

Zuleika shook her head; the perfect mounds of night-black hair didn't quite keep pace but Jezrael thought it was the wind. 'Anything, hey?' she said bitterly.

Jezrael said staunchly, 'Anything you feel you have to tell me. That's what friends are for.'

'You're unbelievable, you know? I'm seventeen and you make me feel like I'm a hundred. All right, but whatever I say, don't make it harder for me. Just listen and don't interrupt.

238

'Well, Jez, I guess they fixed the Martian tan a special way for me, or maybe they were straight about that and I'm just one of the people it doesn't work right for. Like your sister. So my crops kept failing, or people stole them, and the proctors gave me some ace visual effects. Ever seen pain, Jez? It screams down your nerves like a river of fire in colours you can't even dream of – until it's happened to you and then you can't stop dreaming about it.

'No, don't interrupt. I don't need your sympathy. I'd pledged against my quota so I could send some money back home so then I started to steal. I robbed the patches around me, just a little, here and there, so nobody would starve. I stole from your sister. Just a little bit at a time – at first.'

Jezrael couldn't help it. The words burst from her in horror. 'You! You're Leika! Ches would have helped you. All you had to do was ask and she'd have given you anything.'

'You don't know much about people, do you? Or maybe you just don't understand Mars-U. She wouldn't have given me spit if I was on fire. Nobody would. Didn't you learn anything from your Alex? Now shut up or I won't tell you how to get her back.'

So Jezrael made herself stay still and listen, but the words built up inside her like water behind a dam and she was shaken with an anger she didn't know was possible, an anger that was a pressure-bomb inside her head.

Zuleika said impersonally, 'She knew it was me but she couldn't prove it. What's the point in being smarter than everybody else unless you can get what you want?' Zuleika laughed. 'I still didn't get what I wanted, though. I wanted medical treatment to fix the oxyvirus so I could breathe, have a face and hair, nothing to write home about. I just wanted to be normal. But all my garden-master said was that it would be done when I caught up on my quota.

'Alex sold his eye – but it didn't get him anywhere, did

'I went one better. I sold myself.'

Jezrael's eyes flickered upward but Zuleika only smiled nastily. 'Don't bother looking. No, there's no nasty stick of spiderglass there. What do you take me for? I wanted to keep my brain because it's all I ever had to stop me being factory fodder. Don't you think a tower in your head would be worse than shifts full of subliminals? It would be brain-death instead of brain-sleeping.'

No answer. *How can I when to speak is to risk Ches?* And the name was not just a syllable but a sensory image of shared whispers in the dark, giggles and alliance against the perfection the groans demanded, each sister's body interposed to save her other half from any threat.

'Good,' sneered Zuleika. 'You're getting the hang of it now. I had to leave Mars-U but I kept my brain and I still send money home. I suppose you're dying to ask me how? Go on, ask me, but don't you dare say a word.'

Hating her, Jezrael nodded, and now in her vision Zuleika's elegant robes were a mummy's wrappings that gave off exhalations from beyond the tomb.

'There's a good Jezrael. You're beginning to understand. How I make my living is' – she left a dramatic pause and laughed at Jezrael's anguish – 'I sell people to the Company. To Spiderglass. To the Tjerssens themselves. To the Tjerssens who invented towers.'

Jezrael made to speak but Zuleika forestalled her. 'Oh no, Jez, don't spoil it. There's an awful lot of spiderglass, not just down at the pole, and the depot out by the airport. They've got places in half the industries of Earth, and Crystal City, and out in the asteroid belt, even in your ridiculous hanging cities in the Trojan orbits. You talk now and you'll never find her.

'And you know what else?'

Jezrael did. An awful sense of foreboding filled her and she realized that this hideous girl was between her and the entrance to Hell. One hand rushed up involuntarily to check that her mask was still firm, the contacts still shielding her eyes from the vicious suck of the low-density atmosphere as she stared at Zuleika.

'That's right, Jez. Now I've told you all this, you'll never be able to use it, because I can't let you go, can I? Or I'll never get any other trade. You're my bonus that'll pay for the oxyvirus, maybe even for the skin-grafts. You're mine.'

21

Red smeared across Karel's vision like spilt wine. He made no sense of it, everything had been black so long. Clangings and shouts made a random assault on his hearing. Something was pouring cold as a river into his chest.

'Are you all right?' someone said, and lifted his head in clumsy concern. It amplified his dizziness, the nausea clumping around in his guts.

'I got a headache the size of Steel City,' Karel answered and the words tore in his throat.

'Anything broken? I mean, landing without strapping in is pretty stupid.'

'I couldn't.' Even to himself Karel sounded defensive. 'I was –' but the other had already put him down and was moving off, exclaiming about the piled-up riches to some woman who was shouting about her own treasure-trove.

It put Karel in an extremely bad mood, besides roiling his stomach. Cossetted since before he was born, he didn't like being cast aside in favour of a few old tins of food. He lay waiting for the people to come back and help him, rehearsing a few sharp reprimands, working out how to throw up with dignity. He could hear dozens of them chattering and moving about.

But nobody came back.

Eventually he pulled himself up, discovering aches he didn't know he had. Most of the crates seemed already to have gone, except for the plastiface. The hold seemed bigger, echoing, without the stacks of goods.

Painful light shafted in from the open cargo-hatch on a gale that smelt of snow. Bit by bit Karel wriggled out of the smelly air-suit – one of the mysterious somebodies must have pulled off the helmet or he'd have died – and made his way to the hatch to vomit.

He stood shivering in the doorway, thinking about death, squinting out at a tapestry of whites and greys and turquoise. The sky was an impossible, unearthly aqua and away to his left clouds trailed emerald shadows across a zircon sea. The flinty rocks were all right but the vegetation shimmered bluer than the grass of Kentucky Coal. The air was sharp with frost and stung his nostrils; an odour between citrus and cider made him swallow two or three times to keep down his bile. Wherever this was, it wasn't Earth. Or anywhere Karel should have been. But he was too dizzy to work it out right now.

'Get out the way, mate,' a man said behind him, shoving at him with a sharp-edged crate when he didn't move straight away.

It was too late to step aside. Already wavering with dizziness, Karel stumbled over the sill and half fell on to the blue grass that wouldn't stay in focus. He picked himself up and straightened his shoulders, preparing to give the imbecilic worker a tongue-lashing the oaf wouldn't forget.

The worker spoke first from behind the huge crate in his arms. 'Bloody heretic! Stop slacking and do something constructive, will you?'

Karel literally felt his mouth drop open. 'Nobody speaks like that to me! I'm a Tjerssen. Give me your serial number.'

The man turned sideways with his burden so that his wrinkled face appeared behind the crate. 'I couldn't give a whale-fart if you're Ivan the Terrible. If you wanna eat, work.' Hefting his load, the man went on his way, muttering to himself.

The last thing Karel wanted to do was eat. Have a nice hot bath and get warm, yes. Then be hypnotized to sleep by someone who'd make him feel well again. But eating – his stomach churned again – no.

Trailing erratically behind the man – *He's got to live somewhere, hasn't he?* – Karel made his way down the hill

243

and across the plain towards the crystal lake. A tiny dazzling sun slipping down to the horizon was doing nothing to warm him. Neat round fields lay with their grey earth already turned to the winter frosts; a woman was driving a seed-drill behind a hand-tractor in one of them, walking a spiral path outwards from the centre. She didn't even see him, let alone answer his hail. Every now and then she stopped to throw stones at a flock of chickens before they could gobble up the seed.

Karel could feel the cold air really getting to him. He wished he'd gone back for the air-suit; at least that would have been some protection but he hadn't thought of it at the time. His cheeks were stiff with cold and the wind dragged moisture from his eyes. Thin sleet began to fall from nowhere, or at least not from any cloud overhead. Karel thought, *That's all I need.* The leafless orchards on the hillside offered him no shelter. He put his head down but the wet snow melted on his hair and trickled into his eyes and nose. It was beginning to get dark.

The path wandered upward again to a – *well, a wall, really*, Karel decided, though it didn't look like any of the neat reconstituted stone walls he'd ever seen. Rather, it was like a series of restless medallions. In an untidy collection of colours that might be called green, spirals pulsating to the height of a man, a few of them vertical and others at all angles. At first Karel thought they might be mechanical but as he got closer he saw that they were restless forests of green waving arms that looked as if they would strangle him if he came too close. They were up to a metre long, some of them, with sticky odorous buds growing at their tips. It was like nothing he'd ever seen. Despite the ferocious ache clouding his head, a terrible suspicion began to grow in him.

As he trudged closer the smell grew stronger. It was as if a season's apples had been left to rot on the ground. Karel tried not to breathe deeply because the vinegary reek was thick as water all around him, but his walk uphill had left him out of breath. He couldn't help panting. His nausea returned.

Making one last great effort to stride out and look

impressive, Karel walked between ordinary concrete gates. He squinted through the dregs of twilight. From this close he understood the secret of the medallions: they were cores of rock from some excavation or other, dumped any old how at the edge of the township. The tentacles must have grown on them later, some the shivering silver of olive-leaves, some turquoise and others bright as jade in the owl-light.

Reality was beginning to hit him as his concussion and asphyxia receded. He realized how stupid he had been to leave the empty ship. Maybe the crew were still there and would leave without him.

Maybe the ship had been taken by pirates.

Maybe the pirates were the ones he was walking towards, and he'd been stupid enough to give his real name. *What a chance for Berndt! To buy me into his power. Or just not pay the ransom.*

Ice-water ran down his back. Leprous blue lichens wriggled on the low stone hovels. He heard a squeal of wet wood and a face peered out at him from a window in a rain-slick house.

But it was too late. Knots of emaciated people stared at him, turning away at his approach. From a dark hole in a flint-gnarled shack a very large woman was watching him walk closer through the sleet. She didn't seem very impressed. Karel swallowed the acid in his mouth and looked her in the eye.

'You look cold, brother.' Her own face was red with heat and steam was stealing past her from indoors.

'I am. And sick and sore.'

She interrupted. 'We don't like whingers here. No good never come of railing against God's plan. Are you coming in then?'

The icy rain slanted into his eyes. Karel said simply, 'Yes.'

She turned away without a word, leading him down a dark hallway. Even when he'd shut the door it was like a wind-tunnel. His grey suit clung clammily to his skin. Turning a corner he was just in time to see her disappear through a round doorway. An unsteady red light jumped around her massive silhouette.

Inside, he closed the solid slab of rock and drifted between antiquated kitchen furniture to an open fire. Other than the glow of logs there was only a handful of candles in tin reflectors to alleviate the smoky gloom. They smelt bad, too. He barked his shin on a low stool and swore.

'We don't have no blasphemy round here,' she said, reaching into a cupboard beside the hearth.

'Well, could you put the lights on then?'

The woman turned and pushed past him to slam a flat cake of bread on to the table. 'What's wrong with your eyes, boy?'

He tried to keep the anger from adding acid to his tone but failed. 'Nothing,' he said aggressively.

'Then sharpen them lot.' Pulling open a drawer at one end of the table, she dropped a handful of knives clattering on the boards then tossed a whetstone at him that he totally failed to catch. It caught him in the breast-bone.

'I think perhaps you don't understand,' he said, holding on to the shreds of his temper. 'My name's Tjerssen. Karel Tjerssen.'

'Then sharpen them knives, Karel Tjerssen. Even Saint Paul never begged when he was fit enough to earn his keep.'

And with that she bustled out of the room, leaving him – and his clothes – steaming by the fire.

The thick soup bubbled as she laid the pan on the table. Seven children crowded the benches at either side, one of them a girl almost as old as Karel himself. When he reached to help himself the girl nudged his arm and shook her head slightly. Then the oldest son – a youth with his first moustache and an incredibly pious expression – began to say a grace which seemed to cover just about every person, animal and crop in the known universe. Before he could go on to ask blessings on their relatives the girl interrupted with a hasty amen while the boy was drawing breath.

Katja, the old woman, cut the bread as the girl ladled out the soup. It was cold.

'You've only give the knives half a lick with that whetstone,' Katja complained. 'Nor you haven't said thank you for us feeding you out of our own stores.'

Karel chewed his way through some grain in the dish before him. 'I was about to say that I am Karel Tjerssen –'

'So you said. And I said I was Katja Manikow. What do you think of the soup?'

'It's very tasty only I think maybe there's too much salt.'

'I need the salt. You think I got fat by eating in a place like this? Hah! It's thyroid. I need all the iodine I can get.'

Karel persisted, clinging on to his patience. 'But I was going to add that as heir to one of the greatest industries in mankind, I can reward you well –'

This time it was the pale, pious boy who spoke up. 'Only God can give us the just reward for our labours.' Then he relapsed into contemplation.

Katja beamed at him, an alarming sight with her goitred chins red as wattles. 'Amazing, ain't he? He can pray by the hour together and half the time don't no-one know what he's talking about, he's so full of grace.'

It was no use. Karel couldn't make them see that he deserved special consideration. Or perhaps he was already getting special consideration and he couldn't see it.

In the end he said, 'Do you know when the ship is due to take off next?'

'Didn't know it was coming let alone when it's going. And by the seeming of it the captain didn't know neither. We don't get above a ship every four or five years out here.'

'Er –' said Karel, his suspicion solidifying colder than the soup – 'where exactly is "out here"?'

One of the little urchins said scornfully, 'Don't you even know that? I do, and I'm only five. This is 'Lysia.'

Elysia. Berndt's brainchild, a colony out past Alpha Centauri to spread Spiderglass power through the worlds. Eight light-years from Earth and the board-meeting Karel was going to rock. Eight impossible light-years away from where he had to be.

247

'How –' he began but the words scraped themselves raw in the constriction of his throat – 'how did I get here?'

'It was a merricle,' Katja said, gazing skywards.

Karel glared at the ceiling too but his upward glance was one of exasperation.

'He don't know what Elysia means,' said the pious boy. 'It means like heaven. And everybody's saying that you come through Heaven's Gate to save us.'

They let him sleep on the table in front of the kitchen fire. 'Too many young 'uns to let you double up on one of the beds,' Katja explained. 'I'll bring you down some quilts.'

'I can pay for a bed,' Karel said coldly.

'It don't make a speck of difference how many beds you can pay for. We ain't got none to spare.'

While she was shooing her brood up the stairs Karel took a candle to the front door. The rock slab was solidly shut and in the yellow candlelight frost was glistening around the cracks. He was feeling worse by the minute. For the life of him he couldn't have walked back to the ship. He just hoped desperately that they wouldn't go without him.

Katja brought an armful of ancient patchwork that looked – and smelt – like it had been chewed by half the animal kingdom. Then she said, 'Blessings be on this household, Karel, and on you. Don't you go roaming round in the night after my daughter or you're liable to get bit.' Not saying what by, she slammed the door.

He settled painfully among the quilts on the table, since the floor was stone. Alone, he felt his isolation at this far end of mankind. Back there, a moment and eight light-years away, was his life, carrying on without him and there wasn't a thing he could do about it. God only knew what Theresien, Oskar and Berndt were doing to his stocks.

A log rolled in the fire, sending sparks shooting up the chimney. The sound of it dragged him back from the borderlands of sleep. His headache was worse, if anything, and there was no nurse-chair to ease it away.

The ship will still be there in the morning, he told

himself. *They wouldn't leave me behind. They wouldn't, would they? Not Karel Tjerssen, heir apparent?*

But they had left him to suffocate in the cargo-hold and they hadn't come to find him since.

Morning was a dreary affair which started far too early. Katja came in, one long greying plait hanging wispily over her plain maroon dress. 'Rise and shine, Karel Tjerssen. I need the table for breakfast.'

Outside the sky wasn't even grey. 'But it's not light yet,' he said.

'Of course it isn't. D'you think I'm going to let my kids burn daylight just sitting about stuffing theirselves stupid? Can't do it if we don't hustle. It ain't hardly like food grows on trees out here, though we got our hopes, God willing. Now come on. I need that table and if you want to eat, you need to chop some wood. Just out the back, nearest door to the kitchen,' she added helpfully as he peered blearily through the window. 'And scrape the mould off 'fore you chop the logs. It smells something awful if you burn it.'

After a breakfast of some repulsive stuff Katja called porridge Karel borrowed a quilt since there was no coat big enough to fit him and walked back to the ship. He still saw two of everything unless he concentrated but his headache had become almost bearable.

He found two or three of the officers sitting glumly on the bottom step of the flight-deck gangway. Neither the captain nor the pilot was any help at all.

'No. Haven't got a clue how we got here unless it was Heaven's Gate like all the yokels seem to think. We know where we are all right. But that's Sol right over there, squitty looking yellow thing except you can't see it now the sun's come up.' The pilot pointed towards the southern horizon. You could see how depressed she was by the way her arm drooped. 'And this is us here and we haven't got anywhere near enough fuel to get back. In fact we haven't got enough fuel to reach escape velocity.'

She studied Karel's face. His obvious alarm seemed to

satisfy her and she went on, 'We don't usually land, you see. We just dock at one of the orbital cities and tenders ferry the load back down. I hope you haven't got any pressing business to attend to because we're stuck here.'

Nothing he said could budge them from that opinion.

'Could you at least let me on board to get a change of clothes? Or a cup of decent coffee?'

The pilot shifted over a little, spreading her arms in an expansive gesture. 'Be my guest. But they've taken everything.'

Karel stepped between her and the captain and bounced up the gangway. He was certain nobody would have dared take his things.

They had. Even the bed-clothes had gone. Even the toilet-paper. The only thing he could find on his wild search through the ship was the plastiface, and that wasn't the real thing. He kicked the crate moodily then swore at the pain.

Glumly he went back to sit and talk to the officers. One of them produced a hip-flask hidden inside the console where the navigation manuals were kept, and so they were at least able to take some of the edge off their maelstrom of bewilderment and frustration.

Along towards noon the sun came out from behind the blue-green clouds and warmed them a little, though by that time Karel was sharing his quilt with the pilot who could have been worse-looking, all things considered. The other officers had wandered back to their quarters and Karel accidentally-on-purpose let the pilot know who he really was despite his disguise.

'Oh, yeah,' she said. 'And I'm the Ayatollah of OPEC.'

There wasn't a lot he could say to that.

The sun was setting when Karel's hunger brought him back to Katja's. Dinner was on the table, an even thicker version of yesterday's soup. The scrawny kids hunched up a little to make room for him. He sat through a grace – mercifully shorter because it was one of the urchins' turn to gabble it – and waited for his bowl to be filled.

It wasn't.

'Excuse me,' Karel said. 'I believe you've forgotten me.'

Katja glared at him from the snapping black eyes in their rolls of flesh. 'And I believe in the Lord God Almighty. No, I haven't forgotten you. But when I give people food I expect them to earn it.'

'What about them?' Karel pointed his chin at the children.

The next-but-smallest said, 'I picket the cows and keep the ticks off of them.'

The little one added with great dignity, 'And I c'lect the eggs. You're a grown-up. You're supposed to go fishing. 'Less you're any good with a plough.'

Karel clenched his hands into fists. Well, could I please have something to eat tonight and I'll work tomorrow?'

Katja considered. 'Well, the Good Lord brought us all this stuff off of your ship so maybe it would be mean of me not to share it. We don't usually see this much food from one year's end to the next. But you do your part tomorrow or it'll be dry water and fruitless pie for you.'

So Karel went fishing in a cockleshell boat. That first day the lake was verdigris, spume flying from the crests of the waves like pennants in the wind. They rowed – his hands blistered on the splintery oars – over the paler waters of the sand-shallows out to the green-black depths. The fishers, men and women both, showed him patiently how to fix the rods together. Their bony, callused fingers seemed inured to the cold.

Section by section Karel fitted the joints together until he had a semi-rigid spiderglass probe that jigged in his hands when it touched the bottom a hundred metres below.

'Good lad,' Katja said, for it was her turn to share the fishing that day. She spoke exactly as if he were a child and Karel resented it utterly. 'Now just kind of stir the tip of it around in the mud. If you hit up against anything solid, try it again to see if it moves. If it does, you've got one. Just give us a shout and we'll do the rest.'

251

It was boring and the spindrift numbed his hands and stung his blisters. They rowed a little, stopped a little, but nothing happened. He kept looking round at the blue-green hills but the view never changed; the far end of the lake never came in sight. When the clouds broke apart in the lowering sky light splintered on the waves and the splinters seemed to pierce his eyes. He wished he were back on Earth playing in his palm-fringed lagoon, or baking himself on the hot white sands at its edge with Magrit keeping watch over him while she fixed something sweet and spicy for his mid-day meal. All of a sudden he missed her fiercely.

The day wore on and the lake seemed to steam a little where the waters were darker yet. Then a vile stench erupted from a series of enormous bubbles and all the fishers were on their feet, stabbing electric currents down through their rods to the bottom, shrieking encouragement to one another.

The gunwhales came alarmingly close to the surface of the water as the boat dipped and tilted and Karel clutched desperately at the sides. His rod, forgotten, fell into the lake but the fishers were all jabbering anxiously at the same time and nobody seemed to care. Karel wondered if it meant he wouldn't get any supper.

Something vast and shining came spinning up through the water. Karel shouted a warning but nobody noticed that either. When it proved to be only another bubble that burst its vicious odour over them Karel was glad nobody had heard him.

Finally everyone sat down at once and began rowing furiously towards the shore. When he joined in he didn't quite time his strokes right and his oars fouled the next man's. The boat began to turn in circles.

Real panic spread. Katja yelled at him, 'Now, boy, now!' giving him the stroke but it was more the fear in her voice that made him row in earnest.

His oar hit something. Oddly he found himself dreading her reprimand as he tried to free his oar. But it wouldn't come free. It shoved upwards out of his grasp and some huge emerald monster blasted up fast as a champagne cork to soar overhead like a mountain. Mud-crusted scales the size of armoured cars tipped the boat over. People fell into the ice-green sea.

Something grabbed Karel from behind and he tried to throw it off but a voice gasped, 'Swim for it, boy!' and he thrashed along in terror, the others outpacing him. A shadow clouded the waves around him but it moved faster than any other cloud.

Katja screamed 'Dive!'

Karel dived. The force of the monster's plunge pushed him sideways, the current bubbling green-black and silver in confusion around him. He wished he'd had time to breathe.

He pulled for the air so far above. He could see the sunlight shining like mirrors on the dancing surface just like at home. But at home he could reach the wave-caps easily. The ice-cold water numbed him, leadened his limbs. He remembered the suffocation in the space-ship when Heaven's Gate pulled him out of himself. The water compressed him in its hideous embrace.

Then the monster was coming back up again. Greater terror was beyond him. He had reached his limit. His diaphragm tried to betray him into breathing the glassy sea; he didn't have strength to outswim the emerald death. But he tried.

A floor of green scales pushed him upwards and he found himself floating on the monster's back. People were screaming 'Get off! Get off!' as they watched him in horror.

Karel scrambled over the slippery scales but not fast enough. The monster blew itself to pieces with an outrush of foul gases and Karel was flung twenty metres to land almost on top of a fisherwoman. He clung to her so hard he almost pulled her under and she shouted, 'Get off!' again, embarrassingly loudly.

Treading water, Karel said, 'Does that always happen?'

The woman nodded. 'If you don't get out of the way quick enough it does. People get killed that way. See the

253

'lectric does something to it so all the gas in its gut swells real fast. Then up it comes like a rocket and the gases just naturally blow it to kingdom come. You foul up on the oars and you get a lot of wet fishers who are madder'n Jezebel's husband. Was I you I'd keep mighty quiet for a day or two. Now let's see what's left of the boat.'

Every night Karel went up just to see the ship, just to make sure it was still there. He suggested dozens of ways they might fuel her but the officers laughed him to scorn as they chewed some tasteless stringy lizard-thing they'd roasted. He wouldn't touch it although he was as hungry as any of the villagers now the ship's supplies were gone. Spring crops weren't in yet and the winter's stores were almost gone.

Karel sat on the foot of the gang-plank, a step above the others. He made another suggestion. The captain didn't react, just sat staring off through the gloaming, waiting for Sol to rise.

'Don't be stupid, Whale,' Fionnall, the navigator, said again. 'You need a proper nuclear reactor.' He'd stopped actually calling Karel 'Whale-fart' like the fishers did because Karel couldn't beat all of them but he sure as hell beat the navigator. Fionnall pantomimed an elaborate search of his ragged clothing. 'I guess I forgot to bring one with me.'

The captain said nothing at all.

Karel stayed long enough to soak up the fading reality of the ship then went back alone through the moonless night to Katja's.

The pilot had found that one of the widowers in the village was a better provider than Karel so after dark Karel was on his own. Katja and her brood went off to bed leaving him the warmth of the kitchen.

He had never been lonely before. All his life he'd had companions who'd amused him, servants who looked after him, bodyguards he could tease but who never teased him back. Of course, when he was younger they were all on the payroll, he realized, but they'd all looked up to him.

Or seemed to. Somehow it had never mattered before.

And then there'd been Magrit, and her predecessor, what's-her-name. The first towers. The first ones into whom he'd actually programmed loyalty.

Striding through the blossoming orchards Karel looked up at the night sky through the frieze of petals. *That star, that yellow one, a pale golden glimmer not as bright as the starlight on the leaves, that's where I come from. And they all think I'm dead by now. They probably think it was pirates. Ole probably thinks it was Berndt. Theresien's probably jealous that she didn't think of it herself.*

Would Magrit miss me if I hadn't built love into her?

A shooting-star streaked down into the shimmering lake leaving a ghostly trail of fire that died across the waters.

It's four years 'til the next Company ship's due. And eight years back home again. I'll be old. Even if I can convince anybody that I'm me they won't want me back.

For a long moment Karel wove grandiose plans for his return. He missed the speed of thought in the computer matrix but his black box had disappeared along with the rest of the stuff the villagers had salvaged. For all he knew it was half-way round the planet by now. But even without the crystal-sharp song of the symbols he still had a brain.

It couldn't have been Theresien. Or that bunch of hangers-on. Not a senator in the inhabited worlds has power enough to drive a ship past the speed of light. But they'd be back there muscling in on his territory, shoring themselves up, the murderous bastards. Just wait 'til I come home. I'll fix you but good.

He sighed and picked up his pace. In the meantime there was a long day's work tomorrow and not much to eat now 'til the first crops were in.

It was in one of the lengthy Lord's Day services. Karel was sitting in the coolness of the little church, not listening to the groaning testimonies ('Oh Lord I was a sinner and you lifted me up' – the usual line), just enjoying the relief of resting and trying not to fall completely asleep because

255

Katja would probably say he didn't deserve to eat if he wouldn't accept food for the soul. There were the first wild raspberries ready hulled and washed, waiting in the kitchen for dinner-time. The first fresh pungent radishes. So he didn't fall asleep.

The captain ran in. He didn't even slow down, just ran right in in front of everybody. The testifier wound down, obviously hurt by the interruption.

'We're going!' the captain shouted. 'I can feel it! Come on back to the ship quick.' He was capering in his anxiety, a scrubby, grimy little figure in torn clothes. His lank hair was flying about his head.

'I mean it, son. The pilot's already back. She felt it too.'

All eyes focused on Karel, not quite hostile but not too pleased either. Embarrassed, he mumbled an excuse about calming the captain down and pushed past people's knees until he got to the aisle. Then he hustled the captain out.

'What's all this about?'

The Captain – his crew had never called him anything but his title so Karel didn't know what the man's name was – began running through the little graveyard that would have been bigger if the ship hadn't come. It had been another hard winter and folks that would have died without them had lived because of the food and medicines. 'I mean it,' he called over his shoulder. 'Either we go now or we don't go at all.'

So, sceptical but suddenly caught by the captain's anxiety, Karel ran too. He was thinner now but what was left of him was muscle and his legs were longer than the captain's. He got there first, winded a little by the slope.

Fionnall had switched his computers on; there was a muted humming about the ship that had been silent for so long. The pilot was walking little tight circles of worry at the foot of the gangplank. 'You know,' she greeted him. 'You tell me. Should I go or should I stay? Jack's been good to me.' She rubbed her swelling belly.

Karel stopped. He wasn't prepared for this. Mostly she'd hardly spoken to him since she moved in with Jack. To give himself time to think he shoved the long blond hair behind his ears. 'How should I know?'

'I'm pregnant and my kid's going to be twelve years old by the time I get back. What are my husbands going to say? What if we go back as fast as we came, down the Gate?'

Karel shrugged. 'You want to stay here and starve? Or maybe die in childbirth?' He laughed sardonically. 'Or maybe go back a skeleton after eight years' starvation on board? What do you want to do?'

'I don't know!' she wailed, but Jack came up before the captain did and she fell into his arms. He led her away.

And watching the captain puffing up the hill, Karel thought of his dead grandmother. His dead father. The mother he couldn't even remember. Because of Theresien. Or Oskar. Or Berndt. Or maybe even Ole, the smooth-faced liar.

Karel waited, fretting. Now that he might really be going back his problems surged up vivid inside him. It was as if he'd never been away.

Who knew what the Board might have been doing while he was junketing around the universe? He just prayed that the Gate would send them back instead of onwards to some unknown destination. Now he thought of it, he hadn't stopped to bring so much as a sandwich. They might die out there, a hulk floating forever cold between the lonely suns. *If I ever get out of this alive I'll head straight for Mars. I have to get to my double-edged weapon before they do.*

As soon as the doors were shut, without even taking off, the ship turned inside out through time. Karel screamed and heard a ghost of himself scream, another pale shadow ahead just opening his mouth to scream. He saw his hands moving stroboscopically. The terror arose in him that this was just some con: somehow the Board had found out where he was and this was a missile and he didn't know he was dead yet.

Past, present and future co-existed.

Somewhere the Gate was laughing.

MIDDLE RING

1

Light.

Chesarynth was drowning in light and it had a message. Peace. Love. Security. Acceptance. Beauty inside her, and the beauty was light that came in sizes which spanned the galaxies or spun inside electrons. Beauty was communication, each mote of light shaded with one nuance of meaning and each meaning had a colour. There was a grammar of colour and shape and size, and each shimmering evanescent bubble was ashine with love. With peace and security and acceptance that had no limit.

At first there was no top nor bottom to this universe of shining love and she floated at peace in its centre, gazing at infinity. She was not falling; there was no place to fall to.

Then there arrived a rainbow of stronger colours and she could have wept for its strident spectrum that came to disturb the pastel gavotte of suns, but it had a strength she could not resist and a hundred thousand pullulating meanings that tugged at her.

She didn't want to get closer to it but there was nothing else she could do. Its crassness repelled her but it slid inside her because she recognized it as her name and suddenly there was a dark pit, a chasm, a void, and the gravity of being dragged her down into the dark heart of weight. Chesarynth.

Her hand twitched. Her body jerked out of endless sleep. Her eyelids flipped open, and the world was hard-edged, dull and ugly, and so big, so big it squashed the tiny meanings out of sight but still they hovered on the borders of her mental vision and she would have dreamt her way

261

back into that faërie ether but a harsh voice slurred a saw of sound at her.

Her face sketched a query.

'Are you all right, Ms?'

Now Chesarynth's throat worked – she hadn't known it was going to, didn't know why it should – and her own voice scratched the poor air that smelt only of hospitals. 'I want . . .'

But how could you speak the constellations of wonder with the coarse geometry of sound?

'I know, I know,' soothed the face that swam above her. 'But you can't go back there yet. Soon. When we've fixed up your plumbing.'

Oh, 'soon' is a glimmer in the darkness. The rest doesn't matter. But soon. . . . And *soon* was a flame, a fix to an addict.

She shut her eyes, waiting, hiding from their giants' toy-shop of beds and cubic rooms. Every time she closed her eyes they prodded her awake with their cold-smelling hands or their metal-tasting equipment. Or shook her. Or slapped her gently, until a scent that was perfumed with tea sang through the real air to her and she identified one of the sea of aches as thirst.

Since they wouldn't let her sleep, she drank tea. She felt regret undulate through her system as the hot sweet stuff soaked into her cells and the ethereal stars of meanings left her farther and farther behind. Without them there was a gulf between her and every other thing.

So she clung desperately to 'soon'. Obeyed the nurses' every request. If she was good, maybe 'soon' would be sooner still and she could dance in the meanings. . . .

She learnt to feed herself. To walk. To talk. To face herself in a mirror without flinching: neat mid-brown hair that grew in orderly waves, a little longer than her father would have liked, almost to her shoulders, but not the shaggy bird's nest it had been on Mars. Best of all, though, was her skin that was no longer puffy red mottles of failed Martian tan. *A pity,* thought Chesarynth, *that it still makes the same pathetic face with its weedy pointy chin.* But nobody told her that her face was a pretty heart-shape. They all thought she saw the same in the mirror as they saw every day.

As for the gold ring that sheathed the end of her left fore-finger, a tubular nail that ran smooth and hard all round her finger-tip, Chesarynth wasn't sure how she felt about it. Some days it was a deformity, a stigma that proved she had sold her humanity. Just to look at it was to do penance for her failures.

Then, on one wonderful day, it became the key to that magic box where infinity welcomed her to the crystal harmony of the spheres.

And, strangely, they taught her to draw, copying symbols in cross-section or front elevation, predicting three dimensions. For each accomplishment they rewarded her: they put the jack-plug on the end of her forefinger into a socket on a box they wheeled to her bedside and when her eyes closed, the reward was a vision of her scintillating meanings.

But each time, too soon, they withdrew her finger from the socket. Then she cried like a child in the dark for her loss. 'Just one more minute. Please. Even a second?'

But they took no notice and jacked her out anyway, and the hospital was crammed with the odour of disinfectant and medicines and mechanical solidities that drove the pretty meanings away.

'You hate me!' she raged.

And always they replied, the nurse or the technician or the woman doctor, 'No. You hate yourself.'

Then tears would slide down her face into her hair as she lay crying all alone, remembering how horrible it was to be Chesarynth. Because Chesarynth carried the weight of other people's expectations – pass this exam, wear this suit, mind your manners – oh, you've spilt your dinner, just look at my clean floor. Don't mix with those boys. Ignore them. You have to be better than that. Don't let me down. What would your father say? I won't tell him if it never happens again. Make sure you're back by ten. What will the neighbours think?

Then the – the garden-master? She hadn't been good enough to keep her plants alive. She'd killed them, almost all her little seedlings. Thrown away what Jez had so lovingly grown for her in Nutristem back at home. By her neglect and stupidity Chesarynth had stolen the food from starving Martian babies. Anger was forgotten; the long habit of self-flagellation came roaring back as she remembered the – *the puppet?* (Horror: her mind stood on end, backing from the thought. *I'm wrong! I didn't mean it, the garden-master was right to punish me. I deserved it.*)

And my tutors.

And Alex.

And poor, poor Loretta.

All my fault.

'You hate me.'

'No. You hate yourself.'

But it's you who take the meanings away! Only she never dared say it. Because surely if 'they' knew how wonderful the spinning diamond meanings were, they'd know the box was far too good for the likes of her.

She walked as far as the cafeteria on her ward – they told her to – and walking was a strange bouncing glide. But there was never anyone else there when they let her go that far. It was always dark outside and the stars were vague and shifting. Chesarynth began to wonder where it was. For one thing, the gravity was wrong for Mars. When she lay in her bed, weary with just being, there wasn't that painful drag of Mars weight. Nevertheless, she still weighed more than when she had floated in Witwaterstrand.

She was alseep – there was a little island of light over her bed in the side-room of the empty ward – and someone said in a professional whisper, 'Do you think she's ready for the next stage?'

And another whisper. *(That's a voice I don't know. Some man. Should I turn over and see who it is? No. They'd think I was eavesdropping. And I am. They might punish me. . . .)* 'Oh, I think so. What is it now – four weeks? Five?'

Someone clicked the keys on a wrist-memo – it was the nurse with the lop-sided teeth, because one of her keys always squeaked a little – 'Yes. Five weeks and two days.'

Soft footsteps padded away – *Were there three sets? Can't have been.*

'Right,' said the deeper voice. 'Start her on syntax tomorrow.'

Only nothing happened the next day and Chesarynth knew she was right not to trust herself because she couldn't tell waking from dreams of an endless corridor with people whispering about her behind locked doors.

Time for sleep. A whole day without the meanings and it wasn't fair because she'd done everything they'd asked. *Why can't I have the next stage? Why can't I hang in the night of infinity for ever with the meanings wheeling like stars? Out there I don't have to see myself....*

On the borders of sleep she heard the sluff of the box being pushed to her bedside. Forcing herself to stay still, not to complain because her mother had always said complaining was bad, she waited, trying to contain her impatience so it didn't spill out from her body and spoil everything.

At last! The nurse took her hand – Chesarynth left it limp – and slid the contact in her finger into the socket of the machine. The nurse's soft, slightly damp touch faded and darkness sprang into being inside Chesarynth's head.

It seemed that some of the constellations were less random than they had been. Or maybe the meanings were a little brighter because where their radiance spilled out into the darkness, the rose and jonquil and lavender and jade washed into each other and each mote changed a fraction to accommodate the contiguities, and a perfumed necklace of logic darted away, jewelled shooting-stars too fast for her to catch.

But when she woke up she couldn't tell them because they might take the meanings away.

It was while she was reading one of the books they gave her – by a philosopher called Christ – the next day by the lamp-light that she suddenly realized what that gemmed necklace had said. It said, 'Love thy neighbour as thyself.' Only the beads were intertwined somehow. It was as if it meant that you should love yourself as much as you should love other people.

Chesarynth thought about that for a very long time.

That night, in the starshot silken galaxy of the meanings, Friend came to her.

Far off, Friend was amber and musk, velvet and rose. Of course, she didn't know it was Friend yet. It was only a pattern of meanings that textured one whole meaning and it danced in her night, circling about her, near enough to see, far enough for her to be safe.

Chesarynth felt her own coarse fabric ripple with uncertainty but the bubbles, the prisms of meaning, twinkled cheerful and saffron, and she stopped vibrating. Then, bit by bit, the shining, scented constellation sailed closer, promising – Chesarynth didn't know what. All but poised for flight, she held herself steady.

The nuances of being irised through the strange pattern. Its essence stayed the same but now there was something new in its texture, and it became clearer as it approached. There was the emerald perfume of moss and the gold of oak that spread a sheltering canopy out to her.

Of a sudden Chesarynth recognized a hollow inside her. It was a longing that had been in her for always. Shyly, she crept under the invitation that was sunshine and leaf-jade. And Friend made her whole.

She could taste him, round and warm and citrus, deep and cinnamon. He felt strong as bronze, he encompassed her in a reach broad as a chestnut tree. Yet the caress of his meaning was delicate as the first green fronds of spring.

His texture stroked hers, wove through it until he knew her and she knew herself as he discovered her. Almost, the wreath of her meanings trembled apart.

Because in his shining colours he reflected her back in coral and violet, a shimmer of organdie, pearl and secure. She was harmony in sandalwood, a citrine that sang. She was beautiful.

266

She was Chesarynth and with Friend she was complete.

When they melted apart and the nurse pulled Chesarynth's finger-connection from the plug, Chesarynth felt tears skating down her face, looking for what she'd lost. Quickly though she dried them on her wrist.

What's the point? she thought, drinking the fragrant tea that the nurse held out to her. She smiled at the nurse, or rather, her own smile beamed out to glide over the nurse, over the island of light that hung above her bed, the box with the socket that jacked her into magic.

She sank down into the smooth embrace of the sheets, at peace.

Even if I never know Friend again, I know him inside me. He'll always be there. Because he's given me the greatest gift of friendship. He's given me myself. And he's part of my fabric now....

Chesarynth slept and her dreams were peaceful, strong.

The rose of dawn breathed wakefulness over her. Chesarynth tiptoed to the window, curious now as to what lay outside. There was a garden hazed over by sunlight and held in by a dome. What lay beyond the dome, though, she couldn't tell. It had never mattered before, this world that was too big to hold the meanings. Now it did. Out there, somewhere, was Friend.

In her white hospital gown – *I'm wearing a gown. Where did that come from? Where am I?* – she drifted soft-footed down the corridor to the breakfast room and the balcony she'd seen but never really looked at. Now she found there was a window-catch; she slid it aside and her feet whispered out to the balustrade, scarcely touching the ground.

A freshness in the air spoke of dew. Its moisture felt cool on her face. Like a child she wanted to explore.

Cool stone steps were smooth beneath her bare feet. She danced down them in almost weightless pirouettes to paths that wandered between the flower-beds. Each one led her back inwards to the balcony.

Faster now, the tiles sharp-edged under her heels, Chesarynth turned outwards between the pomegranate trees, the larkspur. There couldn't be much more time before someone found she was missing. The arching symmetry of shrubs wasn't beautiful any more. It was a barrier too tall to jump. And maybe on the other side of the barrier there was Friend.

She abandoned the tricksy paths, forcing herself through a tunnel between purple rhododendrons, trying not to leave footprints on the soil. Branches clawed at her hair and she felt like she had done years ago, waiting for Jezrael to catch up, knowing she was going to be late for school, but she couldn't leave her sister to struggle in on her own. Only now she had lost Jezrael for ever. She had contracted. She wondered in horrified fascination what they were going to do to her. Involuntarily, Chesarynth lifted a hand to her head but there was no disfiguring tower. Yet. At least the socket in the tip of her left forefinger hardly showed.

Only where was Friend? Brushing aside looping clematis, she poised to run but her head smacked full-tilt on a wall of spiderglass. She had reached the edge of the garden and it hurt.

For a moment she was dizzy. Her forehead was sore; there'd be a lump there for sure. She'd be caught out.

Peering past the leaf-dappled reflections that had fooled her, Chesarynth saw only white rocks and black shadows. No life. If there were stars above, they were hidden by the light that streamed from the dome. No, wait – what was that?

Straining her eyes, Chesarynth squinted up into the sky outside the neat polished world of the dome. A blue-green crescent hung there, cupping a light-gemmed blackness between its horns.

Earth.

So I must be somewhere on the edge of – of Steel City.

But it didn't feel right. The dark, down-curved horizon which surrounded the bubble-garden was too far away for this to be some man-made asteroid like home.

268

Wondering, she whispered to herself, 'Then this must be the Moon!' Suddenly, beyond, in the black solidity she could make out the pattern in the sun-whitened rocks: the lips of craters.

'I didn't even know they' – *They who?*

It hit her again then, with force. This beautiful dream-state couldn't last. Couldn't be intentional.

Oh, God. I'm in Spiderglass! I shrank. I'm – a thing. Their thing.

Then the sound of her voice echoed back in memory to frighten her. She pulled through the clutching shrubbery and skimmed back up the steps, realizing she was leaving footprints of damp earth. She stole the time to brush them clear with the side of her hand then slipped back inside, hoping no-one would notice her.

But there wasn't anybody to notice. Chesarynth washed, stuffed her torn and dirty hospital gown into the recycling chute and stole another, even brushed her hair (she checked again; no tower growing through her skull – yet) and then had to find a place to hide the dead leaves and twigs that had cascaded from the tangles.

She peeped round the corner. No-one there. In a moment she had jumped into bed, dragging the thin covers up. Under them, her breathing sounded very loud.

But no-one had caught her. No-one said or did anything out of the ordinary, but still guilt made her jump when the nurse came in with lunch. The day went on as normal: drawing lessons, reading – philosophy again, but no ideas that caught fire in her soul. A whole day.

No torture. No tower spiking down through her brain.

She began to hope that maybe she'd already been rescued and this wasn't Spiderglass at all.

And all of it waiting. Just waiting, because she dared not hope. For the meanings, and most of all, for Friend. Because perhaps – just perhaps – he was the one who'd come to rescue her from the clutches of Spiderglass.

Friend never came while she was in the real world. That's what they called it, the nurse, the woman doctor, the technician: the real world. Chesarynth felt sorry for them. How could they know how much more real and beautiful was the infinity inside her with its constellations of meanings, and the comet-blaze of truth that was Friend, who taught her to arrange the meanings in patterns of logic?

But she didn't dare ask him about Spiderglass and what he was doing there.

He showed her how to weld the ideas she read into structures that were sculpted from beads of meaning. *This rainbow gleam – here. Now put this shine of blue spirals here. And the glistening ruby that means longing – set it in the crystal frame.*

Friend stood back – or rather, his pattern spun off a little way so that she could see what it was that they had built inside the black of infinity.

It said, the stable spire that hung in the void said, *We need just this quantity of silk to make perfection.* And intertwined was the pang of longing for that perfection, with the shimmer of signature that meant Chesarynth.

In the real world, Chesarynth didn't understand. Dressed in flowing trousers and a tunic of billowing rose – they let her have clothes, now, providing she chose them herself by drawing what it was she wanted – she spent hours sitting at the table in the artificial sun over the balcony, the day's book-cube dangling forgotten from her fingers. But the puzzle wouldn't come clear.

The palaces of meaning that she built with Friend in the endless night inside her – what were they for? Why silk? What perfection? What had all this got to do with the cruel terrors of Spiderglass that kept Mars-U as a garden of torture (she couldn't even think of the garden-master; somehow he just kind of disappeared from her mind) so it could pluck poor students into its web of inhumanity?

And though she cherished the times when Friend soared in companionship beside her through forever, always – reluctantly, it seemed sometimes, but always – he would pluck new motes of light and weave them into new shapes for her to read, but the shapes only made sense in their beauty, not in the real world where the coarseness of eating and cleaning and going to the toilet squashed the meanings out of the corners of her eyes.

It was all very puzzling.

But it was what Friend seemed to want. Only – wasn't there a hint of impatience inside his patterns too? The private parts she didn't know how to read? *What does he want? Is it – is it something I'm supposed to do? I would! For Friend I would – if I only knew what it was that he wants me to do or be.*

So one night, when she had jacked into the sudden heavenly night inside her, Chesarynth watched Friend appear with less than her usual eagerness. She had been over all this a thousand times in the real world, the world she privately thought of as the world of things. She desperately wanted to fill in the hollow of longing that pierced Friend – but she was afraid she would offend him. What if he didn't want her to intrude on his being? What if it was her feebleness that made him impatient? If she asked, would it drive him away?

For once she didn't follow his building. Instead, hesitantly, terribly afraid she was doing the wrong thing, she plucked meanings from the firmament. In colours that were crude she wove a strand that said, *I am sorry. You have taught me to read the fires of meaning but I am inadequate. I don't understand what it is you want, or what you have to do with Spiderglass, or even how you got me away from them. You are Friend* – she studied the symbols of Friend's identity with all that he meant to her of acceptance and caring, frightened that she was showing the nebulae of her longing for him too – *but I cannot read you perfectly. I am not as good a pupil as I should be.*

Again he mirrored her meanings back, and he held up the distorted black lumps that were her errors of syntax. Then he built another pattern beside it, one that shone through the darkness, the bright complement to hers: *Here you can't lie, or only to yourself. This is what you built, this forest of meanings, but you don't see it clearly because you don't see yourself as you are.*

She constructed back: *You know what I am, and so do I.
There, the blackened wrecks of meanings, that's me, and
you know it because you built it back for me.*

*No! That was your perception of what you built. This
pattern* – he indicated the gleaming iris of colours – *this is
your meaning as it is perceived by others than yourself.
And you have the right to ask.* Friend's triumph flared like a
lightning flash. *I was incomplete and your asking brings
completion. I wanted you to wake up.* (His meanings were
tinged with the sharp edges of anxieties that she couldn't
comprehend, and joy laved them all away.) *To wonder about
your worlds and what place you can make in them.*

Then, she asked, *you will tell me who you are? And
what will happen when Spiderglass* (a dark, tentacled
threat) *finds out where I've gone?*

Mirth, the laughter of the arcs of heaven. But there was
no mockery, and she shared the fun, the edges of her
meanings meshing with his so that he must have felt her
ecstasy but somehow there was no embarrassment.

I am Spiderglass, he signed, and this time the symbol
was a sunburst reaching out to help the benighted. *But
many more people are Spiderglass too, not all of them
good, not all of them human.*

He spun symbols bright as sugar-crystals: the poor,
dim brothers who were not human yet who spun the
glassy fibres ten times the tensile strength of steel along
which optical messages could be sent, for surgeons, for
miners; or incredibly strong strands to link the orbiting
colonies.

Witwaterstrand! she painted. Childhood security, her
longing to return to that simpler time when her mother
cherished her as a bright-haired toddler. But the edges of
her symbol were darkened by the unholy fires of self-
doubt.

Spiderglass, he said, and showed homes for the home-
less. *And spaceships to bring others to their new-found
lands* – he showed the world beneath its triple suns – *to
bring wonder and mystery and knowledge to Earth. Medicines. Food. Maybe one day, even, instantaneous travel that*

272

we can actually control. And his meanings were hazed in a golden future.

Fear quavered dark mists through her symbol: *Towers?*

Yes, there are towers, and the mechanisms are built of spiderglass. Such towers exist, cruel, enjoying pain. They're not all like that, though. His towers rejected the fear she had of the hideous, dehumanized sadists she had known at Mars-U. They were not puppets like the garden-master.

Just the way he presented this, though, and the fact that he was Spiderglass, struck fear into her. Her mind stumbled over the new/old certainty that the garden-master she had loved was indeed a puppet. She had been made to forget that.

And the meanings that were Chesarynth collapsed inwards in a deathly vortex. Her pattern shrank from Friend in terror.

Friend tried to get her to open up, but she would not. Curled tightly, foetally, she turned inwards, focusing only on herself.

He pulled away from her then, and fearing rejection she shrank still farther.

So, from a safe distance, he plucked meanings from the cosmos and wove them together in reassurance. *I didn't know they had blocked that from you. Yes, your garden-master was only a puppet, and yes, the mechanics of it were built by others in Spiderglass. I can see him, your garden-master, though you try to hide how you felt about him. But he was a trick, Chesarynth, and I am not.*

You're doing the same! How can I believe you?

Can't you believe me because I am Friend? And he resurrected the symbolic pattern she had found in him, the amber, the velvet, the musk and acceptance.

No answer. Coiled in on herself, Chesarynth reeled dizzy across her endless night.

There was a wound in him now, ripping across the light, warmth and fabric of Friend. A world of sorrow scattered the sharp scent of wet ash and brimstone from him and curved rejected from her closed, tortured pattern. Even trying to shield herself from him, she could feel that void

273

in him that he wanted her to fill.

Chesarynth, wherever you go, believe in me. Believe in yourself. Believe my pain. It was a dark, tearing scar across his constellation of meanings, and from its charred edges bled horror and self-disgust.

Because I created the garden-master.

2

Behind her the killing cold of night; in front of her, black silhouette limned with jade and ruby, stood Zuleika. And before Jezrael started to react Zuleika lifted one hand to tear away her fountain of black shiny-rippled hair. It was a wig. With it came strings of skin, leaving Zulei's skull pitted with the strip-mines of her disease.

The wig flopped to the ground. Now Jezrael saw that Zulei had taken a short blade from the coiffure. The knife-blade was a cheerful out-of-place red.

Jezrael's heart beat faster but she forced herself to slow the shallow breathing of panic. Some of Jezrael's confidence lingered around the edges of her mind: she was bigger, older, faster with the reactions of laser-dance. It was frightening but the possibility of her own death was too remote to accept. Death was something that only happened to other people – except there was the ragged hole that the shadow-voices had opened up in her and Zulei was tearing at it and there was death behind.

Zulei pointed the blade towards her and it sent lances of red and green light into Jezrael's eyes. Jez, half-fainting, fell into a fighting crouch, as seen on holopics. But Zulei made no move towards her.

Jezrael wrenched at her heater-cloak, bundling it protectively around her right arm. Still Zulei didn't attack. But there was no noise from behind, only the distant wail of music from the zigzag city, and Jezrael began to wonder if there was some threat she didn't know about.

'She won't recognize you, you know,' Zulei said, her teeth shining evenly in the dark. 'She'll be some brain-dead clerk somewhere, just an interface that isn't even

275

human any more. Or some proctor who can slice someone in two without caring. I don't know what sort of tower they'll put in her.

'But you beg me, Jez, and I'll tell you where she is. And then I'll sell you down the galaxy, and you won't know her either. But I'll have skin again all over, nice young skin and the mind to appreciate it.'

Jezrael said nothing. She was sure this was some trick of Zuleika's to get her off-balance, slow down her reaction time.

Zuleika laughed, and the knife – Jezrael assumed it was a knife – wove hypnotic spells on the air. 'Not even a pretty please with sugar on it? You don't really care about your sister, do you? It's all just part of some act to show the world how wonderful you are, how loving. They can't see you like I do, wanting only your own safety.'

Still Jez didn't dare answer.

'You think they'll miss you? The Magyar will send out word that his precious prima donna is missing? Fat chance. He won't wanna stir up trouble. Besides, enough people go AWOL on Mars that one more won't make any difference. You're nothing, Jez. Absolute zero. You're just a piece of shit and if I stepped on you I'd scrape you off my shoe. You're not worth bothering about.'

Echoes inside her subconscious memories slashed Jezrael until her mind bled: *Mother. Father. The shadow-voices trampling her self-worth.* But she didn't say a word. Letting the words flow over her Jezrael waited, standing loose, as though this were some jam dance session.

Zuleika didn't like it. 'She's in the *Southern* –' and at the same time, she aimed the directional blade of her stunner.

Yet a tiny movement of her arm had telegraphed her intention to strike and though Jez hadn't understood how, still she had swayed and spun.

Her heel struck Zuleika on the thigh. Zulei hopped backwards, trying to regain her balance, her mouth a rictus of hate. But Jezrael launched herself, rolling, this time her feet slamming into Zuleika's middle just as

Zuleika wildly stabbed the button on her stunner.

An agony of numbness robbed Jezrael of one arm; it flopped heavily into her side, dangling from her shoulder, but Zuleika had dropped the stunner as she fell and Jezrael stomped it. The broadcast blade split into mirroring fragments and she kicked the red tube of its handle at Zuleika's head.

'You weren't going to tell me anyway! It was just a trap for you to catch another body. You don't know!'

She knew she should hit Zulei. Knock her out if not kill her. But so many people all her life had told her how wrong it was to hurt others, so Jezrael penned inside her the rage that crushed its poison outwards through the walls of her veins, not knowing the harm she would do herself, knowing only that if she killed Zulei she would be as bad as Zulei was. Her left arm still dangled in painful paralysis.

So Jezrael left her enemy shivering with the nearness of death – for she had felt the fire of fury that radiated from Jezrael – and walked back into Hell. Stepping over the jagged icy rocks towards the bowed walls of Hell, she heard Zulei laughing, but she wouldn't give the mind-catcher a second chance at her.

She should have done.

As Jezrael slipped warily into the waiting tapestry of neon, stone and shadow, Zuleika said, inaudibly, 'In the *Southern Cross* ship on her way to Earth, dummy.'

And the rage in Jezrael was a pain that tightened under her ribs, squeezing upwards to wrench at her breathing, drag at her racing heart. It was a force that she tried to hide away tidily, as her mother would have done, because it was a dark and hideous thing that shook her violently.

And in the last hours of night, Hell's streets teemed with the addicts, the muggers. But Jezrael walked unevenly yet unharmed, because the watchers in the jet and neon ghetto saw her dangling arm but they also saw her face and the ire in it was barely leashed.

Her mind was still seething when she reached Maggie's;

it took her two attempts to key the code into the computer-lock right-handed. The dark in the bar was like the darkness inside her: terrifying. Jezrael knew she *wanted* someone to attack her so she could tear them apart, glory in their blood, and she hated herself. She was scared of what might be hiding in the shadows but she was terrified of her subconscious. The urge to murder split her mind like an abyss luring her to jump into its raging depths.

She walked shakily to the bar through the coral and saffron reflections of light from the sign outside. Reaching over the ink-black counter, she helped herself to a tumbler of Spanish coñac and drank it between shaking teeth. Its stored sun-power fired through her, steadying her nerves; she poured another shot and stumbled towards the stairs to her room.

From a dim alcove came Maggie's voice. She started violently. 'Not sleeping with me tonight, then, Jez?'

She put one foot on the first step. 'Just not sleeping.' Jezrael couldn't keep her tone even.

'Me neither.' He waved a languid hand; the pale material of his sleeve caught the light and she turned her head fractionally toward it. 'Let's keep each other awake, hey?'

'I can't!' But she wasn't sure what it was that she couldn't do.

'Then don't. But whatever it is, why don't you come and not do it here.' No demand, just an invitation. And she weighed Zuleika's words, and the shadow-voices, against her own uncertain judgement, and put her boot-toe on the next step up.

'If you don't trust someone, Jez, it's better to keep an eye on them, wouldn't you say? If it makes you feel better, you can even pay me for the drink.'

That sounded like Maggie.

She stepped down to the level. 'Anybody ever call you mercenary, Maggie?'

'Ah, a compliment. I love compliments. Come and sit down before you fall down.'

Swearing as her dead left hand crashed into a chair in

the dark, Jezrael made her way across the room, sat down facing him. She took another drink. The glass in her right hand still clashed against her teeth.

Her body absorbed the silence that swelled through the darkened room. Slowly the stillness rose in a tide that lapped at the rage within her; her breathing steadied. She felt her pulse ease its vast and painful thudding. This time she could drink with scarcely a tremor. All the same, she was glad she could hide from Maggie in the artificial night, though he waited patiently, non-oppressive.

He waited a very long time before saying, 'Talk, talk, talk, a man can't get a word in edgeways.'

She burst out laughing at the absurdity of it, laughed until she cried, and when the tears came he groped across the table to touch her hand around the empty glass. Jezrael gripped his fingers fiercely and he slid along the padded bench until he was beside her and she wept into the haven of his shoulder.

Eventually she pulled away a little, mopping her cheeks with her wrist.

Handing her a crumpled serviette, he said quietly, 'Here, you dreadful urchin. Use this.

'So where's your sister?'

'I don't know exactly – somewhere in the south. Zuleika told me. She – she sold her to Spiderglass. And her face!'

When he had heard the rest of the tale, Maggie said, 'Your arm'll come back to you soon. Me, I think I'd better take an interest in this philosopher person. Can't have her going around taking away my trade.'

'Is that all you ever think of? – No, of course it isn't. I'm sorry. I'm just finding levity a bit hard to take at the moment.'

'You have to laugh or you'd cry. Try it sometime. Now can we get some sleep?' he added plaintively. 'All this listening has worn me out.'

'But aren't you going to do anything now?'

'Of course I am. My profit's at stake. Ouch!' Because she'd swiped him. 'You use the bathroom first, Jez. Unless you still want to go upstairs?'

In the dark she could forget the inhuman perfection of

279

his plastic face. In the dark she could ignore how he repelled her in the light. But she could not disregard the friendly warmth of his arms that held her safe from herself until, impossibly, she fell asleep.

Magyar skimmed the hired ground-car to a stop behind a ridge. 'Are you sure this is a good idea, Jez?' he asked.

'Nope. But I'm doing it anyway.'

Maggie peered through the frost that was already forming on the canopy. 'Well, I don't like it. You sure you got the right place, Antoine?'

The blind man nodded, spoke up against the weary roar of the airstream that broke like surf on this rocky spur deep in Antarctic Mars, and in his voice was a smile, the first emotional response he'd given them. 'I'm sure, Maggie. I can see the lights dancing bright as a river.'

'Well, make sure you don't show yourself on the skyline up there. Even Spiderglass isn't trusting enough to have no watch on its perimeters.'

Antoine Eyeless still smiled at what he saw; he hardly bothered to mumble an absent reply. 'It's not up there, Maggie. It's down here.'

Impatiently, Jezrael pushed the canopy back and an icy blast of wind snatched it from her grasp. The car's hydraulics soughed as they tried to compensate for the sudden shift of the bubble but against that gale they were all but useless, and the bubble-canopy clanged on the car's shell. All three of them ducked but there was no burst of fire from the ice-bound hills.

Magyar tipped the packs over the rim of the shell: tent, food, oxygen, a mound of technology that was wrapped in layer on layer of padding. Still the hired spider in the back clucked and unwedged himself as fast as he could to go and check his beloved bits and pieces by touch. There was a layer of insulation covering his skull; it looked like cotton wool beneath his crown of star-beads and wire. His movements were stiff and angular.

Maggie claimed Jezrael's attention. 'I still think this is a big mistake.'

280

She leaned on the side of the shell, trying to ignore the fact that already she was shivering. Carbon-dioxide ice smoked all around, making a freezing fog that glowed eerily where the rising sun was trapped in its skeins. Squinting against the gale, she looked unflinchingly into Maggie's face. 'A woman's got to do, et cetera.'

'Oh, preserve me from a woman's corn. It's a good job I've got you away from a lifetime of crappy holopics.'

Jezrael wasn't sure what emotion he was hiding under his alleged repartee, only that she was going to miss it when it wasn't around. 'That's not what they say when the heroine lands dirtside.'

'Sorry, I must have lost my place in the script. Well, see you tomorrow morning. Look after yourself, will you? This could have a drastic effect on my turnover.'

'Oh sure, I love you too.'

And the words quivered uncertain between them until she straightened and waved him off.

The ground-car's whine died away in the distance, eaten up by the wind-ripped fog. The jury-rigged tower, Antoine, hovered around, getting in her way as she cleared rocks from the most level part of the hillside. Jezrael hated calling him a spider. Ever since she'd seen a real arachnid close up she shuddered just at the word.

'I'm sorry,' he said in a voice that was more masculine than his flabby, characterless appearance. But it didn't stop him bumping into her every five minutes as she set up the slithering plastic tent, the heaters. Seeing his ineffectual bumbling, Jezrael wondered how much use he could be, and why he had been made.

Where Maggie had found him she didn't know, but once she had dragged the equipment inside the shelter she was very glad that he had. Antoine might have been blind on all normal frequencies but he knew how to assemble his do-it-yourself rig by touch and she marvelled at his deftness. It was the mechanical accuracy of an automaton. The machines grew around him, balanced against the unevenness of the shiny plastic groundsheet, a blue-black hemisphere of amps and circuitry.

When Antoine finished he looked like a floodlit gantry. Wires upon wires wove around him, binding him to his amplifiers. Jezrael could smell the ozone from his crackling crown over his scent of fresh male sweat. He said hastily, 'I'll be going away for a bit and I guess I'll be ravenous when I get back. I usually am. See you, Jez.'

She sat very still, washed with the absurd embarrassment of the able-bodied in the presence of the lame as he said, 'See you.' Then the feeling faded as the sun's light shifted round through the billowing walls of the tent. The tent was all colours and none, odd flurries of snow snaking over it sibilantly; hardly exciting. Gradually her muscles filled with the aches of motionlessness but she was loth to make the slightest sound which might break his concentration.

At first she tried not to stare at him, knowing how the feeling of someone looking over her own shoulder made her clumsy, but soon it became clear that he was no longer aware of her at all. Antoine's brown eyes lost that blind unfocused look; she noticed a faint smile wander over his face as he began to see more clearly. The nodules standing proud on his skull started to glitter in shifting patterns that she couldn't understand. It was like watching a dance of colours that flowed with emotions faster than the light of her vision. It made her want to cry, the way he suddenly seemed whole and human. His red, lumpy features were transfigured and he stopped being a badly assembled mass of fleshy fragments and became instead a vital man. She wondered who he had been before – and if Chesarynth might be the same inhuman thing. Tears stung her eyes a moment at the thought of her sister losing her identity; Jezrael asked herself if the grief was for Ches or selfishly for her own loss.

Antoine focused on a faceted crystal that was the centre of his banks of equipment. His blind-filmed eyes stared at it, all but unwinking. It was as though he held his breath, his whole being concentrated on that chunk of gleaming piezo quartz centred, as he had told Jezrael, above one of

282

the underground cables laid between Spiderglass Southern and their base on the populated equator.

'So why here?' Jezrael asked, giving an artistic shiver that he missed, even as he had missed the sight of the ice-cliffs all around.

Antoine looked up from his crystal, not masking an expression of impatience. 'The cold,' he said, 'obviously. It has to do with superconductivity.'

Then his opaque eyes stared once more at his resonator, cutting her out of his attention, and Jezrael was obscurely jealous of the quartz which glowed with fleeting internal light. For a while he seemed a shy figure hovering on the borders of a conversation, longing to take part in it, to belong. Then it was as if his eyes were speaking and Jezrael was the one who couldn't fit in, a child among adults. *Memory: the kids in school whispering until I came poling up. Were they talking about me   or was it some great secret that I wasn't allowed to hear? A party they wouldn't invite me to? And Ches would keep me company when nobody else would. . . .*

A cloud blotched the plastic walls of the tent, drew her into the present and still she was excluded. Glancing at the plump figure of Antoine balanced against the slope, she wondered just what was happening. She saw the crystal in front of him flicker with pale lights, and guessed that to him it was no pallid, ice-sheathed glimmer. So what was he seeing? And what did it mean? Did it actually hold some clue about Chesarynth – what she was doing, where she was – and if she were still ... whole? Or was all this just a wild stab into nothing? Had Zulei lied even about this?

Jezrael sneaked a look at her watch. One hour and fifty metric minutes. Boredom suddenly unmasked itself and she started to look ahead. *If he's going to be hungry, maybe I'd better get a meal together.*

Then she realized it was her own desire to be valued, noticed even, that made her want to do something that wouldn't take a minute once she'd started. She eased to a more comfortable position against the angle of the ground and schooled herself to wait.

Four hours.

Five.

The short polar day died in bloody shadows. Antoine sat, colours still fidgeting through his crown, that smile still lighting his face.

It's no good, she thought, *I'm going to burst if I don't empty myself soon*. And though she recognized that some of it was rebellion at the hours of inactivity, she could not ignore her bladder. Pins and needles hit her as she moved upslope to the entrance and her numb foot skated on the glossy groundsheet. She saved her curses until she could shout them into the night – then swallowed them anyway out of paranoia.

It must have been seventy below zero outside; Jezrael wondered how much worse it would have been if Mars were at aphelion. It seemed that the wind had dropped a little with the fall of night. Now the carbon-dioxide snow gleamed white beneath the icy disdain of the stars. Already frost was whitening every wrinkle of her sleeve. Even through the contacts the cold dragged tears from her; they froze on her lashes. Jezrael knew that without shelter she would die very soon and there'd be no cheating here. She couldn't smash the freezing antarctic as she had beaten Zulei. Rage swamped her briefly, sharp and red and black. The crunch of Zulei's head pulping beneath her heel was an ugly lust –

Jezrael fought to fold the anger away, tuck it down so deep inside her that she would never feel its corrosion again – she hoped. She despised herself utterly for being the sort of person who could contemplate the slaughter of another woman with savage joy. Turning away didn't take the burden from her.

Only a moment outside yet the tent's welcome seemed a homely, glowing thing. Its warm radiance drove the shivers from her and she was glad to see that she hadn't disturbed Antoine. The rapture of vision was still on his face as she hunkered over the heater, trying to get the chill out of her fingers. The torture of not knowing what had happened to Chesarynth was sharpened by the realization that maybe he already knew. She wished she'd brought something to do that would take her mind off her anxiety if only for a moment.

Surely he won't be much longer? I'll get the food on. If he didn't hear me go outside, he won't hear me open a can or two, will he? And she acknowledged that part of her longing to be bustling about was to try and snap him out of his trance so that he could tell her where her sister was.

So, soup to drink. And bread that would also have to be thawed. A cannister of stew and one of some sweet and sticky thing that Maggie had said she would love, *trust me.* She wondered if she did.

While her hands were busy rooting the ingredients out of their packs, Jezrael tried to work out just how she did feel about the Magyar, but that was a niggling discomfort blunted by the stone weight of her worry about Chesarynth – and about Antoine.

Pulling the tabs on the thermal cans to heat up the food, she glanced over at him but he was exactly as he'd been all day, close yet remote, unreachable.

Maybe something's wrong? Otherwise he'd be back out of it by now. Maybe the Spiderglass network has got him? Maybe they're closing in on us right now and all I can do is mess about playing cook? And all Antoine did was sit there like a Buddha with that irritating smirk on his face.

Annoyed, she picked up one of the cans – and dropped it again. Obviously the inner layer was punctured because the outer skin was burning hot against her chill fingers. The can rolled sideways down the hill and she scrabbled across the tent for it.

All she succeeded in doing was knocking it farther over the slithering groundsheet. It rolled down into Antoine.

For a moment longer he sat frozen, then just as Jezrael cannoned into him he knocked the scalding can away. He fell back into the amphitheatre of his machines, sparks writhing from his crown to his chest and arms.

'I'm sorry, I'm sorry,' she cried desperately, risking electrocution to yank him to his feet. The fountain of sparks died; he staggered, swinging his head back and forth as if to drive out the pain. Jezrael held him, still trapped in her words. 'I didn't mean to. Oh no, what have I done?'

Antoine shook his head where the glass beads now were filled with smoke; a few of the ampoules glittered still like lightning through storm-clouds, but worst was the anguish on his face. He had seen and now he was blinded. Another of the ampoules shattered; glass spattered her.

'Oh, Antoine, what have I done?' she said again.

Now he held her, his plump hands with fingers like sausages trying to steady her. Behind them rose plumes of steam lit from below by the crackling death of his amps. Sliding their arms around each other they clung together, and it didn't matter that he was bloated, nor that his tired sweat made his clothes stick clammily to his bulges.

He said, 'It was beautiful, Jezrael. So pure, the crystal stars singing a paean of rainbows and each tiny prism was a world unto itself, rich with knowledge.'

Unbearable loss wrenched the words from him, biting into Jezrael with acid grief. 'If only they'd taken me! To be part of that melody of infinite chimes of light! But I didn't know! I didn't know and I hid from them in the semantics lab when they came to shrink me, and I sold myself to someone who didn't know how to do it. My eyes -- my eyes weren't supposed to burn out. They said I'd never know pain again, or hunger. Look at me, Jez!'

He averted his face. 'No, don't. I was young and strong. People said I was good-looking. My girlfriend – oh, yes, I'd had lots of girlfriends, but never one like her – she said she'd always love me. Then I was blind, and fat, and ugly, and my hair sprouted into wires with cold, glittering dandruff.' Antoine faltered, sagging against her so that she could barely sustain his weight. But he had to tell someone of the joy dying inside him. 'And I couldn't see, so we couldn't do any more the things we used to – just little things, like watching the sunset, or laughing at a holopic when we turned out the lights in bed, or me reading a poem to her. And she didn't like going out with me any more because of the way they all stared at me – anyhow, I couldn't go most places looking like this, could

I? What the proctors would give – she was scared, and I couldn't blame her.

'Then one day she was different, and the next day she was gone.

'But at least I could come close to the song of electricity. I could see the dance of electrons. I could feel it, and they let me join in. So pure, so beautiful – it didn't matter to them what I was. It was a fire of wonder, and no-one else could see it. I had no-one to share it.'

Antoine held her close so she couldn't see him weeping, but she felt it. Somehow all his rolls of fat were invested with dignity as they shook to his sobs and his weight pulling at her was a part of it that would be a part of her life forever.

Outside, before his grief had time to clot, the wind yearned a different plaint, but it didn't matter. Jezrael held him, her tears mingling with his. 'It'll be all right, Antoine. They'll fix you up again, you'll see.' She heard her stupid phrase clunk but she hurried on, trying to plaster over his wound. 'You'll be able to dance with the electrons again, you'll be better than ever.'

The endless roar of the ancient winds grew more acute.

He fell, and she rolled with him, cradling his fire-strung head across her lap.

'You should see her symbol, Jez! A matrix of colours that sing of tenderness and acceptance of everything except herself. I'd like to meet her, your sister. She could look at me and I wouldn't feel that horror, people recoiling from me – your Chesarynth wouldn't do that. Only there's a wound in her that I want to plug. Her beauty's aching and I want to make her whole.'

Jezrael leant lower over him, straining to hear the words that he was straining to tell. 'Where is she? What have they done to her?'

'She's on Earth, close to the heart. She's in Asia –'

And the long-dead wind of Mars erupted in a howl of powered transport. It was too deep and ominous a sound to be Maggie's little hire-car.

Spiderglass.

Jezrael stiffened, her head cocked to distinguish what was happening.

Antoine said faintly, 'I thought there'd be more time. I'm sorry, Jez. I was too long. The song caught me – I shouldn't have stayed to watch it. And then they heard me tearing out of the sound-web. I didn't have time to fix it. Run, Jez.'

'You come too.'

'Leave the people who could connect me up to that melody forever?' Antoine smiled at such madness, winced at the fires in his brain. 'Go on, Jez. This is destiny – for me. I'm coming home.'

A shudder passed through Antoine and he lay like one dead.

Jezrael called him shook him savagely, but he only flopped, a limp thing. There was no will in his body any more. She couldn't even feel a pulse when she laid two fingers beneath the angle of his jaw.

Footsteps began to crunch across the frozen rock towards the entrance. Snatching up one of the heaters and her cloak, Jezrael slashed her knife horizontally through the tent-wall, low to the ground. With a couple of tins in her arms she rolled through into the whirling darkness of the antarctic night and pegged the billowing plastic down with a handful of icy stones. It wouldn't fool them for long but it would do for a moment.

Cursing herself, she snaked a hand back inside for an oxygen cylinder.

Then she ran, tears freezing like diamond on her lashes until the periphery of her vision was a refracted blur of irised light, out into the frozen night-desert of Mars.

Ran through the thin black air until she couldn't breathe. Gravity stifled her, hammered her red blood cells. Gasping, she tore off her mask to drag oxygen out of the cylinder.

And fell, comatose, in the deadly antarctic night.

3

In her dream, someone was stroking her cheek with a touch as delicate as a snowflake, only it was softer, more loving, totally sensuous. Jezrael's body arched languorously; her dream-self believed she was nestling closer to the Magyar.

Only the caress stopped. Almost she rose through the strata of realities to wakefulness, but then her lover glided his fingers gently over the curve of her jaw to mine pleasure from her throat. Her momentary sulkiness fled as she relaxed into his embrace, an embrace too pervasive to be Maggie's.

Abruptly she jerked out of her dream, slime congealing on her skin. Revulsion shook her. Jezrael forced her eyes open.

When she woke, the world was blue.

The tall fluted walls were blue.

Their arched apex was blue.

Even the air was blue. It came to her that she could tell where the walls stopped being her skin only because the blue shaded down a spectrum from azure to sapphire.

Jezrael felt the crusted stuff on her face and was frightened. Yet there was no-one around that she could see. Still she wondered who it was that she had been responding to. Obviously some misshapen warped creation like Alex; shame flushed heat all through her that she had been willing to give herself to some disgusting pervert. Revolted, picking the scabbing slime from her face, she strained all her senses.

She was on a couch of some silky padding that opened to her contours in a way that was obscurely obscene.

Nobody else was even audible in the blue boudoir all around. When sound came to her, it was only the whispering of blood in her ears, the gentle huff of air in and out of her lungs. Jezrael didn't even notice it. Gases rumbled in her stomach and she was ashamed.

Dreading to think what the stuff on her face might be, she clawed at it with trembling fingers, trying to interpret the strong odour in the turquoise air around her. Whatever it was, it smelt biological. Hormonal. Jezrael could feel her embarrassment gathering physical momentum inside her, turning into nausea.

But mostly she was confused. One moment she was running and dodging through the striations of ice and carmine and sloe, with the fear that the walls of Spiderglass could see through the ancient cliffs of Mars to where she finally crouched, exhausted. Her throat still stung with the rasp of knife-keen wind, her eyes were sore with the dry suck of the freezing night. In her muscles was the memory of the oxygen her exertion had dragged from each cell despite her labouring mask. She recalled ripping the mask off to breathe more freely of bottled air.

Then –

Blue?

It's a blue tent, she thought. *Cutting off the rest of the light.*

But then the columns of moulding moved in soundlessly and it wasn't a tent after all. For the pulsing of the walls was slow and vegetal and the pillars soared and rose in a tracery of veins and she was in a hollow in some living thing with no way out above or below nor escape to the sides.

She screamed. Her scream rang back to her in a thundering descant whose bass-line was so deep it vibrated each organ of her body and she was sick.

Heaving over to one elbow just in time not to drown in her own effluent, Jezrael was so involved with her physical self that it was only after a moment that she noticed the base of one wall oozing forward to cover her vomit. A ripple of lapis lazuli and there was no sign of it. And the living rafters had closed to little more than head-height. Indeed, they seemed to be leaning over her to catch her every breath, closest by her panting mouth, reaching to her eyes, and the air was thick with poison sap and sharp with vomit.

Jezrael shrank into herself, hiding from the blue. But there was no escape. On her face, beneath her nails, the skin stung blistering.

She kicked where the cornflower walls faded to a thin azure; maybe there would be thinnest. But the stuff took her boot, swelling with a strange elasticity, and thrust it back. And where for a moment a gap had shown between her boot-top and her heat-suit, a midnight vein swooped across the wall to form a bulge that thickened out towards the naked skin of her leg.

Jezrael screamed again; she couldn't help it. Then she groped at her shoulder to where the oxygen tank was moulded around her tricep. Fumbling, fingers clumsy in her panic, she dragged at the plastic retaining clips.

Too long! It's taking too long! Feeling the whole blueness shutting in on her, walls running with cyan drops whose stench was acrid and bile, she wrenched and wrenched at the straps and at last the curving bottle came free.

In desperation she slammed the stop-cock open and precious oxygen knifed outwards in an icy cloud that she aimed at the farthest point.

And the plume of vapour was blue, but the blueness all around it bellied inwards to encyst it in peacock and midnight, and while it was busy she slashed at the palest of the azure walls with the tongue of her belt-buckle.

The blueness split with a sound like tearing wood. Its breath fled outwards into snow-bright dawn and it spat Jezrael through when she would have stuck in the slit. Whatever else it may have wanted, the blue tent wouldn't let its precious oxygen go willingly.

Jezrael inhaled freshness, trying to rid her nostrils of that cloying, heavy scent. She scrabbled away unbalanced, going too fast to stand up. Her face stung; she scrubbed handfuls of wind-blown snow on to her skin, knuckling at her eyelids where the enzymes still clung in crunchy clusters. Most of the snow vanished within seconds, going straight to its gaseous state, but some of the crystals were the hexagonal sweetness of honest-to-goodness iced water.

She only stopped when her fingers felt they would burst with the pain of freezing and, as the adrenalin of escape faded, a lethargy swooped over her. Shrivelled Martian air brought weariness into her. The spinning streamers of fog trawled for sunlight that wouldn't be here for a while, and the snow had piled the purest of pillows at the foot of an ice-cliff. She could sleep here until – until Maggie – came – in the morning.

Anxiety speared her awake. *The last time I slept, the blueness swallowed me.* Then Jezrael shivered again with the memory of the sick lust its touch had awoken in her as she lay dreaming. 'Guess again,' she croaked. 'No more sleep for this child until I'm safe back at Maggie's.'

The only thing was, she couldn't work out which way to go.

Half in panic, half in the laughter of release, she turned and turned on the same spot. *Where's Maggie going to meet us – me?*

But there was nothing in the shifting canyons of frozen carbon dioxide to tell her. Avalanches shook powder into the air; it caught fire in the nascent sun and leaped into blushing fires above its opal roots. Spires of crimson and carmine and blood were the rocks, changing colour even as she watched the new day burn off their sugar-frost coating. The wind caught the spindrift and flung it as a jewelled and treacherous veil into the depths of the ragged sky that dizzied her when contrary winds ripped the clouds this way and that.

Lost.

And the hump-backed blueness behind her spread a flat sheet of flesh as the first sunbeam touched it in the valley of shadow. Any direction was as good as another – so long as it was away from that thing.

Lost again.

Why don't I learn! she thought savagely. *How many times do I have to tell myself not to get lost? What am I, stupid or something?*

But she knew all the same that no-one had thought she might leave the tent which seemed warm now and dense with the presence of Antoine – *Only he's dead now, isn't he? And I killed him. If he hadn't come out here to find Chesarynth for me. If Ches hadn't shrunk without trace. If I hadn't been too dumb I could have come to Mars-U as well, then I wouldn't have been alone.*

If.

Hoarse breaths rasped in and out of her throat but none of them was satisfying. The shifting mist was choking Without the mask, her eyes were dry and sore. She became aware, dimly, that her distant body was freezing.

Maybe, she thought, her mind half-frozen slush that squeezed ideas apart, *maybe I could find Spiderglass even in the fog. Wouldn't it be better to be alive, maybe see things like Antoine – or maybe not see things like Antoine. Not such a hot idea, after all.*

Maybe I'll hear Maggie's ground-car swooshing over the hill to rescue me.

She heard only the wind conversing with the ice, the dawn thaw, the shush of tiny rocks dragged free by the first-light gale, each one a whisper but so many it was the shout of a breaker on the shore.

Then again, maybe I won't.

Jezrael dragged herself wearily up a nearby pinnacle, hoping to climb above the billowing mist so she could see something. Cold bit into her. Her fingers were numb, her palms aching with the sharp chill. Still she pulled herself upwards, beset by thoughts of falling, of breaking a leg, of dying all alone in shadows of vermilion where Maggie would never see her.

The spire reached upwards into invisibility. The curse of permanent gravity. Tired, tired, lungs aching for oxygen. But that was in the blueness. For her mask – but that was in the blueness too.

And finally as she hauled herself on to the ice-slick rock where the sun pulsed fire into her eyes, she saw –

No tent.

No Spiderglass walls.

No Maggie.

All there was around her was endless waves of ruby and ice with the fog crawling beneath her feet.

OK, she thought, *You got me. I give in.*

But it wasn't a game. Even if it had been, they never let her win. *I was the one in hide-and-seek that you never came looking for and I hid for hours from no-one. . . .*

Still, there had been Maggie's arena (the tiny sun was like some red-gel spotlight blazing just to highlight her). *Only there's no audience. But Jesus! If I could dance this!*

If I could live to dance this.

OK, you bastards, you haven't got me yet.

Down the pillar of rock, head afire and limbs like ice. Too scared to look down.

Then her groping foot jarred on flatter ground. Amazed, she looked around and saw the valley surrounding her, its garnet shadows scarfed by nacreous mist, but it was definitely lighter now. She could see where she was going.

The oxy-bottle was clear in her mind, alluring. She thirsted for it, imagining the cool wind of it cascading life into her lungs. *If I last long enough to get to the air. . . .*

Purpose hard in her, she staggered back to the flat sheet of the blueness that was spread to catch the warmth of the sun and in her frozen hand was a knife sharpened by erosion from a rock. It was so cold that it burnt her, so cold that it stuck to her fingers.

Her shadow marked her target. She lifted her arm –

'I never seen anybody come back for a second dose of the blue,' said a man behind her, for all the world as though he were safe reminiscing in some bar of his old age.

Jezrael spun, feeling as though she'd been caught out. She squinted at his sunstarred silhouette. 'Who're you?'

'I'm deliverance,' he said. And shot her.

4

Eight years.

No. Not even eight months. It made Karel scared that he was going insane to think how the Gate had bent and folded his time inside his head. Aurel couldn't trust himself. His mind betrayed him.

It took him a long while before he could face Magrit again. Sure, right after he'd made the captain of the vital supplies ship *Antares* promise never to talk about Heaven's Gate – he didn't like thinking about how he'd done that – he'd called Magrit over a scrambled beam. He'd cut brusquely through her anxieties.

'Of course you didn't know where I was. I was in hiding, remember? You weren't supposed to know.'

He saw the hurt on her face. Abruptly he'd ended the transmission just as she was saying, 'But you look so ill! What –'

But now he was going to see her in the flesh. Here, an anonymous Company shrink checking out the efficiency of Spiderglass Southern, he was going to see the woman he'd enslaved to him by playing God in her mind. Meet the bundle of emotions he'd created with just one of his psych-tech tricks.

It was hard to face. He wanted to see her, to enjoy her puppy-dog welcome, but he kept wondering how she would react to him if he de-programmed her affection. He was glad of the plastiface disguise he was wearing. It would help to hide the feelings that were too close to his skin.

Sooner than he wanted, the sensor at the door of his quarters chimed softly.

Magrit rushed in, the same soft-curled hair between brown and auburn glinting around her face, same soft green eyes misted with tears. Her anonymous worker's suit didn't entirely spoil her figure. 'Oh, I'm glad to see you, Karel!' she said, holding her hands out to him.

He turned away, swallowed, but composure was far away. The picture wall in his underground burrow seemed to absorb him; it was a holo of the South Seas, forested hillsides plunging down to warm waters and punctuated by the vivid exclamation marks of birds.

Still staring at the wall he asked, 'Did you find her?'

Magrit became business-like. 'Of course I did. She was hanging around with a bunch of amateurs in Hell. Some woman tried to poach her but she seems to have got clear of that on her own. By the looks of it she has all the potential you foresaw.'

'So where is she now?'

'Um ... I don't know.'

Karel whirled on her, furious. 'What do you mean, you don't know?'

'I mean,' Magrit said apologetically, 'that we caught up with her at the ice-cliffs just beyond the perimeter. Only before we could get a team out to intercept them she disappeared.'

'What do you mean she disappeared?' It was a measure of his upset that Karel didn't even notice he was repeating himself. His grandmother's training seemed to have deserted him.

'I'm sorry, but somebody else got there first. We found a spider but there wasn't a trace of her.'

'Well, don't just stand there! Go find her! Jezrael Brown is mine. My personal adaptation.'

'Of course. At once.'

When her hand reached to palm the door-switch he said, 'And don't forget. The local workers aren't supposed to know about any of this. Not even her alteration. So we can't keep her here anyway. Assuming you do find her.'

5

When Jezrael woke, the world was blue – and it hurt.
Frighteningly, the whole fabric of her being was distorted
into shades of midnight and lightnings of pain sheathed
every nerve in her body. Even the weight of agony in her
head was blue.

I'm back inside the bluetree

Jezrael clutched at the panicky thought even though it
was obvious she was not. The low, primeval scent of living
plant was absent. No sharp notes of sappy odours textured
the blue air. There was no inhuman obscene caress, no
acid caking on her flesh. The clammy feel of slime on
fabric was gone. She was naked, and inanimate textiles
lapped her skin.

She opened her eyes again, not remembering closing
them to shut out the blueness, but it was still there and her
mind was spiked with pain. Air of azure, her hands
sapphire; a thousand tiny nibblings of alien awareness
pecked at her intellect like so many starving bluebirds.

Hiding inside her head, Jezrael refused to accept the
world of blue. She hunted for memories: the rose and
umber reefs of Mars lapped with Antarctic snowfields.
But it was all hazed over in endless mists of blue. There
was her shadow, stone-chip held high to slash into the
spread sheet of the bluetree to steal back her precious
oxygen, with carmine and frostwhite hemming her vision.

Now all of it overlaid with azure and hyacinth, however
hard she squeezed her eyelids shut.

Hadn't there been a man's voice: 'I am deliverance'?
Then he shot me. . . .

A voice (realtime. Sharp as sunlight on zircon was time-

297

sense that she had never known before. Exactly seventeen point three hours had passed since he –) said, 'How you doin'?'

Waves of data seethed in at her filtered through recognition systems that had never been hers. In emotions that were not her own, waves had a liquid pounding substance to them culled from the beaches of Earth's Pacific Ocean. The voice was sun-warm, rough smoothed down a notch with sympathy; the accent had a home: Santos Angeles. He had been cooking because beef-flavoured steam droplets fell into the air around him in the fractional gravity of Mars, and mingled with the tiniest hint of sweat on his fingers were odiferous particles of fresh garlic. He smelt clean, of soap and shampoo. It wasn't the same voice.

And she hadn't even opened her eyes yet.

He let the seconds slide between them, freighted with gentle sounds. Enmeshed with her jagged, nervous breathing was his own strong rhythm of peace that climbed inside her autonomic systems to calm her – though the pain stayed.

He said, 'I can hear you're awake. I guess you're wondering why the blues have got you.' (Did she hear the muscles of his face slip into a smile?) 'Don't be scared. I'm not gonna let anyone hurt you.'

Jezrael fluttered her eyelids to see him but the blue light still opaqued her vision. All he was was a silhouette that was another density of blue. She slammed her eyes shut again.

'You're safe, honey. And you know you're not in the bluetree.'

(Was that the noise of other people out on the fringes of unknown perceptions?) His voice was a husky purr of reassurance and the shapes of it in her head deepened to an indigo rock of security that she knew, without knowing how, was going to guard her.

She heard the sluff of soft plastic clothing; she tensed but there was no threat. Down by her feet the mattress tilted and steadied beneath his solid weight but he made no move to touch her.

'I seen you dance one time. Your body was like fire and you painted the freedom of Hell. I seen the love you wanted and it renewed me. I'd forgotten all that. You lifted me up, Jezrael Brown, and I'm gonna do the same for you. But I'll never touch you less'n you want it or you're hurt. Because you gave me back to myself. If I kilt you, I'd be killing me.'

She heard a smile reshape the resonance of his mouth. 'And I guess your head feels so bad you think you're pretty close to dying right now anyway. But you're not. I promise you, you're not. You'll be OK. I won't let a one of them touch you again.'

He let his voice drift away and her mind wandered, roaming the cool empty spaces between the homes of Witwaterstrand. Shining beads of silver and jet looped in the sunlight of space – but now they were blue diamonds on cobalt. Her breathing quickstepped.

'I'm going to hold your hand now, if that's all right with you. But don't worry. The blueness goes away in a day or two. No. I won't lie to you. It takes more than a few days but it goes again, just about. I promise you that. Only maybe you'd like a little reassurance right about now.'

She felt the warmth of his hand over hers before he touched her. She flinched but didn't move her arm away and the wash of colour behind her clenched eyelids shifted a tone or two down the fifth arc of the spectrum. Fingers, warm and strong, skithered over the back of her left hand. Sitting there, stroking her, the ball of his thumb soothing over and over but never so long in one place that he made her hand sore, he let his voice caress her into sleep whose dream-depths crushed her in peacock and navy.

Still the blueness when she groped back towards consciousness, but different now, as though the first time had just been her mind trying its new colours out. This time when he came back in to see her, the air was darkest around his form, but when he grinned over the noise of the men in the room behind the door – a woman's laugh punctured the air beyond – and he sat down peaceably at the foot of her bed, the blue paled to a translucence like a robin's egg. Was it vision-ghosts or was there really a cascade of glass-clear strands around his head, rooted in a graceful sapphire stem?

'Hi,' he said. 'How you doin'?'

Jezrael raised her eyebrows in a facial shrug, gave a faint nod: *I think I might live.* Her self-inventory wavered through lapis lazuli.

'I'd imagine you've got one or two questions.' His irony invited her approval and despite herself, Jezrael's lips quirked. 'First, though, I guess you'd like something to drink. OK?'

She nodded again, her throat feeling rusty and in-hibited.

In a moment or two he was back with a warm bulb. He perched beside her and held the plastic container. She didn't have to move far; she took it and sucked.

It was good. Tea and herbs and lemon to sharpen it, not too sweet but sweet enough to put some energy into her.

She looked directly at him.

His hair was a lighter blue than his skin – but still blue. Slavic cheekbones caught the gentle light; one eyebrow was incomplete but the other was angled like a circumflex. It gave his features a curiously innocent air. There were laugh-lines around his mouth and eyes, and he seemed indefinably weary. The skin under his midnight eyes was shadowed but he seemed wholesome, somehow. Fresh, though he couldn't have been less than thirty and Jezrael was still young enough to think that was old. With his pointed chin, he might have been an elf out of story-land. *Mind-picture: her mother, towering from a toddler's perception, changing the story-cube for her daughters. WHERE'S CHES?*

She husked, 'Are you deliverance?'

He smiled. 'Good one. Makes a change from "Where am I?" You want to sit up?'

Jezrael nodded.

He lifted her, tender-clumsy, keeping the shiny covers chastely up to her shoulders. A mechanical whine and the mattress inflated behind her back. *(Another memory: the mattress changing shape while she slept so she didn't need to move.* And panic: *How can I remember what happened while I was asleep?)*

She sucked again from the tea-bulb, feeling its plastic smoothness dent as it emptied, knowing it came from a floating colony like she did but not knowing why it should be used on a steady-gravity planet like Mars. On the point of framing the words 'Am I on Mars?' she stopped, because she knew (*How? God help me, how do I know?*) that he was just going to tell her.

'You're still on Mars. Less than a hundred klicks from Spiderglass Southern, out on the ice-desert. You're underground, in a hunters' burrow. I guess you'd think of us more as wildcat miners, but we follow the bluetrees, among other things, to lead us to whatever we're prospecting. And when you went back to the bluetree for your air-can, Rod prospected you. I guess he's the one who told you he was deliverance?'

Jezrael nodded, then wished she hadn't.

'Nothing I could do about it, Jezrael. I wasn't even here when he brought you in. They'd already started towering you.'

He slipped one hand forward to restrain hers even before she'd started to lift panicked fingers to her scalp. 'Don't touch it – it'd hurt even worse.'

Jezrael looked at him groggily, comprehension bringing fear.

'Yes, you're a tower. But not like the ones at Mars-U, or in Spiderglass. There's different sorts, see. What you've got, you've got imminence. You've got all your other senses, sharpened up nicely. But you've got imminence as well. So've I. See?' He turned his head a little and she saw the blue glass flowering from his skull, its silken stamens drooping elegantly as he moved. 'We know what people are gonna do before they do it, so maybe Rod was right and he has brought you deliverance, though he didn't mean it for you.

'Anyways, I know that you still wanna ask 'bout a

301

thousand other questions – don't need imminence for that – but you need to use the facilities while I'm here, and then I got to go hunting to keep the guys off my case.'

She began to slide her feet off the bed, then stopped. 'I –'

'I know. You come from a modesty culture. Work ethic, and all that. Here, lemme tuck that in for you.' And he wrapped the end of the spun-metal blanket around her back like a sarong. The gesture was both intimate and impersonal and it reminded her of Maggie's physical friendship that never grew into love.

The facilities were a tank in the corner, the top removed as a concession to feminine geometry. He left her by it, that smile in his voice again inviting her to share his levity. 'Back in a minute. Don't go 'way now.'

Because where could she go?

Emptied, washed – now she smelt the same soap on herself with her own feminine tang underneath – she hobbled back to the island of safe territory that her bed had come to represent. And waited, tired out from the effort, (raised voices outside, muffled by the plastic curtains of the door), until he came back in with another bulb.

This time he didn't sit down. From the precise speed of his movements she could tell he was in a hurry. Spurs of deep blue light crowned his head, weaving in some restless pattern like speech that she had never learned to comprehend.

'Better now?' he asked. 'Have some of this. You'll be out swinging a tiger by the tail in no time.'

He was already by the door when she managed a belated thankyou.

Looking over his shoulder, (his tower gleamed, fronds dancing), he grinned. 'No problem. My name's Ember, by the way. Was I you, I'd stay tucked up in bed. See you around.'

Jezrael let her aching body melt back on the mattress. Ants of knowledge were pick-pick-picking at her brain, fighting their way in, and she had no defences against them, but the data they brought were swirled and fragmented pixels that frightened her with their strangeness. One thing she did know, she was not going to attract the attention of the men out there beyond the panels of the door. Whatever else he had left her, Ember (the name was oddly freighted with inferences of his mass, his power, the clean safe smell of him) had let her know indirectly that they were a threat.

Still the deluge, the patter, the trickle of endless blue facts in a world whose colours she didn't understand.

Over and over again she shifted restlessly, the long nerves along her spine protesting, but she couldn't drive the alien thoughts away whatever she did. Finally, in a movement of panic that was her body's scream, she dragged up her leaden hands to smash the invaders from her head.

One hand collided with the glassy tower that spiked into her brain. A storm of pain ripped through her like the indigo fingers of a tornado and carried her out on to a midnight sea.

First, she could walk to the facilities in the silence of her empty room. When Ember was away, no-one came to see her, though sometimes she could hear them arguing outside. She thought maybe they were arguing about her.

One time the memory of Antoine came to her, his heavy body lolling and dying in her arms. But hadn't he thought that Spiderglass would save him somehow, plug him in to the endless dance of electrons? All that day Jezrael was in a fever of impatience for Ember to come back.

Late that night, she greeted him with, 'What happened to Antoine?'

'Explain.'

When Ember had heard her out, blue fire gelled into sapphire around him. 'I guess Spiderglass got him. If I can get away, I'll go look for him, OK? But I can't promise. I'm not exactly flavour of the month right now. Where was it anyhow?'

Old impotence rushed up in her. 'I don't know!'

Then a sudden thought came to her. 'Wait a minute. Yes, I do.' And, frighteningly, her night-run through the reef-cut snowfields replayed in blue inside her mind. *Where did that come from?*

Ember accepted it as normal. 'If he's there, Jez, I'll find him.'

But three days later when he managed to get away without anyone suspecting his real purpose in skimming down south, and Jezrael lay weakly fretting until he got back, Ember could only whisper, 'The Company must have got him. They didn't leave anybody behind.'

'Couldn't it have been Maggie?'

When he said too readily, 'Yeah, could be,' she knew the blue haze of his need to reassure her, and wished she could believe him.

Then she could dress herself – though Ember was right: the others laughed at her for wearing clothes in the burrow, even the other two or three towers, and their mockery made her retreat in teenage confusion when she walked shyly into the crowded common-room. After that, she stayed isolated behind her plastic doors until the day-shift cleared the common-room outside. Only Ember cared enough to come and talk to her; from what he told her of the others, both the towered and the plain, she was glad.

There came a time when he doubled back after the others had gone on the trail taking their cyan hardness with them.

Jezrael was pacing up and down her room in the emotional protection of her old innersuit. There was nothing else to do; on her prowls through the empty burrow she'd already viewed the geology cubes and there was nothing else but tasteless pornography. Sometimes she wondered if Ember watched those too, but she'd never ask. It just wasn't something she could do.

Lecky, the cook, was singing off-key in the kitchen; he was lewd as an octopus but no trouble if she stayed out of sight. He had no short-term memory, which made for some strange dishes but it kept her safe from him. Mainly she was bored, but she knew she hadn't the strength to get away on her own. Yet. So she walked to limber her muscles. Each step was a step closer to running away. Ember wouldn't even tell her what from, but she could sense through the flux of data that came from her paling blue awareness that the others had something planned for her, something that she didn't want. Some obscure threat needled her; Jezrael couldn't stop worrying at it but it never burst into knowledge.

So, oppressed by the sullen silence beyond her territory, Jezrael walked around the obstacles in her room: five paces along, four across, five along –

She started when Ember slid through her rattling door-panels one empty forenoon.

'What are you doing here?' she gasped. 'I thought you were out with the others.'

He hushed her. 'Time we started training you,' he whispered. 'The teams are all out – got a big strike maybe. I came back for you. Nobody here but Khor and he's dead drunk.'

'And Lecky.'

'He don't count. C'mon, will you?' and he gave her a hand suiting up against the outside cold.

'Are we escaping?'

Ember stopped fastening the seals on her utility-webbing. Suppressed tensions were unreadable in his face; all around his head, a flickering crown that also veiled his eyes, blue lightnings wreathed and knotted.

'Of course not,' he told her. 'I can't just let you go.'

Depressed, she finished adjusting her protective lenses and trailed after him, still smearing insulating oil over her face.

Above ground, walls of harsh bright air smacked into her, sending her off-balance. She knew Ember's hand would steady her elbow before it did. And the solid indigo of his intention shocked her.

Because, so gradually that she hadn't noticed it, the

blue had faded from her sight. The frozen tide of rock was russet spumed with amber and sparkled with snow in the antarctic summer light. So the sudden lightning-spark of indigo that jumped from him even as the thought crystallized in his head struck Jezrael with an intensity that shook her.

'You OK?' asked Ember, and his hair was a dark untidy blond whipping from under his pointed hood.

Jezrael said, 'Yeah. It was just –' She turned to face him more fully, curious now to see him in technicolour. The skin of his face was weathered to an even, ruddy tan, not dark. And not blue. His eyes were Celanese, almond-shaped, liquid brown with tiny thread-veins, and fringed by black lashes that were almost feminine in their length.

'I know. You saw my intention, right? That's imminence. That's why they planted the spiderglass in you, see. That way you know where danger's coming from before it hits you.'

She tried to edge in a protest but Ember talked fast to forestall her. 'See, Jez, there's not so many people even here on Mars who can do it right. And the one they got to fix you, he did it real good. No infection, no personality warp. Khor, he said it was some guy they know in Spiderglass itself – you know, they pay him and he sneaks out and does it right here. I only saw him when he was leaving. Real tall guy he was, looked meaner'n a junk-yard dog. He don't have no tower himself, but Khor said he had like some socket on his finger, just plugs it in to some surgery-box and the machine fixes you up real good. And when he'd finished, he sticks them for another two hundred credits – danger money.' Ember laughed. 'He works for Spiderglass and asks for danger-money!'

'What was his name?'

'Karl, I think he said. But I wouldn't go too much on that. You think he's gonna advertise?'

Jezrael filed the information in her mind anyway: Karl, Spiderglass. Maybe he was the one who'd fixed her sister. She walked away a step or two into the frost-sharp wind, then spun back into the lee of the burrow-mouth to face

Ember. She was heavily aware of the point on her own hood that matched his. It was how their towers were protected.

'Look, Ember, I don't like this. I didn't ask for any of it. You seem like a nice guy. Can't you just take me back to the life your friends stole me from?'

Again she saw blue, paler, more transparent, stringing out from him and knew he meant to touch her in reassurance but didn't know if he should. Hunched against the sub-zero air, she watched his hand begin its journey but she ducked backwards and his gesture died into azure.

His lips quirked but didn't quite achieve a grin. Ember seemed almost embarrassed as he said, 'One, you can never go back. Even if you did, it wouldn't be the same. And the only guys who might even attempt to take your tower out are the same kind of ones who fixed Alex. Is that who you want walking around in your brain?'

She remembered Alex's petrified, ulcerating eyeball. 'No!' she shouted. 'And I don't want this bloody thing in my head either. What right have you got –'

'I didn't do it, OK? But you're stuck with it, and I'm stuck with it and there's nothing either of us can do about it. Get used to it, Jez. This is the shape of your world now.'

'I don't want to get used to it!'

Ember just looked at her with his beautiful eyes; a dozen forget-me-not threads of intent died on the cold wind around him.

Embarrassment grew in her. 'I know, I know. I'm sorry. I sound just like a kid. It's just –'

He nodded in sympathy. 'Yeah. They bought me three years ago when I got dropped out of Mars-U before my geology finals. I didn't like it much either, but it gets better. Really.'

The walls of the tunnel-mouth were dark, restricting the pale rose madder of the sky. Jezrael felt hemmed in; her snow-suit felt heavy, the air-bottle on her bicep dragging at her as she sucked on it.

'Can't you at least let me go?'

307

Ember shook his head. 'No, Jez. You think the guys'd let me? I'm no match for seventeen other people. Face it, will you? It wouldn't be safe for either of us. And while we're at it, you can't just slip unobtrusively into mainstream. That tower isn't just gonna go away. You seen the way even the guys here like Khaur and Danjit and Mijnheer – hell, all of 'em – don't take to us towers.

'And before you ask, no, you can't saw it off either. Believe me, I've tried. Acid, everything. That's a Spiderglass special. The only thing that'll touch it is an arcwelder – and it's pretty conductive stuff too. With one of these, "Go boil your head" isn't funny. Believe me – in a while you'd miss it if it wasn't there. Hey, come back!'

For Jezrael was striding out under the pink-brown dome of the sky, knuckling away the tears that spilled out from her protective lenses.

Ember caught up with her and matched his pace to hers. She walked faster. He paced her. Again she speeded up until she was almost running, then laughed at Ember's wry expression as the whole thing developed into a silly race.

'All right. Fine. I give in,' she yelled over the windscour. 'So where do I go from here?'

Their boots crunching over the skim of snow, Ember began to teach her imminence.

'You know what a wolf is, right? Or a dog?'

One corner of her mouth pulled down in acceptance of the irrelevant.

'Well, say you saw a wolf running at you, winter-lean, snapping.'

Jezrael trudged on.

'This wolf – he's a big old fella, right? You only got one shot left. He stops out of range, hangs around a while to check you out, then he starts kind of sneakin' in.'

'What's his name?'

'Arthur. What do you care?'

'I just wondered.'

'Well, wonder quietly. I'm serious about this, Jez. I can imagine there'll be one or two unhappy people if they find out I've even taken you walkies let alone tried to help you plug the blueness into reality. So shut up, OK?'

He looked across at her through the frost and rose of dawn. Jezrael grimaced but kept on striding over the ice-desert towards the shattered Antarctic horizon.

Ember nodded. 'Good girl. So there's Arthur, yards of red tongue drippin' out of his slaverin' jaws, teeth the size of –'

'Of big teeth.'

Ember clicked his tongue and rolled his eyes in exasperation. 'Will you cut that out?'

'What with? Wolf-teeth?' But she subsided.

'OK. Well, anyway, you see old Arthur there crouch down, muscles quivering. His eyes are fixed on you and you know, you just know that he's about to spring. Got it?'

'Ah-huh.'

'So how do you know he's gonna spring?'

Surprised, it took her a moment to find something to say. 'Because you told me.' But underneath her smart-alec answer she could see a mental picture of the wolf. Jezrael swung herself breathless over a bar of rock and down into the wind-shadow of a huge erratic that faced the sharp-cut sunrise. 'Because he's all tensed up. He just looks like he's going to spring.'

Ember squatted, patting the ground beside him. The gleam of insulating oil shone bright on the prominences of his face, dimming and brightening again as she moved past him to hunker down at his side. Ahead, the low morning sun kissed an ice-cliff and a spindrift of snow scarfed brilliantly in a slow-motion avalanche.

'That's right. You can tell what old Arthur's gonna do by his stance, the way he moves his muscles. Trick is, to know just when and how he's gonna move so you can kill him before he kills you. And that's why we got imminence. That and a lot of other stuff.'

'Wouldn't it be easier just to stay away from wolves? I mean, there aren't actually that many out where I come from.'

Ember ignored her sarcasm. Absently he squeezed

309

more insulating oil on to his fingers and passed the tube to Jezrael. She watched the play of sinews and veins over the backs of his hands as he massaged the cream in. Somehow, when she did the same, there seemed to be bits of grit scratching her uncomfortably.

'Doesn't matter, Jez, whether it's a wolf or an animal that's a lot more dangerous. A man. A man, now, he can lay a trap with words, or press a button in his desk and shoot you where you stand. And that's what we got imminence for – but you can use it for a lot more than that. It's fun, Jez, once you get the hang of it. You ever jam with your dancing?'

'Sure.'

'You ever get it totally screwed up so it comes out like shrieks and coloured vomit?'

'You mean there's another way?' Her flippancy helped her distance the odd reality of the blue that wove through her vision. But under her assumed indifference she felt interest sparking into life.

'Think of this, then. You want to see imminents laser-dance. Up to now you always done solos, at least that I seen. And you didn't even notice me though I must have come five or six times. But think what you could do with an imminent! You paint a picture like that Mars now I saw you do one time, empty with loneliness. But if you had an imminent on your side you could have had the ache of the wind and rain crying down from the clouds.'

'I didn't want all that. I just wanted the loneliness.'

'Is that all dancing is to you? A way of jerking off? Don't you know how to be with someone else? Don't you ever want to paint a different picture?'

'I don't know how!' she shouted and rose to her feet to get away from him but he twisted there before her, his hands on her shoulders and his brown-black eyes blazing down into hers.

'Jez, you ever think what loneliness is if you go turning down offers of friendship? I mean, is that loneliness or is it just some arty pose?'

Before she could pull away from him he jerked loose his

310

grip and started back the way they'd come. Not knowing what else to do (though now, suddenly, there was an awareness in her of where the burrow lay, point nine of a klick to the south-south-east, and the trail unscrolled before her taking forty-seven metric minutes at the pace they'd come), Jezrael drifted along behind his back.

All the way to the burrow he didn't speak to her nor wait if she got snagged. Ember moved with an ease that soon took him out of sight among the frost-clawed rocks and left her panting, furious with him but unable to catch up to say a single one of the angry remarks cartwheeling through her mind.

Her fury faded, leaving her bereft. She kicked a spurt of gravel moodily.

Jezrael felt full of sorrow but soon it was eclipsed by the memory of dancing with Maggie, giggling like kids when their picture-harmonics clashed. And that would never happen again. Now even Eiker wouldn't say she couldn't keep up with him – having seen the speed of Ember's reactions, she knew that imminence was sharper than studs. And it was another Jezrael that Eiker had left behind in Witwaterstrand in shreds.

Ahead, Ember turned into the tunnel-mouth, not even looking over his shoulder. *And the way he tells it, it's not even his fault!* He wouldn't talk to her now. Lashing out at him that way she'd cut off all information about who and what she'd become, and why.

No. Not all information. Because the air around her crackled with it, temperature, oxy-content, the very flavour of the rocks. Her own confused purposes shimmered in blue at the edge of her vision.

She had lost herself. *Even if I do get away from here, what the hell am I going to do?*

Loneliness of a different flavour bit into her.

6

For days Chesarynth closed herself inside her mind. She would never commingle with Friend again. Instead she lay listlessly on her bed, rejecting the box with its magic socket when the nurse wheeled it over.

Or at least, that was the tragi-romantic picture Chesarynth had fluffed up in her mind. It didn't work that way at all.

For one thing, it was boring, just lying there doing nothing. Behind her eyelids hung retinal afterfires of the meanings' beauty. She couldn't ignore their entrancement. When her mind's eye tired of the ghosts of memory, her gaze skipped above her bed to the ethereal mobiles whose charm was always changing.

And when the nurse slid a cube into the player on the wall, Ches couldn't help but be sucked into the story. It bespoke action, not passivity, its companionship was better than solitary brooding.

When it finished, there was lunch and music: all her favourite foods calling her with their rich odours of spiced meats and pasta. Handel's music showed her a silver trout gliding through a sun-splashed river in the mountains. And a tall, slim glass of passion-fruit juice reminded her of Jez. Then nostalgia for her sister was a warm memory flying across her mind. She pictured Jezrael back home after a shift at Nutristem, laughing and ranting over some petty injustice, wry with self-mockery, a crusader with no shield but a vivacity she couldn't even see.

No doubt Spiderglass had sent her parents some message of reassuring platitudes. None of them, not even Jez, would be worrying about her. She wished she could go back in time, to when she and Jezrael had shared a room and secrets after Mom put the lights out. She wished she could tell Jezrael about –

Friend? she whispered to herself, and grieved that there was no answer. Because the horror of the garden-master puppet belonged mostly to someone else now, to the person she had been before she saw that meanings were the most important thing in the worlds. And somehow the regret in Friend's banner of meanings cancelled out the bitter mould-taste of failure that the garden-master had cultured inside her.

They wheeled the magic machine over by her bed and though she willed herself to keep up her pose and reject their plain black box, the astral song of meanings drew Chesarynth's finger to the socket. She jacked in before the nurse had time to say a word.

The dark galaxy spiralled around her, each constellation pricked out in delicate shades of fragrance. She melded into it, observing her own flight of colours. Only a handful of her shades had deepened despite her urge to grieve.

And though she half hoped that Friend would wheel alongside her so that she could ignore him, he didn't appear. But what he had left her was the key to untangling the harmony of dancing lights and that let her in to a place which like a child she had always stared at unknowing before.

The universe inside her mind exploded her out from its centre of *I* and other beings poured into her so that she knew their inner selves. The history of Spiderglass began in flesh and blood, but even more in physical minds. She saw the first researchers, long-dead now but their essence still lived, frozen in the flow of electrons. She could not communicate with their static sky-fires but she watched/felt/learned of the realities of Spiderglass on the Earth of a century before, back when industry meant manufacture or service and didn't encompass its environments or political power.

For the tensile strength of monofilament spun by arachnids was the key. *Modify the arachnids,* said the researchers. *Change their bodies and conditions, and you could get fibres like glass, still monofilament, but with logarithmic progressions of possibilities of strength and flexibility, and the ability to resonate light-particles or sound-waves undistorted, scarcely weakened over thousands of miles. Who said the arachnids had to be totally organic? Who said their glassy strands should be wholly of what was called silk? Alter gravity and you could lose the limitations of size. A single thread that could tower to the silver eye of the moon – if you could convince the spider of its need to do it.*

And Per Tjerssen, the founder, had impoverished his life, his family, until his Spiderglass Company put out the first shoots towards immortality. Because spiderglass now webbed the Solar System and reached out to the stars. Company colonies stretched and mewled and grew. Spiderglass could not die: a chain of spiderglass hubs girdled the orbit of Earth. After Steel City and Crystal City came the Metropolis of Glass. Moon-colonies, a fountain of star-frost asteroids, cities and lands from the tundra of Mars to the blooming deserts of Earth: Spiderglass.

Per Tjerssen: there was awe of him in the flock of bubble-gleams that were the meanings of his name. A scent like the roots of an oak in autumn, hard, but contaminated with the spores of fungi in the mouldering of ochre leaves that fell, layer upon layer, where branches of the Company still leached its old power to spread ever wider....

And underneath its weight (were the meanings tinged with suffocation not meant for anyone to see?) were the nepotistic directors back-stabbing for power. Ole Tjerssen. Theresien. A score of names she couldn't afterwards recall. Killing each other with the ruby of poisoned wine. Discrediting their enemies, watching their friends.

Beneath them were the workers. (A sound like the mindless drone of bees; the sound whispered to Chesarynth and she strained her perceptions to hear its sub-text: *like bees they'll sting unless you sate them with*

314

security and dull the thoughts from their minds.) Below even that, the gentle longing of the spiders to spin to the ends of the worlds, forever doomed to frustration.

Chesarynth wanted to comfort them.

Later, real-time, in the depths of her self-abnegation, she didn't connect that with the doctor's brisk statement on her round. 'We've made excellent progress, haven't we? You're fit for duties. Be ready after lunch.'

Spiderglass treated her well on the trip to the spiders of Earth but that was no compensation for ripping her out of her own charmed cocoon.

Chesarynth asked, 'Will I still be able to –' and floundered. How close she'd come to betraying the warm brilliance of the meanings! *Careful!* she warned herself while the nurse watched her curiously, trying to guess what she meant. *If I tell them, they'll take the meanings away.*

Chesarynth gritted her teeth, her lips clamped on half-formed phrases that would give the game away, knowing she wasn't good enough to deserve the shining wonder the meanings sang inside her.

The nurse grew impatient. Chesarynth couldn't help but be aware of it. How long had she and Jezrael observed their parents to forestall their anger? So even without intending to the nurse could not help but give out signals Chesarynth could read: the heavier exhalation, the pale tightness round the lips.

Hastily (so she didn't annoy the nurse more and drive the box of infinity quickly out of reach), Chesarynth stuttered, 'Will I – will you be sending the black machine with me?'

The nurse raised her eyebrows in adult surprise at such a childish worry. 'Of course not. We'll be needing it here. Now hurry up, will you? We've got a lot to do if you're going to make the shuttle.'

The royal 'we' of the medical profession.

Chesarynth didn't miss the impersonal attentions of the technician and the nurse, but the magic box stayed firmly where it was in the suite in the house on the 'dark' side of the moon. However pleased she was to revel in the shimmersilk robes of garnet and lavender, their perfumed delight was as insubstantial as light through caramel compared with the security of the only place the freshborn Chesarynth knew – and the gateway to the starscape of meanings called through the tides of her blood. Mars was merely a sad story that somebody else had told her, but leaving the meanings was worse than unrequited love. Not even her nervousness about travelling on her own could make that go away.

At least she could revel in the bright meanings in which Friend had painted her, had accepted her.

First there was the curving trip in a white car that rocked through the mag-lev tunnels to the spaceport. All alone on the snowy contour-couch, she clung to the thought that she was going to comfort the spiders; to twine the jewelled rain of her meanings through the web of their unfulfilment.

So there has to be another black box, doesn't there? Please? Or how can I look after the poor things?

Chesarynth tried to swamp the thought that the box might be only a therapist's tool. *I'm supposed to be cured but now I'm an addict as well as a failure. . . .*

And who is Friend anyway? What if he's not real?

An idea she couldn't accept. She veered from it, remembering the human warmth of him. *He – he wouldn't leave me in meaningless dark forever. He's not that cruel.*

Is he?

He said he made the – the garden-master.

Only I got angry with him and he didn't come back. What have I done?

She tried to cling to her comforting belief that somewhere in the Company was Friend with all that his glow of meanings implied; the feel of him was still clear in her mind. *Out there I'll find him.* The desire for his total understanding was the bright song of a chanticleer to greet the longed-for dawn; she had no idea that the longing had been seeded amongst the far-flung auroras of the meanings he had programmed into her magic box. It was a hearth to comfort her, a homeland up ahead beyond the lonely journey in the tunnels of claustrophobia beneath the surface of the Moon.

The white carriage swayed, slowing. Other cars shot out of side-tunnels, frightening her with their suddenness.

Abruptly, signs for the Earth-terminal glowed red. The speed of her car was still so great that it took Chesarynth a while to realize the signs weren't complete. In fact they were partial letters of rubescent neon repeated over and over again that blinked past too quickly to separate each one from the next fragment. They blended together to form one flowing alert.

Never quite stationary, the mag-lev decanted her on a windy platform and whined away into the cavernous tunnel. Above her, the vault seemed so high it should have had rag-clouds like Mars, but it was unearthly white.

Everything they had given her (except the finger-plug that jacked her into infinity) fitted into one bag that didn't seem to belong to her. Chesarynth gripped it convulsively at the strange sight of people milling around. It had been so long since she'd seen so many people all at once.

I mustn't miss my flight!

Feeling small and insignificant, Chesarynth summoned up the courage to move. The skirt of her lavender robe flew trickwise round her legs, fielding her first step before she could quite make it. She almost fell, almost flew.

She stood a moment, collecting herself, and a thought coalesced like the red signs had: *I'm a baggy now!* Fringing this stunning awareness came the long-forgotten knowledge of status.

In the seconds when Chesarynth was coming to realize that she actually mattered, another white car distorted the draughts with its brake-force. Someone else was blown out by the cool-warm gale, tottering into her as the car howled away.

Is it Friend? thought Chesarynth, sure that something about him would give himself away. But from the tall, hawk-faced man beside her came nothing of the subtle serenity she hoped for, only a sense of controlled power

317

that dispersed when he said prosaically, 'I'm sorry, did I kick your ankle? It's the wind in here.'

'It's OK. Excuse me, do you know which is the way for Earth?'

Already half a stride ahead of her, he threw the words over his shoulder. 'Up the roll-ramp and keep left. You can't miss it.'

She followed him, buffetted by the gale of other cars arriving, but she couldn't walk that fast in her new-won skirts. The tall, dark-faced man seemed to have no problem managing his robes, though his haste didn't do him much good. He was still at the barriers that funnelled the mob into a line under the cynical eyes of a guard when she struggled up behind him.

Waiting her turn, trying not to feel overwhelmed by the noise in the bustling concourse, Chesarynth watched how long it took each person ahead of her. For each one the clerk jacked in to his unit to check their ID and match it to their personalized ticket.

'That's progress,' said a fat man behind her to a child. 'Everything takes twice as long now they got so much data on the computers.'

Chesarynth shuffled forward a place as the serpent line moved up. She reckoned it must take all of eight or nine metric minutes per person. That meant maybe point six-four of an hour.

Only the hawk-faced man ahead of her just side-stepped the line. He waved his ID and smiled and the clerk didn't even jack in to check it. The woman guard almost fell over herself dropping the barrier-field to let the guy through. Chesarynth followed him visually until his white robes disappeared into the VIP lounge. She wondered who he was to have so much power.

That still meant she had fifty-six metric minutes to wait until they scrutinized her ticket-chip.

But what would happen once she got to Earth she had no idea.

7

A pinwheel of impressions: the crowded shuttle with a curry-scented woman overflowing the seat beside her; the drag of acceleration and the ponderous fall to Earth, heart-stopping jolts as atmosphere tricked the craft. The tedium of disembarkation while she booted her carry-sac in a full one-gee through the murmurous shuffle to Customs.

Something about the air smelt different. Dense with non-mechanical smells. Unknown.

And over all hummed and shimmered the warring coloured adverts for Spiderglass and Madreidetic and Usines du Rhône with a dozen others belting out music and olfacts that dizzied her to nausea.

Someone around her – she couldn't see who in the dark forest of heads and frame-bags – was talking a different language. Unease stretched out in Chesarynth's body; a pulse beat in the side of her head.

'Have a nice stay,' said the customs official, but it wasn't to her.

What am I supposed to do now? she panicked in the vast, echoing hall. *Where am I supposed to go?*

'Ms Brown Chesarynth?'

She spun to find a little bald woman – Chesarynth's mind seized upon the woman's finger-socket as though it were the badge of some sisterhood – and said, 'Yes.'

Satisfied but not human enough to be a sister, the woman held up a tiny version of the black box. Chesarynth felt conspicuous; people around were staring at them, but it was the first time in her weary day's travel that she had seen a box and it called to the echoes of

319

firesong that the one on the Moon had left in her mind. A vertical lust shivered through her, connecting mind and viscera. She couldn't help it. All the centres of pleasure flared with longing and Chesarynth jacked in.

The hall winked out. Instead, from the spangled endless night that dimmed the hall, meanings shone. They were not the musk-and-amber subtleties of Friend. Hard-edged, smelling distastefully of banknotes on snow, they sketched for her, faster than light, a helix of numbers. The symbols had a tinge of feminine superiority, an aura of vast power that was taken for granted. A neat dollop of anxiety cored the figure and stoppered it with a ridiculously short time-limit. Hidden among its sunburst symbols was an obscure, sadistic pleasure. Chesarynth was sure she wasn't supposed to see that.

The message disappeared leaving only the galaxy of her own thoughts in the infinite night of meanings.

Time-limit. Anxiety. A message I've got to work out. Time-limit.

It's a test, she realized. *If I make a mess of it that woman is going to be so glad. She doesn't want Friend to be right about me. (Amazement: she doesn't like Friend. She wants to prove him wrong so she can slap me down. She hates even using the meanings the way he helped design them. She can't hear beauty singing through them like I can! She doesn't even know I can read her sub-text!)*

Chesarynth wasted precious moments on amazement that she could appreciate something the powerful woman could not. Echoes of Friend's admiration came back to her, explained now. *So that was why I had all those art lessons! To teach me to perceive the shades of beauty and the shades of meaning....* And the shaven-headed messenger was just that, a messenger. The symbols didn't originate from her.

Time dissipated. *I've got to solve it or she'll just re-route me to some tedious filing-clerk's job! I can't let Friend down after all his faith in me.*

Quickly Chesarynth re-hung a memory of the helix in front of her mental gaze. It was imperfect. Its slight irregularity could be either intentional or an accident due to the hard-edged woman's discomfort with the beads of meaning.

But it was all so obvious. From the taint of sadism, the hint of superiority, the woman evidently wanted her to fail. And the cryptic little message offered Chesarynth just enough information to do something – *if only I can decide what. Where am I supposed to go?*

Triumph: that was it. It was clearly some sort of code. Co-ordinates. An address whose doors would be forever shut unless she got there soon.

With an artist's skill Chesarynth conceptualized the hard-edged grey-green symbols in different arrangements, in different colours and shapes. Only one arrangement looked as though it belonged together: *those two lines of dots and blanks, they must be binary numbers. And that, then, all that must be the name of the strand. The street, or whatever they call it here. So if it's a name, and not a visual identification – no, doesn't look like anything I've ever seen – then if it's letters, it must be . . .*

Hating to, Chesarynth still jacked out, leaving the meanings aglimmer in the prison of the magic box.

Suddenly the spaceport hall crowded in at her with light and noise and shadow. The box itself was only a small black weight in the bald woman's arms.

'Take me to' – Chesarynth fumbled with saying the words whose symbols had been so clear – 'Kärtnerstrasse seventeen. Director speed.'

And, wordless, the woman did.

The Company jet-copter dropped them off two blocks from the ancient heart of Vienna. Even Spiderglass wouldn't risk damaging Austria's heritage with powered transport: the steep-gabled buildings were a source of revenue for the Company. The grandmother of the present Tjerssen had been fully alive to the possibilities of tourism.

Or at least that was what the smooth-skulled guide said when Chesarynth asked why they couldn't land closer.

Untempered sun-heat weighed Chesarynth down as she

jumped from the copter. A sky vast and cloudless blue magnified the immensity of the sun, a mother to the tiny star she'd known from Mars. The patterned cobbles reflected its heat and the buildings bounced it back and forth. Tourists smelt of sun-screen and beer; their clothes were garish but the worst thing was the haphazard barrier they formed to Chesarynth as she raced heavily through the dusty street. They sauntered and stopped without warning and she had to duck and weave through their chattering bunches.

Some twentieth-century vandal had ripped out the latticed windows of number seventeen. Plate glass, thicker at the bottom with the weight of decades, glittered; a display of diamonds and spider-gems refracted the sunshine with painful intensity. Above the door the name *Spiderglass* was painted in spiky gold-leaf. More opulent was the holo-sign with its fantasy of opal on quartz; baroque music stroked arpeggios on the air. Even its perfumed olfacts smelt expensive.

Chesarynth remembered her first awe at the township of Ecoville. Dwarfed by Vienna and time, it now seemed crude and static. But she had no time for resurrecting memories, not if she was going to fulfil the promise Friend had built in her. A surge of longing for meanings nova'd inside her and ebbed as suddenly, leaving her shaken. When it dropped her back inside the moment, the external realities of Kärtnerstrasse seemed a pastiche of the Middle Ages.

The guide led her into the air-conditioned jewellery shop and held out the box to a sales assistant. Jealousy jagged through Chesarynth as the girl jacked in. At that moment she hated the bald guide with her one lock of blond hair curled in the hollow of her nape. *That's my box!*

Jacking out, the saleswoman slid her finger into a socket behind the counter. Three doors sprang into view; the guide led Chesarynth behind the display of savage gold and through the right-hand door. As she stepped into the humming elevator, Chesarynth realized that the other doors were holograms for security. The excellence of their design meant an interloper would be slowed for a moment to decide which was the real one.

At the top of the building Chesarynth stepped out under a vaulting skylight. The receptionist's desk was empty; a beam of raw sunlight gleamed on the patina of its age, leaving the chair behind it in darkness. There was no sound from the double doors beyond it. An eerie feeling of isolation wafted through her as she heard the unspeaking hairless guide slide the lift back downstairs. She was alone.

Waiting.

Chesarynth rested at first from the relentless heat and gravity of Earth. Her breathing slowed. She began to wonder if the woman who had sent the box-message had tricked her here into this dead-end room.

Or did I get the answer wrong? Don't tell me – it's my fault. I've spoiled it all. I'm not supposed to be here at all. What have I done to Friend?

And, as time melted the sunbeam and dripped it moment by moment from the desk to the floor, Chesarynth had only her dubious belief in Friend to sustain her. Because he had faith in her – she had seen it in the colours he painted her.

But Friend had made the garden-master. So how reliable was his judgement? And why would he make such a hideous puppet-thing?

How will I know if I'm in the right place? There's nobody to tell me.

There were no answers. Waiting was all she could do.

Except suddenly she thought of the receptionist who would normally be at that desk. Doing things. Jacked in to do things.

There must be a socket.

Chesarynth was across the room before she'd even finished the thought. For a heart-constricting moment she wondered if somebody would catch her out. But there was nobody. *And surely I'll hear the lift if it brings my inquisitor up?* She knew it was a lie.

The trouble was, caution didn't matter. Because there was the socket. Round, gold-hooped, delectable.

Chesarynth walked away from it, stopping only when the chill metal doors of the lift were a smoothness under her innocent fingers.

What, me?

The socket was a siren-song.

She drifted closer. Resolved not to do anything but wait like a good worker. Still, she moved closer. Leaning her back in a façade of patience against an ancient painted wall. Part of her trying to look merely idle.

From here she could see the socket. In the shadows its gold rim funnelled darkness through from the black night of meanings. It was a connection.

A tingling fire of lust coursed from its counterpoint in her forefinger. It was a clear silver flame that hollowed her with its hunger. A pulse of desire burnt in the cavities of her body, beating as she imagined orgasm must.

I could just . . .

And she did.

Smooth as rainbows in oil the socket embraced her finger. Lips apart, she remembered-anticipated the cool sweet darkness of infinity, longing for the magic gems of meaning that swept ionizing tides of fulfilment through her every cell.

But it didn't happen.

Instead there was nothing but a pale mist-shadow pearling between the surfaces of reality. One fragment of her mind reeled in shock but a rational response formed even as the connection spun its thread: *Of course. It would be no good having a receptionist blacking out every time they jacked in.* (Pictures spun fractally through her mind: the clerks at the spaceports, the saleswoman in the treasure trove below. They could never know the fire-opal of her meanings. Her reason coloured the images with pity.)

In the micro-seconds that had passed, the connection achieved itself. Chesarynth discovered her senses. In this anaemic echo of her own box on the Moon, her body still had substance. Nervous trembles ached in her legs and the floor was vibrating fractionally with the movement of some train deep underground. She could hear something whir and stop inside the reception desk, but most of all she could hear voices from the room behind the double doors. The oscilloscope graph of both voices was flattened in the lower register: tension was restricting the movement of their vocal chords. But the woman sounded calmer than the man.

(Wild hope: *It's Friend!* Instantly dispelled. Age creaked this man's throat. She knew without seeing him: *There's none of the vigour that glows in Friend's pattern.*) In her disappointment Chesarynth missed what he had been saying.

The woman answered, 'And I tell you it is dangerous, Berndt. We can't have Karel planting his creatures willy-nilly through the Company, let alone giving them who knows what orders through his little black boxes.'

'No, it's not likely he'd dare –'

The woman ignored his interruption. 'It's one thing to have brain-dead clerks amplified to efficiency. They're no more than extensions of their machines, hands to do the computer's will. You can tell them to fire the building and they'll do it and watch themselves burn. I know.'

Horror quavered the old man's voice. 'You mean it was you who . . .'

'Don't be such an old woman. He was getting too powerful.'

'But all those people –'

'Spineless, aren't you? Where would you be now if it weren't for me? I just clipped his wings a little, that's all. He'll be a little less adventurous for a while, and that gives us an advantage.' A sigh. 'Ole should never have given him Security.'

'Ole thought, we both thought, the boy wouldn't be able to do any harm there. It's not like he can make command decisions –'

'It's just like he can make command decisions! Yes, he holds the least votes on committee in Security. So far, we've been able to keep him in check. But he's not going

325

to just sit there for long. Ole should have thought of that but he's too feeble for executive commands. Think about it, Berndt: who makes the final selection for management?'

In her nacreous haze, Chesarynth was trying to puzzle out who the speakers were and what the boy Karel – whoever he was – had done to raise such spikes of hatred in the old woman's tone.

The old man, Berndt, laboured to a conclusion. Chesarynth could practically hear the elephantine tread of his thought processes. 'Security.' For the first time he came to a horrified acceptance of the woman's view. It dragged down the timbre of his voice to a gruff murmur. 'The boy.'

'Yes, Berndt.' Her irony was icicle sharp. 'The boy. Ole's harmless pet, Karel. Not so harmless, is he? Now do you see what I've been saying all along?'

There was a feeling of wordless assent, tinged with Berndt's growing apprehension. Chesarynth sensed it and realized for the first time that what she was hearing was nothing but verbally-trimmed ideas. Even worse was the knowledge that the whole conversation fitted her so ill because it was wrapped in the distinct flavours of a different language. A kind of mechanical telepathy.

It must be because I'm not reacting to the socket like the receptionist would. Her own horror burst out of its chrysalis. *If that woman's the sort who'll incinerate a whole building, what will she do to me when she finds out I've heard all this? Christ, she won't dare let me live. I ought to jack out now!*

But if I'm going to work for these people – and what choice do I have? – I need all the forewarning I can get. Chesarynth didn't jack out.

'Kill her now!' said the old man vehemently.

Chesarynth's stomach leapt with a spasm of fear. She tried to control it, telling herself, *Don't be so egocentric! Why would someone I've never met want to kill me? He must mean –*

The old woman said derisively, 'What would that accomplish? Karel knows she's here. Whatever else he is,

326

he's not stupid. He probably reprogrammed the courier I sent for her, insisted on a hidden message-box to record her arrival, the whole works. It could even have been disguised in that box I sent. Now I know the things work. I just don't know how well. Who knows what's inside that girl's mind? We've got to decide now, before she realizes something's going on.'

(A lightning bolt of fear convulsed Chesarynth this time: *They do mean me!*)

The murderous old woman went on, 'I know I would if I had that much invested in her. We kill her and Karel will know we're on to him.'

'Perfect, no? He won't dare do anything!'

A long, pendant sigh. 'Berndt, do try and use the brains you were born with. If the boy knows we're alive to his threat, he'll just keep his schemes out of sight until it's too late for us to do anything about him.'

Chesarynth's mind reeled with a sudden intuition. *The boy, Karel? Do they mean Friend?* As suddenly, she rejected the idea. *What would some dangerous member of the board want with me? It can't be Friend. He's not like that. They probably don't mean me at all. I'm just being paranoid.*

Berndt said, as though it were his incisive wit alone which had arrived at the nub, 'The question is, what do we do with her in the meantime? If the message you sent her was as cryptic as you said it was and she's still managed to get here, she's smart enough to be a danger to us.'

'Oh, well done, Berndt! Do you have to state the obvious? Why else did you think I sent for you – to discuss the weather?'

The old man was angry now at her cavalier attitude. (Chesarynth wondered in frustration why he never used the woman's name. *How am I going to find out?*) 'If it's so obvious to you, dear,' he said, trowelling on his own measure of irony, 'I'll leave you to deal with it, shall I?'

'Sit down, Berndt, and don't be so childish. I need you here because training's your bailiwick. I just wanted you to be sure that she's dangerous to us. A little accident during

327

her training, hey? That way we'll have no full-sentients spreading Karel's childish revolution through our systems.'

'Won't he suspect –'

'Not if you're careful. Remember, we're playing for control of the Company here. If I go down, I'll take you with me. No more jollies with little girls in Brazil until this mess is sorted out.' And the vicious indifference of her nemesis impaled Chesarynth: 'Deal with it, will you?'

Chesarynth jerked her finger out of the socket as though it were burning. Two half-run strides took her to the only way out: the lift.

It didn't come when she slapped the call-stud.

Behind her, the double doors slid noiselessly open.

8

In the dark wind-tunnel of the burrow-mouth Jezrael pulled up short. Her breath was laboured, the oxy-bottle moulded round her shoulder all but exhausted, but it wasn't that that made her back-pedal, twisting her heel on a rock, smothering her shout of pain. She backed up out of sight, stone rough on her shoulders.

Mijnheer and Danjit had their blades at Ember's throat. Peacock lines of probabilities crowned their harsh faces. Mijnheer switched off his knifeblade and sent the haft spinning before Ember's eyes.

'– done with her?'

'Nothing!' said Ember, twisting his neck to avoid Danjit's blue-sparked knife. 'I was just showing her imminence. She's got to know –'

'We decided, huh?' interrupted Danjit, his greasy, crinkled hair hiding no tower. 'Having her fixed up is enough for delivery-specification. Why waste time on her when you could be out making money? Let them train her.'

Ember's gaze slid out of the corners of his eyes. It was the only way he could see Mijnheer with Danjit's knife angling his head against the rocks. But Danjit was only the hand that held the vibroblade. Mijnheer was the man who counted.

'Tell him, Mijnheer. This way she'll be more valuable.'

Mijnher wasn't a tower either. He stared down at Ember's glass-crested head dispassionately. 'She'll be worth nothing at all if she runs out on us. That's why we agreed not to train her. We don't want to give our golden goose a head-start. Everybody gets a cut, not just you and your emotional wallowings. Weren't you listening?' The Dutchman nodded fractionally; Danjit pressed the tip of his vibrating blade into the pad of flesh beneath Ember's jaw. 'Now, Salembere, what have you done with her? Where is she?'

Blood slid darkly over Ember's skin. The muscles of his straining throat trembled with the aftershocks of the vibro-blade. Medusa-threads of blue shaded away around him, concreting to the dense midnight of one single possible action: Ember told the truth. 'I told you, she'll be along in a minute.'

'She'd better be. If you've let her get away from us, the only cut you'll get is with this.' Again Mijnheer spoke; again at his Olympian nod Danjit slithered the knife against Ember's naked throat. Danjit's Mars-tanned features smoothed in a sensual grimace of pleasure. His tongue flicked out as if snake-like he could taste the scent of Ember's blood

'Don't worry, boys. You'll get your cut.' Night-blue intention flared from Ember's head; even Jezrael, hidden behind the flank of the burrow-mouth, could sense the threat in that midnight lightning.

Answering spires of black-blue force speared from his attackers. It didn't take imminence for Jezrael to know that violence was only skin-deep in each of the three men, hidden like lava, waiting to erupt. Neither Mijnheer nor Danjit was a tower.

If they kill Ember there'll be no-one to protect me. I can't get away yet – I need supplies and they'll be watching for me. And I'm not strong enough. If Ember'll teach me how to sort this God-blasted bluelight out, I'll be in a better position. He owes me.

The computation of probabilities took Jezrael only seconds. Where once she had dithered over choosing a suit for a new day at school, now imminence brought her fast to action – at least in the short term. Even as self-disgust welled up in her like pus for using Ember, even as the jellyfish threads of azure darkening around her made her want to mewl in repulsion, she was stepping forward.

330

She wondered if the sapphire strands of her pretence at unconcern were legible to the miners, then kicked herself for her stupidity. Of course they weren't. Wasn't that one of the things straights had against towers? On the other hand, who knew what weird senses they might have instead?

'What's going on?' she said, and hoped her thoughts were transparent to the point of invisibility.

Danjit reluctantly pulled the knife away. It was the sullen withdrawal of an unsatisfied lover; she could see the blood-lust engorging his half-lidded eyes. Tendrils of blue fire writhed above his head, indecipherable to her, but one thing she knew: at the slightest provocation Danjit would let his knife-love drink.

Ember twisted his head to ease the strain in his neck.

A smile dropped on Mijnheer's face from the blueness she could see around him. It looked out of place. 'We just thought Ember here was ripping us off. We don't like that.' A sheen of cyan tattered to azure around him; he had decided to do something but dropped the idea for some reason. Instead the tall, black-browed Dutchman flicked his vibro-blade on and off so that the rocks behind it seemed to tremble into and out of existence. He said, 'Remember that next time you want to go for a stroll.'

Mijnheer sketched a mocking courtesy, indicating that she should go inside first. Her back felt unprotected when she stepped past him. Danjit stumbled forward so that for a moment she felt his lubricious body-thrust. He laughed silently when she recoiled.

Now she knew the safety of her room was illusory; it was just that they couldn't be bothered with her. Yet. If they wanted her, they'd come and there was nothing she could do to stop it. Jezrael still went there, staring at the walls of her prison. *Where else can I go?* In a fragment of mirrored plastic glued above her bed – *Whose was it before mine? And after me?* – she saw reflections of her milling thoughts: truncated spurs of alien blue.

Sickened, the memory of violence unnerving her, her mind a traitor, Jezrael twisted her face in an attempt not

331

to cry. Or at least, not to be caught crying.

The panels of her door crackled open. Smearing her eyes on her sleeve she turned to face down her enemies.

But it wasn't an enemy – if she was lucky. It was Ember. And blood he had paid to teach her how to cope with imminence was crusting on his collar.

'I'm sorry –' they both said at the same time. And laughed.

Jezrael asked in surprise, 'What have you got to be sorry for?'

He shrugged, embarrassed. 'Getting you into more trouble. You were in enough to start with. I just ...'

'I know. You just wanted to teach me how to cope with this horrible bastard blue stuff that's invading my head.' She was crying again.

'Hey, c'mere. Don't cry – I don't know what to do about that. Makes me feel helpless.' His arms slid about her in a brotherly embrace that she wanted to trust.

From the muffled, plastic-scented hollow of his shoulder, she said, 'You? You're about as helpless as a hurricane.'

But he wasn't in the mood for jokes. It fell flat on the floor. 'Listen, Jez. In a week or so we're due for recall. It's –'

Her face was still pressed against the shimmering fabric on his chest. Through it she could feel the steady rhythm of his heart-beat, only now it held a threat: the fragility of life. Depression and uncertainty thickened inside her throat, tightened her breathing. 'What's recall?'

'It's when we get called in from this patrol back to base. When we get paid. You know, get our cut' – the word sliced through her mind like a blade of ice – 'from all the strikes we've made this season. Party-time.' He looked down at her; feeling the movement in his upper body, she lifted her chin to meet his gaze. 'And you know, don't you, Jez, the best strike we've made this season is you.'

Wavering blue threads flamed around her head. Trying to ignore what they might be saying about her, she held on to silence as her only control. But Ember still understood the question.

'See, we've found a few seeps of underground water that's close enough to the surface for things to grow. Found a few new life-forms, too. That's why we follow the blue-trees. They home in on to anything damp, even the moisture in something's body. Someone's body. First assays showed that some of the plants are viable oxygen producers, edible, medicinal, that kind of thing. We get a rake-off for anything Mars-U says will help the terra-forming. Or if we tell them about anything dangerous so they can get it before it gets their precious settlements. With what-all they're doing to this planet down at the equator, there's some weird stuff happening up here. Like the bluetrees, for a start.'

'A-huh.' It was the first sound of only partial accept-ance; Jezrael was waiting for more.

'And mineral deposits. Got a fair bauxite strike and some low-grade iron ore, but it's standard. Won't hardly cover the cost of the survey.'

Jezrael knew what was coming.

'Don't look at me like that!' he yelled. 'We can't all be fancy dancers. Some of us got debts. You know what that's like?' Ember was angry now, angry and desperate. Broken spurs of blue light spat ugly in the air around. 'The guys won't keep me on the team. Out here they don't just send a polite cube over to your bank manager to cancel your pay. This is my last season, Jez, and I just haven't made the grade. This time, unless we sell you, they'll sell me. Turn me into a drone. Or maybe use me as the basis for tissue culture, body-bank, whatever.'

'Is – is that what they'll use *me* for? Why can't they just ransom me? Maggie'd pay, I know he would.'

'Don't talk wild, Jez. They've invested a lot of money in your conversion. Bribed some top-flight mind-tech from Spiderglass out here to put your tower in. They don't wanna waste you for spare parts. The people I'm workin' for, they're not a big operation. They got a lot of over-heads just keeping the big boys off their necks – kick-backs, blood-money, you name it. If anybody finds out who shouldn't, they'd have to kill to keep them silent.'

Behind her diamond eyes, Jezrael was seeing the plants she'd maimed in the name of cultures. What Nutristem had done to plants, these people could do to human beings. To her. 'Maggie wouldn't talk! He could pay a lot of cash, too.'

'Your friend would know they'd kill him. Maybe –'

Jezrael shouted in desperation over Ember's continued catalogue of horror. 'He could go somewhere else, run away! Just ask him! Ember –'

But Ember was saying with a quiet despair of his own, 'Or maybe chop a little off his brain to grow some cortex material for a rich man whose head's on fire with cancer. They're not gonna ask, Jez. Forget it!'

'You slime-ball. You diseased mutation!' Her whole being radiated revulsion.

Ember shook her fiercely. 'You think I don't know that? I told you, didn't I? You think I can look at myself in the morning with a damn great blue glass spike in my skull yelling at me, "Hey, you're a freak"? You think I chose to be here?'

Jezrael's tirade stumbled over itself and faded. 'Didn't you?'

'No! I didn't want to wake up with blue lightning any more than you did. Only there wasn't but one way I could survive Mars-U and that was by gambling. I did pretty good at it too. Beat my quota. Even got myself a nice little vacation landward of Seattlefish on Earth – hills, rivers, air you could breathe, that sort of stuff, and the sky so clear you'd figure you could see forever. Never saw nothing like that in Santos Angeles.'

He shrugged. 'Sorry, Jez. I think about it a couple of hundred times a day and kick myself for not staying right there. But no. Not me. I had to go round planning to be some rich corpo. Delusions of grandeur.

'Anyway,' he went on, trying to find excuses for himself, 'I reckon I always had some sort of imminence because I'd feel a hunch rolling up inside me like a breaker on the ocean and I'd just know what was going to win. Anything with people in it, or animals. I never had no luck with numbers, but real flesh-and-blood races ...

'Trouble is, my bookie figured I had it too. Even when I played through proxies he must have still known it was me, because one day, 'bout the end of my second year on Mars, I woke up with the blues just like you did. I figure the bastard sold me out.

'And once you're a tower, nobody but nobody at Mars-U wants to know you. You're gonna find out what that's like, Jez, when we get back to the civilized belt. You think it's bad here in the burrow? Down round the equator, nobody'll even accept that they're seeing you. Not even the fine citizens of Ecoville who have to get their rake-off too, or they wouldn't turn a blind eye to it. You ever figure that? Did your sister? Even the weirdos in Hell, they don't want you. "Hi," you say. "Nice day. How you doin'?" and they don't even look at you when they're taking your money. It don't feel too good.'

Behind her the door-flaps clashed tiredly with the wind of someone's movement in the common-room outside. Once the sound would have made her nervous, but not now. Her conscious mind didn't even register it, nor the weeds of blue awareness that tangled at the edge of her mind. She could tell he was close to some revelation that would explain what was going on.

Ember said more loudly, 'So now it's either sell you or sell me. And frankly, you're worth more.'

Jezrael lashed a hand out to punch him hard on the jaw. Imminence: of course he saw it before the impulse had even taken the first step on its journey from her mind to her body. In slow motion she saw the jagged indigo from his mind outpace the reciprocal movement he made. His strong hand cupped her fist and held it. Before she'd begun to swing up a knee into his groin he jerked her towards him. Off-balance, there was nothing she could do.

Her mind clenched in terror before his alien violence.

But Ember clamped her limbs against his own and whispered, 'So we've got to get away. You need me, right? And I need you. Act terrified.'

Jezrael did nothing; for a moment she was too stunned.

Ember thrust his face at her as if in concupiscence. His shaggy dark blond hair pivoted to tickle her cheek. 'Go on,' he hissed. 'Hit me.'

And when she did, he stopped the stab of her free hand and twisted it up behind her shoulders. His weight toppled her to the air-bed that shushed and bounced beneath them. Her arm stuck into her spine; she wrenched it free.

A harsh laugh grated from Ember's throat. 'There's nowhere you can run, Jez. Five thousand airless klicks to the equator and winter comin' on. The Company after you because of that stunt with the blind spider. And believe me, even your friends from Hell are gonna fade out when they see you with a lightning rod through your brain. There's no place to hide.'

Ember slithered more firmly on her body, his hands mashing hers helpless behind her head despite her attempts to free them from his grasp. Jezrael was frightened. She didn't know which side of his double game Ember was actually playing.

He reared his torso a little way above hers in a pose that connected their loins in frightening intimacy. Jezrael thrashed to get free but it didn't work. He shook his head a fraction and his gaze slid to the door and back – but even searching the hyacinth radiance around his head she could not guess what he really meant to do. With all her fear-sharp energy she tried to pierce the secrets of his imminence – and failed.

A smile split Ember's face. His position had torn Danjit's knife-cut again and blood spiralled through the labyrinthine folds of his collar. 'But if you're nice to me, now, I can maybe help you get a cut of your own when we sell you. What d'you say, honey?'

Outside the door, footsteps mimed drifting away.

9

Chesarynth turned round guiltily, so fast that she almost overbalanced, her toe catching in her hem. A soft-faced old man was framed by the double doors that opened on to a room of unparalleled luxury. The old woman was not in sight.

'I'm – I'm sorry,' Chesarynth said automatically, trying to look as though it were normal to stand on one leg with her skirt round her knees.

'No, no, young lady, it is I who should apologize for startling you.' His voice was soft too, a padded sound that cloyed in its assumed sympathy. Wasn't he the man who had said he would kill her now? Or rather, have her killed. He didn't look like he could do anything more strenuous than spit out a grape-pip.

'I'm happy to welcome you to Spiderglass Europa. It's Fräulein Brown, isn't it? I am Berndt Tjerssen, head of training. I'm so glad to see you managed to pass our little initiative test.' In his harmless blue eyes there was no sign of his murderous intent. His cheeks were round and innocent as a choir-boy's.

'If you'll step into my office, Fräulein Brown? I'm so sorry to have kept you waiting. For some reason I haven't got to the bottom of yet, I have only just been informed of your arrival.'

Chesarynth hung back, not wanting him behind her, but he ushered her in with little shooing motions of his manicured hands and she had no choice. A frisson wriggled down her spine but the room held no other occupant and though she turned round as soon as she decently could, Berndt Tjerssen contrived to look like a sweet, chubby old man. Certainly he made no threatening moves. In fact, he seemed quite taken with her.

Chesarynth wondered where the old woman had gone. There was still a flower-and-citron fragrance in the air but as Tjerssen fussily set a chair for her, she realized the fragrance was coming from him.

So whom had he been talking to? A telephone call? No – surely they'd never commit something so dangerous even to a Company Spiderline. And would I have got so much just from a voice? So where's the old woman?

Berndt stopped talking. Only then did Chesarynth realize that he'd started, so wrapped up in her anxiety was she.

He waved her to sit back more comfortably and took another of the gilt-and-velvet chairs, dragging it closer to hers. Under other circumstances she might have found it avuncular but now it was oppressive. Even as she replied, 'I'm sorry, I didn't catch that. It was such a long trip,' she couldn't help craning her neck to see where the old witch was.

She could have been anywhere. There were ancient, faded tapestries sprawling over the pale-pannelled walls. Huge blue-and-white urns stood sentry in niches. Vast and unidentifiable pieces of furniture cluttered the room, their curlicued carvings filmed with dust. Over the parquet *(Wow! That's real tree-wood. What a waste of natural resources)* were scattered ancient carpets made of pastel silks. Any of them could have hidden a secret staircase. Even the sunlight was blocked out by layers of muslin, and the air was thick with perfumed smoke.

Meantime Berndt gushed with the oil of social graces, pouring her a glass of wine she had no intention of drinking, (she remembered the Tjerssens as Friend had shown her them, smiling as they gave you ruby venom), pouting when she refused his macaroons. Chesarynth perched on the edge of her seat, fearing a poisoned needle in the cushions. *Pull yourself together*! she thought. *He's not supposed to kill me now, the old witch said. And the boy Karel knows I'm here.*

Just knowing, though, that Berndt meant to arrange her murder was enough to rattle her wits. She was glad of her long skirts at last, because they hid her shaking. It was hard to stumble through polite replies as to her health and her first impressions of Earth.

'But wait 'til you see winter in Spiderglass Scand!' he said, moist lips curving in an ecstatic smile. 'The frozen waterfalls and the children skating on the fjords.' Berndt's gaze hovered embarrassingly on a level with her bosom and Chesarynth felt again her lack of development. That was one thing Jezrael had that she had never attained.

But Berndt didn't know any of the layers of discomfort he was pressing on his new trainee. 'That's where our family home is, you know, and they say home is where the heart is. Someone as beautiful as you, I suppose your heart is with some young man?'

The question hung delicately on the swirls of incense in the air and Chesarynth's mistrust deepened. *How can he lie like that? I'm not beautiful and I never have been. What more does he want of me?* She didn't know what to say. *If I tell him there's no-one my life's even more at risk, but surely he must know from my records? And if he doesn't, the old witch will. What can I say?*

Mind skittering, conscious of the seconds layering thicker on the antique dust of the room, Chesarynth finally settled for a half-smile. 'Ah, that would be telling!' she said coyly, and was instantly sure he knew the hint was a lie.

An uncomfortable pause followed. Chesarynth almost drank the wine just to fill in the time, but the thought of poison halted the crystal-stemmed goblet half-way to her mouth. The gesture died meaningless, awkward.

Berndt soothed the gap by laying another pitfall. 'I'm so sorry, my dear, but your sweet face has entirely driven from my mind the details of your file. In fact I can't say for certain that it ever arrived. You haven't got it with you, by any chance?'

'No. Was I supposed to?'

'Not to worry. I expect it'll turn up eventually, if it hasn't

339

already. Where exactly were you adapted for interface?'

Doesn't he know? Chesarynth looked at his sybaritic features and decided his laziness had made him prefer fleshly pleasures to work. He might even have lost her file-cube between the islands of venerable desks. It fitted in with the way the old witch had treated him. *And as for all that rubbish about my sweet face.... Only if he doesn't know, and he and the old bat are hostile about the way Karel had me adapted –*

Wow! Karel's one of these murdering Tjerssens! He can't have known how Friend slid in to change my adaptation!

Confused now at all the permutations of possibilities, Chesarynth decided on the safest course: *I'd better not give too much away.* She wished there were someone here to support her and her soul cried out in longing: *Friend!*

'I – I'm sorry, sir –'

'Oh, please call me Berndt.' The old man's round face hovered between a smile and a leer. 'Much more friendly, don't you think, my dear?'

'I'm sorry, Berndt. It's all – well, hazy, all that part of my life. I know I was contracted but I can't really remember.' Tears weren't far away and she didn't discourage them. It made her hate Berndt even more to have to descend to such a feeble-minded stratagem. 'It must be what – what they did to my nerves.' She realized she was fiddling with her finger-socket as she so often did, but it was a useful habit now and she didn't stop.

'What do you remember?'

She paused to consider. 'Well, I remember going to a holo-bar that I couldn't afford very often. I get a sort of impression of black and bright colours but it was always different. I'm sorry. It just won't come.'

Watching her play with her handkerchief, plucking at it in distress that wasn't faked, Berndt smiled a little plastic smile. 'No matter.'

'Oh, but sir, I mean, Berndt, I'm sorry I can't be more helpful. Only I was really upset at the time and when I think of them drilling into my head and peeling back my skull and –'

The white-haired cherub shuddered.

Chesarynth piled it on. 'I wish I could remember, but I don't. I do remember that I left a sort of note for my family telling them not to worry because I'd got a good job and I might not be in touch for a while, but then it all gets kind of overlaid with a memory of a headache like you wouldn't believe, and shock at being connected to all these horrible machines and −'

Berndt looked distinctly sick. 'Yes, yes, that will do.' He cleared his throat and tossed back the wine red as blood in his goblet. 'I understand you've been recommended for business training at our school here. I trust that's agreeable to you? We can't, of course, settle your future exactly until we've had you tested out, aptitude and so on, you know. Let's get down to details, shall we?'

She wasn't about to give away Friend's plans for her. *They were Friend's, weren't they? Oh God, what if I've got it all wrong and Friend's just some trick of Karel's like the garden-master was?* 'I'm sure I'd be happier just going back to one of the Company offices on Mars,' she lied.

He wasn't having any. 'No, no, my dear. We have to make certain that we fit you in the proper niche. I couldn't permit someone of your abilities to moulder away in a backwater. You wouldn't like that, I'm sure.'

So much for trying to get away. She made a last-ditch attempt. 'You've been so kind to me that I don't want to put you to any trouble.'

He reached forward and touched her knee in a way that wasn't wholly reassuring. Chesarynth remembered what the old witch had said about young girls. 'My dear, it's no trouble at all. If I can suit you to the Company needs, I know that will be best all round. Job satisfaction is so important.'

Mmm − yours or mine? she thought, and simpered a reply.

So for the next few months she used a variant of the tactics she had tried to perfect with her parents: do what you're told and keep your head down. Only this time

Chesarynth did something she never had before. She played down her abilities, fluffed tasks that should have been childishly simple. Being important in Spiderglass could terminally damage her health and the best way to avoid that was to show she wasn't too bright. And she had to live through this to justify Friend's faith in her. The poor unhappy spiders were waiting for her help. She clung to the belief that Friend had sneaked down the wires through Karel's network and one day he would come to rescue her....

Of course, it was a tightrope walk; they must have profiles of her from her school and Mars-U. *(If I ever find them, I'll junk them.)* Using that as their base-line (or why would they have contracted her?) they would expect a high performance in her theoretical IQ. Applied intelligence might get them a completely different result, she couldn't be sure. Echoes of her multiple failure at the university shook her faith in her reasoning, but if she were as thick as they'd made out there, surely Spiderglass would never have shrunk her? So her performance couldn't be too low either – especially with the risk of being relegated to the brain-dead clerk-level. Chesarynth remembered her sister's stories of the lowest levels at Nutristem where subliminals ate away the whole shift from your mind. *Maybe a quick death would be better than that?*

Endless lessons jacked in to a computer without even the star-dance of meanings to cheer. Bland little symbols were only mirrors of colour and shape that she had to push around into the order her teachers wanted. None of it was real or important. Even the cash-flow predictions they cared about so much were nothing to her but answers she wanted ticked.

Her health suffered; vagrant aches camped out in different parts of her body but she didn't dare go to a Spiderglass doctor. That would be handing them her life on a plate. Her flesh melted, leaving bone and tendon beneath her grey skin; she hated what she looked like in a mirror, but then, she always had. Fear stalked her sleep, because however far she could drive her anxieties from

342

her mind by activity in the daytime, she had to relax control when she sought sleep. And between the shores of waking and slumber lay sharp reefs of nightmare. Even when she was too tired to read she sought escape in romance-cubes she spent all her wages on at the Madrei-detic shop. With the safety of evening fleeing behind her, she forced her burning eyes to watch cubes until the stars paled. Crossing each night became an epic voyage.

And in all that time she'd never heard from Jez, nor even from her parents. Arranging strings of symbols in the computer tanks at the school, Chesarynth could not ignore her hurt. Even if they didn't know her exact address, they never answered the little notes she sent care of the Company. Assuming they arrived. . . .

Afraid to make friends with the other students (*Is it him that's the spy? Or that girl with the Esquimau nose?*) and not daring to spend the time she used to in study lest she be dangerously good, she now had hours and hours in which to brood and her old pains came back to life. Growing burrs and hooks, reaming her snaggled, sleep-starved nerves, her fretting longed for the relaxation of talking to the one person who had always taken her part: her sister.

Only Jezrael doesn't care enough to find me, does she?

And that became the seed-crystal around which her tensions solidified.

Maybe three months into training, when the captive trees behind the hotel complex burned into autumn flame and the air smelt of bonfires that they told her didn't mean danger, Chesarynth shivered across to the school. Crisp yellow leaves scrunched satisfyingly underfoot, giving off a sweet sad scent. The very sky smelt of frost though a sun bigger than she had ever seen on Mars still shone remote between gold-fringed clouds. Up from the river came the moist, dirty smell of its swollen waters. Yesterday, after purple thunderheads had bled rain over the hills for the third day in succession, the air had dried up. The tutors had led the business pupils on an organized 'social' – a walk to the Prater. Silent, untouched by the presence of the others that she couldn't trust *(that hurt)* she had crossed the Danube bridge. It spanned the water-meadows but the grass was deep under water. Opaque scummy floods lapped only a metre below her feet; a foul smell made her nauseous. It was a dead sheep, caught on the buttress of the bridge, and its dark-swollen face was fish-nibbled. Its yellow-black devil's eyes haunted her.

Now, back in school, Chesarynth hoped that jacking in would drive this dreadful melancholia away. The other twenty students listened with Teutonic thoroughness but not Chesarynth. She sat impatiently listening to the teacher's drivel about the fault in the program he was about to network. Find the fault, he said. We'll enter a merit on your records.

What do I care about your pointless merits? Stop jawing and let me get on with it. At least there are the ghosts of meanings in there and I can dream in the space between electrons. Even if Friend never comes back to me, I can dream.

'You can jack –' said the tutor, but Chesarynth heard no more.

Faint dark mist was the background, with the symbols only crude and faded opal scars. But, unlike the other students, she stayed fully sentient while her finger was in the socket thanks to her Friend-engineered connection.

It was a real program, she discovered, with a real fault. Something to do with Company cash-flow, stuff they'd hardly touched on the course. It wasn't the egotism she feared that told her none of the others would understand just what the program was, or its significance. It must be something serious to turn the students loose on it.

Interfacing, she slipped the colours of her awareness into the non-space of symbology. Like some antediluvian mouse Chesarynth roamed the corridors of files. Or, more aptly, she flew between pinned butterflies of ideas. None of it held the magic of her communication with Friend; even here, jacked into the shadows, she ached for him but reason told her she wouldn't find him, long before she

344

stopped looking. With a mental sigh that dimmed her meanings, she turned her attention to what she should have been doing all along.

Assets – that clump of symbols, rich as distant gold. Investments tempered with the vagaries of stock-markets. Overheads. Turnover. Profit that glowed like beads in a smoked-glass display. Cash channelled to each arm of Spiderglass – *I never realized there were so many! And why so much to that one stuck out deep in the hinterland of Asia? I'll solve that one another day....*

No obvious fault. *I'd better check the figures.*

Later, brain-fatigue smearing her concentration as she tried yet again to make the balance positive: *I'm not wrong. Something's eating the profits and it's not entered here.*

It was better than an analgesic in her blood. Chesarynth concentrated on the maths of it so hard that for a long time she ignored the awareness tugging at her subconscious. Checking and rechecking her figures, she had no time to give in to the promptings of the irrational. Only somewhere there was the bubbling upswell of a hunch.

But her bladder demanded attention. With a grimace of irritation, Chesarynth jacked out.

Before she could fully withdraw her finger from the connection, a fire possessed her, bright as magnesium fireworks. Just for a second, while part of her still jacked in, a sun imploded around her.

But she had begun the withdrawal and her synapses knew enough to carry it out even as thousands of her brain-cells died in the nova.

Her finger came out smoking. Burn-blisters reddened, popped, raining juices from her hand. She convulsed, collapsing to the floor with the pain that danced down the paths of her nervous system.

Chesarynth thought it was her own screaming and embarrassment boiled through her but when she looked round, bodies were twitching and smoking everywhere as the computer-banks sparked into flame. Panic filled the classroom.

She dragged other students from their places, freeing them from the killing connection. Groans and sobbing wove through the smoke-reeked air but the sprinklers were already pouring foam on to the consoles and the power cut abruptly.

The room dived into darkness, shrinking Chesarynth's world to the chairs and benches shining pale in the moonlight from the window. She had no idea she'd been in there so long.

A torch spat light that splashed dazzling between the shadows. The tutor holding it yelled, 'Is there anybody else still jacked in?'

One or two shapes moved through the darkness but most people – *There's not that many*, Chesarynth realized. *Most of them had already gone home* – were slumped in shock on the floor.

'Everybody make your way to the door,' the tutor called, his voice trembling. 'Don't leave until I tell you.'

One by one he checked them off on his register, letting them stagger out into the corridor where the ghouls who liked disasters were already forming a pressing crowd. Chesarynth leant back against the wall, holding her throbbing hand and waiting for the knives in her head to dissolve. She had lost one of her shoes; broken glass had cut her bare toes.

The tutor's tired authoritarianism wavered to a stop. Almost to himself he said, 'Power-surge. It could have been worse. It could have happened this morning when all of you were in there.' Chesarynth could hardly hear him above the questions of the throng.

Confusion peaked with the arrival of the rescue teams but they led or carried the survivors to the relative peace of the sick-bay. Under fierce lights that did nothing for her head, a doctor and a technician examined them one at a time. They gave Chesarynth two painkillers and told her she was lucky. Some of the others would have to be rewired; some would never be rewired again, but all she had was a headache. You'll be all right in a couple of days, they said, and in her disorientation Chesarynth thought,

Days are geography not time. But here she was the interloper. The knowledge saddened her all over again.

Then, as she stumbled outside into the frost-gleamed blue of the night, an idea seized her. For her life's sake Chesarynth turned reluctantly and made her way back to the tutorial room.

Back at the scene of the disaster the confusion worked to her advantage. If anybody asked, she could say she'd come back for her shoe that had fallen off in the stumbling mess of wrecked furniture.

But nobody did ask. The ghouls had all been sent away and under the fierce new glare of naked lights, carctakers were clearing up while someone pushed a trolley of glass-eyed computer-monitors that got into everybody's way. Chesarynth felt as though there were a huge sign over her head saying she shouldn't be there. Afraid that at any moment someone would shout 'Grab her!' and drag her off to some unspecified yet ineluctable torment, she forced herself at least to look calm while she sat at the console on the dais. The memory of the towers' electro-sticks back at Mars-U made her fingers fumble at the keys.

Nobody noticed.

It wasn't hard to sneak a copy of the tutor's program and take it back to her room. Even if anyone saw it under the charred fringes of her robe, she could say it was homework. They wanted her to be keen, didn't they?

Well, maybe. Because there were two answers to that. The possibility of a real power-surge she discounted. Surely a place as organized as Spiderglass Europa would have resistances built in to protect against just that?

So either Berndt had begun to kill her, and to hell with anybody else who got in the way.

Or the program itself didn't like being investigated.

10

Ember transferred his grip on Jezrael's wrists to one powerful hand. Pinned as she was beneath his weight she hadn't even the leverage to free her arms or buck him off – though she tried desperately. The air-mattress soughed and sucked to their frenzied movements. Out of one eye, through the curtain of his rough blond hair, she could see their bodies in the mirror on the wall. It seemed sick, perverted. Already she hated herself, and he hadn't even begun.

A muffled voice faded in the common room outside. The dense blue fire of solid intention arced from Ember's mirrored head and collided with the lightning that sparked around his face only inches from her own. Its dark meaning terrified her.

Jezrael strove, whimpering. It was inconceivable that she shouldn't be able to throw him off, but she couldn't. Her limbs were wracked with the aches of her first trip outside since the bluelight had punctured her brain, and he was whole and strong.

Not Ember! Surely he wouldn't –

He arched his body, pressing down on her with his hips. He swung his free arm sideways, parallel to the ground. Down and round to the level of her breast.

Tension rived through Jezrael. Her imagination jagged with tumbling violent images of what he might do to her. She tried to kick him, but he only grinned more widely. More wildly. And his hand picked up a dropped boot to hurl it against the crackling plastic doors.

They bulged out, connected hard with something

348

outside in the common room. A man exclaimed, 'Shit!' and went away for real.

And Ember said softly in her ear, 'I'm not really gonna do it but it's gotta look good, OK? Can you reach the light-switch from there?'

Jezrael nodded, uncertain – *What am I doing placating a rapist, for Chrissake?* – and when he slackened his hold on her upwrenched arms, groped fractionally for the remote.

Ember seized and aimed it at the control panel beside the door and the room went as dark as it could with the little amber safety-lights glimmering in case of accident.

Biolight. Banned on Mars, realized Jezrael in hysterical irrelevance.

Ember mouthed, 'Could you just shuck off your outer suit, Jez? At least the top?'

'How real –'

'Just do it, OK? Then we'll skinny down under the covers. It's gotta look convincing.'

Then slow relief flooded her as in the giggling, whispering darkness they mimed the act of making love. The hem of a distant Marsquake shivered through the walls of the burrow, and Jezrael had to stuff the back of her hand in her mouth to stifle her laughter as Ember cried out in artistic mock-orgasm. She just knew he was thinking, *Did the earth move for you?*

Faint noises from outside dwindled into the peaceful black chasm of sleep. She heard his words floating out to her, pale clouds in the darkness: 'So now we can get time alone to plan.'

She had to chow down with the others in the common-room now she was mobile. Jezrael hated being the only one there who wore a bodysuit but she would have hated more the embarrassment of displaying herself with all her imperfections to the crude and lumpen miners. Like Lecky, the cook, many wore no clothes at all in the warmth of the burrow; others wore a cache-sexe. Just looking around at acres of tired, naked flesh made Jezrael squirm; she stayed in her room as much as possible.

Mealtimes were hell. Danjit liked to get in pointed little jibes like, 'Hey, bow everybody, her ladyship's actually gracing us with her presence!'

Around the table or squatting on whatever box they could along the burrow walls, the others reacted in their different fashions. Some, like Khaur, were indifferent. All he cared about was booze, but he still got the job done before he got soaked. He'd carry on eating, one elbow on the table, through all the racket.

Erin, though, the other woman, wouldn't let any dig lie. Lolling on the bench beside the monitor, one foot on someone else's chairback, she said, 'Maybe she'll grace you with a little more than that, Danny. What do you charge for renting her out, Ember?'

Jezrael's face burned. She stared down at her plate, wishing she knew what to answer, wishing she were somewhere else but they never let her out of their sight. Someone was always watching her.

Some pimpled boy whose name she didn't know put one finger coyly beneath his chin and snickered, 'Oh, look, she's blushing.'

Jezrael felt her heart swell with her smothered rage. It felt like it would strangle her from inside. *Déjà vu.* Yet she was just as impotent as all the other times.

It didn't help when Lecky the cook said, 'Gimme the cube rights –'

Before he could finish Erin sneered, 'Forgotten what it goes like, Lecky?' Fat Trask choked with laughter, spattering half-chewed pasta over another man who slapped him upside the head.

Ember grinned knowingly. 'If she ever gets tired of me, Erin, I'm sure she'll put you high on her list – right after blue-tress.'

More laughter. Jezrael could feel stupid tears forcing their way through her control. It was worse than school.

Mijnheer yelled, 'Hey, Salembere, does that make you a bluetree?'

Ember stood up, striking a parody of a muscle-man

pose. 'Nope. It makes me dessert.' He reached down to take Jezrael's hand. 'C'mon, you. Let's leave these guys – all they're good for is talking about it.'

The chorus of catcalls faded as Jezrael's door-panels flapped shut. Ember ducked his head to whisper in the warm, secret tinge of biolight, 'Don't pay no mind to them, Jez. It's only six more days to pay-off at Placerco and you're nowhere near up to strength. We've got to get this sorted right or we're iced.'

The lights of the equator sprang up, spangling the sun's race from the night-side. Jezrael didn't want the flight to end. Not that the freighter's jumbled hold was pleasant, crowded with the noisy, dark shapes of the mining team who thought of her as cargo to sell.

She eased her legs sideways in the tiny space between rattling crates, shouting, 'Cramp,' to Ember, but it wasn't true. All she wanted to achieve was an excuse to feel the human warmth of his arm against hers. There was no other emotional support she dared to ask for. Either the rest of the gang would hear her and sneer, or Ember might turn away. After all, how grateful could he be for her dancing weeks – no, months now – before? He'd barely begun to teach her to interpret the wreaths of imminence, the meanings of nictation and stance. She still couldn't tell what made him tick just by looking at him.

Jezrael wished she could. Imminence didn't seem to have helped her at all. All her life she'd thought, *If only I knew what so-and-so was thinking I'd know what to do....* Now she did. But if anything, it had made her even more indecisive. *Even if we do get away from these guys, where am I going to go? I can't take trouble back to Maggie. Besides, he'd just tell me that having a tower around was bad for business. What can I do?*

Cocooned in noise, the hostile presence of the rest of the miners oppressing her, she felt fear thrusting in at her with the decibels of the freighter's flight. *If I could be certain of Ember, it wouldn't be so bad.* She glanced at his half-seen profile with the sunset flashing over his cheekbones as the ship banked for landing.

He shot her a grin and she thought of what he'd been to her in the last week and a half. *Everything good about this whole horrific mess, he's given me. To the others I'm just meat on the hoof.*

Yet Jezrael knew he'd been one of them for longer than she'd been on Mars.

She thought of the jokes they'd shared, bundled up chastely in her bed, and she wondered what it would have been like if they had made love. *He never even kissed me....*

A smear of red sunlight bounced across her eyes as the ship completed its landing approach. The moment Danjit, jostling the pilot, shouted back, 'We're home free, guys!' the hold erupted with ravelling cheers. A stampede broke out, people pushing past Jezrael to the cockpit to see the first signs of other human beings through the canopy. Even Jezrael hauled herself up by the strappings on a crate: silver lights shone through the mists of twilight.

The ship's nose dived; bodies fell, laughing insanely. Jezrael hung on only because her hands were twined through the strapping. Gravity sucked her feet forward and across to the doors. Panic slammed around in the cavity of her body.

She could just about hear the pilot yelling for silence. Then he slapped the speakers on and a solid weight of noise crashed against her head: the pilot's amped-up voice thundered, 'Back to your positions! This is a cargo-ship, not a frigging Gateliner.'

Gateliner? wondered Jezrael, but whatever it meant, it worked, either that or the ship's erratic plunge. The miners scrambled back up the hill of the slanting deck and the ship steadied. Erin kicked Khaur over to where he'd been told to sit when the pilot first landed at the burrow to ferry them back to headquarters.

'Civilization!' somebody shouted.

It looked very small.

Jezrael could still see the lights of sunflowers strung out like mercury on rose satin. The land around was crumpled with shadow valleys, a corduroy of fields. Greenhouse roofs rippled from salmon to garnet with the cold winds of sunset. She could almost smell the rich fermentation of silage like there'd been around parts of Ecoville, or the green alkali of the air-plants. A faint haze of heat-differential shimmered the lights of town but the thin mist meant visibility was quite good. A wedge of frosty light clove a farmyard as someone stepped out to look at the stars in the russet sky.

Freedom. Jezrael shivered in anticipation.

But the rumbling hulk of the ship was dense with the sounds and smells of men on pay-day – and she was part of their pay. It was a lot to get through.

The pilot jounced the ship through turbulence – Jezrael felt the gravity drag at her limbs, making them a dead-weight that her feeble stamina couldn't shift. Terror hit with the enormity of pitting herself and Ember against the seventeen members of the patrol – no, eighteen if you counted the pilot. *And what about all the ground-crew when we touch down at Placerco? Oh, shit!*

But Ember contrived to nudge her reassuringly and a gravity-shift bounced her high and maybe it was all possible after all.

The ship's braking-jets roared, vibrating the hold into cacophony and falling objects. Then they were gliding in to a crown of diamond lights and it was time.

Jezrael couldn't work up any spit. *What was it Ember said? Pretend it's just another show?*

What if I bomb out? We won't get an encore....

The deck lurched and steadied, creaking, to a chorus of jeers. *What if we crash?*

Then the door clanged open and she thought in surprise, *We're down!*

A river of cold air fountained into the hold, drenching everybody in sudden condensation. Dazzling lights knifed at her vision from the docking bay. Ember dragged her to her feet and she limped stiff-legged through the hatch and on to the landing-ramp. Only a couple of guys had got there first; Ember had picked their position well.

A couple of silhouettes emerged from the glare of light. Jezrael stopped on the top step, yawning and stretching, one hand flung up to shield her face against the cold hard radiance. Someone jostled into her, cursing. Exactly as Ember had said.

Now the other two were almost at the bottom of the ramp. Half-way along it, Ember whipped round to yell, 'Go, Jez!' and vaulted over the hand-rail.

Before he hit ground Jezrael spun to slam the hatch-door shut. Ember shoved the wheeled ramp sideways but it was all right because he'd told her to hang on and she had. The two guys near the bottom fell tumbling and Ember hit the first one hard on the neck.

Behind her the miners had wrenched the door open angrily. One pitched out, hitting the ground with a sick-ening thud; Erin yelled, trying to hold on, but she fell too, attempting to roll, but she couldn't make it to her feet with one shin-bone staring whitely at her through her pant-leg. Blood began to splurge out and her screams pounded Jezrael with a different rhythm. She was paralysed, staring at Erin.

'Jez! Quit that and get moving!' Ember yelled.

Guiltily she ran down the bouncing shallow steps, jarring them as hard as she could to off-balance the last man on his feet. Somewhere out in the sheet of light black shapes began to react.

Jezrael leaped at the man in a balletic kick, somer-saulting as the back of his neck snagged her foot for a second. Fast as laser-dance she rolled and recovered. Shots spiked the air and night plunged down on them as Ember shot the lights out. In the vacant dark Jezrael aimed another kick, blindly. Her boot collided with some-thing high, she didn't know what. Afraid she'd left her victim mobile, Jezrael hesitated, waiting for a clue. This time he didn't get up.

'Hit it, kid!' shouted Ember. His footsteps were hard to pick out in the roaring darkness. Other men were running now, and yelling; she heard the unmistakable sound of the ramp being rolled back and felt its nearness before it could actually hit her.

She ducked under the belly of the ship, scuttling low to the ground, but she still managed to slam her head into some unseen landing gear. Lightning flashed across her vision and she thought it was concussion but it was the pilot putting on his cabin-lights. Vague shapes were running in counter-directions.

Ember whistled, thin and high. She sped into the half-light, aiming well to the left of the sound.

The sound of her boots changed as she left the edge of the fireproof field. Sparks spat through the gathering night ahead of her; she slowed unconsciously as friction rubbed bright answering wires of electricity from her boots.

Here the ground was uneven limonite and she stumbled. Her new sense of time told her that a scant three minutes had passed since landing.

Hope flamed in her. *Maybe we'll make it!* Wordless images of a new life expanded her, making her feel an incandescent love for life. Her feet kept on blundering along through the darkness and a stitch stabbed at her side but she blinded herself to exhaustion and ran.

Me and Ember, we'll go to Maggie's and he'll help us and we'll find Ches and everything'll be fine –

Four minutes. A minute sooner than Ember had said, emergency lights blazed on. She saw him ahead of her, hopping up and down in his anxiety. Multiple shadows of him fell on the perimeter wall, leaping like pale giants. Jezrael could hear the wires that crowned it humming with power.

She forced herself to go faster, her hand reaching out to him.

He took it, saying, 'Well done, Jez! I knew you could do it. Let's split.'

Not even a proper force-wall above the barrier of regurgitated rock. Ember had said Placerco couldn't afford one yet. He blasted the wire with his third shot and the ends writhed sparking.

Their pursuers were close now. He boosted her over the wall and scrambled up behind her, dropping to safety as bolts of power spanged past them.

Breath wrenching in their lungs, Ember pulled Jezrael along hand in hand. The last glow had gone from the sunflowers now and they hung their heads on their spindly supports. Jezrael let go and dodged weakly beneath the first one. Frost was beginning to whiten the ground beyond the rustling greenhouses outside Placerco, but the underground thermal grids laid a net of darker squares across the fields.

She stole a glance from her future and turned her head. Behind them torches were bobbing through the night.

Ember pivoted, gun well out from his side. One shot brought a barrage of answering cross-fire that burned angrily around them but just like he'd planned, Ember and Jezrael had separated. At least the torches went out. None of the miners wanted to be a target.

But there were still the heat-sensitive beams and she couldn't see them.

Ember angled towards her, dragging at his oxy-bottle as he ran. A sunflower belled upwards not fifty metres away; the one they'd passed was twice as far behind them. From what Jezrael could tell as she snatched rags of glances backwards, their pursuers hadn't reached it yet.

So far, so good. She hated to consider the alternatives.

Almost level with the last sunflower and she didn't think she could make it. Ember was still ahead, waiting. Pains like hot iron poured molten through her legs and her throat was raw with the icy emptiness of the air she was gulping. Under the sepia of the sky only starlight shone on the frost around her.

She didn't think she could make it. Back there somewhere she could hear the miners' grim shouts; they were closer in the mahogany night.

Stumbling with weariness, she forced herself to stagger towards Ember. Each lurching stride printed *I can't, I can't* on her mind.

Ember gave up waiting for her and signalled frantically. Jezrael dropped where she stood, on the cold wet soil above a thermal. Ember ran to her, scooping dark mud over her to blind the heat-sensors to her. Not a perfect job but enough to fool the miners – she hoped.

Face in the damp mars, she could hear their pounding footbeats. 'Go!' she hissed at Ember, but he stopped for an agonizing moment to cover her better. Jezrael's fingers crisped into the grit beneath her; even her face worked with the adrenalin that surged up, so much did she want to shove him away and make him save himself.

Only if she did that, all his effort would be wasted. So she lay still, prone, trying to catch the sound of her breathing before it escaped and gave the game away. Eons passed and suns died; at last she felt the ground tremble as Ember sprinted – *Too far! He'll never get there!* – towards the sunflower.

Like interlocking ripples came the shock-waves of the miners' steps. Jezrael couldn't even lift her head to look because he'd told her that eyes shine in the darkness; as well light a beacon. Grit clung damply to her eyelashes as she shuddered closer into the ground. She made herself breathe through her mouth as slowly as she could to hush her own sounds, and inhaled the odours of the earth with her own warm respiration.

Cramp spasmed through her calf. She didn't give in to it.

She hung on to the ground, waiting.

Where's Ember? Oh God, she prayed, beseeching a deity that was only something her father swore by, never something believed, *let him get away. It's my fault he's in this mess.*

The footsteps thundered closer. Gobbets of soil shook down into the cavity where she hid her face. She stopped breathing but her heart kept on thudding its own wild race.

A scatter of miners ran past her, one even stepping on her hand with a pain that burned sharply on her half-frozen fingers. Jezrael clenched her teeth so hard against the torment that her jaws shuddered, but she didn't cry out. *I'm not going to give him away. Oh, fuck, it hurts.*

The knot of footsteps spread thinner into distance. Into silence.

Jezrael waited.

Surely overhead the stars wheeled through the chocolate sky? The cold seeped into her muscles and she couldn't stop shaking but she wouldn't look up too soon and betray Ember who was good to her.

Pictures: *I'll take him to Maggie's after closing-time (the river of lights over the bar, and warmth, and coñac in coffee, and Maggie admiring and relieved). It'll be all right. (Dad, this is Ember. Salembere.) We've found Ches. (Mom saying 'Thank you' over and over again, and her tears of gratitude hot on Jezrael's neck.)*

And Mars travelled a million miles through space around the distant hub of the sun.

Except that in the treachery of silence Jezrael finally lifted her head. Maybe seven minutes had passed but she dared not wait any longer because who knew when the miners might give up and come back?

So she lifted her head and a voice behind her yelled hoarsely, 'I've got her!'

Jezrael lurched stiffly to her feet and lumbered off at a run. From behind her came a spear of light that struck steam from the ground at her feet. She dodged sideways but her frozen muscles wouldn't respond and she half fell, clawing upwards again like an athlete on the starting-block but another shot scorched through the mud in her hair and she slumped to her knees in despair.

The iron smell of Danjit's sweat solidified in her nostrils as he straddled her from behind, one hand wrenching her jaw up, his vibro-blade cherishing the soft skin of her throat.

Up on the neck of the sunflower (peacock flames of imminence blazed his position) Ember shouted, 'Jez!'

And they shot him.

His body flopped brokenly from one strut to the next, cartwheeling ungainly to crump on the earth.

She ran to him. They could have shot her there and then and it wouldn't have made any difference. She still would have gone to him if she had to crawl.

His forehead was ripped dark in the starlight but his

cheekbones still gleamed (an image superimposed: the sunset slanting over him as he grinned at her in the freighter) the way she remembered. His shoulder was crooked, the arm limp.

Jezrael threw herself to her knees beside him, not daring to touch his rag-doll body. It didn't matter that they were coming to stare down at her and Ember with the ugly blueness of ghoulish satisfaction on their heads. Her hand hovered above his neck that looked so defenceless. She didn't know what to say, and then words welled up unstoppable.

'I'm sorry, I'm sorry, Ember, I didn't mean to –'

'Ssh, don't cry, honey. You any good at jigsaws.'

Jezrael didn't even smile at his joke. 'You'll be OK, Ember. They'll patch you up good as new, see if they don't. You'll be fine. Don't worry, it's going to be OK.'

His soft, strained voice stopped her babble. 'One thing, at least it doesn't hurt. Don't blame yourself. It was a dumb plan anyways.'

She reached out and dared to feather her fingertips over his neck in a hopeless caress. His pulse was a distant polka retreating into the unknown. A mandala of electric fires reached out from around his head, stretching, thinning, weaving into the invisibility of the air.

Jezrael hugged him tighter as if to hold the life in him but it trickled out around her. She sobbed, 'It was a great plan only I'm stupid. Oh, Christ, I wish I'd just done what you told me. We could've gone to Maggie's....'

And in the mist-wraithed frosty field, she told his corpse about the good times ahead while Trask and Khaur closed her future in their night.

11

'My tutor's not coming in, did you say? Oh, never mind. I'll catch him tomorrow. Thanks.'

Chesarynth jacked out of the communications network. Her glance slid over the cube she held, seeing it as an object, a thing she met with every day. It shone; its fine veins sparkled where the tiny gold wires crossed but she didn't see wonder in it. Slipping it under a broad embroidered bracelet, she left her room and sauntered over to the business school. Bitter thoughts tangled with her headache.

What did Friend put in my head that they don't put in everyone else's? And if he is a Friend (she remembered the shadow-horror of her garden-master) *why did he do it to me anyway?*

It was easy enough to hang around in the courtyard enjoying the soft splash of sunlight on her bare arms. Late afternoon gilded the granite of the Spiderglass complex. Tiny feathers of cloud drifted over the horizon like a flock of fire-birds. Beyond the railings, a squirrel whisked among the bronzy oak trees and sparrows quarrelled on the hum of distant traffic. Earth was more beautiful than she could have imagined; it didn't seem fair when everyone was out to kill her.

Inside the business school chimed the melody that meant the change of lessons. Students began to spill out of the building, others to stream in. Chesarynth sucked in another breath of the sweet, tangy air and melted into the crowd, shuffling inside with the rest.

Along the corridors, up the tubes, hidden in the

polyglot mass of students. No-one cared that she jacked in to the lock on the tutor's door, feeling around mentally to jig it open. It was easy. In real-time only seconds had passed, not much more time than it would have taken to see if he was in and ask him for a few minutes of his time. It was only part of the communications system anyway, nothing advanced. After all, what strategic importance could an ordinary tutor hide in his ordinary office?

All the same it was a relief to discover that he really wasn't in. Somehow she hadn't quite believed it before. Tension prodded a tic under her eye. From somewhere she could hear a lecturer droning; maybe it needed speeding up a little. No threatening footsteps tapped up the corridor to discover her. Chesarynth hoped all the secretaries were happily jacked in to some routine part of the system, or getting their jollies from the nerve-stimulators some of them were addicted to.

Dithering nervously with the colour coded translucent cube-sleeves watching her intrusion, it took her longer than she would have liked to calm down enough to start. After all, just being in the tutor's office couldn't be that much of a crime, could it? But what she was about to do, that was a real, honest-to-goodness gold-wired sin she might not live long enough to regret.

Chesarynth sighed. Even now, scared of losing her innocence and terrified of being caught, she could still see no other way of finding who was after her this time. Taking a deep whispered breath, she slotted the cube into the console's access.

The tutor's personal machine switched on to the cube. His code was no problem; hadn't she seen it enough times anyway when he powered up the network? Tempted to back out while there was still time, Chesarynth knew she had to find out and quickly if she wanted to stay alive. She jacked in with an anticipation she hadn't felt since Friend had left her so far away on the Moon.

Chesarynth booted in the program, making her own little file with an octopus of dark hollow symbols: a worm that would eat up any trace of her prying, provided she did the whole thing quickly enough that no-one noticed while she was in.

And right where she didn't expect it in the black universe was another dark space, solid with hidden meanings, difficult to see, alien to her comprehension. Now that she knew they were there, they stuck out because they were obviously some different language. A whiff of dirt and mildew stung her awareness with its rank unfamiliarity. If she'd had only the clerical level of interface that she was supposed to have, she'd never have found it.

And maybe the rest of the gang wouldn't have got burned out if she hadn't come close before.

She whistled soundlessly. *I wasn't expecting that. What in the worlds is it?*

But there was a sombre shadow of familiarity to it and after subjective eons of frustration, intuition struck her.

Madreidetic. It had the same feel to it that she knew from the long hours she'd spent experiencing the mass-market romantic slush that Madreidetic packed into their holos.

Her flag of meanings dimmed in puzzlement. *Why me? Why couldn't somebody else find it?*

The answer was obvious – though there was a lot else that wasn't. *Friend. Somehow this is an awareness he's built into me or I wouldn't be able to spot it where nobody else can.*

Does that mean he's from Madreidetic?

Automatically dissecting the problem into the code of coloured balls and prismatic chains that was the symbology of her interface, Chesarynth looked at it from all angles. It seemed very unlikely that Friend was from Madreidetic. Studying their strange, dark language, she found it largely incomprehensible. Certainly it had none of the verve or joyous beauty that she associated with him. And surely he wouldn't have omitted to teach it to her if he had planted her as another spy for them.

Madreidetic.

Madreidetic who made cubes.

Madreidetic who then also sold data-cubes and stored their own hidden programs within the crystalline lattice.

Programs that hived off fortunes into their own coffers.

Now what do I do? Dam the leaks?

If I do that, the Company doesn't have to know I've been interfacing data when I shouldn't. I could tell the tutor I got scent of it before the system went down yesterday. . . .

Then everyone will think I'm some kind of spy anyway because it's hardly going to fit in with my cover of being a moron. So then Berndt and the old witch will know I'm as smart as they don't want me to be, AND that I've been poking around in high-security files.

But what if I say nothing? If Madreidetic's anything like as unpleasant as their language, why should I let them get away with piracy? And who knows what else they've got in here? In any of the Company networks? Vicarious terror gripped her. *Jesus, what might they be doing to our starshipping? To the colonies? To all the worlds dependent on our supplies? And if anybody came close to finding out, curtains. . . .*

Her meanings all but drowned in the immensity of it all. The seas of black space around her took on an aura of dread. Anything might be out there. Even a worm that would kill any interface stupid enough to blunder into it, but fear stoked up a hot red glow of anger inside her.

Before she could investigate further, her own dim worm fired a warning shot. Somehow she had triggered her discovery but she didn't know who was out there hunting her, Berndt's killers or Madreidetic.

At the speed of thought Chesarynth fled through the towering ranks of symbols that obstructed her now with their colour-coded lattices, their confusion of cold money scents. Was it paranoia or could she really feel someone closing in on her? A lethal charge that lurked around the next junction?

She jacked out so quickly the tutor's office swam around her before she knew what it was. Fear shuddered her breath, fragmented her vision of his pale walls, the spectra of his neatly-stacked cubes.

Berndt or Madreidetic. I still don't know. I've got to get out before one of them switches me off.

363

*

Outside, the silver-frosted blue of nightfall wrapped her secret. Her first instinct had been to creep back to the familiar haven of her room, but now Chesarynth couldn't face its bright emptiness. Only there was nowhere else she could go. Or was there?

An odour of dank river air swam up from the river. It decided her; instantly she followed it to the broad Danube. The ghosts of stars were netted in its ripples and she let their feyness layer a skin of calm on her thoughts. Hardly aware of the chill she paced restlessly along the bank, seeing for the first time the way the dew crisped to frost along each blade of grass until the parkland veered from dark to grey to an ephemeral diamond enchantment. A high wind frayed the sails of clouds until a crescent moon limned each shred with white gold. Leaves skirled across the paths, rattling like the click of a dog's paws, but she saw no-one else and the dark trees of the Wienerwald were left alone to sieve their ancient harmonies from the gale. The chill air cooled her face and seemed to sweep her problems into the distance. They were still there, attached to her by unbreakable strings, but at least they retreated enough for her to have a breathing-space in which to resolve them.

Suddenly she laughed, face turned up to the platinum moon. 'It's easy!' she shouted into the rushing wind. 'I'll go where none of them will ever suspect. I'll go where I should be – with my spiders in Asia.'

12

It wasn't like she'd imagined a slave-auction. No stripping off and being stood on blocks for the world-weary rich to stare at in lust or mockery.

Khaur and Danjit simply propelled her – Jezrael could hardly walk, so massive was her state of shock – out of the wintry night fields and back to their depot, leaving Ember's body lonely in the cold. Some female handed them a hypo-bulb and they sprayed it into Jezrael's face, and there was a physical paralysis leadening her without physical pain. Yet even that was cruel because it left her thoughts an active prisoner.

Frustration fastened Jezrael, a solid wall that cramped itself around her body. Shock distanced her horror at what she had done to Ember.

Danjit's hand unsealed the front of her suit in the shadow-hung warehouse in front of everybody and she could do nothing about it, but his lascivious toying with her breast and the perverted obscenities he whispered in his garlic-and-beer breath couldn't make her feel terror now.

I deserve it, thought Jezrael bitterly.

Danjit's hand slid lower, skithered spider-like across her belly.

Jezrael couldn't so much as shudder. Even breathing took attention.

She wondered what Spiderglass would do to Chesarynth when they found out that Jezrael had been trying to free her. She saw baggies, their heads clouded in violent imminence, shooting Chesarynth, who fell with the same gut-twisting thud that Ember's flesh had made. She saw

Chesarynth cast out, begging in the gutter Hells of Earth where she could feel no home as Jezrael had on Mars. She saw Maggie, scooped in and carved up, the proud plasti-skin peeled leprous from his face. Because of Jezrael who thought she was strong enough to meddle and get away with it.

Danjit was licking her now, his tongue slavering lower down her neck. It didn't matter. The laughter, the irritation, of the rest of the team who were unloading while he wasted time – none of it mattered.

I deserve it. All she could hope for was that Spiderglass would never find out who she really was. It was the only thing she could do to safeguard her sister. Jezrael's unblinking eyes grew hot and itchy with tears for Chesarynth, for all that her sister had meant to her of protection and sharing – none of which Jezrael had ever said. *I thought she would always be there. I thought I could do anything. Now look at me. I can't hide myself from them.*

Eventually, someone called through the echoing warehouse, 'Quick! Company squad-car's just rolled up.'

Mijnheer hissed, 'Danjit, leave her alone. How many men they got?'

The voice at the huge door whispered back, 'One woman. And two towers. Big bastards.'

Danjit hastily resealed the suit to cover the love-bites he'd left where he'd slobbered over his prisoner.

Mijnheer said, 'Remember – we're just delivering her. Don't tell anybody anything.' Then he sifted over to receive the Spiderglass buyers. He soon came back, trying not to look intimidated.

Colonel Magrit Welland peered at the immobilized Jezrael. Above the Company uniform her waves of lustrous brown hair were pinned back from her face but it didn't hide the fact that she was also some kind of tower. Her green eyes hard, she inspected Jezrael, peered at the spiderglass tower with its fronds that swayed to her breathing. 'Where did you get her?'

Mijnheer said quickly, 'We're only delivering her.

366

COD.' Nobody believed him.

'It doesn't matter,' the woman said. 'I'll take her. Two thousand credits.'

Mijnheer said angrily, 'You promised five.'

'You got another market, buddy-boy?' The woman was hard with menace. Both towers had their hands on what looked to be weapons. 'Because if you have, the Company might want to ask you a few questions.'

'Four thousand.' Mijnheer was sullen.

'Two-fifty. And your life.'

Angrily Mijnheer held out his hand. The woman dropped the credits where he couldn't catch them; the thin plastic chips feathered down through the air and Mijnheer scrabbled after them, his dignity in shreds.

Jezrael felt the Company's muscle-men pick her up and cart her away. Her body bounced between them in the light gravity.

Closed in on herself, Jezrael felt only apathy during the flight to Spiderglass guard-school, hidden out in the asteroid belt. Put in isolation, she washed when they told her to, ate what they gave her. Then they gave her a battery of psych-tests that plugged straight into her nervous system; though she fought against it, they strapped her down and there was nothing she could hide, no way to stop the relentless tide of data and attitudes they programmed into her, or the probing of her mental set.

And after another sleepless night, the green-eyed woman took her to the commanding officer.

Captain Kandinskaya said, 'Brown, right?'

For the first time in days, something sparked in Jezrael's eyes. 'No. You've got the wrong name.'

'Oh, no we haven't. Jezrael Brown, born Witwaterstrand, 2178 –'

'It's not me!' Jezrael protested desperately. 'That's not –'

'Look, you shipped into Mars on Aust 26 last year. We got your ID, your voice-print, your retina-scan, fingerprints, brain-resonance.... But it makes no difference to

Spiderglass what you call yourself. As far as we're concerned, you became a new identity the moment you were hit by blue lightning. You can call yourself anything you want.'

A little snub nose and short, naturally curly hair complemented Kandinskaya's subtle make-up. She could have been anywhere between twenty-five and forty, but Jezrael didn't care that her boss wasn't wearing plastiface or that her hazel eyes looked like they might brim with mirth. Around the captain's head was the bland curtailed blue aura that meant a controlled openness to anything that might occur but though it was obvious, Jezrael didn't care about that, either. She didn't know what to say.

Kandinskaya raised her eyebrows a little and scrolled through the data cube on her desk-tank. It was angled so that only the captain could see it and Jezrael had no knowledge of what it showed, only her own innate fear of what damage it might cause.

Wires of blue light pencilled patterns on the air as Kandinskaya absorbed Jezrael's history and psych-profiles. Jezrael could see that her personal data was offering the captain a wide range of possibilities but it had no personal significance for Chesarynth's little sister. Once it might have done, but not now. All that mattered was keeping her secret.

Kandinskaya stopped playing by the rules. 'Up to now, Brown, you have been only a cypher. A purchase. But your training's just about to start and your scores are exceptional – perception, reflexes, empathy.... A few little personality defects like indecision but we'll get those sorted out over the next few months. You could fit in in a number of ways. Executive. Quartermaster's clerk.'

No reaction.

'Lavatory attendant.'

Still no sign from Jezrael.

'In other words, Brown, you'll do whatever we tell you. And I could call you Meat-head and you'd still answer. Is that all you want to be – a broom in someone's hands? A weapon for someone else to fire?'

Jezrael shrugged. Her erratic gaze paused briefly on the broken nail she was picking with her other hand. Nothing mattered except protecting her sister's identity, and she couldn't even do that.

'So you won't mind if I run you into the main data-net as Jezrael Brown, hey? See if Spiderglass Central can correlate you with any –'

'Ayesha Marron.'

Kandinskaya smiled faintly. 'I don't mind entering you into our records as Ayesha Marron if that's what it takes to wake you up. And remember, Spiderglass has invested heavily in you from purchase through transport. We're going to train you to be an executive, not some zombie-clerk in Stores. We expect a return on our investment. Now, Marron, let's hear your career decision.'

Jezrael went back to saying nothing, but Kandinskaya had the key now. 'So, Brown, what –'

'Executive.'

Kandinskaya nodded. 'Executive.' She switched off the data-analysis and scratched her snub nose. 'Any comment?'

Jezrael barely shook her head, her clean but tangled hair falling in a mop that half hid her face.

'Don't forget, Marron,' the captain said harshly, 'the bluelight is supposed to increase your ability to select appropriate options – you know, make you more decisive. I want you to work on that one because if you don't, maybe we will.' It was a naked threat. 'You'll get your posting at the end of eight months. And remember the executive's first duty.'

The words were there inside Jezrael, programmed by the cold machines of the night before. 'Loyalty to the Company means get the job done but don't waste your squad.'

'It may come as a surprise to you, Marron, but that includes you. You're Company property now. So don't waste yourself, either.'

13

Eight months later in the lull after the end of training, Jezrael-Ayesha was summoned to Captain Kandinskaya's office. Under the clear astrodome she walked to the admin building, the sensors at Kandinskaya's door showing red. She waited. High above, in the bleak night of space, jagged boulders turned, flashing in the sunlight. Overhead one vast angular monolith spun, its apex seeming about to crash down to shatter the dome. Instinctively Jezrael ducked – and felt foolish. It was probably a hundred klicks away.

The door sensors shone green. Jezrael went in. Kandinskaya put out a hand to switch off the visiphone but the speaker at the other end said hastily, 'Oh, and another thing.'

Kandinskaya raised her brows. 'Yes, Karel?'

'Make sure nothing goes wrong. I want one of my teams on it. There's too much at stake to fool around. I never did trust Berndt's planning.'

There wasn't a lot the captain could say without jeopardizing her standing so she just nodded once and switched off. The neat cap of imminence around her head changed from its suppression to three positive lines of hyacinth signifying actions about to be taken. She turned to Jezrael.

'I presume you heard that, Marron? Yes, well, that's your first mission. To prepare to destroy a target.'

Jezrael was aware of Kandinskaya's scrutiny, and also aware that her own imminence – registered by Kandinskaya's desktop monitors – scarcely flickered.

The captain's eyes narrowed a little; a flare of blue fire shot out like lightning from the back of her skull down

370

towards her left hand. It took only a micro-second, but it told Jezrael to prepare for some movement from Kandinskaya's left hand.

The captain slapped her palm on the desk with a sound like a breaking plate. Jezrael tilted her head fractionally to indicate mild surprise and indifference. The solid blue of Kandinskaya's imminence spiked darker and thinner with frustration and Jezrael responded with an overt – if insincere – display of attention. What she said, though, robbed Jezrael of any desire to mock.

'Your target, Marron, is Steel City.'

Jezrael felt her own imminence flare wildly and fought to control it. Kandinskaya watched her as if she were some lab specimen but eight months of training had taught Jezrael techniques that smoothed her responses to a minimum. Still it was hard when she'd just been asked to blow up an orbiting city with almost a million inhabitants.

I must've misheard.

'It appears, Marron, that Madreidetic are infiltrating our transport security with rigged data-cubes. And yes, it should concern you because what is happening is that our transports are disappearing. Anywhere you go in space, your ship's autopilot could divert to an unknown rendezvous. You could be attacked and killed, and the whole ship along with you, so try and look as if you care, for other people's sakes if not your own. This is not some dumb Gate story, it's real.'

Kandinskaya licked her lips as if stalling for time; Jezrael could see her imminence paling as she strove for greater calm. Kandinskaya stared hard at her and said, 'The first one was apparently plucked out of its route between Mars and Andronicus and whisked away to a place in the asteroid belt some seventy-nine degrees away from here. How it happened we don't know but the flight-recorder said it only took a couple of minutes and the navigator confirmed this. Absolute rot, of course. It would take days at ship speeds. Several minutes even supposing we had faster-than-light propulsion. The navigator claims it was like some sort of gateway through time but his captain died and he's obviously space-happy. As it happens we got that shipment delivered eventually though some of the perishables had gone off.

'Whatever, we've also had three ships in the last five months taken permanently. Gone without a trace. And two weeks ago, one of our colony supply ships managed to broadcast a more reliable report – until transmission was cut off by a boarding party. Our colonies out in Alpha Centauri are in enough trouble without vital food and medicines being hijacked. Madreidetic, of course. They've sold us rigged cubes before. Given their nature we presume they were actually after the drugs, but that is mere supposition. It could have been an attack on Spiderglass itself.'

Jezrael allowed her head to droop fractionally in a nod. She could see that the captain believed all this – there was certainty in the peacock imminence around the woman's curly hair – but whether she herself could accept it she wasn't so sure. It might be some devious take-over bid – especially if the board's strong-arm boy Karel was going along with Berndt Tjerssen.

'You are to report direct to your strike-team leader, Nils Borden, in the Spiderglass Hotel in Vienna, Earth. He'll give you a full briefing.'

Kandinskaya turned her attention to her console, pretending to blank Jezrael's existence out of her mind. Via her bluelight, though, Jezrael could see that it was only a minor game of tit-for-tat. As soon as she stood up to leave, Kandinskaya, as expected, said, 'Oh, Brown.'

Jezrael-Ayesha flinched just like she knew the captain had expected. 'My name's Marron.'

Kandinskaya smiled tightly. 'So it is. If you don't screw up.'

Nils was an arrogant bastard. Though he was shorter than Jezrael, he had a tendency to put back his bullet head and sneer down his nose at her. All the way up on the ferry from Vienna, Earth, Jezrael kept remembering how he had treated her at the briefing.

'Yes, Asheya or whatever your damn name is, I did say Steel City. You know, big thing up in the sky, whirling around the Earth.'

She had stared down at him, feeling the hard disdain radiating from his muscular body and trying not to give way to the sheer physical power of the man. 'The name's Ayesha. Ash, if you can't manage that. And I heard what you said. I just thought –'

His hand lashed out to grip her arm so tightly it hurt, as he meant it to. 'You're not paid to think! It says right here on your records that you might be thinking of wimping out on us. Lacks decisiveness, if you want the exact words.' Nils jerked her off-balance, his two cohorts rising to their feet in case he needed back-up. The deep sapphire of violence speared from all their heads. More, there was something Nils wasn't telling her.

Not liking the odds Jezrael clamped down her anger. 'I know the –'

Nils shoved her hard and she fell into the deep satin embrace of a sofa. 'You don't know shit! And in case you are thinking of reneging let me tell you that we're gonna watch you. All the time. Everywhere. You can't even take a crap without one of us knowing all about it.'

'Lucky you!' she retorted.

'Yeah, I'm lucky and I wanna stay that way. So if you so much as look like you're going soft on us I'm gonna take you apart with my bare hands. One step out of line and you'll be dead.'

Then his cohorts had forced her head back, back, until she could not breathe. On the verge of passing out, she felt them connect her bluetower to the memorizer and Jezrael drowned in someone else's memories, the battle-plans and layouts bulling their way in to trample her personality beneath them.

Now, with the hull of the ferry drumming a different note as the thrusters tuned up for docking, Jezrael-Ayesha felt her hatred for Nils give way to the fear in her.

Steel City. Madreidetic's most vulnerable possession, and

373

Spiderglass was about to blow it and its eight hundred thousand inhabitants to incandescent death that would rain destruction on the Earth below.

Not Spiderglass. Me. And the thought was a terror in her mind.

It was ancient, a nest of shining metal that had been the first cis-lunar colony, the first man-made world that orbited around mankind's ancestral home. Its lights sparkled in the shadow of Earth but even as Jezrael watched its approach, Steel City was wheeling its impressive silver network into the full light of the sun and it became a diamond filigree that flashed like a new-born star.

Despite her fear she caught her breath at such beauty. Even when she closed her eyes they were still daggered by its scintillations. The ferry closed on its starfire, Jez let its luminous wonder account for the flashes of terrified imminence she could see crowning her reflection in the viewports. And even this close, with the knurled extensions showing painted co-ordinates and crystallized dents, Steel City was worthy of wonder. Because, unlike Jezrael's old home, this whole orbital was inorganic. All of its metals had been freighted at colossal expense from Earth; there wasn't a natural curve to be seen, just endless arches and spires designed like a vast piece of jewellery. Jezrael could hardly believe such extravagance. That one organization could own this jewel, that was something else. Spiderglass owned far, far more, but Jezrael couldn't imagine them owning anything so incredibly beautiful.

She began to see small craft darting like dragonflies between the soaring galleries. Inside her a thought was crystallizing, painting her treachery in bluelight on the shining glass of the viewport: *I can't do this. I can't kill all these people. Whatever Spiderglass says they're doing, these people can't all be responsible for stealing freighters. What if it is the Gate anyway?*

And what about reprisals? Won't Madreidetic hit Crystal City in revenge?

I can't do it!

374

And however hard she tried to hide her intentions from Nils they were emblazoned around her in the electric blue of panic over the iridium crown of Steel City in the night.

That was when Nils swaggered over to her. So scared she felt her limbs turning to water, Jezrael tried to cap her imminence into bland indifference. Watching her reflection in the viewport she knew she'd failed. At any moment he would slide a spike between her ribs. She could feel it. . . .

'Of course,' he whispered close as a lover into her ear, 'we're just gonna plant the bombs. We're not actually gonna trigger them unless Madreidetic refuse to give in.'

She turned. He was smiling. Mocking her gullibility. Jezrael-Ayesha opened her mouth to say something but her brain gave her nothing to say. She could feel her mouth trembling with reaction.

Nils smiled more widely and sauntered casually away. As he left she caught a brief flash of sapphire from his head. It meant violence. He turned a brief cold stare on her.

She still could not escape him.

The queue shuffled into a blind spot between two viewports. Jezrael looked obliquely for the rest of her squad.

Over and behind, in a different line, Ramu's head was feathered with electric-blue that he was trying unsuccessfully to tame into urbanity. Nils, just wafting up the passenger-tube past the customs check, of course just looked high, excited, fulfilled even, like so many of the passengers now that the strange air of Steel City was wafting between the decks. Of Thea there was no sign.

Jezrael stepped forward into nothing, allowing the tube to loft her into Steel City. It was just like the tube back at work in Witwaterstrand, vertical strings of graffiti dripping unsuccessfully in multi-coloured smears. Only here the guards were obtrusive. Jezrael-Ayesha saw one woman, laser-rifle half-cocked in her arms, staring at her. She swallowed but no spit came into her mouth. Next time she dared look back, the guard in her niche was below and out of sight but there was another just above.

Steel City: from inside it was nothing but an over-crowded nexus of radials smelling of close-pressed bodies and metal and chemicals. In her head Jezrael saw her route unscrolling through the throng with the sweep of passing seconds. Making herself lean back into her walk as though she had all the time in the world, she paused to rubberneck at the clash of signs and scents and jingles. An old man, flab hoisted by plastiskin into the semblance of youthful buttocks and belly, strolled past in a scanty g-string but the game was given away by the static pads of fake muscle that didn't even twitch as he walked. Never-theless he exuded pheromones and she saw two elderly ladies from the ferry clutch each other's arms and whisper. He pretended to bump into them; Jezrael wanted to turn and watch but her cultural modesty wouldn't let her.

Reluctantly she stepped on to a moving walkway that carried her through a mishmash of exotic atmospheres. Madreidetic had nothing against franchising: there were tawdry oriental souks; Andronican holos where every passer-by became a hero or a young beauty; jungles full of bird-song. In each she could happily have hopped off into the side-streets with their displays of over-priced gauds but Nils had insisted on timing things right. The whole job had to be finished so they could catch the same ferry back. They had to be well clear before Karel informed Steel City of the takeover option.

And overhead, where the borrowed memories said they would be, scanners searched her. Nils had told her Madreidetic hadn't yet stolen the secret of imminence-awareness from the Company but that was no reassurance. Nils would tell her anything.

Jezrael wondered whose memory was being replayed inside her mind to guide her through this metal rat-run. *Was it male or female?* Female, she decided, then wondered how much editing had been done. She could feel no personal flavour but a dirty undertow of fear. *Maybe it was someone who had no personality?*

The implications were frightening. *What'll they do to me if I screw up? Scrub my brain clean?* Only there was a vertiginous attraction in that. To forget the weight of Chesarynth, of Antoine, of Maggie.... Of Ember.

Turning, walking, lofting up or down tubes on her pre-determined course, she tried to keep her mind on the job.

Jezrael shied from probing deeper, thinking, *Who am I to question orders? I can't do anything right.* Vertiginous horror swirled up around her, the riptides of chaos that lay out where decisions spun. Enough death and suffering already laid blood-guilt on her over the old guilts from home. Her fragile sanity crept away from the edge to cower inside the fortress of her orders.

But the damage was done. From the breakers beyond, nightmare thoughts chipped away at her security. *What if it's just a cheap take-over shot and Madreidetic aren't the guilty ones? Maybe this is just some pre-packed Spidurglass motivation? What if Madreidetic won't give in and we really have to blow Steel City?*

The concept reared up fully formed: the sparkling snowflake of Steel City fragmenting from the hub of fire, spilling bodies into vacuum, the debris plunging flaming spears of fall-out on to the dense towns of Earth.

Dangerous ideas. And as it was her first run, a chip inserted into the bluetower in her skull was recording her own performance. Jezrael tried only to skim the surface of her thoughts. Apprehension was something she tried not to acknowledge.

The closer she came to the centre of Steel City the more guards there were. A tall man with an exoskeleton frightened her by demanding a retina-scan but the contacts in her eyes apparently passed muster because he let her through. Just thinking about passing his metal-boned body again made her feel sick. *What if that happens to me? What if he captures me?* She could feel his light-weapon burning off her skin, charring her bones, slinging her on to some meat-heap to be reassembled from scrap.

Jezrael almost fell over a gee-node that hadn't been here when her memories had taped the place. Her weight tripled, fell again. *What else has changed? God, if this is all for nothing and we're going to die anyway!*

The inhuman guard glared at her. What else could she do but go on, fearing that at any moment he would realize she'd tricked him?

Here, gravity was variable. Apparently it wasn't thought essential, but odd leaks from the room-nodes around spilled weight intermittently over her. The few people walked swiftly, or tried to steal time from their employers, hurrying with assumed purpose when they caught sight of her or some other guard. She felt the tall pile of her hair spiring to hide the bluetower, checked to feel that it was still in place.

Jezrael felt conspicuous. *Surely they must suspect something?*

But no. They carried on with their plans, excluding her, and a weird loneliness hollowed her stomach with longing. *Unless it's a trap? Madreidetic know what the Company's up to. They're waiting for us. We're all gonna die....*

But there was no sharp knife of imminence from them. She was almost disappointed. She didn't belong here, but they were too self-involved to see it. A solid ghost, she drifted past their lives. None of them cared about her. The walls, curved or octagonal, gleamed into brilliance as Jezrael passed, dying behind her until the next person switched them on by body-heat. Stray winds brought changes of temperature and smell and her ears popped with shifting pressures. Guards checked on her; machines scanned her. She tried to look as though all this were normal.

Then, to the second, the memories cross-hatched over the entrance to her target. Jezrael's contact-lenses gleamed with somebody else's retina-pattern and someone's plastic palm-print in her hand keyed an old-fashioned door. An oscillator moulded under plastiskin to her throat vibrated her larynx to some official's voice-pattern.

The door shushed open. Surprise hammered her heart, sending it slugging through her chest. Jezrael walked inside, scarcely believing it had all worked.

A young girl briefly glanced up from the action-cube

378

she was playing. She hardly looked old enough to be security. Around her head were fantasms of imminence, the way she'd win if she were the heroine. She could imagine no actual threat here in the steel heart of Madreidetic; Jezrael hated to do this to her.

But Jezrael had lived more than the 3-D heroine and her admirer. She slapped a bubble-syringe into the hair at the base of the girl's neck where the mark wouldn't show. The heroine's image faced fearful odds in the cube but she'd make it and the girl would think she'd just fallen asleep.

Until four hours from now when Karel called Madreidetic. Either they gave in to Spiderglass demands – or they'd lose Steel City and all credibility. The power-room's rigged to blow, he'd say. Jezrael didn't know if Karel would really explode so many people into space if Madreidetic called his bluff. Maybe on Berndt's orders he would. If Nils was anything to go by, he might. Jezrael felt sorry for the girl.

Nothing else to do now but watch in the security-scanner, make sure it didn't record anything it shouldn't. Twenty seconds and it began to do its own action replay. A speck of grit danced over the time-segment at the lower right-hand corner, smearing the rolling figures. Jezrael couldn't even see the rest of her squad at work in the power-room, but they were. The monitor's *déjà vu* meant Thea was on the job.

Guiltily realizing that she hadn't finished yet, Jezrael leaped just in time to rewind the cuber. She hated having to scan it in reverse rather than just rewind to go back to the same sequence the girl had been watching when she came in but Jezrael hadn't thought to check the counter. Nervous, she overshot, almost knocking the illicit cuber from the girl's senseless fingers. *Get it right!* Jezrael told herself savagely.

The girl was stirring. Jezrael's new inbuilt senses told her it was time to fade. She backed gently towards the door. At the last moment she shimmered forward to snatch the tell-tale bubble from the girl's pleat of blond hair. The girl yawned and rubbed the back of her head just as the wind of Jezrael's exit ruffled the yellow curls. Eye to the crack in the door, Jezrael saw the girl's own guilt palm the cuber as though she'd been watching the security scanner all along.

'Is that it?' she mouthed at Nils, 'accidentally' bumping into him as they fell, slower than gravity, down into the ferry.

'What do you expect – a medal? You're not proved yet. Now shut up and leave me alone or I'll report you.'

There was nothing to say one way or the other whether Madreidetic's piratical policies would go on. Nothing to show that thousands of people might go nova in three point one five hours. Nothing but a memory that could be someone else's to tell Jezrael that any of this had ever happened. She left the ferry after the brief trip back to Earth. Nils' team stuck close by her.

Overhead, in the amethyst dusk above the Viennese Altstadt, Steel City was an evening star.

Back in the Company's suite after debriefing – 'You've proved,' said Nils without praise – Jezrael was free to go out on the town. The others didn't invite her along to their own revels. It hurt, but Jezrael told herself bitterly, *Why should they? You've done nothing to make them like you. You're a non-person, remember?*

She headed for the door.

'Oh, and Ash?'

'Yes, Nils?'

'There's a tracer in you. There's no place you can go that I can't follow.'

So she drifted through the diamond-decked tourists who chattered and laughed in the street-lights. Alone, she smelled other people's coffee, other people's cakes. A couple passed her, arm in arm. They smiled into each other's faces, pointing to the same things at the same time, sharing. *They must be seventy if they're a day,* Jezrael realized, and wondered who she'd be with when she was that old. *Assuming, of course, that I'm still alive.* And then, *I wonder if Chesarynth ever thinks of me? I wonder if she can...* At the next tourist-trap, she bought an old-fashioned post-card and paid a small fortune from her new salary to send it to Witwaterstrand. The trouble was, she didn't know what to put.

Discontent and guilt settled into a sour mood. She used her eye-muscles to flick her time-sense on; even if Karel was going to blow Steel City, it wouldn't have happened yet. Jezrael needed someone, but the only people she knew in Vienna were killers.

Like herself. Finally she nerved herself to go and have a drink. At least she could be near other people, even if she daren't get close.

It was on the news in an olde-worlde bierkeller where the volume couldn't compete with groups of arm-linked drunken singers. Steel City, a dark, starred lace black against the silvery moon, and a voice Chesarynth would have recognized: an old woman, Theresien Tjerssen, smiling plastic teeth in her old-and-modern face. The singers' chant frayed as they began pointing at the Spiderglass Europa logo, and in amongst the strangeness of a foreign tongue Jezrael heard the triumphant old woman say, 'Spiderglass' and 'Steel City'.

Jezrael laughed, a little drunk herself. The cuber on the shelf in the corner showed Spiderglass ships on a rescue mission; a star-map cut to the Madreidetic colony out Alpha Proxima way, with shots of swollen-bellied children. And gallant Spiderglass was taking them food and medicine. The shot cut again to Joint-President Hans Tjerssen, looking stern and fatherly, saying something about a Gate.

The ball-game resumed its monopoly of the cuber but the singers competed with its spectators' roar. They sang something noble and uplifting about Spiderglass and the atmosphere of pride swelled Jezrael's emotions until she was swallowed up by the crowd's euphoria. A man had his arm around her, rocking her from side to side as the singers swayed with their patriotic song.

She belonged. For now. Her arm tightened around him, her other hand resting loosely on the shoulders of another singer. People were buying her drinks; she was lifting her glass in time with the others, banging on the tables like they did. What did it matter that she couldn't understand what they were saying? Their imminence was a furry outreach of robin's-egg blue embracing her in their number.

Jezrael-Ayesha laughed when they did, their feelings carrying her above herself on clouds of alcoholic freedom. *I did that*, she wanted to say. *Planting a bomb means saving the children that Madreidetic was leaving to starve. That was me. I did something right.*

But she couldn't say it. It was a secret. And the thought of her doing something right dropped her with the suddenness of beer-induced mood. *Chesarynth. Ember. Antoine. Mom and Dad. Dael and Eiker and Maggie and Ember. All the things I didn't do right. All the people I've let down.*

Violent fractal pictures broke in her mind – what would have happened if Madreidetic hadn't given in: the bomb exploding, the light-starred gem of Steel City bursting charred with the flames of burning bodies.

Ember, thumping down from the sunflower against the bitter chocolate of the Martian sky. Any good at jigsaws?

And she knew now why Nils had let her leave the hotel this evening. They had the testimony of her own brain showing what she had done; she could never deny it. She was an outlaw.

Only Spiderglass could protect her – if she were one of them.

Company property. That's me. I could've killed someone else. Ember was only my admission price.

Strangely, a comber of exhilaration lifted her, spilled acid bright in and over her, tangy and lethal as the vastness of ocean. Jezrael felt immense, immortal, swelled by the rage at herself that grew when she realized the deaths she had diverted from herself to her friends, to Company enemies. The sensation augmented in roaring octaves of bitter power until she hung at the edge of being where something – some eternal truth – hung clear and untouchable as the luscious stars.

'I'm a spider,' she told the man beside her, and her smile glittered reckless like a knife.

He didn't understand but he heard the word 'spider' and laughed, and she laughed too, until she saw how the light slid over his cheekbones and dropped luminous on his hair like Ember's, then she was crying into the warmth of his shoulder and he took her through a linden-scented night to a place where her tangled feelings speared through tawdry lust into oblivion where she wasn't alone.

That was her first job.

Her second was to protect Chesarynth – if she still lived. If she were still a person.

Three months after the Steel City affair, the training-school in the asteroid-belt blew. Not all of it – just the administration block. Jezrael had learned a lot in her training. She knew how to rig 'accidents' that couldn't be traced back to her. A power-duct gone crystalline where some fault in the rock had let in the awful cold of space. Couldn't be helped. No lives lost. And surely they'd be able to replace all the training programs stored in the computer, all the memory-recordings.... As for the files on past students – well, they weren't that important in the cosmic scheme of things. Spiderglass could live without them.

Jezrael felt her glands pour rivers of adrenalin into her blood as the emptiness of space swallowed the flames, smothered the roaring lungs of the explosion. The adrenalin hurt: her shallow, panicked respiration frizzed in her brain and her heart beat so fast she felt sure it would burst.

It wouldn't have mattered if they'd caught her. If the fire had been the hot womb of her death that called siren-like. Not to Jezrael, it wouldn't.

But even when the shuttle she was on turned back to answer the mayday, she made sure her disguise – patterns of others' skin and hair, eyes and voice and figure – yes, she had to make sure her disguise held, and deny her longing to be cleansed in the fire. Otherwise they might connect her with Chesarynth, and Chesarynth would suffer. She didn't even dare look for her, let alone make contact, but at least Chesarynth was as safe as Jezrael could make her.

What else had all this been about?

The injustice of it all, the knowledge that Spiderglass possessed her and there was nowhere she could hide from them with their tracer in her head, the certainty that Karel could blackmail her with her string of crimes pushing her ever deeper into the mire – it all added up to just one thing.

The bluelight was supposed to give her foreknowledge so she could act decisively. But foreknowledge meant more choices for Spiderglass to take away. She hated herself. But she knew she could do the next job. And the next. Forever.

On a beach in Bangkok-Ivoire, feeling the sun's heat pushing light through the grottoes of her muscles and bones, with the sky a great raft of blue, Jezrael watched two girls build a sand-elephant beyond the sun-danced lapping blue of the Indian Ocean. The girls chattered briefly in Thai and the scent of coconut oil blurred past Jezrael as the younger ran down to catch the sea in her bucket. Then the elephant and its shell-jewelled howdah were an island, and the father and two mothers cuddled the children in pride and laughter.

Jezrael cried.

Faces and flames. Heavy breathing in shadows. Trivial enjoyments that never quite roofed over the abyss of guilt and indecision and fear for Chesarynth.

That was all there was.

That and Nils, to keep her on her guard.

14

Chesarynth pieced together the fragmented red lights that whizzed by: Kandahar-Spice. The white car rocked around a bend and slowed at a station that swelled white and vast as a glacier.

So soon?

From Spiderglaß-Vienna she had shuttled herself to Sears-Nyork beneath the ocean, to Seattle-Fisheries, Kamchatka-Power, back to Mexibean City. Sallow young kids, thin as sticks, had tried to sell her drugs or their young brothers, or Aztec artifacts that said Made in Mexico in computerized ancient script. Down to Antarctican Waters (by appointment to the Emperor of Nippon Electric). She hoped she was untraceable after all that.

But Kandahar-Spice, nexus of danger, after only forty-eight hours? Wouldn't Berndt have Spiderglass on alert all around every outpost, searching for his escapee? Chesarynth wasn't ready for it.

The doors shushed open and the car swayed slowly the length of the platform. Hastily grabbing her bags she stepped out. Already the car was shooting off on a cloud of hot air that wafted alien scents around her.

Tiredness, strangeness, the relativity of standing still, conspired to make her stumble. One hand grabbed inelegantly to pull her printed silk robes away from her legs so they wouldn't hobble her. She was learning. Her hair whipped at her face, its smooth, mid-brown waves knotting into a matted tangle.

She examined each stranger, expecting at any moment that they would wheel and fire at her on Berndt's orders. Terror was a scarf drawn tight around her throat.

Chesarynth walked into the wind. Even the signs were in four languages she didn't know but the picture for exit was standard. She was glad; she hadn't dared play the language cube in the mag-lev car in case somehow it was monitored and gave her away. Thinking of the burnout that had hurt dozens in the tutorial lab made her feel she wasn't being paranoid but cautious.

Even after so many stations she wondered if her ID cube meant safety or discovery.

The clerk let her through with a yawn. A timetable on the wall (she knew the timetables by heart but still she felt so insecure she had to check) gave the time of the next mag-lev to Spiderglass-Asia as shortly after dawn. The figures were international, the symbols for her destination long-rehearsed in her mind.

Kandahar was a strangeness that stepped out from behind its label. Standard prefab blocks reared their tiers of balconies to the night, but there were dark cataracts of plants from the windows and wailing music drifted lines of pale washing back and forth like signal flags. The streets were alive with lights, some electric and some the sharp-smoked fires of burning acacia. The sky was a dark mud of midnight that she couldn't believe in. Supercilious camels grunted and dunged in dusty squares next to modern transport trucks each with boys squatting on top, and each boy's profile showed a rifle soaring above his frayed burnous. The boys called high-tongued insults back and forth and mooned and giggled.

And over all shrilled the tapestried scents of the spices that gave this ancient trading-centre its name.

Stepping between the shadows and over the broken-limbed beggars who reeked of bhang, Chesarynth could not help but be moved to pity. She opened her purse and was besieged. Cultivated sores stank for her attention, eye-sockets gaped and plastic scars wept, and all of them demanded, 'Baksheesh,' 'Caridad,' 'Money money money.'

Frightened, she tried to run along the streets and urchins trailed her, laughing at her fear, their hands

386

outstretched.... She felt more than alone. Chesarynth wished there were somebody with her, someone always on her side. Like Jezrael. *Only now I'm an interface. I'm less than human now and that's all long ago....* A child scooted forward to trip her; another snatched at her bag but she managed to get to her feet and shove them away.

Then at a firelit café where men squatted around low tables watching a cuber set in the branches of a tree, someone rearranging his belt stepped between her and the mob of children, yelling louder than they. The children quieted.

'I am Nazrullah. Are you for Spiderglass?'

His tongue whistled between stained teeth on the r's and s's and a cheroot stuck in the corner of his mouth made him still harder to understand, but the children's catcalls and disappearance earned her gratitude and she said, 'Yes.'

'Then join our table and I will guide you there in the morning, insha'Allah.'

After that the man ignored her, chattering to his friends in a language she hadn't learned yet and gesturing derisively at the story on the holo. When she had finished the hot and sickly mint tea, the beaten earth pulled her body down on to it. Little by little, against her will, Chesarynth fell asleep on her pack.

A hand on her shoulder shook her back into her body. Blearily Chesarynth made out the man, his waistcoat still a spangle of red and gold when he pulled his jacket tighter.

'Is time now, missus lady. Mak-a-lev train coming soon. You have tikkut?'

Her tired anxieties sprang up like soldier-bones from dragon's teeth. Renewed with worry, Chesarynth went through her ritual, patting her pockets, rootling through her bags for things she had seen only seconds before but still couldn't believe she hadn't lost or had stolen.

The man said again, 'Is time now.'

Climbing up from her knees, she hoisted her bags. 'OK, OK. Yes, I've got my ticket. Where's the station?'

He led her off. Between the buildings in the space where night had been, rolled the desert, dawn-licked, shining bleak and rose and brown. Pale streamers of cloud vanished in the white of daybreak and the cinnamon air was chill with the sound of cock-crow. Her rescuer didn't offer to help her with her packs and when she caught up with him he hurried all the faster, leaving her struggling behind.

Suddenly a weird shriek rent the bustle of the street and everybody fell to their knees, heads bowing to touch the ground. He pulled her down beside him. After a brief moment the shrilling stopped and the man dragged her up again as though nothing had happened.

In the mag-lev he lit a cheroot and grinned beneath the NO SMOKING sign. 'My name is Nazrullah, missus lady. I am gate-guard for Spiderglass.'

The car sped along the white tunnel.

'I'm Chesarynth Brown. I'm the new interface.'

'Inter –?'

'Interface.'

He shrugged, curling his feet up beneath him. He too had the barrel of an old-fashioned rifle pointing up behind his shoulder. When he shifted it aside she noticed the bandoliers under his jacket, the brass bullets sharp and gleaming. Stubbing out the cheroot on his boot-heel, oblivious of the sparks that scorched brown patches on the hem of his tunic, Nazrullah composed himself for sleep.

His eyes flashed open, bright beads in his tanned skin. 'Face?' he said, patting grubby fingers over his forehead and nose.

Chesarynth shook her head. 'Interface. Interface for the spiders.'

His whole torso moved in an eloquent gesture of incomprehension and he went to sleep, leaving Chesarynth to stifle her coughing in his tobacco fog.

The car swayed to a standstill at the subterranean terminus and only when it was quiet did Chesarynth realize how the wind had rushed around it.

388

'Is time, missus lady. Spiderglass Asia.'

Chesarynth woke without knowing she'd been asleep and stumbled out of the car. Armed guards, some still in headdresses though something told her they were deep underground, stood around eyeing up the passengers, bullying the brain-dead who were unloading other cars.

Nazrullah spoke to a man in yellow and brown striped robes, a conversation in some high-pitched tongue where the hand-movements flew like birds, as important as the phonemes.

Above the chaos of the unloading – no, not chaos, but an intricate choreography hindered by the milling guards, she realized – the tough man in the stripes called peremptorily, signing at her in irritation when she didn't move quickly enough. He led her away, not bothering to check that she followed. Over her shoulder, Chesarynth saw Nazrullah wink encouragingly at her.

With the tubes busy ferrying the supplies, the fierce man glided to the end of the platform and along a corridor. Chesarynth wondered if he were on wheels, so smoothly did he move.

Then up stairs, the lower flights modern and angular, made of artificial stone. Higher and higher, with the ventilation shafts occasionally pouring pools of golden sunlight down to fade in the man-made glare. Higher still and the treads were natural rock hollowed at the edges with a thousand years of footsteps. It seemed dimmer here, and the green smells of living plants came clear and spicy into the dimmer corridor. Dimmer, she realized, because the lights had been switched off and blinds of thin canes tied in sheets blocked off the windows. Chesarynth longed to lift one and peek out but her guide was just turning a corner and she hurried to catch up with him, her pack banging against her thigh.

He left her in an antique elevator, pressed a button and said, 'Sikander' before the doors trapped her inside alone. For a second she felt the tiny room shrink skintight but it didn't happen. That was replaced by a moment of fear when her weight surged. Her centre of balance sank below her knees and rose again with the creaking of the lift.

'It's all right,' she told herself, then wondered if she had spoken aloud. And if so, who had heard.

When the doors clanked open, her ID cube *(Will it fail? Have I made an error?)* overrode the clerk's programming and she trembled with reaction. The beautiful boy jacked out and led her straight to Sikander.

Chesarynth would never have known it was her boss. The boy-clerk let the draperies close off the arch behind them but he said nothing and neither did Chesarynth because she couldn't think what to say.

Sikander Bahadur, misrepresentation of Alexander the Great, was swaying round the room scattering rose-petals on the marble floor. He wore a sharp cut in beach-shorts that may have been fashionable but did not hide the cracks his belly's bouncing caused in his plastiskin slimmer-sheath. A laurel crown sat precariously on his balding cranium and from the cadencing of his voice, he was reciting poetry to the dark-haired girl who stood stock-still on the rose petals when she saw the clerk bring Chesarynth in. But Sikander still had no notion they were there and he fell to his knees and grovelled, sliding his hands imploringly up the girl's bare legs towards the exotic ruby and gold fringing that was all she wore.

Chesarynth backed up and collided with the clerk, who dutifully announced, 'The new interface, your excellency.'

Chesarynth would have killed him if she could, but the look she gave him was nothing to the one Sikander shot his way. The clerk, naturally, was impervious. Of course the brain-dead were not really brain-dead or they couldn't have functioned at all, but higher levels of autonomy were stifled when they were on duty. It was doubtful whether the boy realized anything was wrong.

Sikander got to his feet, dragging the shreds of his dignity around him by yelling, 'Get out! Get out, you son of a diseased camel and a one-legged whore.'

The clerk calmly obeyed and Chesarynth hurried after him, skidding on a rose-leaf and almost bringing the curtains down. She spent the next few minutes dreading what her boss might do to his new employee after such a dreadful start. *But it won't be as bad as what Berndt has planned. Or Madreidetic. Or the old witch, whoever the hell she is.* While the clerk jacked in and Chesarynth longed for that same haven, she stared through carved stone lace at the mountains in sunlight on the edge of the world.

Sikander Bahadur stalked through the curtains some twenty-five metric minutes later. Elaborately stiffened business robes hid the imperfections of his figure and his beard and remaining hair gleamed with attar of roses. Ignoring Chesarynth completely, he had the clerk activate the cube's message on a private display.

Chesarynth knew her credentials were impeccable because she'd programmed them herself. Some of them were even true. And she hadn't needed to fake her dedication to the glass-spiders because it was her one remaining link with Friend. So long as Sikander didn't spot that her authorization was false.... For Berndt would never think of her hiding here, inside Spiderglass.

But Sikander didn't realize. Either because he was too rattled to think straight or because she had woven her credentials skilfully enough to deceive him. Being Chesarynth, she inclined to the first belief.

'We don't need another spider-interface,' Sikander said querulously.

The swarthy perfection that was the boy-clerk looked up deferentially. 'Our interface has been sent on sick-leave, your excellency. Nervous strain.'

Sikander slapped the boy's head. 'He's only just come back, you moron!'

Only marginally aware, the clerk went on impersonally, 'The doctor's report stated that the interface is still not up to par, your excellency. It came through two days ago – the eighth of Octover. I brought the matter to your attention –'

'Typical. Well, I won't have the spiders upset. We have to keep our output up after that débâcle last month.' A

391

thought struck Sikander; worry wrinkled the shiny skin high on his head. 'Do you mean there's nobody interfacing with them now at all? Why wasn't I informed?'

Steamrollering over the clerk's mechanical assurance that he had been, Sikander shouted, 'Well, what are you waiting for? Put this new thing to work straight away. You know what happens if the turnover drops.'

The boy-clerk never thought to escort Chesarynth to her room personally. What he did, knowing she was an interface and this the most efficient means, was to jack in and summon up a map of the palace. Then he told her to jack in beside him. She accessed the map with its line of red fire and thanked him, but his awareness was already busy with the scores of day-to-day matters Sikander left to him and he didn't even notice her colours withdrawing.

Chesarynth found that like all maps this one had very little to do with reality. Side-doors that the boy hadn't bothered to mark became significant when you were looking for the third on the left. Rooms turned out to be broom-closets and half the time the stairs weren't where they were supposed to be. The whole layout of the place was illogical. Someone who'd been sleeping threw a cushion at her when she disturbed him. A man in a bath laughed at her embarrassment when she burst in on him.

Feeling small and childish, she tapped on a door she thought might be the right one. When she got no answer, she opened it tentatively, still thinking what a waste of space these hinged doors were compared with the sliding panels everyone had in Witwaterstrand. Feeling inadequate always made her think of home.

Whether it was her room or not ceased to matter. Splashed with a pattern of sunlight was a magic box almost like the one back on the Moon. It shone at her, a zebra jewel of black and gold. Throwing her bags on the bed against the wall, she kicked off her shoes. They skithered across the inlaid stone floor to crash into a carven table but she didn't care. Hope swelled beneath her like a wave under a surfer.

So many longings weaved through her that her finger trembled. Already she could feel the cool burn of the socket, the endless night of infinity with its galaxies of meanings. Friend. Her poor spiders that no-one was taking care of....

Let this not be one of those pale computers like the clerk's downstairs. Don't let me have forgotten, exaggerated what it was really like. Let it be –

It was.

Her finger slid into the oiled silk caress and the circling planets spiralled her into their singing dance. Rich in the ebony space sang stars of lapis lazuli, round moons of silver velvet. Tears of honey gleamed between crystal swords that smelt of eucalyptus and the plaited coiling structures seemed to welcome her into their abstract of her world.

At first she sailed between the knots of concepts, joy filling her for the sheer pleasure of reading their meanings, of recognizing the artistry that shaded a concept into its resolution by the mere addition of a clove-headed bead, or a thread of sun-warmed citrus. Then she recognized an unbalanced sheaf of light here, a sour chorus there, and her exploration changed to the homelier pleasures of housewifery. She knew it was not really home-making; rather it was the tidying up of problems and answers to make the running of Spiderglass Asia more efficient.

It was too much to hope for that she would find Friend, but there was delight enough without that. And it didn't take long to set up a warding worm for her own protection.

Then she turned her awareness back to the wondrous skies around her.

It soon dawned on her that a lot of the off-key castles of meanings were shaded with the same warm, furry musk. The bead-symbols representing that deep and spicy odour weren't always the same shape, hinting at a deep problem in approaching whatever it meant. A hint of familiarity tickled her mind, coming from something she couldn't quite place.

393

Chesarynth expanded her awareness, leaving her colours wide open to anything that might be. Because even in these ghosts of their real essence she recognized the distillation of the glass-spiders that Friend had given her. Just thinking of him brought a ripple of sun-sheened gratitude to her colours.

And with a faint and distant chittering, the spiders themselves slipped their colours between hers. They drew close to the warm, hearth-red symbols that meant her urge to mother them, and she wrapped herself protectively around them, amazed at the gentleness of their minds. Though their thoughts were dim and fuzzy as a kitten's, they were as sweet, and she embraced them, glad when they blended into her. She was amazed at the welcoming recognition they seemed to have saved just for her. She felt unworthy of it, but their attitude wouldn't allow such self-doubt to linger. Their trust was total and it deepened her feelings to acceptance of herself.

Gradually their intangible melancholy matched and locked into her previous memory of it. Now it wasn't just homecoming, a beacon in her loneliness and theirs. Now it was a knowledge of all their needs and wants. Chesarynth their earth-mother, egg-sac of food and purpose, would provide.

Their pollen-soft essences shook when she thought, *I will – if I survive.*

Simple shapes spelt out *How long since your mating? You taste better than the last one. Don't die,* in urgent, muted colours.

She wondered how to explain it so they could understand. *I have an enemy,* she thought. *I'm hiding from him. He feels like this*: bloated, incense-reeked, grey-old and decayed, his symbols overlaid with death-white webs of deceit. *But I don't know all his colours yet.*

Chesarynth felt their security glow brighter in the yellow fuzz of their minds, and knew that to them murder was less certain than the inevitability of death by reproduction.

We'll spin our webs around you. We'll keep you safe.

Touched by their simple faith, Chesarynth thanked them and slowly disengaged.

When she jacked out her room was flat by comparison. And chill. And the darkness was made of walls that kept her in. Without the spiders' loving acceptance she felt her fear of Berndt and the old witch lurking at the fringes of her mind, waiting for a moment's inattentiveness so that they could pounce and seize her once again.

Unsettled, she drifted to the stone lace of her window to watch the moon rise over the plain. Beyond the flat roofs of the palace's other wing, acid lights illuminated the walkways round the sheds where she knew her genetically engineered spiders spun their monofilaments in isolated safety. The basis of Spiderglass' wealth.

Chesarynth couldn't stop thinking. Inhaling the night sweetness of the gardens brought a balm to her; a nightingale trilled and pomegranate blossoms showered the air with their fragrance. Past the shadowy mounds of bushes where white moths flitted lay the perimeter. Down where she supposed the gate to be – the road stretched pale across the desert beyond – a tiny flare of red glowed and faded. She smiled, wondering if it were Nazrullah with one of his cheroots.

Still her thoughts circled. Her stomach growled hollowly and the room-lights were too cruel to leave them on. She jacked in briefly to find the admin circuits but there was no-one in the kitchen and it was obvious she'd missed dinner.

Sleep was far from her and she was experiencing that clarity of perception that overtiredness brings. Booting in the cube she'd copied she jacked in once again, only now she constructed a timer-worm to fetch her out of it so she didn't miss breakfast too.

Covering her trail, Chesarynth stretched out across the miles to creep into Spiderglass Vienna. It was suppertime there – she had forgotten that on Earth there were time-zones; how strange – and only a skeleton staff was on duty. Laying erasers the way she'd worked out before, she checked that no-one had missed her, that Berndt hadn't sent out an alert. But it seemed her programming had held.

Then she set out to unravel the puzzles that might save her life or end it. Like who and what Berndt was really, and who his allies. Who was in Madreidetic's pocket. And who Friend might be.

It never occurred to her that she was pitting herself against the vastness of Spiderglass.

Or that that might be what Friend had put her there for.

15

Ayesha-Jezrael laughed at Nils' challenge. 'Why not?'

Above her growled the bronze-green paint that was Andronicus' sky in the empty studio. It had been a smart idea of Theresien Tjerssen to have her new-formed squad meet up anonymously in a neutral company's floating city. Trouble was, La Tjerssen had drafted her with Nils and with his typical arrogance he'd already annoyed the hell out of Liu, Theresien's squad leader, and they'd only shipped in two hours ago. According to the gospel of Saint Nils, he was the only one of Karel's troop who deserved promotion to this crack squad.

So Liu, masking his irritation, had said casually, 'Why don't you two join us for a couple of beers? I know a great place. . . .'

Now here they were on the set of an Andronican cube-epic and Liu had smoothly introduced a game of chicken. If Jezrael won out, she'd secure a high rank in the pecking-order.

Then Nils, playing for dominance, had upped the stakes by producing a handful of capsules and Ayesha-Jezrael didn't dare back down. Besides, in the golden euphoria of the drug, her base of self-hatred and indecision tilted her mind sideways. She thought, *What the hell. What's so special about life anyway?*

Rocking to her feet she clinked her noisy-labelled beer-bulb against Nils'. Angling round the control-area a little so Nils had his back to the set's meta-jungle, Jezrael shot him a smile of diamond-eyed malice. Even Liu was taken aback at the way Nils risked his partner's life but he kept quiet. After all, an initiation was an initiation.

Ayesha-Jezrael smelt the chemicals of death oscillating from acrid to enchantment at the back of her throat; already her hunger for them was punching holes through her reason. That was part of the game, to drag the wanting down into her every cell and then deny its lethal conclusion.

If she could.

Liu unobtrusively damped the safety-barrier round the set and the green world burst through.

Past Nils *(Oh, no, you're not jealous, Nils?)* screamed the banshee jungle, fraught with semi-sentience. Shivering palm-fronds hymned their malevolence. Hostile vines lashed out with bursting pods of alkaloids. One brown-veined liana crept towards Nils but he was relaxed, facing his female prey. He had no idea the creeper was creeping towards him.

Jezrael and the others, beer-bulbs in hand, watched it and damped their imminence so he wouldn't guess. The vine exploded its ichor over Nils' ear and they burst out laughing at his pain, then it dodged his angry backlash which made them laugh all the more. Clumsy with the poisons he'd taken, the peacock serpents of his imminence scourged fiery round his head.

Nils dashed the goo from his ear before it had time to eat deep into his skin. His blood, carbon-monoxide scarlet from the side-effects of the euphoric, dripped through his fingers. Now wars were packed in cubers, this was the place where ancient gung-hos came to be filmed in action for their fans – but it was far, far worse than the rain-forests of the old wars had been. Pickled first in celluloid and then on holocubes, mere leeches, malaria and tigers had not been enough for the kids who'd never seen real war. They wanted not human suffering but superhuman. Steroid-muscled berserkers with star-burst explosives. Preferably tortured to the limits of agony, but still battling, still winning. Atavism to bolster the punters before their next shift. And all of that was produced here in Andronicus, in this very studio. Jezrael was only glad this wasn't the set of one of Madreidetic's snuff-movies.

Nils stamped around, the psychotropics breaking him out of his usual control so that for once he cursed in hot anger. The drug-laced blood oozing from his torn ear sent his battle-fatigues crazy trying to boost their camouflage to day-glo scarlet. Seeing Jezrael laughing so hard that she choked on her beer, Nils couldn't stop his jealousy over-taking him. It knifed sapphire-cored lightning towards her, but stopped short of overt murder and she knew he had a plan.

He snarled, 'You're so smart, you should know why not.' The word 'chicken' lurked unspoken.

Jezrael, Liu and Sylvain fell about laughing.

'I do know why not, Nils my little garden of delights. The point is, to know and still to do it.' *Who wants to live forever?*

'Four to one you don't make it.'

'Done. And boy, you have been.' She clawed through her fragmented mind to reclaim the rules. 'Snap another capsule and get a bulb of beer you planted on the far side, right, Liu?'

Liu nodded, grinning in anticipation.

'And it's right the other side of this souped-up jungle, yeah?' She gestured at the tossing vegetation beyond the safety of the studio floor.

Liu smiled even wider, stretching the pale rim of his skin-graft that splayed across cheek and jaw. 'Yeah. And there's no way you can do it.'

Liu's partner Sylvain leant forward from the director's console by the banks of cubers. He knew what Liu had in mind and he wasn't happy about it. 'Don't do it – Ayesha, right? You won't –' He was so spaced out that the warning hand he would have slapped on her shoulder missed alto-gether and he overbalanced, sprawling undignified on the studio floor.

Liu put one foot on his partner's neck with enough pressure to hurt. His face was cold as stone, his voice low with menace, but still he smiled. 'Don't spoil the game, Sylvain. The little lady wants to play. Don't you, sweet-heart?'

From his body-language, the electric-blue flicker of his imminence, the way Nils stood close to Liu, Jezrael knew he was trying to cook something up with Liu. The drugs were only Nils' way of spicing things up a little so she failed. But it didn't matter. So many people had died for her that seeking death *had* become a game with the long sleep as the only real prize. So far it had always had somebody else as its target.

'Sure, Liu,' she said. 'Hey, Sylvain, you've got –' half turning as a blind, she flicked a low kick at the back of Liu's knee and he was forced to roll into Nils to save himself – 'some bug on your neck.' Jezrael stooped to give Sylvain a hand up, making sure she'd left no opening for Nils' envy to attack her. In her bluelight-powered manoeuvre she had got what she wanted from him. Palming the small, flat remote, she stared at Nils. He staggered upright, fury cloaking his awareness.

Keeping Nils in sight she said, 'Oh, it's OK, Sylvain,' not friendly but at least half-way open. 'It's gone now.'

Not waiting, she snapped another capsule and inhaled its euphoria. Instantly the colours of the studio began a ballet before her eyes, each shade of green blending into a symphony of hot colours. She could feel the dance echoed in the tiny granules afloat in her semi-circular canals. Lurching momentarily to find her balance, she stepped as briskly as she could towards the low barrier separating the theatrical jungle from the cuber-crew's safehold.

The orchestrated riot of emerald, jade and spring-leaf tried to mesmerize her into stillness. Solid depths of viridian sang sleep at her with the pastoral lilt of gold-splashed sunlight on beryl fronds chanting peace. Snakes of sound hissed from the hungry swaying of the lianas and she hung swinging between the safety of one step and the next.

But if she gave in to the green incantation and slowed to the drug's hypnotic ululations, she would die for sure. Only aerobic activity could break the drug's lethal spell. Still the siren lullaby cymballed the long sleep of death through her and she wanted to listen....

Each pulse of blood crashed like a comber through her ears, washing her closer to her own star-distant mortality. Her body was very far away. There was only her blood that reverberated through the green-tangled overture of death.

Jezrael's autonomic systems completed the step for her before she could fall and she tumbled back into her body as her foot jarred the floor. Startled, she took another ragged stride and then the self-preservation of the very drunk took over and she leant forward, walking rapidly to stay on her feet. The low barrier lay inert before her. Then, past a deceptively peaceful clearing, the wall of the jungle reared in a frozen cataract of greens.

The meta-jungle knew she was there. It lashed its tendrils, sensing that she was tacking towards it.

Nils, a deadly smile on his face, readied himself to stab the control that would power the barrier. But Jezrael had known him a long time. She knew that once she entered the engineered green hell, he wouldn't cut the current to let her out. 'Hey, Ayesha,' he said, a drugged smile of triumph on his face as she crossed the barrier on to the acid-green turf.

So she slipped the emergency remote from her sleeve and walked backwards a pace or two over the frothing grass. 'Looking for this, Nils?'

Liu and Sylvain studied the by-play between their new squaddies but it didn't stop them swigging at their beer.

Nils sneered. 'Think you're smart, don't you?'

She took another step backwards, hearing and dodging a roaring man-sized frond. 'Sure do, Nils. Better than being like you.'

'Trick is, Ayesha, not to get cocky.'

Faintly perturbed that his imminence grew new hatred from the frustrated stumps of the old, she still grinned mockery at him. 'Don't worry, Nils. I leave that strictly to you.'

A spear of meta-bamboo shirred through the air behind her. Jezrael heard it as just another note in the emerald opus of death. The drug pulled her centripetally to icy aphelion, far from the sun of her egocentric universe, far from the knowledge that she was about to die. Hot arias of blood sang in her ears.

Nils smiled, crowned with midnight triumph.

As through a telescope, some tiny rational part of Jezrael-Ayesha's mind decoded what she was seeing into images that had some meaning. Awareness zoomed in from its orbit, somehow acquiring the mass to shove her sideways and laser-dance reactions span her into a cart-wheel that saved her life. The bamboo arrow fell, a flat coda to the song.

She slithered forward to rescue the remote and on her second attempt raised the force-barrier so Nils could not get at her unprotected back. The rainforest was happier now, the thrashing rhythm of its branches settling to a steady contented throb. Without true mind, it still held a limited awareness; the barrier was instinct with light and gravity and electrons that shimmered ripples inwards through the very currents of the air. How pleased the jungle's creators would have been if they could have seen it stalking its human prey. Jezrael didn't need imminence to know its intentions.

Still not trusting Nils, Jezrael skimmed zig-zag over the sward and slipped between the trees, glad to be out of his range. Only she wasn't.

Scanning the director's main console, Nils touched pressure-pads at random.

Heat drowned the jungle. Jezrael saw it as an amber density in the air, pushing apart the minstrel walls of greenery. The twining songs pushed up a key and the percussion of smells struck harder: foetid bass-notes, a weight of emerald growth spiced with floral sparks.

Jezrael-Ayesha ducked along what might have been a path, a sort of green tunnel that was a shifting chiaroscuro of shadows. A shoal of flies swam up from sweet metallic blood on a fallen log; it was only a reminder of the cube made in the second shift of the day. She brushed their frantic buzzing from her in childish frenzy and her vision jumped as her battle-fatigues spun from green to green.

Sweat rivered from her and she saw her own odour as the peat-brown of someone else's holocubed pain.

A scorpion approached her in an arabesque of death. Jezrael danced around it, warding off a hail of needle-seeds. Roots writhed to trip her, branches to slash. Already her perspiration stung in dozens of leaf-cuts; she remembered her work at Nutristem and knew it was only just.

Nils pressed harder at the console and the mock sun burst with solar flares. Lances of light pierced the naked skin of Jezrael's face and throat and hands. Heat was hard, fierce waves that were prisoned by the force-wall. Her heart sprinted. Sudden fear sparked darkness into her mind. Euphoric confidence slid into a pit and she began her ancient flamenco with death; lover and threat. Purpose was hard to remember in the shout of colour and motion.

Massive mahoganies reached out through the nets of plantlife. The thick milky scent of gum oozed from rubber and tropical eucalyptus. Beneath her boots, broken fungi squirted rank smells that were whirled away on a mazurka of mazed air and storm-winds threshed sound from the winnowed branches.

Fear was solid now in Jezrael. Death wasn't serene; it was a dangling shriek of agony. She felt the heat would burst her apart.

Nils saw only the frantic treetops grow more frenzied as he turned up the heat. It was bad enough where he hunched over the console and he hadn't had the extra capsule. It wasn't him at the focus of the jungle's inimity. He grinned unpleasantly and cracked another bulb. Liu and Sylvain watched what the initiation revealed and grew wary.

In the jungle arena a red-banded spider spat venom from its web. Dodging flechettes as she straddled sharp rock, Jezrael hadn't seen it. She felt the liquid coiling down her temple and dashed it from her, but the palm of her hand was cut and the spider-poison speared its way into her blood.

Her world narrowed to a place where pain was the only truth. It was red as the sunlight burning through her closed eyelids. Her blood-light flickered darker; it was the wind lashing the green canopy, but she didn't know that. The darkness, the crimson darkness of her blood in her eyelids was death at last. She couldn't open her eyes to look away.

Injustice burned in her, a volcano that shook the foundations of her fragile sanity. *It's you, Chesarynth. Your fault. If I'd never come looking for you this wouldn't be happening. I wouldn't be dying. Everything I ever was, you killed. Every time I fed the walls, you cleaned up and made supper and Mom never even noticed what I'd done. Every time I got an A, the teachers called me by your name. Mom and Dad liked your friends but I had to skulk out to Dael's or the Wasp's Nest to meet people who only put up with me 'cos I could dance. You were so smart they sent you on a wave of praise to Mars-U. They wanted your future to shine with their approval but they said my only hope was to marry somebody rich. I even threw my name away to keep you safe. I was wrong in Vienna. It isn't me that's the spider. It's you and you've killed me.*

A vast and alien cruelty rived through her, splitting her old self apart. In the warped light of the drug and the spider-venom, Jezrael saw the shards of her old self spinning off into outer darkness like fragments of a dying world. *But I'll get you, you bastard.*

Her eyelids sprang open and the world reeled in on her, the green shriek of the meta-jungle. Jezrael smashed the spider with a stone. Its legs scattered writhing on the slick crimson of its blood. Jezrael smiled in satisfaction.

Above the canopy she could hear the mock sun crackling and roaring itself to shreds. The heat shattered great limbs from stands of ebony and their fall scattered twigs pattering and tearing through the lower gallery of the rain-forest. Humidity pearled the fans of palm-trees, glistened on the loops of foot-long leeches. Swirls of cloud hid the burning sun but the heat was still prodding the meta-jungle to kill. The whole emerald orchestra whipped itself to new heights of vicious frenzy.

Stiff-legged, the urge to kill Chesarynth luring her through the nets of tangled vision, Jezrael lurched through the forest. Only now it was serious. Its menace buzzed through her, so low that her belly shook and she was sick.

When she stood a vine had encircled her ankle in hooked tendrils. Jezrael couldn't shake it off; couldn't cut through its tough bark that formed even as she struggled to yank it loose. A great branch tore loose in the screaming storm-wind and she couldn't entirely duck it. Throwing herself backwards, leg still tightly anchored, the armoured weight of it smashed her down into the insect-seething loam. Shivering grass unleashed a new flight of flechettes at her that stung her face.

Wonder: *I'm going to die! I haven't done anything I really wanted to in my whole life, and I'm going to die before I can. All I've ever done is react to other people. Even laser-dancing because the groans didn't like it was dancing to a tune they played.* She thought of all the things she'd done, sick things, to punish herself for Ember's death and Chesarynth's captivity, to fit herself for the rôle she'd been forced to choose and her disgust was the colour of guilt. *Now it's too late. But it was Chesarynth's fault and I'm the one that's going to die before I've lived!*

Until that moment it had seemed impossible, remote, that she could ever end and the world spin on without her. Now, shin scraped raw, with the monsoon god aiming the rainforest at her, ants swarming over her escaped blood, and the god's own tree spearing her captive, death was really going to happen. Her imagined flamenco with death the lover was just that – imagined. More than anything else, she didn't want to die. Too late she'd discovered a reason to live: Chesarynth's days were numbered. And, when Jezrael finally figured out where she herself could run to, Spiderglass would find they'd lost their hold on her.

But all that would come later. It would take time and planning. In the meantime she still had to get out of Nils' trap.

If I get out of here, I'll fix him too.

405

Nils. Playing the controls. This is his storm and I've locked myself in it.

Suddenly the lump sticking into her hip resolved itself into the remote. *Easy,* she told herself, and commited self-torture to wriggle the thing free. Not even the most desperate actor would let himself die for fame – if he could avoid it. The remote would override the controls where Nils smiled in anticipation of her death.

She cut the sun – cold winds whirled – and the clouds glowed down through blood to black. Fear of the dark came to haunt her as it had when she was a child. Only now no ghost was going to come and steal Chesarynth away so Mom and Dad would have had to protect her instead. *(I didn't even remember I'd ever dreamed that.)* Instead, the cooling air sent rain rattling through the jungle, hiding any noises that things might make as they crept up on her. When she set her mind to pushing away the log that pinned her down, something scuttled away from her fingers unseen and she screeched. Pins and needles spidered up her leg when the weight was gone from it and she worked desperately to get loose in case the pins and needles were real spiders.

Now it was torpid with cold, the vine round her leg no longer moved. By touch in the night, Jezrael frayed it on a stone with frantic haste.

And ran blundering through the sleepy hostile forest. Without the over-stimulation of vivid colours, the drug too lay dormant in her blood. Her blue-built senses of time and direction clicked in or she'd never have made it. She clambered up a living plastic hill and stopped just before the force-wall. Its dim radiance was a blessing she was determined to deserve.

Easy to block in a faint artificial daylight where the leaves curled brown with cold. Easy to drop the barrier – so what if the jungle got Nils? – and to find the red beer-bulb with its macho label gleaming and humming on pre-planned frequencies to stimulate androgen or testosterone. She picked it up, her face caught between a smile of triumph and a sneer.

Then she assembled herself into a cocky swagger to go and collect her bet. The money was nothing. What counted was the way Sylvain hugged her in front of Nils, the way Liu smiled, 'Well done, Ash.'

In the warm, solid luxury of the squad-room, Jezrael-Ayesha leant companionably against Sylvain. Even by Spiderglass executive standards, their quarters in Andronicus were swish. Real human servants – brain-dead, of course – concocted lavish banquets. Picked men and women could be summoned for their pleasure, and a blood-warm sun-filled pool lured them to swim beside its musical cascade. There was even an automated gym.

But this room was the peak of it, with nightingales singing in potted lemon trees and golden wind chimes ringing above carvings of ancient Chinese jade. Diamond stars spattered the wedgwood blue ceilings. At voice-command any electronic entertainment ever devised would spring into action. Every now and then Sylvain would look round at it in wonder and his sweet face would smile at Jezrael, sending a pang through her. In the thirty-five shifts they'd been here, he'd fallen youthfully in love with her. He couldn't understand why she wouldn't love him in return. He kept saying, 'You will, you know. I'll make you love me.' Only Jezrael knew what happened to people she loved, and looked away from his perfect, unscarred form.

Now Sylvain stroked the soft skin above her collar-bone where her mauve silk robe fell back. Opposite, looking half-asleep on his floater, lounged Liu, feet propped on their couch. Loose-jointed conversation dangled between them, going nowhere, waiting.

Nils sat at the other end of the room, engrossed in a hypno-cube. He might choose to say that he didn't care for their company right now, but they all knew different. After what he'd tried to do to his supposed partner, they were happier without him.

A hum; the soft lights blinked and Nils' relaxation-cube clicked off. Sylvain raised one eyebrow, meaning 'What now?' but Jezrael just stayed where she was, feeling the warmth of Sylvain's shoulder against her cheek. Liu didn't react, either. As squad-leader he needed to look cool, in control.

A larger-than-life hologramatic figure flicked into view, dominating the room. Neat wings of silver-blond hair stretched out from the old woman's patrician features; her graceful robes draped a figure that was proudly erect. She stood still as a pearl in an oyster; it might have been a statue. Behind her, prismatic curtains gave no clue as to where she actually was. There was nothing to show whether the holo was live or pre-recorded.

A woman announced, 'The Lady Theresien Tjerssen, Countess Spiderglass,' and the hologram's old face mazed into a smile of regal condescension. It was obvious the skin was all hers, not plastic.

The huge holo began to speak in her precise, accented way. 'Welcome, Nils Barris, Ayesha Marron, to my team. Nils – may I call you Nils? – we have all heard so much about you. Your operations in Niagara-Moorlands, Silicon Valley, Tycho, Steel City –' she broke off, smiling and lifting her braceleted arms – 'what can I say? Spiderglass owes you so much. I hope that your promotion to my personal team of executives will go some little way to compensating your years of inestimable service.'

Into the pause that lengthened, Nils said, 'Why, uh, thanks, Lady Tjerssen. No problem.'

'And Ayesha.' The hologram's eyes moved, focusing slightly to Jezrael's left. It made Jezrael feel disconcerted. 'I trust that you find your suite comfortable?'

'It's fine, thank you.'

The holo scarcely gave her time to finish. In tones rich and resonant as Venetian glass, Lady Tjerssen carried on, 'Though you have only been with us for four years, you have become an ornament to our Company, a model of efficiency. I should like to believe that my people on Andronicus are looking after you properly. All my people.'

First Sylvain and then Liu found things to fiddle with.

Nils merely curled his lips in the shadow of a grin. It faded when the apparition's gaze locked regally on his.

'If they are not, Ayesha, you have only to let me know.' La Tjerssen smiled and waited courteously for Jezrael to say something, but what could she say in front of Nils that might not rouse him to reprisals?

The tall, glowing figure went on smoothly, 'Well, to business. In the past you have all of you worked against external threats to the Company. I am sure none of you is unaware that your various contributions have, for the time being, eliminated the threat of Madreidetic.'

Now the voice hardened. It seemed to come from all around them, each word cut from dark crystal. 'What we have now to guard against is a threat internal. A certain member of the board, and, we regret to say, of the family itself, is attempting to destabilize Spiderglass – not the daughter Companies here in Europa and Scandinavia, but all our activities, including our colonies in the stars. That man is my nephew, Karel, and as a traitor I disown him.'

Jezrael smothered a grin. Theresien Tjerssen used English like a sledgehammer; without the accusative endings of her native language, she had just made it sound like La Tjerssen herself was a traitor.

But Karel was our boss long before the countess here wheeled us in. Wondering, Jezrael listened again.

'For this end, we have thought it advisable to join you with Liu and Sylvain, who have also never let us down through almost as many operations as you two. We give you unrestricted access to the library. Within twenty-one shifts we expect a modus operandi that will protect not only the Company itself but also our poor fledgling colonies. Ah, with, naturally, the minimum amount of disruption and above all, no attention drawn to the re-shifting of lines. We want no enemies inside or outside the Company to profit from this, you understand? Ole and I will be very grateful.'

It seemed the holo took silence for assent. Yet another gracious smile of noblesse oblige was sent to gratify the peasants and La Tjerssen winked into non-space. The room was much bigger without her blocking so much of it.

Nils leant forward, resting his arms on his knees. 'I reckon –' he began but Liu had other ideas.

'Set up a corporate structure visual, Nils.' When Nils would have protested, Liu stared him down. No-one backed Nils' play for independence; they all knew his place in the pecking order of this unit. Liu's Chigro features showed no give at all.

Nils covered his irritation with a mask of nonchalance. 'Sure, God.' He let the words fall separately so that nobody could tell whether he were complaining about the menial task ahead or addressing Liu ironically.

'Sylvain, sort out the accounts for us. I want to know who's got the financial clout to back this kid or block him. Ash,' he turned his gaze smoothly on Jezrael-Ayesha, 'you used to work for this guy, right? D'you ever meet him?'

She shook her head, dark blond spikes of hair cut to form a pyramid that made her tower stand out even more as she moved.

'Right then, Ash. Find out as much as you can about the guy. I think I heard that he has some sort of personal base on the Moon, so use that as a starting point. And Ash –'

She looked her enquiry

'Don't let any misguided loyalty to him screw you up You heard what Lady T said about him letting the colonies starve. And maybe you didn't know that he's the guy that invented towers himself and from what I hear tell you're none too happy about that. Then as soon as Nils has blocked in the main figures, I want you to track them all down. Know much about the Company in-fighting? No? Well, until then, get yourself briefed on what's going on, because without La T, we're history.'

Nils said nastily, 'What about you? What are you going to be doing, Liu?'

'Don't worry about me. I think I can keep myself entertained.'

16

While Jezrael reived across the solar system delivering death by order, Chesarynth stayed in Spiderglass-Asia slowly unpicking the seams of the Company. The older sister spread her secret tentacles among the electron pathways and discovered everything she could about the executives. About La Tjerssen, member of the board, and the schemes she hid behind her apparent honesty. With the strange skills Friend had bequeathed her she could even taste the black acid corrugations of the old witch's colours. She hardly needed to call down a holo (taken at a Thanksgiving Ball in Sears-Nyork where the Lady Theresien had smiled as the Spiderglass ambassador) to know that this was the woman who would have had her killed just because of the way Friend had planted her immanence.

And she found out about the golden boy, Karel, Chief Executive. So-called because he had people executed. She gasped at the elegant palaces of symbols that were his programming, at the secret controls he had built in to the Board members' areas. Not a one of them knew it. It was a pity he was so lethal. More, it was a terrifying thing. Because if any of them could find her, it was Karel.

And the more she discovered, the more Chesarynth realized that she didn't dare plug the cash-leaks. Madreidetic might be peddlars of porn and addiction; they might blackmail senators and lords in nominal governments and murder the few vice-squad agents they didn't own.

But they were cotton-tailed bunnies in comparison to the Lady Theresien of Spiderglass, and Chesarynth was tied. The way she had left things in Spiderglass-Vienna, Berndt would be looking for her on the outside. If Karel Tjerssen, head of security, was anything to go by, she certainly didn't want to get caught. Her secret sorties through the Company computers all over the worlds taught her that.

As soon as she could, Chesarynth paid an eager visit to the spiders in their sheds. But seeing them close up made her cringe in repulsion: they were a seething mess of tangled grey-and-yellow limbs under the endless lights of their tanks. She couldn't have brought herself to touch one even if they hadn't been behind glass in their steamy environment. When one crawled up the glass (real silicon glass so that they couldn't eat through it) she recoiled. As it happened, one of them died. And seeing the rest devour their dead companion, Chesarynth almost threw up. She practically ran from the shed and it took her a long time before she could make herself jack in and think with them again but when she did, their gentle thoughts were, *We have missed you. We were worried about you. Please don't leave us.*

So, lonely but undetected, she stayed. The safest place for her was hidden here in Spiderglass-Asia, where she could at least share her love with the willow-pollen minds of the spiders. Of course, there was no-one else. Who would want to talk to an interface, and an infidel one at that? Of Friend she had found nothing but tantalizing half-clues in all her long years of search. Without him there was nothing she could do to realign the Company – though she occasionally toyed with the idea of discreetly bribing some member of the board with chunks of the leaking cash. Except, anyone who would take a bribe would hardly redress the Company's policy of solid greed – and she was afraid even to try. *If only Friend were here to help me!*

But he never was. The seasons changed, betwitching her then leaving her behind. An interface. A non-person with a gold socket mutilating her finger, setting her apart from everyone else. Alone.

So she hid away with her spiders, saving her wages, preserving her self.

The first Spring Chesarynth spent in Spiderglass-Asia,

thin-toned skirling flutes lured her to the Samarkand gate. It was late afternoon; already the sun hung brassy in the bleached bowl of the sky, its rays tingling on her skin. A crowd had gathered there, of guards and wives and children, cooks and cheap labour. A shallow drum-roll shook the last petals from a tamarisk tree.

'What is it?' Chesarynth asked.

Someone said over their shoulder, 'The nomads.'

When the gate swung open everybody shoved forward, chattering shrilly. And down at the oasis a sight met her eyes the like of which she could never have imagined. Striped tents and balloon-wheeled trailers were scattered beneath the palms and between the bushes of lilac traders had spread multi-coloured rugs. Pink-fleshed lamb dripped grease above charcoal and the scent of herbs rose with the smoke that made her eyes smart. The cloying sweetness of sugar-cakes stuck in her hair.

Stunned, turning this way and that between the piles of red leather and bolts of gold-flecked silk, she almost bumped into a kneeling camel. Its haughty sneer was on a level with her face and she back-pedalled, tripping on a heap of glittering brass that clanged beneath her shoes. A scam-faced man with one fierce eye brandished a gun at her and swore. And over all the haggling and the wailing songs rose the blare of a satellite cuber's quiz.

By nightfall she'd bought slippers and embroidered blouses, patchouli and coloured glass. Chesarynth hesitated for a while, wondering whether she'd get Jezrael a set of silver goblets or an enamelled dagger. She couldn't help wondering whether Jezrael had ever got that last impassioned message – or if she'd only dreamed that she'd sent it. She couldn't understand why Jez had never so much as tried to contact her. *What did I do wrong?*

Wistfully thinking, *Jezrael would have loved this place,* she settled on the goblets and arranged to have them sent to Witwaterstrand. *After all, what use would Jez have for a dagger?* Then, before the dancing became too wild, (an excuse: they saw the socket on her finger), Chesarynth wandered back alone.

A week later the nomads set off under the last stars in the grey pre-dawn sky. Not once had Sikander gone out to them, not even when the old men had requested a meeting to talk about water-rights. The last she saw of them was a black strand of silhouettes pointing for Sirius.

Spiderglass-Asia settled down into its hum-drum existence. She couldn't even write about what she had seen because her parents must stay not knowing where – and what – she was. To know would place them – and herself – in danger.

Every year after that, on anniversaries and Witwaterstrandfest, she sent her parents guilt-offerings with no return address and made-up tales of a fine social life to save her pride and her mother's anguish.

The mag-lev car would rattle away down the tunnel with her expensive anonymous freight, sucking hot air in its wake to flutter her clothes. Finally, even that would stop plucking at her and Chesarynth would slowly turn away.

Then she would watch for the red gleam that meant Nazrullah was on duty at the gate, so she could bribe him to let her out to weep under the jasmine that hung over the dying oasis.

On this particular day (time and not geography), Chesarynth jacked out of the communications system access in her room, totally fed up but determined for once to get her way. Sikander Bahadur was being more elusive than usual but Chesarynth was more annoyed than usual and she went to his suite to see him in person, first pausing just long enough to leave him a little surprise on the administration network. It wasn't even worth her while calling his clerk to ask if her repeated calls had been passed on; she knew they had been. The fault lay with Sikander.

The nomads were here and they wouldn't wait. Down the corridors and spiral stairs. After almost four years she knew them as well as she knew the power-structure of Spiderglass. Each and every little crack in the white and rose marble was familiar to her, and each and every tremble through the shifting alliances of the Company.

When she burst into Sikander's outer office the beautiful brain-dead boy-clerk was jacked in so Chesarynth strode crossly to the window to while away the time. Once more the spring rains had come to the heart of Asia. Far in the distance the snow-capped mountains glinted white against the towering storm-clouds. Cross-currents in the atmosphere drifted a haze against the foot of the mountains so that the peaks seemed to be floating. Nearer at hand, fugitive sunbeams braved the chill winds to play on one field of colours and then another, spotlighting random patches of red and mauve and gold amongst the green tapestry that was the desert in the waking of the year. The arroyo was a gunmetal sheen snaking between its broken bluffs. Moist earth gave a bass-note to the sappy green odours that the spring flowers sweetened. Normally it calmed Chesarynth when even the gentle spiders couldn't soothe her loneliness or her rage.

Not this time.

The haunting wail of a flute from the oasis was backed by high-pitched war-drums.

She turned to face the desk. 'Arbuckle? Arbuckle!' Of course, the boy couldn't hear her. From the smile ghosting on his face he wasn't even tuned in to the admin frequency.

Chesarynth stared at Sikander's curtain-door as though the sheer anger in her gaze would summon the boss. Not surprisingly, it didn't work. And she knew better than to disturb him when he was 'busy'. Just the sight of her aroused him to rage then and he would thwart any move she made. *Not this time, though. I've got him by the short and curlies.*

Stepping round beside the boy with the ill-fitting name, she slid her finger into the spare socket on his console, knowing a new irritation on top of all the others because she hated the pale imitation of meanings that Arbuckle was fobbed off with. As she had expected, even his machine patience had been exhausted by Sikander's lack of attention. This time the nomads wouldn't wait.

Arbuckle's pattern was coiled tight, woven with the

coarse over-brilliant spears of mechanical pleasure. His brain-centres were stimulated in precise ways that reached even his semi-sentience. A flickering in the top portions of his electron-structure was the equivalence of taste, his prime remaining pleasure. When, out of pity for his hours spent vacant, Chesarynth had made this toy for him, she had found all his hormonal levels set to static celibacy. Even through delicate manipulation she found that his libido couldn't be awoken. Visual pleasure, it seemed, was confined in his case only to the sight of correct business procedures; music didn't reach him. Nor could he understand friendship. So she had made the best of what he had left: taste.

He was reluctant to come away from his enjoyment but she quickly constructed a knot of concepts – shining beads, rough cubes and coloured helices hued with urgency. Sensing it peripherally, he unwound from the long shards of his enjoyment and responded to the shapes she had made.

Slightly appeased that she had accomplished that much, Chesarynth jacked out. Arbuckle's office filled in solidly around her: the graceful arch of the window-grille, the charcoal brazier bouncing warmth off the marble walls, the blue silk draperies hanging behind Arbuckle's desk. Since Sikander was, nominally at least, a Muslim, there were no pictures but traditional rugs hung on the walls and a soft Chinese carpet gave under her feet. The fierce music from the nomads by the oasis was still threading itself interminably into the old palace.

Outside it began to rain again, a steady shower that dripped on to the sill and pattered on the flower-beds below. Chesarynth watched it impotently, fingering her shiny socket. Rehearsing what she had to say renewed her anger. Something had to be done before it was too late.

Finally, knuckling sleep from his eyes, Sikander parted the sky-blue curtains and came in, lank hair awry, dripping a stale scent of attar of roses. He said sourly, 'Where's the fire?'

Chesarynth was so wrought up that she forgot her usual

apologetic manner. She stared him in the face. 'In the spider-sheds.'

Galvanized, Sikander grabbed her arm. Panicking he babbled, 'What? Christ! Allah and the Angels! What are you doing here? Why aren't you doing something?'

She jerked her arm from his sweaty grasp. 'I am doing something. I'm preventing it.'

As the import of her words sank in Sikander took a step towards her, fist upraised. Normally she would have backed off. In fact, normally she wouldn't have provoked him in the first place, but this was different. It was serious, and her precious spiders might die through his inaction. Totally out of character she leant forward aggressively so that her face was only inches from his.

He leaped in before she could say a word. 'You insolent thing! Yes, thing! How dare you – you – you machine.'

It hurt as he had intended. But Chesarynth showed her contempt; harsh lines bracketed her mouth and warped her lips, and her grey-blue eyes narrowed. Anger over-mastered her years of control. 'Taught you that in business school, did they, how to treat your staff to get the best out of them? Oh, no. Sorry, I forgot. Who was it you screwed before you got fat and ugly? That whore Theresien, wasn't it, when she got drunk at a party? She wouldn't have done it sober.'

This time he really meant to hit her. He swept his upraised fist higher but she seized his forearm, digging in her long nails. 'You touch me, Sikander Bahadur' – she sneered his self-given title that meant 'great' – 'and you can kiss your job goodbye. Because your spiders are really under threat. The nomads mean it this time. They'll torch this place and take their water back, and, unless you stop poncing around pretending you're a great lover in your harem – did you know your ladies laugh at you behind your flabby back? – and actually do something for once, the spiders will die. I don't think the Company would like that very much, do you? Especially Theresien – she's probably just looking for an excuse to get rid of an embarrassment like you.'

The broad wings of Sikander's nose whitened with fury. He wrenched free of her but her nails left runnels on his thick wrist. Blood seeped into them and he yelled, 'Look what you've done to me! You're hysterical. We should never have had a woman interface. Too unstable. You're paranoid, you know that?'

Sikander whirled round, catching his thigh on the corner of Arbuckle's desk. Arbuckle himself never moved. He was jacked in again to his pleasures.

Cursing, Sikander ranted on, 'What was it first? An electronic barrier. When the Shah ruled here a two metre wall was good enough for him, but no. You want electronics. You're trying to bankrupt me.'

Chesarynth laughed. 'No, petal.' It was astonishing the venom she could put into that ironic endearment. 'You were doing that with your inefficiency. You were even skimping on the spiders –'

'You and your Shaitan-spawned spiders! Is that all you ever think of?'

She ignored him. 'But since I got here their mortality-rate is down and production's up twenty per cent. We've cut overheads –'

'What do you mean "we"? That was my idea, you stupid bitch.'

'No, I just let you think it was.'

'I could have cut costs even more if you'd stop playing lady bountiful to a pack of filthy savages! They won't thank you for it. They just take your money and laugh up their sleeves.'

'No. Sikander Bahadur. They take your money, remember? After all, you're the one with the investments in Madreidetic. Or rather the one who had them.'

Sikander stopped massaging his bruised thigh. 'How do you know about that?'

Chesarynth smiled. 'I know about your *pied-à-terre* in Filipinas-Turísticas too.'

The short man slammed one meaty fist on Arbuckle's shoulder. The boy fell to the carpet, his finger pulling reluctantly from the socket in the desk. Arbuckle's mouth opened imbecilically. Sikander yelled, 'You, you traitor! I'll have you taken apart –'

Chesarynth slapped him. Sikander put one hand to the palm-print that was pale against his congested cheek, unbelieving that a mere woman should dare to strike a man.

Slipping prudently round the polished desk, she said, 'Don't be stupid, Sikander. It wasn't him. It's you. You're so clumsy and your greed makes you even worse. Ever since I got here you've been hiving off the profits I've made for you –'

'You're fired! Get out of my sight, you filthy sneaking bitch!'

'You can't fire me. Do you think my spiders'd work for anybody else now?'

His answer was to summon his bodyguards and have them throw her into an echoing dark cellar where unseen things rustled. Putting aside her fear, Chesarynth settled down to meditate for strength, a practice that had become much easier ever since she'd been adapted. Visualizing a lily swelling from the tiny nub of a bud to a rich, red-throated flower and then to its brown gleaming seed was easy to someone who could manipulate personnel registers or stock-flow inside the matrix.

She reckoned it would take between four and eight hours, depending how mad Sikander was – and how desperate.

In the mournful dusk the door opened. Two security guards hauled her to her feet and she stretched, yawning. They used Sikander's own elevator to get to his private quarters.

The pain she had put away during her meditation came back with a vengeance; Sikander's bodyguards had left her with a black eye and a cut on her cheekbone. Sundry other aches had stiffened unpleasantly but Chesarynth was largely whole or she'd never have begun the proceedings. She only hoped that her boss's mental sufferings were even worse.

The guards rapped on the ornate, polished door and pushed her inside. Seeing Sikander again sent a surge of anger slamming through her so that she shook physically. For just a second she wished Jezrael were there – *like she was when they bullied me at school. One of Jez's virus delights would make him so sick he couldn't get up for a week.* Only of course there was no biolight to sicken into stench and Jezrael was in the past.

Sikander stood before a silken couch, drawn up as tall as he could in a pose that was meant to be majestic. He had adopted Eastern dress of tunic, baggy trousers and mirror-embroidered waistcoat, presumably under the impression that that was what his namesake, Alexander the Great, had worn.

'You are dangerous,' he said. 'But indispensable. Sit. Drink.'

'You drink first.' Chesarynth sat gingerly on a pile of cushions before the glowing brazier.

Mocking such distrust, Sikander poured a stream of amber Muscatel into two chased silver egg-cups. She watched him drink a little from both then took one of the little goblets, being careful to drink from exactly the same spot that he had. Relaxing a fraction in the warmth of the room, Chesarynth appreciated the heady raisin scent that rose from the wine to mingle with the incense-sprinkled charcoal.

Sikander clapped his hands (*He must have got that from a holo!* she thought sardonically) and a meal appeared. Like him, she dipped portions of pilau and savouries using only her right hand – and in each dish letting him dip first despite the hunger and chill she had acquired in her six hours in the cellar.

'So where is my money?' he said, picking a pine-kernel from between his teeth.

'It's perfectly safe, still in your name, in the same funds, even. It just needs a private withdrawal-code, that's all.'

'Am I to believe you?'

Chesarynth smiled. 'You have a choice?'

Sikander made a ball of pilau and chewed it morosely.

'What about the spiders? They seem to be in some sort of coma. I hope you haven't killed them, because it'll take a while to get any more grown.'

'Don't worry; I'd never hurt them. I just asked them to have a little nap 'til I got back.'

'You can't ask them things – all right, all right, don't say it. Just put me out of my misery and tell me how much you want.'

Shaking her head in smiling pity, Chesarynth sighed. 'How can you judge me by your own measure, Sikander Khan? I don't want money. Not even your money, though heaven knows you've got more than anyone needs.' She couldn't suppress a grin as she added, 'Had any messages from the parent company, boss?'

'How did you – all right, I won't ask that either. But yes. The Chief of Security is coming here in person.' It was Sikander's turn to feel triumph and his dark eyes gleamed with satisfaction. 'Apparently he's not at all happy that such a large sum has been allocated – by your orders, Ms Brown – to build an underground irrigation channel from the mountains to the nomads' oasis.'

A personal visit by Karel, the man responsible for Spiderglass' army? For deaths by order and mass disappearances. The chief executive.... And, knowing Karel's reputation as a hard man to cross, Chesarynth felt dread build up inside her. He wasn't going to like what she was doing one bit. What did he care about the nomads? The Tjerssens cared for nothing but themselves, not even each other. Hadn't Theresien had Oskar poisoned? And Karel was coming here....

That wasn't the response she'd been expecting but she covered her uneasiness in asking for more wine. She took a sip and said, 'Ah, yes. Karel Tjerssen, the boy wonder. He used to be Head of Recruitment, didn't he?'

She nodded to herself. 'Only now his dear aunt' – Chesarynth raised her brows at Sikander, knowing full well that the aunt in question was the Lady Theresien – 'has decided she wants him at her side on the board. We are moving into exalted circles, aren't we?'

'But, Ms Efficiency, our readiness for this visit lies in your hands. I trust you're prepared?'

Chesarynth swallowed and licked her lips nervously. 'When is he coming?'

'Tomorrow.'

'Then, if you'll excuse me, I'd better get on.'

As she closed the heavy door behind her, Chesarynth knew her boss was smiling at her imminent discomfiture. Maybe her imminent death.

Her old insecurities came back full-force to plague her. *What have I done?*

It was a lie. When she jacked in to check everything in the system was ready, Chesarynth found that Karel Tjerssen wasn't really coming for another month. Sikander had only misled her to get her worried, and he had succeeded.

But she knew herself. *If I'm this worried now, think how bad I'll get in a month....*

Then Sikander smugly announced that the boy wonder had blocked her plans for the nomads' water-supply. Furious, Chesarynth jacked in, insinuating her colours along the shining electron pathways to Spiderglass-Vienna. With practice, constructing her concealing worm had become the work of a moment. Her skein of meanings dark and tight with suppressed fury, she checked Sikander's story.

It was true. Not only had he blocked the request, he had dismantled the stacks of data she had sent in to Vienna over the years: not one tiny fragment of proof remained about the way Spiderglass-Asia had selfishly sucked more and more water from the river that sank in the little oasis. The facts, the hologramatic pictures of the dried-up river – all gone. Her studies of the threatened wildlife – obliterated. More to the point, all her interviews (made behind Sikander's back because he didn't want to rock the boat) with the nomads' grizzled war-leaders had also disappeared. Not a word left about how they needed water or they'd die. There was nothing left to substantiate her claim about the dangers in the situation.

When she shuttled her colours to Asia and back to bring copies of it all, the machines in Vienna wouldn't enter it in their files.

There was no way now to make the Company accept that if there was no water left when the nomads came back this spring, they had promised war.

Beating and battering at the problem in dozens of different ways made no difference. Spiderglass-Vienna wouldn't accept the data. Karel had beaten her. She even found a faint trace of teasing meanings that must be him, mocking at her. Though something lurked, a somehow familiar afterglow to his colours. It didn't matter. Karel had won and from the seeds of his selfish intransigence there would grow war.

Not even blending with the fuzzy yellow of the spiders' minds could calm her then.

The novelty of wearing baggics' robes had long since worn off. Changing into the sort of comfortable Eastern dress that everyone wore, Chesarynth took herself out through the mizzle to do some serious worrying. It didn't even have the grace to rain.

Maybe I should just disappear again? I did it once and Berndt never found me. I could dye my hair or something, and the ID cube's no problem ... except it'll have to have my own retina-scan and voice-print and things. I can't imagine La Tjerssen giving up looking for me even after, what, four years?

A worse thought struck her and she leaned her face against the shaggy wetness of a palm-tree. *And Karel's her pet. Head of Security. It's his mob who're looking for me with a bomb on a plate.*

She closed her eyes against the moon-dappled night. *Oh, Jesus, I wish Jez was here now. She'd save me.*

17

'Nils!'

At Liu's peremptory command the broad blond man scarcely looked up from his war-game. He was too intent on loading pressure-charges into the simulacrum bodies of the soldiers in his holo-tank. Annoyed at the interruption, his imminence grew short tufts of ultramarine, announcing his intention to irritate in return. 'Yeah?' he said insolently.

Liu flicked his gaze at Jezrael-Ayesha who had come in to one side just in time to hear this exchange. She called caressingly, 'Oh, Nils.'

That did make him look round. Liu vaulted over the table, catching Nils' chest with a high-voltage slap but Liu had landed well out of range and there was nothing Nils could do about it without having to fight two of them simultaneously.

Liu brushed back his long bushy hair. Around it his imminence was a repressed cap. 'That's three times I've asked you, Nils, if you've got your scenario set up yet. I'm not going to ask you again.'

Not hiding his annoyance, Nils said, 'Sure. A child of three could have done it.'

'That's why I picked you. Put it on the tank now.'

Pushing past Sylvain as though he weren't there, Nils stalked over to the computer and accessed his program so that lifelike holos swam in spatial relationships to each other, each linked with coloured threads. As Nils leant forward, Jezrael noticed the grey hairs beginning to show among the buttery blond. By the deepness of the bluelight around his head she could tell that Nils intended to do

424

something that mattered to him. In this situation, it could only be showing off.

'Clear enough for you?' Nils said.

Liu didn't even bother to reply. Jezrael studied the scenario and had to admit it was good. She could feel Sylvain at her side, his fingers sliding annoyingly over and over one spot on her shoulder. She wished he wouldn't, but the only way to get through to him would hurt his feelings so she leaned forward still further (that didn't work either) and studied the figures floating on the blood-red background.

At the top was Ole Tjerssen, Chairman of the board. He had the long Tjerssen nose but his arrogant expression was weakened by the soft mouth. Hard to believe that he had control of an empire extending from the cities of Earth by way of outposts in the Solar System to the fifteen-year-old colonies out around Alpha Centauri. The colonies whose desperate plea for supplies had taken four years to arrive and whose relief – if any – would take another four years to get back. If ever an instantaneous transmission-Gate was needed, it was now.

Below him, smaller and to the left, was Berndt, who was, in fact, his uncle though of almost the same age. A strong blue line connected them.

On a level with Berndt was La Tjerssen, the Lady Theresien. A line of broken blue led upwards to Ole, whom she followed in theory but would cheerfully have murdered if she had the chance. Nils said impersonally, 'The fact that Ole has food-tasters "because of his weak stomach" is due entirely to her, only Ole doesn't seem to know that. We, of course, entirely support her.' He glanced up at the diamond-starred ceiling, knowing full well that the diamonds hid spy-sensors. 'After all, Ole is getting old and doddery. He's not fit to command Spider-glass.'

Liu growled, 'Cut the primary-school stuff and get on with it.'

'OK. See that yellow line –'

'Yeah, garish, isn't it?' said Jezrael.

'– well, the reason it connects La Tjerssen to Berndt is that he doesn't even sneeze without her say-so. The way I figure it, she's got something on him because he's too scared for executive decisions on his own. His vote on the board always goes the way she wants it to. Up to now, for reasons of policy, that's usually been how Ole votes, only in the meantime La T has been cooking up her own merry band of supporters. See there – and all those down there? And that little girl at the bottom?'

They followed his net of yellow lines whose focus was, though often indirectly, the Lady Theresien.

Nils said, 'Lemme show you something. This was six months ago.' At his touch, the same figures appeared, only the yellow lines of Theresien's influence were thinner or non-existent. Except for the link to Berndt.

'Now look again. See how blagging that little girl into marrying old Uncle Oskar then bumping him off has brought all his supporters over to her? La T must have all of fourteen solid votes on the board and whatever she's planning, she won't have to wait much longer. The girl gets rich, Oskar got his end away, and all her family are right behind La T. That just leaves Karel.'

Karel. Looking into the tank Jezrael saw an olive-skinned man with the long Tjerssen nose. Like most of his family he had high Slavic cheekbones, but in him the recessive Nordic blue eyes were present. Pale as a Scandinavian lake, they were startling against his tan. His hair was a dark, streaked blond, unfashionably long. 'The boy' must have been all of thirty but his personal magnetism made that irrelevant. Jezrael couldn't help staring.

'OK,' said Nils. 'Now just look at his network. Straight blue line to old Hans at the top there. The old man coughs and the boy wonder jumps, and he doesn't like Berndt one bit. You ask me, Berndt helping the old man get Karel made Chief of Security was a big mistake, even if it did restrict the number of votes Karel could swing. And La T knows it.

'Look at this scenario from three years ago. Solid blue *and* solid yellow. Even last quarter it looked like Karel

426

would lie down and beg for either Hans or La T, whichever held out the biggest bone. And look what he's done with it. Those purple lines are him.'

Sylvain whistled. There were almost as many purple lines as there were Lady Theresien's yellow.

Nils said, 'More of the purple ones are broken but the boy wonder's only been in business a fraction of the time that Lady T has. I reckon he must have used murder and bribery and blackmail to get where he has so fast, but there's no proof.

'Only now La Tjerssen says he's too big for his boots.'

Nils was justifiably proud of his summary but Liu squashed him. 'So the boy wonder's bright enough to see that La Tjerssen's going to have to move against him. And he's ruthless enough to have something very unpleasant waiting for the ones who try. That's why you're going in, Nils. La T wants Karel executed.'

'What about Miss Ice-balls there?'

Liu smiled down at him, his imminence the sapphire of a hard determination. 'Seeing as you two are so close, she'll be your back-up.'

18

Which is how, when winter had come early to the northern hemisphere, Earth, Jezrael came to be stamping the snow from her boots outside Karel's office on Earth. Nils had arrived several days previously but of course he hadn't been able to send any messages since then. She wondered where he was now; it was hard to trust him out of sight. And being on Karel's home turf didn't make her feel any happier, though reports said Karel wasn't due back on Earth until the following day. He travelled around a lot.

Looking out of a perfectly normal window in the perfectly ordinary farmhouse, Jezrael wondered where in the dark mass of the Black Forest the automatic sensors were but she hadn't got time for more than the one backwards glance towards the pines silhouetted against the lowering sky when –

A scanner flashed and the door hissed sideways, letting out a homey fug that swept aside the sharp, resin-scented air. From inside a cheery voice yelled, 'Come on in! I've just dialled for hot drinks.'

Jezrael stepped inside and the door slid shut behind her. Something sparkled on the edge of vision but when she tried to focus on it, the crystal brightness slid shimmering out of sight.

She didn't know what it was but the place already felt like home. Strange. Gathering herself together, she saluted smartly and announced, 'Ayesha Marron reporting for –'

The woman sprawled in the floater laughed. 'We don't worry too much about all that round here. I know who you are anyway, or you'd never have got in. I'd pass you a

428

drink but I'm in the middle of this' – she waved a mirror and a small brush that dripped enamel on to the quiet matting – 'so would you do the honours? I'm Magrit Welland, by the way.'

Jezrael dropped her bags and palmed the door-mechanism. Magrit moved far enough to kick a floor-stud and another floater ballooned up. 'Sit, sit. Take the weight off your medals. I'll be with you in a minute.'

Fascinated, Jezrael watched her enamel a tiny flower on to the carven lobe of one ear. Magrit must have been a good dozen years older than she was, but with her shimmer-dusted auburn curls and youthful outfit of gartered cream silk she looked a teenager.

Magrit sighed in content and twisted the brush back into its sheath. 'There now. What do you think of that?'

'It's – it's dripping.'

Sticking her tongue out, Magrit snatched up the mirror and made some emergency repairs. 'Better?'

'Ah-huh.' It had been a long time since Jezrael had known anyone spend so much energy on personal adornment. It made her feel young again.

'Well, to business then. Want another shot of mulled wine?'

'OK, cheers.' Jezrael took the scalding cup and blew; clove-scented steam added to the cosiness that a real log fire and tasteful knick-knacks created.

'Well, the first thing, Ayesha – You don't mind if I call you Ayesha, do you?'

Jezrael shook her spike-cropped head, smiling at the vulnerability in Magrit's way of talking. She couldn't help liking Karel's assistant, though she knew she shouldn't.

'Good. Do call me Magrit, won't you? I hate all this colonel-stuff when I'm not on parade. Well, the first thing is that we know you and Nils Bernstein are assassins sent by Lady T.'

From the depths of her chair, Jezrael sat bolt upright, sending the floater yawing and pitching round the room. Boiling wine slopped down her uniform but before she could unclip the projectile hidden in her belt-buckle –

429

she'd had to pass a weapons detector before she'd got this far – Magrit started laughing in a chummy way.

'Oh, don't worry about it. They call you Ash, don't they, the other members of your squad. I found your parting with Sylvain so affecting. How can you be so hard on the boy?'

Striving to adjust, Jezrael stalled for time. 'I wouldn't be so hard on him if he'd just stop snivelling all down my clothes. He's great on the field but – How did you know?' *Worse than that – why am I blurting everything out like some stupid kid?*

Magrit seemed to have read her thoughts. 'Easy. Don't forget Karel's official title is Chief of Security. He's got light-hypnos hooked up all around here. You know, those familiar little patterns you keep seeing out of the corner of your eye only when you look straight at them they're gone. Notice how I've got no imminence? That's because it's all damped down in here. Whatever else he may be, Karel's no dummy. And neither am I. You don't even remember me, do you? I was the one bought you off the miners. And believe me, you're a clam compared to Nils.'

Jezrael felt her lips move in a fatuous grin of triumph. It had been so long since she went under her own name that even this weird hypnosis hadn't pried that out of her. And to beat Nils the arrogant at his own game, that was even better.

Her mouth said of its own accord, 'Whose side are you on?'

Magrit looked surprised. 'Karel's, of course.'

'But he's a conniving little butcher!'

The older woman shook her head; the shimmer-dust made each auburn strand of hair a separate sparkling dancer. 'A handsome conniving butcher, but he's not little, believe you me. Besides, in his case it's all in a good cause. When he gets control he's gonna fix Spiderglass up to fit humanity, not wreck it. And if we're talking about butchers, let me show you a few little things about La Tjerssen....'

After Magrit switched off the holo Jezrael-Ayesha was

more shaken than she'd felt in a long time. Struggling to steady her voice she said, 'That could have been a fake.'

Magrit shook her head emphatically.

Jezrael-Ayesha went on, 'I've done some pretty horrific things in my time but that ...' She felt physically sick. 'Could anybody really kill their own son?'

'Oh, come on, Ash, don't be so naïve. The way you go on, anybody would think La T is a plaster saint. Yes, she murdered her own son, but that was only to stop him doing the same thing to her. Don't make the mistake of thinking he was the same as any other eleven-year-old, not after his up-bringing. Let's face it, for a Tjerssen that's practically normal behaviour.'

Magrit leant forward to lay a comforting hand on Jezrael's. 'Don't worry about it, Ash. All that's over and done with. What we're trying to do now is stop the old witch doing it any more. Have another drink.'

The pitcher was standing in the hearth, still hot. Jezrael took the mug she was given and slurped some of the sweet, potent wine. As she did so, Magrit said, 'That's better. I'm glad you feel that way about her. I sure do. I've got a feeling you and I are going to be real good friends.

'And now it's time you forgot.' Magrit settled back on her floater, ready to paint her other ear-lobe. 'Forget everything. Forget everything you've heard except how you feel about La murdering Tjerssen and how you and me are gonna be real good friends like Karel wants. Karel's not your target. In fact, you'll really like Karel.'

Magrit put the finishing touches to her other ear-enamel, then clumsily knocked the brush-sheath, sending it spinning towards Jezrael-Ayesha. Jezrael automatically tried to catch it, knocking her wine in a scalding arc down her front.

Karel's second-in-command passed her a suction-wipe. Then, gesturing at her ear, she said, 'There now. What do you think of that?'

'It's – it's dripping.'

A week later, out on snow-drill, Jezrael seized an

opportunity. Letting the rest of Karel's squad pull ahead, she signalled Nils to slow down a little and panted, 'Are you any closer yet to killing Karel yet?'

Nils slowed his run to drop back level with her. 'Nope. The bastard hasn't given me a sniff of a chance. You?'

Jezrael was almost surprised at the question. She shook her head, frightened at the intensity of his imminence. Violence writhed round him in jagged sapphire bursts. In this mood of frustration Nils was liable to take a swing at anything if he couldn't get a clear shot at his target. Allowing the gap between them to widen a little for safety's sake she went on, 'Don't know that we'll – get the chance.' Jezrael wondered if she ought to try and dissuade Nils from assassinating the boy wonder but decided it wouldn't work. Nils would take great pleasure in wiping her out first. Still running through the snowy woods she went on, 'Magrit says he's got designs on this Gate-thing. You know – anything about it?'

'Only what – I've heard around. Seems like – some ship or other – got caught up in it and ended up – way out in the – asteroid belt.' His face hot and red with running through the ankle-deep snow, Nils flung a few more words over his shoulder. 'They say – the ship made it – in about ten minutes.'

'Faster than light?'

'Yeah, Einstein. – Sounds like a load of – crap to me.'

As she was stepping out of the shower, Magrit came in.

'Hi, Ash. Want to hear the latest? Karel's sending that new guy out on assignment tonight. You know, the one that came in just before you did? You said he was good.'

Jezrael paused in pulling her orange ski-suit up, pretending to fiddle with the adjustment. *With Nils gone I'll have to be the one to kill Karel. Why does that make me feel so bad all of a sudden?* Confusion made her fingers clumsy; she jammed the adjustment. It gave her time to arrange her features to mild interest. 'Yeah?' she said not looking up. 'Where's that, then?'

'Well, Ole the Chairman's got a lead on this mysterious

Gate everyone's getting so fired up about. He's told Karel to get it checked out. If we can use it, think of the saving in time and transport costs out to the colonies. I hear tell they're desperate for supplies out there. We think the Gate starts out in the asteroid belt somewhere. Isn't that where you come from?'

'Nah. I'm from Witwaterstrand.'

'Oh? I haven't heard of it.'

'Maybe you know it better as Nutristem.'

Magrit leaned back on the rumpled bed. 'Sure – in complementary orbit to Andronicus, isn't it?'

'That's the one. Only out there, we don't like to think we belong to the Company. My dad – my dad's friend, that is, he grew a lot of the homes up there. One of the very first settlers – went there to get away from people telling him what to do. Cantankerous old feller. Wouldn't spit on Nutristem if they were on fire.'

'I'm from Georgia-Yourt myself. Got any brothers or sisters?'

Jezrael pulled her hair savagely into its spikes, static writhing round her fingers. 'Yeah,' she said fiercely. 'One.'

Magrit didn't ask any more questions after that.

Five weeks later, when the icicles hung thick as arms around the cluster of old wooden houses on the farm, the word went round, 'Nils is dead.' Magrit wouldn't confirm or deny it and Karel wasn't there to ask, but everybody knew. The first thought that went through Jezrael's head was a fierce chagrin: *I wanted to watch him die knowing it was me that took him out.* She'd never forgotten what he'd done to her in the meta-jungle of Andronicus just because he was jealous of her promotions coming faster than his.

That afternoon, when the sun netted in the pine-trees caught fire from the ice, Jezrael filed into briefing along with the other couple of dozen in transit through Karel's headquarters in Bavaria. Like everyone else, she'd felt the rumble of the mag-lev and guessed it meant Karel was back from another of his mysterious trips. It came as no surprise, therefore, when he came in to stand at the front of the hall.

433

What did surprise her was the rip-tide of conflicting feelings that battered at her mind. She meant to kill him. She remembered clear as clear the chart Nils had presented in the holo-tank showing how Karel was subverting the board. She remembered all her hard work to plot out where all of them were, what each of them was doing. Especially Karel, who'd planned the destruction-or-surrender of Steel City. The man, it was said, who was responsible for the colonies starving right now.

The man who'd invented blue lightning and shot it into her head.

Oh, yes, she wanted to kill him, all right.

Only for some reason that she couldn't pin down, there was something radically wrong with the idea of Karel being dead.

And it was a struggle to lash down the imminence of violence that wanted to flare from her head, only she didn't really know who else on the shifting squad had the same kind of tower. Any of them, spotting her, would kill her where she sat.

But gentle, funny Magrit said Karel was all right. And if Karel was going to stop La murdering Tjerssen's deathly games, Jezrael was all for it.

Not understanding her confusion, Jezrael concentrated on the long-nosed man in front of the screen. She couldn't help but be attracted to him. One thing, his stagecraft was certainly effective. Clad in a simple grey version of their combat fatigues, his flowing hair pale around the tan of his Slavic face, he looked like any one of them. But behind him was the red of the Spiderglass flag, rippling in the holotank against a representation of the galaxy. He looked tall and heroic like a figure from some ancient epic that might be titled 'Man against the Stars'.

Scratching one ear like any regular joe, he smiled sheepishly and said, 'Well now, I know you're all thinking that I'm going to start off with, "I guess you're wondering why you're all here". But I don't pick my personal squad from people who are that dim.

'I know you all know exactly why you're here, and that's

to find out what happened to Nils and then go do it back before they can do it to us. Because not only have we lost a skilled executive, we need that Gate. With it, we can stop Madreidetic or anybody else from pirating our colonies and shooting everybody up. We can get supplies and medicine fast to the people out there who need it, and we can bring in the raw crops they've harvested to feed the people starving on Mars and even right here on Earth.'

(Background shot of swollen-bellied children, big-eyed with starvation, too tired even to brush the flies from their faces; another shot of string-muscled students staggering in front of their plastic greenhouses that were scant protection against the frosty wind of Mars.)

'We don't know who's currently got the Gate,' Karel went on. 'But here's what we do know and Nils died to tell us. Let's not waste it.'

Nils' memories. Nils' vision and thoughts from inside his head. Jezrael could hear his adapted breathing, see it freezing in front of him against the silver and indigo rocks. There was the ghost-red of his targeting map overlaid on what he had seen.

Out of the corner of his eye Nils had spotted a movement. He whipped round, firing from the hip, and a jet of tracered fire left something black and ruined. Ash circled slowly against broad grey leaves. The picture scanned left, right and behind, bouncing closer then with the long strides of light gee.

'Some sort of plant,' Nils thought on to the recorder, and it sounded in his old, assured tones.

Strange, Jezrael told herself. *I never dreamed I'd hear that bastard's voice again.*

Along the trail – 'Had to land over the curve of the asteroid,' Nils said. 'They shot at me – don't know what it was but I'm damnwell pleased they missed. I guess the ship's recorders will have all that down, electro-magnetic radiation or whatever. Found a good site, though, where they'll have a job coming up on me. On the ship, I mean. Couldn't see any sign of mechanical transport.'

Another rock moved as his shadow fell on it. No,

another plant with a thick-headed bulb at the top of its stalk. It seemed to stretch up towards the pale light of the tiny distant Sun but otherwise it made no threatening moves. Nils looked at it (they could hear him thinking, 'I'll give 'em a good close-up of this thing' and the thought was coloured with arrogance at the skill with which he did his job).

And then light nova'd. Someone must have damped down the pain in editing the memory-chip but even so the whole room rocked and gasped with shadows of Nils' last moments.

When the squad had quieted Karel stood again, the centre of his stellar epic. 'Maybe you know that I'd already sent out two ships to negotiate with whoever or whatever is in control of the Gate. They didn't even get as far as Nils did.

'Magrit, I'm switching you to active service. The rest of you, you're coming with me. Ash, you stay here and handle communications. You're going to be acting squad-leader for the duration. Come hell or high water, I'm going to fix those bastards.'

Jezrael never knew where Magrit followed Karel for the next six weeks; neither of them reported in except by untraceable messages. And for Jezrael six weeks in the silence of the thawing forest brought her uncomfortably close to herself. If it hadn't been for Magrit, she'd have lit out on day two.

When Magrit came back she flung herself into Jezrael's arms and hugged her. Surprised but very pleased, Jezrael returned the embrace and for the first time she came to learn what true friendship was. HQ was much more fun with two of them there.

Laughing at a catch-phrase that the others didn't get. Sitting up late over drunken boasts that grew more and more outrageous as each tried to out-do the other. Helping each other out with admin that Jezrael was still getting used to. Laughing over the men they admired and the ones that they didn't. Covering for the other if they made a mistake and lying cheerfully through their teeth. Each knew what the other was and that their lives might be short, so they made the most of it.

One night they left the base empty and sneaked out to a laser-dance bar in Munich-Forestry. Another time, on official passes that Jezrael let Magrit write, they went to sit in a darkened church where the tiny lights of Candlemass grew to a blaze of light that shimmered on the skeins of incense, shone on the altar's gold.

It was an easy time because there was hardly ever anyone else on the base. Karel kept his army hopping and Jezrael, despite her arguments, penned in at her post.

Then Karel sent a call.

Jezrael called across the cheerful office to where Magrit was watering a bowl of saffron crocuses on the windowsill.

Magrit heard the catch in her friend's voice. She put down the can of water and came to lean over Jezrael, her auburn hair tangling in Jezrael's spiky crop. 'What is it, honey?'

'Karel. How can he do this to me?'

Silently they watched Karel's tired brown face stare up at them from the holo. 'Ash, send whoever's on base out to the Gate. I want you to stay put.' The message faded, only his bright blue eyes glowing on screen after everything else had faded.

Jezrael looked up at her friend. She said vehemently, 'I don't care what he says, I'm not sending you out there. I'll go.'

'He wants you here, Ash. I'll go.'

'Look, Magrit, just because you fancy him doesn't mean you've got to run all his dirty little errands.'

Magrit coloured. 'That's got nothing to do with it. Anyway, you do too. I've seen the way you look at him when he's around. The point is, you're security, I'm security and there's no-one else here. I've been sick to death of being cooped up at the desk so long.'

'I should go, Magrit. I'm younger than you.'

Magrit's gentle eyes crinkled in laughter. 'Were you always such a silver-tongued charmer?' She reached forward to start punching up transport information.

'Look,' Jezrael yelled, her hand grasping Magrit's fingers in a painful grip, 'you didn't make it this far by being stupid. Why start now?' But she knew she was fighting a losing battle.

'Look yourself. Just order me to go, OK? OK?'

Jezrael knew she had lost. 'OK,' she said quietly. 'Magrit, get out there to the Gate.' Both of them finished at the same time, using the PT instructor's favourite phrase, giggling, 'And that's an order!'

Magrit knew full well that Jezrael intended to slip her a mickey. That was why she slugged her hard at the base of the neck.

Magrit's laughter died alone, echoing sadly in the chimney.

When Jezrael woke up, Magrit had gone.

INNER RING

Cold as starlight the naked cliffs enfolded Ayesha-Jezrael as she passed the spot where gentle Magrit died.

It's all Chesarynth's fault! she thought, and squashed that memory before the chip in her head could record it.

And Karel's. He's the one who should be dead. Confusion and desire cut the thought to ribbons.

There was hardly any atmosphere this far from the sun but she felt the schist grating underfoot and the sound of it came up through her bones. There was only a shadow on the frost to mark her friend's last bed. High on the slope the schist winked silver in the far sunlight; there seemed to be a figure in a cave beneath the stones limned with dark shadows, a pattern like mackerel scales with the figure as the pupil of a cold stone eye. Something paralysed Jezrael.

Ceriad the warrior-woman rode the gravity, crowned with the sapphire imminence of violence. Her poisonous bow-wave rushed outwards from its moving axis, beginning to fall as a deadly stream sheathed in acid light towards Jezrael, who could not escape.

Still some core of hope wouldn't let Jezrael-Ayesha give up. Reflexes trained in the laser-dance and honed in many a battle whipped up her sword and braced its vibro-blade to pierce Ceriad's neck, though she might be dead herself when Ceriad's illegal blade struck. *Maybe....*

If only I can take her with me, I can get the Gate. The millions on Mars and in the colonies might be fed.

Even with Ceriad's poisoned fire licking out close to her neck, all at once a smile burst out on Jezrael's face, surprising her, a joy so fierce it was like a flame while the warrior woman's beam floated, fatal, closer....

441

Fierce sunshine flooded Chesarynth's vision as she peered over the mounds of smoking debris in the mag-lev tunnel. A ragged hole in the roof dangled a fringe of ululating tribesmen (Chesarynth sagged near-fainting) sliding downwards to attack the car that wasn't even due yet. And, on the roof of the rubble-dented car, was Karel, her enemy, the focus of a ring of glittering scimitars. A bullet spanged past his head.

Trembling, Chesarynth aimed at a warrior hoisted high on the sun-gilded rope that plunged into dark and bloody chaos. His ancient rifle was aimed at Karel. Eyes closed, she hesitated, gripped by gut-wrenching fear and a savage satisfaction that it was what the butcher of Spiderglass deserved. She couldn't help but watch through half-shut eyes. She saw Karel fall, sprawling, sliding, finding a bracing-point just as another assailant sliced at his leg. It was in her to shoot him herself, so great was her disgust and rage, but the guards she had known for years were losing and their lives were on the line.

Pulling herself together, Chesarynth fired a heat-seeker at Karel's airborne attacker and a second burst at his assailant on the car. The sweat-robed figure plunged headlong overboard.

'Get to the generator!' yelled Karel. 'Power on!' Then, a lone blond warrior, he was falling under a wave of nomads....

Outside, Chesarynth leapt to the roof of the power-shed, running from shadow into hot light that stabbed at her eyes. As she headed breathless for the trap-door in the flat roof, it was flung open from below.

She fell back, her head ringing on the sunbaked stone. Concussed, confused, she fell back through time to Witwaterstrand and the mob was going to laugh and watch her die.

Jezrael will save me again.

But when she forced her eyelids open against the burning light, a seam-faced, one-eyed nomad was coming

442

at her with a knife and Jez was nowhere in sight. He lifted the curved blade to plunge it into her helpless chest. At the summit of its arc, the curved blade glittered downwards. . . .

The gold of a knife in Asia.

The raging dark of the tunnel.

The midnight and silver of the asteroid.

And linking it all – Jezrael thought – was the colourless, odourless non-substance of the Gate.

Hung between a heart-beat and infinity, Jezrael felt a strange and savage happiness. Not just the fierce knife-edge roll of the dice that might just win against all odds, but a dusty, alien pleasure that seemed to whisper along her frozen neural canals.

A portrait caught at Jezrael. The frame was Ceriad's sapphire intention, the angle of her silver-suited body, the sun-opalled spike of her poisoned rain that shone against the starry black of the sky. In comparison the figure she saw seemed weak: a man, a tower, a spider.

His tower shone with a pale iridescence above the winking heads of his spidery crown. She had never seen both in one head before. He seemed old, old as the first atom; as Jezrael watched, his red-knuckled hands trembled with age. But the pleasure that poured into her tasted of him, and his intelligence was bright as honey in sunlight with his humour.

The oddest thing was that he had no imminence at all.

Then he moved inside her mind and Jezrael wanted to be afraid but she wasn't and that scared her too. She couldn't move. Again she was imprisoned in her body (*I killed Ember!*) and fear tried to reach her with its barbed hooks. For inside her body was silence. Gone were the chugging of her lungs, the pumping of her heart, the rustle of blood in her ears that she had never heard because she had taken it all for granted.

And now it was gone. Even the shades of terror were gone though a faint memory (Alex and the shadow-voices, Zuleika, her Spiderglass missions of death) of learned terror wanted her to acknowledge it. Jezrael wondered if she were already dead.

But Ceriad dangled motionless too and her spear of poison was trapped in a sunbeam.

'Well done, Company,' his ancient voice wheezed, proving (or did it?) that she was still alive to be dancing with death. *Or should I say* – she felt something rummaging around in her mind – *Jezrael Ayesha Marron Brown? You're the first one that's said, 'Let's talk'. Now, what shall we talk about?*

Call this bitch off! she thought, and her larynx wouldn't spill the sounds outside her.

No answer. It was as if she saw him, though, ferreting round in the piled junk-heap of her store of experiences, tossing away ideas over his shoulder. And she was powerless to stop his invasion of her life.

Am I dead?

He chuckled, an ancient, grainy sound. *Nope. It just takes time for the adrenalin to hit your bloodstream. But out here there is no time. You really want to feel scared?*

At least I'd know I was still alive!

Park your agitation in orbit for a while, Jezrael-Ayesha. Lemme ask you something.

If Jezrael could have felt fear then an avalanche of terror would have ploughed her up. For what she heard – and saw – and experienced – was the screaming mêlée swarming over Karel, and in its sweat-and-blood-reeked reality she didn't want him dead. But that was just the *hors d'oeuvre*.

For there lay her sister, paralysed by concussion and conviction of inadequacy, with the great silver sickle of a knife coming down to rip her where she lay.

Jezrael's mind wanted to burst, if that's what it would have taken to let her break loose of her own weird paralysis, and fly to save her sister, even though she knew logically that Chesarynth would be long dead by the time she got there. Because however much she might think she hated Ches for all that she, Jezrael, had become, she could no more abandon her than she had when they were kids.

I thought so, the old man told her in the silence that echoed in her head. *Now, what about Spiderglass?*

Again, his body still sitting cross-legged and grinning inside its rococo frame of violence, the old man went rootling through the piled-up trash of her past. Emotions she had long ago forgotten snagged her through joy and humiliation, rage and sorrow and indifference, as he riffled among her memory-files. There was Nils. And Magrit. And Karel's strong face with its long, chiselled teeth, a face she had not realized had become so dear to her. But that was something she had suppressed even to herself, because she didn't want to tread on Magrit's toes. And because part of her still wanted him dead.

The picture panned back to Nils and for a moment Jezrael thought she had failed whatever test it was that the old man had in mind, but she gave a mental shrug. Then he carried on sweeping aside the haphazard trophies of her life while he looked for — whatever it was.

Just one last little thing, young lady, and then you can have your head back. Mind, so can she.

Her eyes locked unmoving, frozen in the platinum-indigo wastes of the asteroid, Jezrael could still see Ceriad, nemesis falling with a sword of virulence to split her out of life. Jezrael saw her own hands angled to spear Ceriad even if she herself died first. Somehow it was less of a comfort than it might have been. She struggled to move; failed.

The old man was still sitting motionless on the edge of the shadow, thin rags of hair whipped out stiff as his metallic blanket, frozen too where the wind from the air-pump had struck him. Now his mind was picking over Karel, the boy wonder, leader of assassins, maker of the garden-master and lord of the imminence tower. Jezrael felt it all. She even saw La Tjerssen, the old witch of ambition. And suddenly Jezrael felt like she did in Maggie's bar when she was about to dance a message of solidarity, that we were all walking wounded, but she couldn't move —

And then her heart gave one slow and solid beat that

echoed in the vacuum of her chest. Her diaphragm twitched a fraction downwards for the first hollowing of her lungs; the first whisper of cilia in her nostrils signalled the first sighing intake of a breath about to happen.

Fear dappled through Jezrael, streaked with the infinitely slow dance of virus droplets falling towards her skin. She strained but still not a muscle of her sword-arm would obey though a tiny spark of sunlight flashed from the tip of her vibro-blade.

She was Madreidetic, was Ceriad, the man said chattily. *Judging by you two, I still don't think mankind's ready for the Gate.*

Instantaneous thought in Jezrael's mind: *What is the Gate?*

I am.

She flicked uncomprehending past that thought. *But what about the colonies? What about the students starving on Mars?*

Up to you.

No, it isn't! Now panic budded through Jezrael's mind, began its hormonal etching along the nerves of her body. *Anything I ever do for myself, it goes wrong. I thought if I could know what people were going to do then I'd know what I ought to do as well. But it doesn't work that way. This damn' great chunk of spiderglass in my hair, it's useless! I can't do anything right! I'm what my parents always said I would be – useless! So all I do is obey orders. They can make the decisions.*

Who?

Well, them.... Jezrael's thought-chain trailed off, the links unravelling.

You can't blame other people for your life, Jezrael Brown. You want to make the best you can of it, even if you see everything in shades of blue. It's precious, the most precious jewel you'll ever have. Give it a nice setting, polish it once in a while. Make it something really beautiful, do what you want with it. It's your life, your colours, the azure and the midnight, they're yours, get me?

But I'm going to die! And so's Ches. And Karel. And –

We all are. Trick is, to make it worthwhile first. Help people. Make someone else glad you lived. And now, I've got to be going.

Stop! How come you said you were the Gate?

I was a mercenary, just like you. Hired gun – see, I don't tart up the truth with words like 'executive'. See, some bastards caught me trying to infiltrate Madreidetic on Mars. Bet you didn't even know they've got an operation there? Neither did I before that. So they sold me to some bastard who gave me my first-head-job: this spider-crown. He chuckled. *'Course, it didn't work right. Didn't quite fit my thought-patterns or something. And then someone sold me to Karel in his little hidey-hole on the Moon and he put this tower in my head, right? I was a real prize specimen for him. He hadn't ever seen anything like me before, a cheap pirate copy of his invention. He was real curious about what a tower would do with the spider-crown.*

The little old eyes twinkled at her. *You got imminence, right? Well I've got simultaneity.* He stood there like I was a rat in a cage and watched me. *First thing I knew about it I was here freezing to death trying to breathe and then I was back there all at the same time. Man, it took it out of me. I like to died just with the effort. Hard to hold something as small as a person in one place. Not enough mass. A space-ship now, that's got plenty of mass. So every now and then I fire off some supplies out to all those little baby outposts of empire that Spiderglass and Madreidetic and one or two others got all over the option. I ain't about to let anyone starve to death if I can help it. And I'm gonna fix that Karel bastard once and for all.*

So that's me. Now let's get down to cases. What you gonna do about Mars?

But the Gate! At least let me know what –

He smiled enigmatically. *You want to know what? I'll tell you what. . . .*

Strange. Weird. It was as though with the second thud of her heart a part of herself was stripped off, poured away, funnelled down a long dark tunnel in a fall that lasted forever yet only seconds, to end up in a fierce hot jangle of daggered light against the limp blue sky.

Chesarynth's hand came alive, speared forward spade-like to drive into the nomad's throat. Chesarynth cried out, her self overflowing with the essence of Jezrael, even as she rolled aside and watched the nomad plunge off the roof into the green-spiked acacia underneath.

On the asteroid Jezrael's mind was fragmenting, her breath hissing in, her heart dropping in a tango, her thumb too slowly groping for the spread-setting on her blade-shaft. A scream was building up inside her as Ceriad drifted closer, beginning to gather speed, her viral fountain beginning to shoot its fire nearer to Jezrael's throat. Jezrael wanted all her awareness back in one place to keep her alive. She needed it. But part of it was streaking through a whistling chiaroscuro of colours and plunging into a dark and noisy pit.

Karel's dark and desperate thoughts suddenly grew shafts of blue fire, javelins of imminence that crowned the thrusting faces before him. He could see now – and it startled him – which of the tribesmen above him was going to move first. Then it was as if something shoved his thoughts aside, kicked his legs scything against the seam-faced leader's legs. The man toppled, bringing his body-guards down and a rope suddenly swam into Karel's vision. Even as he jumped for it he felt muscles trained in the laser-dance balance his body accurately for the leap and a feminine-scented presence that was Jezrael flashed through his mind and away. As she was dragged back to the asteroid she heard through the break in the tunnel roof the scream of Karel's jet-copters across the bright blue sky.

On the asteroid Ceriad's poison-beam split the sky-darkness, cleaving fast towards Jezrael who staggered a little as her fractured mind returned to her.

Jezrael saw through the pearling dampness of the acid how the old man slumped sideways, then she was triggering the spread-set of her own sword so that the blade arced wider, faster. The first drops bounced off it, unbalancing Ceriad's fall as the warrior tried to duck her own lethal juice.

Then Jezrael was ducking herself, rolling backwards in a light-gee somersault.

Free.

CLASP

Fire: the wild and crazy fire of laughter laced with the electricity of fear. There was nothing left to risk. It couldn't get worse than this. Her blood burned.

But fear was only a taste of darkness that gave substance to her ultimate joy: Jezrael could die now knowing that Chesarynth at least was safe, and knowing from what she and the Gate had felt in his brain that Karel wanted not to kill but to save his worlds; after the battle of Spiderglass-Asia the old Company methods would be discredited. Theresien was in the past, Ole some abstruse preterite that couldn't happen again. It had taken a war that couldn't be hushed up but now even the other hard-heads on the board couldn't risk the scandal of water-theft, the draining of the poor starving colonies.

Death was a long sleep of joy; even as the first acid virus touched her, she felt the Gate pulse in the darkness of her mind: *I am Dwillian and you, Jezrael, are the Gate now. Time is yours, all of time. Create the future, rewrite the past. Winners do. Survivors.*

A mental storm twisted her mind like lightning through cumulus. Power surged through her and echoes of her self danced through the fleeted years, the busy days to come.

There was Maggie, too scared to step from behind his plastic skin. But not too scared to hire a dancer – Jezrael will see him as Eiker, no, better still Dael – to fly the banners of freedom across the chocolate skies of Mars. There was Ild, strongarming the drunkards out of Hell. Cheap rotovators chiming energy to lure the students of Mars across their ripening fields.

Karel the gentle beside Chesarynth, restringing the Company's meanings in opal on midnight. There were the nomads, sitting cross-legged on jewelled carpets of Astrakhan, the sheik's brown glass stare belying his pleasure. In Chesarynth's Oasis swam fish while a hundred fauns danced at their moonshadows in the waters of diamond and health.

Jezrael's heart burst to the pain of life. Breath returned, the scream of a newborn into the isolation of being. Ceriad's droplets hit her like quills of vitriol. Jezrael felt them burn into her, smoulder in her tortured flesh. A thought rose in her, an indignant shriek: *But you said....*

Dwillian's mind showed his old body shaking its tired head, a fraction, a massive arc of pain. *No, you thought I said. Ceriad is your problem. Chesarynth and that Karel. Doing what you want with the life your parents made you, that's your problem.*

His head slumped, eyes too worn to close. A necromancer's fire sparked through his broken crown of thorns; the Gate was wrecked. His vitality paled within her mind even as the black silhouette of Ceriad swung her rainbow death in an arc across the sun.

Dwillian said inside Jezrael, *The future of Mars. Feel the blood in your veins, Jezrael. You can stand and watch them die of quotas; doesn't everybody else? But you got the power of Spiderglass – ain't you an executive? Hasn't Karel's two-edged weapon cut his heart? And you got more than that. Feel the heat of your blood tingling power through you to let you know you're not dead? Taste the immanence that roars down blue into your mind? Use it.*

Didn't I say your life is a jewel? Then put up or shut up, Jezrael. Care or don't care. Simultaneity dies with me; there'll be no more timeless trips to the stars. So polish your life and make mankind its setting. Join life. Join the rest of the human race. Become, he thought mockingly, *a Gate into a future you choose.*

There, starring high in the void, was the blue ocean symphony of Earth that spun wider, dizzyingly closer, into the beige and gold steppes of Asia. And below it, a ruby that Maggie once had sketched, was the quivering throb of red Mars.

Stretching out her blade she slammed Ceriad sideways into unconsciousness, swept her weapon down.

Acid ate hissing into the asteroid, vipered through Jezrael's flesh. Fast poisons raced through her blood-stream but *There must be antidotes.* Wings of ecstasy and terror swept through Jezrael.

She kissed the sleeping dream of Ember waiting in her darkness and looked into the light.